Innocence Waning

Chezdon Mitchell

First published in Great Britain in 2019 by Chezdon Mitchell

Text copyright @ Chezdon Mitchell, 2019

The moral right of the author has been asserted.

A CIP catalogue record for this book is available from the British Library.

ISBN 978-1-9999612-9-9 (paperback)
ISBN 978-1-9999612-2-0 (ebook)

First Edition

www.innocencewaning.com

Contents

...everything in moderation, including moderation.

1. Chezdon

Staring out the window after a session of vigorous masturbation is complete, I notice for the first time that the season has changed from summer to autumn. It wasn't just a memory evoked by the sound of the last bell at school that liberated our class of teenagers from our daily scholastic duties and associated mundane tasks that sounds in my head. The feeling of semen begins to run down my thigh, prompting me to clean up the mess that I made with my underwear as I acknowledge that time is on my side for a change. The last bell at school rang well over a week ago and it has provided a temporary feeling of freedom to enjoy 'school holidays' which are conveniently scheduled to align with Easter.

When I ponder the colloquial term 'Down Under' or what people usually outside of Australia refer to as the largest island in the world, I think about it in perspective whilst wiping sperm off my thigh. Australia is the size of the continental United States and it is daunting to think that it is an island. The city of Melbourne is referred to as the 'Paris of the Southern Hemisphere' and others refer to it as 'The Sporting Capital of the World' whereas I just think of it as a city that gets cold in the winter and very hot in the summer where there is always good coffee being served somewhere. When I noticed the leaves starting to change colour earlier in the week, I could still be comfortable wearing a pair of shorts with a hoodie outside. It was then that I realised just how much I enjoy this time of the year living in Melbourne.

Whilst on school holidays I enjoy an additional aspect of freedom as my father considers himself too important to take any time off from work. He must run a company and boss people around who mainly reside overseas. This 'offshore labour' gets paid in the day what it costs me to buy a coffee and a Big Mac. It is quite common for the parents of my peers to take the school holidays off to spend it with their kids and because of this, the traffic congestion eases in this major city. Even the rabble that 'rally' or should I say protest about the government also take a break. Most Aussies seem to take a vacation in their lounge room. Sitting in front of the television watching the football, shouting and screaming at the various players as the sun sets and the day turns into the night is one of our national pastimes. I don't mind the football but I don't obsess about it like some of my mates do. We certainly never have just a quiet night in watching it with so many other interesting things to do virtually on our doorstep. One girl that I know of became infamous as she was ejected from the footy at the Melbourne Cricket Ground for shouting racial abuse at an aboriginal player called Adam Goodes. Much like how my father enjoys providing expert commentary on the sport and how he demeans the Chinese that he must remotely work with by using various colourful names and slurs, I decided long ago that we are all just a little bit racist. This inherent tribalism, in turn, makes watching the sport interesting. We just don't watch it together as a family.

In the distance behind my closed bedroom door, I hear my father shouting something presumably into his phone followed by the front door slamming a few minutes later. The almost daily morning disturbance motivates me to get my naked body up from the bed. The sun is shining and there must be something to amuse me besides the online antics of my friends or just wasting time looking at silly videos of cats. I am keen to avoid the melodrama of Facebook having just jacked off. I haven't done any physical exercise for a few weeks since we were forced to participate in an athletics carnival at school. Feeling sloth-like as I wander around my room scratching my stomach and yawning, I fondly recall the last athletics carnival. There is not much to do besides undress my peers with my eyes, talk shit and post photos via Instagram every third minute. Being rather competitive, I take these events very seriously and I strive to run faster than the others. Talking shit and giving a shit are not mutually exclusive when it comes to me. Rather than waste yet another day of my break from high school and feeling motivated after pondering the last athletics carnival, I slip on my black Nike trainers and my associated gym kit and decide to go for a run. At first, I was thinking that I was losing my mind. Nobody that is sixteen years old wants to do anything active or productive at 7:30 AM during school holidays. I know that I am a little bit different though.

Although it is cold outside, I decide not to wear a hoodie since I get hot very easily. I jog towards the footpath that leads me first behind the Crown Casino in Southbank and then on to the pedestrian trail that is shared with cyclists which I follow to Beacon Cove at Port Melbourne. My jog evolves into a run, and I easily finish the four kilometres stretch in twenty minutes. Calling into the café opposite the pier where the Spirit of Tasmania vessel is docked, I order a much-needed coffee and wipe the sweat from my brow using my shirt as I wait for a mug of coffee to be brought to me. Sloth again begins to overcome me as I sit back and watch the tourists disembark from the huge boat that just arrived from Tasmania. Checking my phone for new tweets and text messages lead me to identify a void in my digital life so early in the morning, I then realise that I really shouldn't care about what is happening out in my virtual world. I need to just live in the moment. I don't need music or any distraction and I put my phone into flight mode. After gulping the coffee and doing a cursory scan of a newspaper that someone kindly left behind, I leave the café and decide to run a stretch of Port Philip bay which takes me past a sandy beach and then finally to Westgate Park. This nature reserve not only has a private go-kart racing track but also a saltwater lake and a curiously a freshwater lake. It also seems to be the home for many birds and diverse wildlife. Since it hasn't rained in greater Melbourne for a few weeks, I thought I would continue my jog through the park since the dirt tracks should not be muddy and I will not ruin my shoes. Spotting the public toilet before the dirt paths diverge toward the Westgate Bridge, I venture inside.

Urinating is just part of life and it is such a waste of time. It isn't until I complete the mundane task and after pulling my sweaty black cotton Bonds underwear over my flaccid cock that I notice another bloke staring. He is playing with his engorged dick whilst standing at the metal piss trough. Probably because I am going about my business dutifully with the intention to use the facilities for what they were designed for, I didn't even notice this gentleman enter the brick shithouse and stand next to me. My heart begins to beat fast and I can feel my blood pressure rising as I realise that he is getting off whilst leering at me.

I feel like time has come to a stand-still. His hard cock is just a few metres from my hand. My body is seemingly frozen and I am in a state of shock but I am also perversely excited. As I begin to salivate, I watch the stranger push his foreskin over his cockhead and then back down, exposing the pink mushroom head. "Want me to suck you?" The stranger whispers to me in rural accent. He continues to caress his boner with more rigour as he waits for me to answer or to react.

I can only make a guttural sound which emulates something like the wildlife that calls the park home would make. Freeing myself from this wrinkle of time, I retreat through the open door and back into the daylight. I begin to run down the dirt path and toward the Westgate bridge at the opposite end of the nature reserve. I stop once, looking behind me to see if the stranger from the toilet block is running after me. I feel slightly disappointed when I discover that he is not. Feeling like I need to overwhelm my senses and distract me from the filthy thoughts rushing around in my head, I push my headphones into my ears. I find the debut album by one of my favourite

Aussie bands, *5 Seconds of Summer* and hope that once I start the music, it will drown out my lurid thoughts. I start to run again and wonder what it would have felt like getting my penis sucked by the stranger. I smirk as I imagine jerking off the bloke and visualising him cumming on the floor gets me further aroused. I force myself to think about aging politicians, terrorism and other horrible imagery to banish the lurid thoughts from my mind which then tames my erection after some long and painful seconds. I continue to run as if possessed by some unknown force that is willing me forward as fast as I can humanly go. After regaining control of my body, I turn around and sprint back the way I came from at top speed until fatigue begins to overwhelm me. I want to get back to the toilet block and see the stranger again. More importantly, I want to grab his big throbbing dick. I make a noisy entrance as I stumble through the door of the public restroom and I am absolutely gutted when I find nobody inside.

Feeling both physically and emotionally drained, I retreat into the sunshine again, abandoning the potent smells of bleach and piss and sit on a wooden bench. I pull my phone out my pocket and take it off flight mode. The device then greets me with numerous alerts and message just a second later. Multiple queries appear asking me if I want to hang out – the requests stream in at the early hour as the rays of the sun begin to burn my face. Nobody ever sends me a message reading 'Want a blowjob?' or 'Come and fuck my tight arsehole senseless' which is very disappointing. Obscene thoughts fuelled by my over-active imagination quickly return and is accompanied by a sense of regret for deciding to run away from potentially my first sexual experience that did not involve my hand or a piece of fruit. I am reluctantly sucked back into reality when my phone begins to vibrate, announcing that a caller with a "Private Number" wants my attention.

"Hello, this is Chezdon."

Silence.

I repeat "Hi, this is Chezdon." However, this time I add additional emphasis when saying my name.

More silence. I end the call and begin to jog slowly back towards home.

2. **Jayden**

I am roused from my slumber by a familiar voice shouting through the wall that shares the common wall with my bedroom. A vivid memory of a dream about being in a public toilet begins to fade from my weary head as I stretch, knocking a pillow onto my cluttered bedroom floor. My father has an irritating habit of using the speakerphone functionality on his mobile so he can type on his laptop at the same time he shouts at people, thereby disturbing the early-morning peace in our happy household. Why he is up at 6:45 AM on a Saturday morning working instead of nursing a hangover is confusing me at this early hour. Slowly emerging from my sleepy haze and after wiping crust from my right eye it dawns on me that my dream was in fact linked to a very intriguing reality. I remain in stasis after picking up my pillow and holding it across my bare chest like how I dreamed what I would do with the throbbing cock that I watched dance yesterday.

A cold shower is followed by using the hair dryer on my blond mane which tips off my father that I am in fact conscious. He sends me a text message querying if I want to go out for breakfast. This is how he prefers to communicate with me when I have my bedroom door closed. I assume he is afraid of throwing open the portal to my realm and seeing me pleasure myself as he has on a few occasions. Instead of shouting through the common wall and my closed bedroom door, we agreed that messaging via our telephonic devices is the most prudent, especially when it is such a god-awful early hour on a relaxing weekend. I respond with a straight-forward 'sure' to his kind invite to 'brekkie' as Australians call it since it has been at least a week since I have even seen my father. I begin to rummage through one of the many heaving bags that are filled with clothes that I have yet to wear that rest on the floor of my closet. These unworn items of apparel were recently purchased using the spoils of the cash winnings that I gratefully accepted from my father after the outcome of a few horse races were successfully bet on. He generously passed me a wad of sweaty cash and told me to go on a shopping spree with his winnings. I expect that Flemington Racecourse will be his destination again today and selfishly I not only want him to win every meeting so I will profit, but it will mean that there is a good chance that I will have the apartment all to myself. Since he wants to get breakfast and bond, it is a tell-tale sign that he will be going to the track all day to shout at the beasts that run around in circles all afternoon with his mates.

We dine and chat at a café on Southbank Promenade which overlooks the murky Yarra River which is near our residential tower. Breakfast turns out to be a very sedate affair as my father is occupied with sending messages to his mates and reading the latest tips on the horses that will be running today. I enjoy a plate of roasted chorizo in a watery and flavourless tomato sauce along with two poached eggs. When my father is not distracted, I simultaneously field a thousand questions about school, my friends, girls and share my thoughts on current events as I chew on the components of my breakfast. The conversation evolves to the point that he begins to disparage the names of horses that are running later today and like a galloper himself, he suddenly bolts to meet his friends after I give him my sincere wish that he backs many winners today.

Before leaving the riverside restaurant, I order two more cups of black coffee and occupy myself by sending messages to my friends. My best mate Jayden is the first to respond saying that he will take the train into the city centre to hang out. With some plans in motion, I relax holding a glass of water and watch people stroll down the promenade whilst my best mate navigates the intricacies of the Melbourne public transport system. After he sets off from his home in the suburbs, we agree to meet at Federation Square, which is across from the iconic Flinders Street train station after some hearty negotiation.

Federation Square is a short walk from the restaurant in Southbank and is a popular meeting place because of the many bars and cafés. There is also a huge outdoor television screen in the plaza which broadcasts every iteration of the sport. There is an abundance of improvised street furniture so tourists, teenagers and the corporate lunch-time lovers all have a place to chill out and relax. This is also a great place to people-watch. Lately, I have found more people watching me and my friends hanging out in this public space compared to the other way around though. I have been chatted-up by trashy girls that can barely string a sentence together since I am often there waiting for friends to turn up. These admirers all ask me silly questions which prove tedious, but as I learned from my father, it is always best to be cordial to everyone since you never know how silly words or abrupt actions will impact you in the future. I also would prefer not to get my arse kicked by a group of girls, so I consider my politeness an act of self-preservation.

Like clockwork, Jayden turns up at the agreed time. He is my most punctual friend. He even found a few spare minutes to purchase a blue Slurpee from the nearby 7-11 convenience store. "How can you drink that shit?" I shout at him when he is some distance away after I spot him with the fluorescent drink in his hand.

Jayden matches my volume and returns serve. "It is good to see you. You bloody fucking arsehole! How is my anorexic best mate?" His question encourages the nosey tourists taking photos in the immediate area to stop and stare. I feel uncomfortable for a change after the question which a feeling that I don't experience often. To have some fun, I make loud retching noises and bend down holding my stomach. The routine doesn't entertain those that are milling around me in the public area as much as it does me and Jayden. The spectators quickly move along but not before a few take photographs memorialising the wayward youth and how they spend their downtime on a lazy Saturday morning in central Melbourne.

Jayden is wearing black skinny jeans which I suspect belong to me and an over-sized white shirt. As a slave to the latest fashion trend, at some point, he cut the sleeves off his shirt, which have left his pale shoulders at the mercy to the morning sun. As we embrace and slap each other on the back repeatedly, I wonder why he is dressed like a slut. "Are you going to walk the project runway? Are we going to try to sneak into a club or something?" Jayden has a girlfriend who also complains about how he dresses. He wants to appear like he is fashion forward but just comes off looking like a teenage male whore outside of school hours. What I do find refreshing is that he doesn't care what anyone else thinks. His nipples, chest and shoulders all alternate being on display since he cut out so much fabric it is hard not to stare at his exposed body.

After sucking blue ice through the straw, my friend stares across the road. My eyes follow his and I look at the mob of people exiting from the train station. Jayden groans and then clears his throat. "I don't care what we do today, but I am not getting on that goddamned train again. Every idiot in this city is coming in to watch the footy today." He takes another slurp of blue ice and then coughs.

I scratch the back of my neck and then push my dirty blonde hair forward over my ears, before interlocking my hands behind my head. "Screw the train and the fucking footy today, mate. Why don't we head down to Port Melbourne?" The suggestion spits from my mouth without giving the logistics much thought. I am not going to tell him what happened in the public toilet block which borders Port Melbourne but I am keen to go have a look at the nature reserve again. I really doubt he would be very supportive if I told him that casual sex may be on offer in the public toilet though.

Jayden stares at me with a disturbed look on his face. "Why the fuck would you want to go there? There is fuck all to do in Port Melbourne." He takes another slurp from the cup of blue ice and coughs again.

"There is a beach!" I exclaim feigning confidence in my plan. "It is going to be a nice day for a change so let's take advantage of the last of the warm weather before the season changes." I sound like the bloke that reads the weather report on the silly breakfast television show that I watch. "The sun is shining; the birds are chirping." I look up in the sky hoping to find birds overhead. Jayden notices me roll my eyes as a Channel Seven helicopter passes overhead.

Jayden chortles. "Look at me, mate. Does it look like I am dressed for the fucking beach?" He intently watches a middle-aged heterosexual couple walking past us holding hands. "You know I am not much of a beach person."

I cross my legs at my ankles and balance on my toes. "It is something different to do, I am bored. It is not as out of control there as compared to St Kilda and you did say that you wanted to get away from the idiots here in the city. I just don't want to sit around here all day like an arsehole." Paying for my friends to partake in various activities, feeding and hydrating them seems to be an expectation now since my father started giving me large amounts of money. He calls it a bonus to my allowance as the result of his winning streak at the horse races as of late which makes me try to bribe my friend. Oh, my father gave me two hundred dollars so hey, we can spend it. Let's just go."

"Fine. After you, sir." Jayden bends down and outstretches his arm in the direction of the closest tram stop.

Innocence Waning

Jayden continues to slurp the blue ice from the cup as we casually walk to the tram platform on Collins Street. I notice him walking with shorter strides, his gait being inhibited by his very skinny jeans. In between gossiping about our classmates, I briefly wonder how musty the smell of his crotch would be after walking around for a while on this abnormally warm autumn day. Garish thoughts quickly turn into ones of self-preservation as we jaywalk to the tram stop avoiding speeding taxis, which is positioned in the centre of the busy street.

The tram arrives and is packed with travellers and their belongings. The commuters were most likely residing at the Grand Hyatt and the Westin hotels which are in the immediate area and are travelling to Port Melbourne to catch the Spirit of Tasmania which I assume is leaving at some point later today. My father always rubbishes that boat and refers to it as an overpriced tourist trap. You can fly from Melbourne to Tasmania for around eight dollars in just over an hour. Why would you go to all the effort to take the bloody boat that hauls both humans and cargo on an expensive overnight trip? The rationale doesn't make much sense to me but the gullible tourists still reckon it is a good idea since the service remains in business.

We travel on the tram southbound without saying a word. We endure the abrupt stopping and starting of the tram which jolts me from side to side for the entire twenty-minute journey. The tram tracks follow parallel to the pedestrian footpath which I ran along just yesterday. The journey ends at Beacon Cove where frazzled tourists pull their bulky bags off and onto the platform and we follow. I suggest that we buy drinks from the café that occupies the former train station, where I enjoyed my caffeine hit yesterday. Jayden agrees. Quickly, one coffee turns into four and with some urgency in my voice, I announce that I am ready to go. Jayden expresses his interest in languishing on the deck and basking in the sun like a lazy seal which immediately frustrates me. I want to go and explore the nature reserve and not sit around here any longer.

Not only did the owner of the café look at me with a curious look as I powered through the fourth mug of coffee like a man obsessed with imported beans, but Jayden provides a running commentary to amuse himself. "The boy won't eat but will live on a diet of coffee and Coke. You should go into politics or try to be a model!" Jayden likes to stir me up, sometimes so incessantly that he just sounds ridiculous. "Did you eat anything today?"

"Why do you care that I drink so much coffee? I like it. You drink so many goddamned blue Slurpee's that you probably single-handedly manage to keep that 7-11 franchise open in Federation Square." I pause long enough to finish the last of the coffee in my mug. "Of course, I ate today arsehole. I don't know why you have this idea that I never eat anything." I scoff before abruptly standing up and swat at a fly buzzing near my ear with my hand.

"Yeah sure, you eat. I never see you eat anything." Jayden winks. "Prove it." Jayden pushes his chair back, stands up and follows me as I walk down the stairs which leads to the foreshore.

"What is wrong with you? It always seems like I am eating. I just don't eat the shit that you like to eat." I pause and watch the tram that we arrived on glide away from us along tracks back to the centre of Melbourne. "Speaking of food, I read a tweet earlier saying that the taco truck will be in this area right about now, so I will shout some tacos if you want and prove to you once and for all that I actually do eat." Being an average height with a low percentage of fat in my body, I could have easily pulled on the skinny jeans that Jayden is wearing and not struggle to walk. His discomfort is no doubt fuelling his attitude.

I lied when I proclaimed that the taco truck is in the area. It does randomly turn up in the industrial estate not far from here as I have tracked it down on multiple occasions in the past. I really like Mexican food, but I have no intention of walking into the industrial estate today. Most of the streets are not even pedestrian friendly and it is the last place that I want to spend my Saturday. I want to stroll along the beachfront and end up at Westgate Park after all.

We follow the footpath that deviates from the edge of the sandy beach that borders the bay. Walking near the industrial estate which borders Westgate Park is when Jayden starts to whine incessantly. He claims that he is hot and demands to know how much longer we must walk. "Where is this damned taco truck, mate?"

I fob him off with a suggestion. "You can use my key to tear up your skinny jeans and turn them into skinny shorts." He looks at me like I have lost my mind.

"Fuck you. Where is the taco truck?" Sacrificing comfort for fashion seems ridiculous. There are only a few people around and who will judge him?

I point at the footpath that leads to Westgate Park. "I need to hang a piss." It is not a lie. I really do need to use a bathroom.

"Maybe you shouldn't have had so much coffee." Jayden lifts his shirt up and wipes his face with it. "Just go ask them across the street."

I roll my eyes and continue to walk towards the nature reserve and Jayden follows. "It isn't like I can walk into one of those warehouses and ask them to use their toilet mate." I continue to plod along the footpath. "Jesus Christ. Let's just go to the park. There has to be a toilet but if there isn't, I will just piss on a tree." Jayden nods his head and I feel satisfied knowing that I am getting my way.

Being high on caffeine and acutely aware of my surroundings this time around, I notice that the small car park is filled with motorcars as we walk into the reserve. Most of the vehicles have a mere single male occupant just sitting in their car and everyone is staring at us. It is weird that these blokes just drive to the park, only to just hang out in their car. Then I have a light bulb moment and assume something far more sinister is afoot. I am glad that I coerced Jayden on this adventure as I begin to feel very wary of my surroundings.

Jayden gleefully points at the now familiar public toilet block even before I catch sight of it. My head is turned and looking over my shoulder at all the men sitting in their cars leering as he taps me on the shoulder and points in the direction of the shithouse. My best mate leads the way into the toilets which shocks me. This wasn't part of my master plan. I really wanted him to innocently wait outside this public facility and read his social media feeds. I wanted to spend time inside and hope that someone would be in there wanting to touch me. Disenchanted, I follow my friend through the open door and into the public toilets. I immediately notice the strong stench of bleach and piss. Jayden skips into a vacant cubicle and slams the door shut. I hear a latch snap, securing the door from the inside. I scowl as I look at the graffiti on the walls of the structure. My eyes follow the vandalism on the floor and then to the ceiling. After sighing, I stand at the metal trough alone wondering why I thought something erotic would happen in these squalid conditions. I take a deep breath and release another audible sigh and wonder what is wrong with me. Who aspires to hook-up in a dank toilet in a park?

A trifecta is when you place a bet on three horses to finish the race in an exact order. Gamblers can make massive returns betting money in such a way; however, I think it is too complex and risky. Why bother adding extra variables when it hard enough to pick just one winning horse? I stand at the trough and decide to just piss. I unzip my skinny jeans and pull down on the band of my sweat-soaked boxer briefs, liberating my cock into the musty air. I release a stream of piss so mighty that it splashes off the back of the aluminium trough. I quickly side-step on the metal grate so that my urine doesn't splatter back on me. The sploshing that my piss makes off the shiny metal distracts me and I do not immediately notice when someone walks into the five-star facility. When I first notice the bloke stepping onto the grate next to me, I jump. My heart begins to beat faster as I watch him spread his legs as he balances on the grate. He stands a mere metre from me and begins to unfasten his belt. After fiddling with his jeans, he frees his soft thick cock and begins to piss. Behind the closed toilet door, Jayden releases the longest and loudest fart that I have ever heard in my life. The release of gas lasts for at least five seconds and sounds absolutely eerie.

"Goddamn! I feel like a new man!" Jayden shouts. The words echo through the chamber of old piss, shit and bleach. "Yeehaw!!!" He yells like a cowboy in the wild west would.

My phone begins to vibrate unexpectedly in my back pocket. I recognise the custom rapid-fire vibration I associated with my father's contact card. "Jesus," I mutter. He gives me nearly limitless freedom if I remain at the top of my class but more importantly if I answer the phone promptly when he rings. Time is money or so he says. I try to hold onto my cock and finish urinating. I desperately try to suppress my laughter as the commentary that Jayden is shouting from behind the closed stall door is hilarious. I struggle to retrieve my phone from my back pocket with my free hand. I end up pushing my skinny jeans down to my bent knees as I struggle to pull the phone from my pocket whilst feebly attempting to keep control of the stream of urine. The bloke standing next to me, who I suspect had untoward intentions at first begins to cackle. Jayden starts to sing a song, clueless as to what is taking place on the other side of the closed door as the words echo through the room.

When I finally get my phone to my ear, I greet my father in a huff. "Hey, dad." My jeans rest on my knees and I desperately try to pull them up with one hand, much to the amusement of the stranger who begins to laugh. I wedge the Samsung phone between my ear and my shoulder and grab the sides of my jeans and yank them up after putting my cock back in its prison.

I step away from the trough desperately trying to fasten the top button of my jeans, embarrassed as the stranger is still watching me with a smile on his face. "Where are you? You had better not be at some pub. Who is singing?"

"Chezdon's father is my hero!" Jayden sings in a falsetto from behind the security of the closed stall door. "There goes my hero, watch him as he goes!" He decides to channel Dave Grohl of *Foo Fighters* fame as I scurry outside, leaving the chaos that the restroom has devolved into behind so that I can have a conversation devoid of distractions.

"No, don't worry, I am near Sandridge Beach with Jayden, and honestly I was just hanging a piss if you really must know." I am confident that my father would have detected a fair amount of agitation in my voice as beads of sweat start to tumble down the centre of my back. "What's up?"

"Why are you in Port Melbourne of all places? There is nothing to do there!" My father exclaims in a bemused way. I explain that we are on the hunt for the taco truck and that we just had coffee in Beacon Cove.

Too much information quickly bores my father. He proceeds to announce that he backed some winners running the first race at Flemington and if I want to buy a new phone that I can today. He continues to say that he bet on a trifecta and there are only good times to be had. I consider telling him that I seemingly won a trifecta also. A random guy was getting his cock out next to me. Win. Jayden farting, commentating and singing in the public toilet. Win. Me losing control of my trousers as my beloved father decides to randomly ring. Win. Trifecta.

I watch the horse bolt from the public toilet so to speak as my father lets me in on where he hides a stash of cash in the apartment. The stranger who just a minute ago was smiling at me whilst standing at the trough leaves the shithouse and walks past me laughing. Before ending the call, my father insists that I enjoy myself and to look after Jayden. If he only knew what his only child had on his mind when he rang, I am sure he would be mortified.

Jayden emerges into the sunlight wiping his brow with the back of his hand. "Why are you so red?" My face turns red easily when I am warm or when I am embarrassed. "What is wrong with you?"

My eyes go wide and I think of something to say to distract him. "Why the hell are you sweating?" It was cold and clammy in the public toilet after all.

"Who do I complain to mate? What Council oversees this area? There was no goddamned toilet paper so I had to wipe my arse with my socks and my underwear. Whoever has to clean that shithole will have a surprise waiting for them." Jayden stretches his arms over his head and locks his hands together which reveals his dark brown armpit hair.

I smile and am at a loss for words. "Oh god." Images then come to mind of Jayden wiping his arse with his clothes and I begin to laugh hysterically. "Oh fuck!" I screech.

"Yeah, I left the shit-soiled underwear and socks on the floor, mate. That is right, laugh you fucker. I am sure there is some sick fuck that will get off in there with them too." Jayden yawns and then smiles, knowing that he is amusing me. "I don't even want to think about what happens in that shithouse. It is disgusting."

I continue laughing like a lunatic. A plethora of bizarre thoughts has managed to converge in a matter of minutes. I can't stop chuckling at the sheer ridiculousness of the situation. Morbid curiosity pulls me back into the public toilet to inspect the carnage that Jayden abandoned. I open the door to the cubicle that Jayden used only to see two socks with shit smeared on them laying innocently on the concrete floor next to a pair of pink Bonds underwear with a black waistband that is also soiled. The smell of shit makes me gag and I retch.

I scamper outside into the bright light of the autumn day and begin to snicker. "Pink underwear?"

"Shut the fuck up, I like them." Jayden turns around and starts to walk in the direction of Beacon Cove and the tram platform. "I am over this shit, let's go."

I continue to giggle and briefly jog to catch up to Jayden and slap him on his back. "You did like them you mean."

Jayden looks flustered and wipes the sweat forming on his upper lip using the back of his hand. "I never should have come to this shit area. Now I am going to get a chafe."

"Whatever, let's just go. Do you want to go find the taco truck?" I take a deep breath and hope that he will not want to go into the industrial estate and try to locate the truck that I am confident will not be in the area today.

"No, I am over it. I just want to get out of here." He lifts his shirt again and wipes the sweat off his face.

For the next fifteen minutes, Jayden complains that his skinny jeans are now rubbing him in all the wrong places. He provides me with a blow-by-blow commentary like you would get when watching a boxing match on television. It only takes a few minutes to walk to the waterfront, but Jayden's mood has turned feral. "Stop whining! Jesus Christ!" I cry. "That is what you get for wearing skinny jeans that are too small for you."

"Whatever arsehole." Jayden sits on a wall that partitions the shared footpath and bicycle path. He leans back and puts his rests the palms of his hand on the dirt and looks thoughtfully over Port Philip Bay.

"Look." I point. "There is an IGA. It is a shit grocery store, but they probably have some socks at least." I have stopped in this IGA before to buy Gatorade during one of my previous runs through the area. I vaguely recall that they sell some basic items of clothing.

Jayden quickly walks into the small market and I follow. He locates a pair of underwear that is devoid of any style. He has found plain white briefs hanging on a hook next to where mops and brooms are displayed. We both hunt for socks and given my surprise that they have underwear for sale, I am surprised not to find any. Jayden grabs a pair of scissors from the office supply aisle and I follow him to the checkout area. "Get out some cash mate and pay, please." I pull a fifty-dollar gold-coloured note from my pocket and hand it to the attendant and he returns some cash and coins to me.

After walking outside, Jayden points at my feet. "Give me your thongs." I methodically kick them off and they strike him on each of his shins. He sits on the low brick wall nearby and unties his black Converse shoes. He kicks them off with such force that they hit the Westpac ATM machine mounted on the wall of the grocery store. I am sure many things, including foul language, has been thrown in the direction of that ATM, but never a pair of shoes.

"What are you doing?" I ask. "Can I do anything to help?" I scratch my head.

"I'll be back." Jayden walks away.

Barefoot, I carefully stride to where his shoes landed. I never walk on the pavement or anywhere without shoes which have made my feet unnaturally soft and sensitive. "Where are you going?" I push my blond fringe out of my eyes and off my damp forehead. I wedge the longer strands of hair behind my ear.

"Look!" I follow the direction that Jayden is pointing at. "You see that toilet block next to the café where you drank a litre of coffee? You could have used that toilet and we could have avoided all of this drama."

Jayden walks away with my thongs on presumably because, without socks, walking was painful wearing only the Converse. He disappears into the toilet block which gives me an opportunity to catch up on my social media feeds. Not finding anything interesting, I pull his shoes on, which are a bit big for me but not so ill-fitting that I must walk like a clown.

My best mate eventually emerges and I immediately notice that he took my original advice. He has cut up his skinny jeans and made them into skinny shorts. His snow-white and hairy legs contrast somewhat against the short black skinny shorts that he has produced on a whim. He looks a bit silly but I don't make a comment as I don't want to be abused. Besides, who am I to judge?

My phone begins to vibrate in my back pocket once again. As my own clothes are properly fitted to my body this time, I retrieve the device without much effort. "Hi, this is Chezdon." There is no response once again from the 'Unknown' person who is calling me. I repeat myself again and then the other party terminates the call. "What the fuck," I mumble.

"Who was that?" Jayden scratches his knee. "You look pissed off."

"I don't know. I keep getting calls from a silent number and the person just hangs up. It is getting annoying." I push my phone back into my rear pocket.

"Oh well, fuck them. Let's go spend your money. What did your father want?" Jayden yawns again. His mood has noticeably improved.

I smile and recall my father saying that I should buy a new phone and celebrate his win. "His wager paid and he is partying." I notice the tram gliding towards us along the tracks in the distance. "The bloody tram is coming."

"He is always in party mode. I love your father!" Jayden exclaims with a newly found sense of vigour and enthusiasm. He follows me to the platform. I hear my thongs making a clicking noise against the balls of his feet as he catches up to me and slaps me on the back.

Jayden walks past me taking an interest in his phone as someone taps me on the shoulder "Excuse me mate, you dropped this." A voice from behind me says. I turn around and recognise the man as being the stranger that was thoroughly amused by my antics in the public toilet earlier. He has a smile plastered on his face. He hands me a folded-up piece of paper which I accept and shove into my pocket. "Thanks, mate" is all say as he walks back to the foreshore. My heart begins to race again as I am desperate to know what is written on the piece of paper. It certainly does not belong to me.

When I am confident that Jayden is completely engrossed in the world that exists on his phone, it is only then I stealthily remove the piece of paper from my pocket and read it.

Tomorrow. 10:30 AM. Same place as before.

With some subterfuge, I roll the scrap of paper into a small tight ball and shove it back into my pocket.

"Look at this!" Jayden thrusts his phone in front of my face. I briefly see a photo of his girlfriend's breasts. I admire the photograph and notice the elderly couple behind us having a look.

I push the phone back towards Jayden's face. "Nice. Do you want to go shopping or something? I can buy you some new skinnies and some new pink underwear." I snigger and yank my phone from my back pocket again. "I can't believe you wear pink underwear."

"Don't take the piss mate, but yeah. Let's go." Jayden again takes interest in his social media feeds as we board the air-conditioned tram. "I really did like that pair of underwear. It is a damned shame I had to lose them."

I resist the urge to say that I would have thoroughly enjoyed seeing my best mate wearing just that pair of underwear.

Innocence Waning

3. Bryce

The journey by tram into the centre of Melbourne seems tediously slow as I sit in the cool carriage with my feet resting on the seat in front of me. The air conditioning blowing onto the top my head isn't sufficient to cool my body down though. Musing that I should have followed my own advice and cut up my own skinny jeans would certainly have made this excursion more comfortable. The morning sun is quickly becoming excruciating as it traverses the sky above and shines through the window on my lightly tanned arms, face and neck.

Jayden looks up from his phone and stops tapping on the screen. "What the hell is wrong with you, mate? Your face is bright red." He tilts his head to the side and seemingly finds me more interesting than whatever is on his Twitter feed. "You look stressed out."

I begin to rub at the nape of my neck and feel the damp shirt sticking to my back. "Nothing, it is just fucking hot." I rub the side of my head on my shoulder and cross my legs at my ankles, which is my signature pose. "I should have worn shorts."

Jayden rolls his eyes. I am sure that he is thinking that he was the clever one after making alterations to his wardrobe and I should have taken my own advice. I am jealous of his newfound comfort. "You are a strange kid, Chez." He returns his attention to his phone and begins to tap and swipe at the screen swiftly using a single digit.

My imagination kicks into overdrive. Graphic imagery of what the stranger who passed the note wants to do with me inside the public toilets appear like a PowerPoint slideshow presentation in my head. The bloke doesn't want to just talk about footy or the weather, that much I know for certain. I am equally intrigued and terrified at the same time. These oscillating feelings are causing me to sweat profusely and have introduced unneeded stressors into my relatively sedate life. The stranger knows what he wants and I have no idea what to do or what to expect besides just turn up for our date. "Why am I strange?" I scrutinise Jayden from head to toe and try to distract myself from my vivid thoughts. "Look at you. You define the word strange, mate."

Jayden smiles. "I am colourful and eccentric." The tram suddenly grinds to a stop on Collins Street, delivering our sweaty bodies back into the centre of Melbourne. We fight our way past the pole-huggers that selfishly obstruct the open door of the carriage and try desperately to push our way off the tram. The next battle is past the influx of rude commuters that try to advance into the carriage before all of the passengers completely alight. It is a bit like a game of rugby I have found. I just put my head and shoulders down and if people don't get out of the way and let you off, they get knocked in the process. It helps to have a fully laden school backpack on weekdays though as you can casually hit people with it. I let out a groan that is drowned out by the noise of the commuters and the sounds of the city as I finally shove myself off the tram. "Emporium, food, coffee?" Jayden shouts. "I am hungry."

"Reverse the order and I will buy," I yell. Jayden then quickly takes the lead navigating past the pedestrians on Collins Street and I follow my comrade.

I am not sure if I really need more coffee since I am already firing on all cylinders, but I do like trying new places and enjoy it if it is brewed correctly with exotic beans. "Let's get lunch at Emporium after coffee," Jayden suggests.

We stop momentarily and watch a busker who is performing a cover of a *Green Day* song in front of one of the many shopping arcades. Jayden taps me on the stomach. "Come on. Nothing to see here, this bloke is shit. I still haven't heard back by the way." Jayden has been on pins and needles since trying out for *X Factor Australia a* little over a month ago. After the original try-out, he was called back to perform again so whenever he hears a song by *Green Day*, he becomes anxious as that is the band he covered in his first audition.

I follow Jayden through the maddening crowd of shoppers and dawdlers. Whilst walking, I check social media and respond to notifications feeling as if I can walk, type and read at the same time, that I am a true multitasker. I read a message from my mate, Bryce. He writes he is in the city and is keen to meet up for lunch. I advise him that we plan to have lunch in the Emporium food court and invite him to meet up with us.

I have known Bryce for a little over a year and first met him at one of the many athletic carnivals. I first approached him and made small talk about what he was drinking, Cherry Dr Pepper. I thought I was the only one in Australia that enjoyed drinking this beautiful carbonated drink. Originally, I simply wanted to know where he bought it. It is a rare find outside of the United States and I seldom find cans of it for sale in Australia. Bryce educated me as to where I can source the soda in bulk, and even directed me to an online forum that tracks oddities like Cherry Dr Pepper in Australia. Bryce doesn't attend our school so I found it easy to foster a friendship with him because he is not caught up in the political dramas, social circles and gossip rings that affect not only my peers but me. He has hung out with a few of my mates, including Jayden, and finds him tolerable. Since Bryce isn't directly involved with my cliques, it was easy to admit to him that I am gay. He asked me what my sexual orientation is a few months ago after first articulating that he wasn't trying to hit on me or demonise me in the lead up to the question. Bryce, like Jayden, has a girlfriend and despite my penchant for the same-sex, I never felt sexually aroused by Bryce. He just isn't my type. I tried to explain what I am looking for to him but I could not really describe what I really like. At the time, I had to just say that I was simply looking. He did make the sage statement that when the right boy comes along, I will know it though.

Jayden and I continue to dodge a phalanx of weekend shoppers, tourists, mothers pushing baby carriages and more buskers. We stumble into one of the last surviving Starbucks in Australia, escaping from the crowds. I now need more caffeine and I expect Jayden to spend most of the time Snapchatting. We queue up, order, give our names and wait patiently staring at our respective phones.

"Bryce is keen to meet up," I mumble and lean against the window. "Do you want to get some Mexican for lunch?"

"What does your boyfriend want?" Jayden takes a selfie with me as I raise my middle finger. He sends it to someone via Snapchat. "Do you blokes hang out every weekend now?"

"Just to chill out and get lunch. Nothing too sinister mate. I suggested we meet at the Mexican place at Emporium." My eyes scan the customers sipping from their coffee cups. "I am hungry, mate. I am shitty that we didn't get anything from the taco truck." I raise my voice just to reinforce the fact that I not I do eat food and am in fact hungry for some Mexican.

"I finally get tacos!" Jayden screams with unexpected enthusiasm. "Tacos! Tacos! More tacos! Give me tacos!" Jayden chants and points at the ceiling. He shouts as loud as he can, "tacos!" Everyone around us scowls at him. He must have had his heart set on enjoying the spoils of the taco truck. At least I wasn't caught out in a lie about my earlier intentions for visiting Port Melbourne. "Jesus Christ, I love their tacos!"

"Really, I never would have guessed." I smile. Jayden's antics are entertaining.

A Starbucks employee with a stolid face and flat nose barks from behind the counter, "Jayden! Grande Mocha with cream."

"He loves the cream, give him extra!" I shout back which makes Jayden grimace. "He will show you his nipples for more cream." Jayden stands at the counter and expresses his appreciation to the worker. He offers his apologies for his obnoxious mate and I, in turn, offer more words to further embarrass him. "Don't worry, he shows his body to anyone who wants a look for five dollars." I laugh hysterically. Jayden quickly walks back holding his cup and shoulder charges me, knocking me against the window. His reaction encourages me to continue laughing.

The now familiar voice from behind the counter barks. "Cheese-don! Iced Caramel Macchiato." I quickly stride to the counter, grab the drink, thank the server and jog through the open door of the store before Jayden starts to mimic how she pronounced my name.

Jayden catches up with me outside the newly renovated Emporium building. We navigate the corridors passing high-end shops and travel on many escalators which take us to the top floor where the food court is. It isn't a typical food court that you find in a shopping plaza. The big-name franchises do not have a presence here. Speciality food outlets that cater to those that want a more refined dining experience after shopping are on offer. We join a queue of other hungry people and wait to order tacos from the Mexican place that I previously suggested. When we finally get to the front of the line, Jayden orders frozen margaritas, however, the clever server behind the counter requests his identification and then is promptly refused service. "Maybe if you dressed a bit more conservatively, someone might believe you are eighteen and not try to card you, mate."

"Fuck off." Jayden shoves his hand inside his shirt and scratches his chest. "It doesn't hurt to try."

After locating an empty table and sit amongst the feeding herd, we eat our tacos, making guttural sounds in the process. Wiping my mouth, I notice Bryce wandering around. "Bryce! Mate!" I scream and wave my arms.

Bryce spots me and waves back. He casually walks toward our table. "G'day boys, what's shaking?" Bryce asks with as much enthusiasm as Jayden had earlier when tacos were mentioned. "No tacos left for me? I am cut." He sits on the chair next to Jayden.

"You know how it goes, eating tacos and talking shit. The usual, mate." I lament and notice that Bryce is wearing what appears to be the same skinny jeans as Jayden, however with all the material still intact. My eyes are drawn to his shirt, which is a lightweight hoodie with all the buttons undone which reveals his chest. He catches me checking him out and I feel my heart to start beating faster. I am confident that my face has turned red. "Yum. You turned up too late fool." I hope he doesn't confuse my appreciation of the tacos with his exposed chest.

"Hey man, how have you been?" Jayden asks Bryce whilst taping the screen of his phone. He then tosses it on the table and extends his hand.

Bryce shakes Jayden's hand. "I am a bit fucked off actually. Thanks for asking. You blokes will have a good laugh even though it isn't funny. I was woken up at around 4:00 AM. My parents were shouting at each other. I overheard my father say that my mother farted on him whilst he was sleeping. The fart woke up my father. He wasn't pleased so he started shaking her and swearing at her whilst she was still asleep." He tells the specifics of the story a bit like a newsreader would report the weather. "I guess my father has a habit of holding my mother at night when she sleeps. A bit of spooning that went wrong. I guess it has happened before at least if the hysterical shouting that I overheard can be believed. She got pissed off and left as she will 'not be shaken like a goddamned rag doll whilst in a deep sleep' and drove to our holiday house."

Jayden begins to laugh and I take a drink from my bottle of Coke. His laughter combined with Bryce's sardonic tone breaks me down and I join in and add to the hysterics. Tears flow from Jayden's eyes as his mirth reaches the volume you would expect from an aeroplane. Diners in the food court begin to stare at us, no doubt curious as to what is so bloody hilarious. "You have to admit, it is funny. Tragic, but funny." I offer in between sips from the straw protruding from the plastic bottle of Coke.

"Yeah, have a good laugh. It is funny. Sort of." Bryce stands up and stretches his arms out and yawns. "I am going to buy a burrito. Do you boys want anything?"

Jayden continues to laugh and recounts parts of Bryce's story in-between gasps for air, slapping the table with glee and wiping his eyes repeatedly. After some time passes, he manages to speak in coherent sentences. "No mate, I am fine. That is a brilliant story though." I shake my head and Bryce immediately understands that I don't want anything else from the Mexican place.

By the time that Bryce returns to the table with a burrito and a bottle of Coke, Jayden has calmed down. "That is the best story ever." Jayden continues. "It beats the article that I read earlier about a woman who lost custody of her children in the United States because she decided to party with her sixteen-year-old daughter and her male friends. The funny part is that they played naked Twister if the media can be believed. The mother thought it would be a good idea to get out a dildo and use it on herself before doing some drugs with the kids." Bryce and I begin to chew on our fingernails at the same time as Jayden begins to speak again. "She later got fucked by one of the sixteen-year-old boys there. I guess it became too real for her daughter as it was reported that her sixteen-year-old boyfriend. He supposedly has a ten-inch cock which he tried to put in the mother when she was passed out after she fucked his eighteen-year-old mate in the toilet."

"Jesus Christ, that is mad." Bryce blurts out and begins to chuckle, spitting rice from his mouth. "Did the daughter complain to the cops or something? How did something bizarre like this end up in the news anyway?"

"From what I read, the mother decided to turn her life around after that party and went to Alcoholics Anonymous. She told the whole sordid story to her sponsor. Her sponsor rang the coppers and tattled on her." Jayden pauses and stares at me. I start to giggle which causes him to laugh like a maniac once again. Bryce chews on his burrito, seemingly lost in his thought.

I start to ramble without considering my audience. "That is fucked up. I would think that the daughter, when she saw the ten-inch cock at one point in her life would have said that it wasn't ever going inside of her. Period. I wonder what would have gone through her mind when she saw her supposed boyfriend try to shove it into her mother." I notice professionally dressed gentlemen at the table next to us are all intently listening to our conversation and chomping on chicken burritos.

Bryce touches Jayden on his arm and leans towards him whilst staring at me. "Chezdon, doesn't Jayden have a ten-inch cock? Does it hurt when he rams it up your arse?" Bryce laughs. I am at a loss for words as Bryce is rarely crass. The diners next to us start chuckling. We collectively look at them and they find their lunch all the sudden to be much more interesting.

Jayden smiles. "Mine isn't ten inches. I will happily admit to that. I wouldn't want one that big. What I have already has scared a few women so I wouldn't want it any longer." I roll my eyes. I must be confusing porn that he watches with real life once again. "I know my girl wouldn't want something that huge in her anyway," Jayden claims to have had sex with his girlfriend. I don't believe it.

"Where did you read that story mate?" I pick up a morsel of chicken that previously fell out of my soft-shell taco and toss it into my waiting mouth. "It is hilarious."

Jayden rubs his eyes and yawns. "It was posted on the Murdoch news website. I read the story when I was taking a massive shit in that nasty toilet block earlier that you took me to." Jayden grabs the bottle of Coke that is resting in front of Bryce and drinks from it. "Thanks, mate."

Bryce verbalises what I have been thinking. "Farting, shitting and ten-inch cocks. Such lovely conversation to have whilst I eat this fat thick uncut burrito. Hey Jayden, are you going to Commercial Road later?"

"No why?" Jayden looks confused and scratches the top of his head before crossing his arms. "Why the fuck would I go to Commercial Road?"

"I thought since you are dressed like a whore today that you would be joining the other prostitutes walking that street tonight offering your shit to the highest bidder." Bryce starts chuckling again having amused himself. It took a while for Bryce to comment on Jayden's outfit today. I expected the prodding to start as laid eyes on him.

"Are you jealous of my hot body mate? Have you had a good look?" Jayden stands up and pushes his arse out and towards Bryce and starts slapping it repeatedly. "I know that you check out my hot arse. Have a good look mate. Want to grab it?"

Bryce pushes Jayden away and he sits down. "Are we going to go shopping or something or are we just going to spend the day fucking around here?" I break the silence. "Let's get the hell out of here."

"Why don't you just say what is really going to happen, mate." Jayden stares at me which foreshadows that he plans to stir the pot. "This is how it will play out if we go, as you put it, shopping. Let's say we are silly enough to follow you to the Armani Exchange. You will then buy a shitload of clothes in five minutes flat and then whine that is taking too long to pay. You will then proclaim that you are over shopping and will want to go home. Does that sound, right?" Jayden kicks my leg under the table. "Am I right or what?"

I wince and then kick the leg of the table hoping my foot would contact Jayden's shin. "Am I really that predictable?" I pick up another morsel of chicken and toss it into my mouth and then interlock my hands behind my head.

Bryce and Jayden simultaneously shout, "Yes!" They look at one another and then scream, "jinx!"

I roll my eyes and stand up. "Jesus. Whatever. How about I go follow your script and meet you boys back here in fifteen minutes?"

Bryce and Jayden agree that following me around shopping isn't very fun. They don't have any money to buy anything anyway. I am left to my own devices to explore the Armani Exchange shop by myself. I am very brand loyal and like what they usually have on offer, mainly because I know my size and

I don't have to waste time or suffer the indignity of trying clothes on. As my routine never changes if my friends can be believed, I walk into the store, browse for items that I like and strategically not remove anything from the racks until I am ready to leave. I then make a mad dash around the shop and remove everything that I want so I am not hounded by the workers who try to engage in banal conversation. After walking only a few steps from the food court, I casually enter the Armani Exchange shop and begin to browse. I give a cursory look at the price and size tags attached to the clothing as I continue to browse. Mere minutes later, after inspecting everything available in the relatively small shop, I begin to execute my plan and methodically remove clothing from the various racks. The nearest sales associate notices my frenzied activity and literally sprints over and asks me if he can assist me in finding my size. I politely inform him that I know my size and start handing him one item of clothing after another as he follows me around the shop. "I will just buy these." The sales associate suggests that other items in different colours stored in the back room would match my green eyes. I brush off his upselling tactic and for once I am honest and say that I am in a rush to meet my friends. He immediately begins to scan the clothes using a wand located at the terminal and beings to remove the security tags.

"Do you have our VIP club card?" The sales associate asks as he repeated clicks the mouse and starts at the computer screen. He is roughly the same build as me and I find his blue eyes are very soothing.

"I don't have the card on me but can I give you my phone number?" After he replies in the affirmative, I say the digits of my mobile phone number. He successfully retrieves my profile from the database. He confirms my name matches what is in the system and then continues scanning tags. When he finishes he begins to carefully fold the clothing and places each piece of apparel carefully into a large bag.

Innocence Waning

The sales associated looks up at me and smiles. "Did you know if you spend a mere sixty dollars more in this transaction, I can give you a VIP discount card today so the next time you come in, you will save one hundred and fifty dollars?"

"Oh wow, fine. I am sure I can find something else to buy." I rub the back of my head. My eyes scan the store as I contemplate which way to walk.

"Give me a minute, please. I have a suggestion." The associate quickly disappears behind a door which slams shut. True to his word, about sixty seconds later he appears once again holding a shirt that immediately reminds me of what Bryce is wearing. "This will go nicely with your green eyes and your dirty blond hair if you don't mind me saying." I take the blood-red shirt from him and hold it up, admiring it. I really like it.

"Sure. It looks good, I will have it." After the final amount owing is calculated and complete the transaction using my debit card, the large bag of clothes is handed to me along with a card and an outstretched hand.

"It is good to meet you Chezdon, my name is James. I hope you will come back soon and see me. Here is your VIP card. Don't lose it."

"Thanks, mate. Later." After taking the VIP card, I shake his hand and examine his scruffy yet professional appearance. He is dressed in black Armani Exchange branded clothing from head to toe and is an attractive guy. "Take care." I turn and walk out of the shop.

Upon returning to the food court I find Jayden chewing on a taco. Bryce is speaking to someone on his phone and has his feet resting on the chair that I was sitting on earlier. "You bought the store I see." Jayden smiles. He grabs the bag of clothes from my hand and starts to scavenge around in it.

My phone begins to vibrate in my back pocket. "Jesus. What now?" I mutter. Jayden begins to pull clothes from the bag and tosses items on his chair. I am positive that he is making mental notes of the clothes that he will want to borrow. He stays overnight at my apartment frequently and always borrows clothes and rarely returns them. "I like this shit!" Jayden roars as I place my smartphone against my ear. Whoever is calling would have heard Jayden.

I scoff and grin. "Hi, this is Chezdon."

"Hi Chezdon, this is James from the Armani Exchange store at Emporium Melbourne. You were just in here." I am confused as to why this bloke is now ringing me. Did I leave my debit card in the shop? I shove my free hand into the depths of my pocket. "How are you?"

"Fine. Okay. I am fine." Bryce ends the call he was on and watches Jayden sort through the clothes that I purchased. Finding my debit card in my pocket, I quizzically ask, "what's up?"

"I just wanted to say thanks for coming into the store today." With added enthusiasm, James continues. "Your purchase helped me make my sales target for the week, so I just wanted to say thank you again."

"That is good to hear." I really don't know what to say and feel like I am bullshitting for the sake of it. I recently read an article about Richie Benaud, the cricket commentator and former captain of the Australian Cricket Test team. He only spoke when he had something of value to add to the conversation. I thought the article was apt considering we seem to live in a society where you feel like you need to be constantly communicating in one form or another.

James clears his throat. "I am hoping that I can buy you a drink sometime to say thanks." I am momentarily stunned and at such a loss of words.

I fumble some words together. "Sure. Cool. Great. That sounds good." I pay some attention to Jayden who continues to wave my new purchases above his head. "What do you have in mind?"

"How about we meet up tomorrow after I finish work?" James asks. "Drinks are on me." I like to think that I look my age and wonder how old James thinks I am. If I was wearing the outfit that Jayden was wearing, there would have been no doubt in his mind that I am sixteen.

"Fine. Just message me, I have got to go as I am with my mates. Chat with you tomorrow." I end the call as James begins to say something.

Bryce tilts his head to the right and licks his lips. "What is wrong, mate? "What happened?" Bryce demands. Jayden begins to shove my clothes back into the shopping bag.

"Nothing mate. It is all good." I resurrect the details of my limited interaction with James and go over it in my head. I was going out of my way not to engage with him or even look at him inside the shop. I assume that he is in his mid-twenties. I fondly recall the black studs that he has jammed into his earlobes. My phone vibrates in my hand momentarily, interrupting my total recall.

A text message appears from a number that is not part of my contact list. It is coincidentally from James who suggests that we meet at the Transport Bar at 5:00 PM tomorrow. Transport Bar is in Federation Square, spitting distance from the 7-11 where Jayden buys Slurpee's. That bar takes the responsible service of alcohol very seriously. Not only I but most of my classmates have been denied trying to order booze at that bar. I message James and suggest an alternate venue. The one pub that my friends and I have found that doesn't usually ask for identification. It is easy to relax in the low-key beer garden at this place, especially when you have someone else buying the rounds. James quickly responds in the affirmative and agrees to meet me at the pub that I suggested.

"What are we doing?" Bryce taps his fingers on the back of his phone. "I don't want to sit here all day watching Jayden eat tacos. How many can you eat mate?" Bryce tosses his phone on the table.

I lick my lips. "We can go back to my place and watch a movie or something." I offer my own hospitality as I selfishly want to drop my big bag of clothes off at home and not carry it around with me. "There is booze there and I don't think there will be any adults around." Bryce and I offer one another a wry smile whilst Jayden shoves the last of his chicken taco into his mouth.

"Sounds good!" Bryce yells and slams his hands down on the table in unison. "Let's get the fuck out of here." He grabs his phone and walks off obviously not wanting to wait for Jayden to swallow and offer his opinion.

We walk the less travelled path to Southbank, meandering along the laneways that give the city a distinct character. Ironically, we walk past the bar where James agreed to meet me tomorrow. Horse racing is being broadcast on the wall-mounted television in the beer garden. The afternoon revellers appear to be enjoying their pints and are smoking cigarettes under a large tree. I wonder if I should just order a juice when I meet James tomorrow. It would be awkward getting caught out and being refused service. Acknowledging the fact that I am only sixteen-years-old and embarrassing me or him begins to play on my mind. Is this a date or if it will be two mates enjoying a beer, talking about footy and his sales targets? I rub the sweat off the back of my neck and wipe it on Jayden.

Banter makes me lose track of time. We arrive at my apartment tower in Southbank in what feels like minutes when it has really been a half an hour since leaving Emporium. After riding in the elevator and unlocking the front door, we enter my climate-controlled home in the sky. "Chezdon?" I hear a woman's voice. "Is that you?"

"Oh dude, have you ever met Melisandre?" Jayden asks Bryce whilst tapping on him on his chest with his open hand. "She is so cool."

Melisandre is the 'Red Woman' in the *Game of Thrones* series. I once told my father that the woman who he has been dating for many years resembles the 'Red Woman' in the television show. My father agreed and even bought her a red robe that she wears around the apartment on occasion. She has never bothered to watch *Game of Thrones* so I am confident that she doesn't get the inside joke. "The bitch from *Game of Thrones*? What does she have to do with anything?" Bryce asks.

Melanie walks into the living room and offers her greetings. I didn't expect her to be around and thought she would be out with my father at the races. "It looks like you have been shopping. Can I see what you bought?"

"Sure, go for it." I hand her my large shopping bag.

Mel goes out of her way to act like my friend. She is cool and never tries to take on a motherly type of role. She goes out of her way to treat me as her peer and speaks to me like I am an adult. She has a great relationship with Jayden and they share many inside jokes, most being at my own expense I would assume. Since she doesn't want to bear children I suppose it makes it easier for us to treat one another as friends. Besides even if she wanted to have a child with my father, it would be difficult since he had a vasectomy after I was born. My birth mother has suggested that he got the operation because he didn't want a child to begin with and I was, in fact, a mistake. She is an evil bitch. For a mother to say something so heinous to her child is just pathetic.

I leave the bag with Mel who happily begins to sort through the clothes in the same way that Jayden did earlier. My friends and I retreat to my room once Jayden and Bryce exchange stop snickering. Jayden walks into my bathroom and takes the fingernail clippers off the basin. He cuts the price tag off the blood-red shirt that he absconded with before Mel took the bag of clothes from me. He pulls off his slutty cut-up shirt and tosses it on the floor. He fumbles pulling on the shirt that James went out of his way to sell me. I touch the impression of the VIP discount card bulging in my pocket next to my penis which twitches against the pressure of my skinny jeans.

"Thanks for the shirt," Jayden unbuttons three of the buttons so he can continue to fulfil his destiny to represent all the trashy looking teenage boys in the world. "I like this. Good job, Chez."

"You are such an arsehole mate." Bryce summarises what I am feeling with only a few words. "You have some balls though."

"It is no big deal. I didn't even want that shirt." I lie. "It was forced on me at the last minute so I could get a one hundred fifty-dollar voucher. I really don't give a fuck." Although I want the shirt and feel like ripping it off Jayden, I decide to brush it off. "It does look good on you Jayden. You can have it, mate."

"Aren't you going to buy a new phone today?" Bryce looks at me. "You have been carrying on about it for weeks."

Innocence Waning

"Oh shit. I almost forgot. Thanks for reminding me." My eyes go wide and I push my hair behind my ear again. "I will be right back."

"Where are you going?" Jayden asks as I walk from my bedroom and quickly walk down the hall and go into the room where the adults sleep. I spent all the money in my savings account on clothes so I need to get raid the stash of cash that my father told me about earlier. I rummage through the middle drawer next to his bed and discover a neatly stacked under a book. It must be leftover winnings from gambling but I really don't care. I begin to count out multiples of fifty dollar notes so that I can purchase the Samsung smartphone that I have been talking about for weeks.

I am poked in the side. "Jesus man!" I jump after Jayden startles me. He leans over my shoulder and I momentarily lose my balance. He points his finger and I look inside the open drawer. "We could have a good party with that."

I continue counting money, making a mental note to tell my father later how much I took. "Mind your own business mate," I demand and continue to count currency, ignoring Jayden. His hand dives into the open drawer. "That isn't your business mate, fuck off!"

"Wow, look at this!" Jayden holds up a small sealed plastic bag which contains white powder. "Want to guess what this is? We could have a good party, hey?"

"Put that back mate!" I raise my voice and shove my body into Jayden. I didn't know that my father dabbled with party drugs. "Give it to me."

"Let's do it and see what happens." Jayden slyly suggests.

"I really doubt my father would be too pleased if his stash went missing." I try to reason with Jayden. I can imagine some awkward conversation days or even weeks from now where my father musters the courage to ask me if I stole his bag of cocaine from his bedside table. "Who will be blamed for taking it? Mel?" I giggle thinking about how that conversation would go down.

"If he says anything, just blame it on your cleaner. She is Columbian, isn't she? Oh, I know, we can replace it with flour. Is your father going to write a letter of complaint to his dealer? He will just put the flour up his nose and be none the wiser." Jayden pushes the small plastic bag into his pocket. "We are doing your duty to help him. Think of it that way."

"Jesus," I mutter as I push my father's money into my pocket and close the bedside drawer. Jayden follows me back into my room and pulls the small plastic bag from his pocket. He dramatically waves his score in front of Bryce's face. "Let's get fucked up mate. Let's party."

"Where did you get that you idiot?" Bryce asks incredulously. "Holy shit!"

"Chezdon's father is drug-fucked. He has a drawer filled with cash and coke. I love it." Jayden is really hamming it up and begins to sing. "I am so excited, and I just can't hide it."

"Shut the hell up," I demand. "Jesus, do you think you are one of the fucking Pointer Sisters? The last thing I want is Mel coming in here and asking questions." Jayden starts to laugh. "You make it sound like my father is some version of Walter White. This isn't *Breaking Bad*, mate."

"No, it is *Game of Thrones* judging by who is in your living room." Jayden and I both chuckle. "I wonder how much that coke is worth," Bryce asks quizzically. "My sister would probably buy it."

"Let's do it later," Jayden declares and then changes the subject. "Are we going to go out again or what? Chez can buy his phone."

"Yeah, let's go." Bryce is looking at the poster of the four boys that make up the band *5 Seconds of Summer* which is affixed to my bedroom wall. "Is there a JB Hi-Fi around here?"

My phone begins to vibrate again. I glance at the screen and sigh when I see that the caller ID is blocked and divert the caller to my voicemail with one tap. Seconds after the phone stops vibrating, it starts in again. Exasperated, I accept the call this time. "Hi, this is Chezdon." I am not surprised when there is no response. "Goddamnit! Why do you keep ringing me and not bother to say anything? Jesus Christ!"

A voice finally speaks. "Those are some pretty harsh words from such a little boy." My friends look up at me. Jayden taps the small plastic bag against his nose repeatedly.

"Who is this?" I ask tersely. The male voice sounds vaguely familiar but I can't identify it. The call suddenly ends and I quickly get lost in my thoughts. Bizarre phone calls, a scheduled hook-up in the public toilets, a date of sorts arranged at a pub, my best mate holding a bag of drugs and a wad of cash in my pocket. What could possibly go wrong?

4. James

Bryce swipes and taps on the display of his iPhone erratically. After remaining unusually quiet for what seems like an eternity, he finally speaks. "I just checked the Bureau of Meteorology's website and it looks like it is going to rain in forty minutes."

I vacillate between venturing out and staying put. Do I lead my friends to the South Wharf shopping precinct so we can browse the electronics superstore? Purchasing the phone of my dreams is on my mind, however, my thoughts revert to identifying the voice of the nuisance caller. His voice was that of an older bloke, which adds to my frustration. Who the hell could it be?

"Let's just watch a movie or something!" Jayden mumbles after taking the prime position on the corner of the lounge. He grabs the integrated remote control and powers on the Samsung television along with the other audio and subservient components by tapping a single button. My father invested a fair amount of time automating this system. He would frequently become flustered having to look at five different remote controls which just added to the clutter on the glass table which he could not tolerate. "Just get the phone from the Samsung shop the next time you are at Melbourne Central." Jayden offers a suggestion most likely because he wants to avoid being rained on. "It isn't hard."

I cross my arms and ponder what to do next. "I was given a gift card for JB Hi-Fi and I want to use it. It is going to expire in a few days." I patiently wait for my friends to show a hint of motivation to budge off the lounge and stand up.

Bryce follows Jayden's lead and assumes a comfortable position on the lounge. He places one of the red pillows between his arm and torso and stares out the window. Dark clouds are slowly creeping towards us from the southwest. He pulls off his Converse shoes and then peels the socks from his feet. He isn't going anywhere. "Fine." I simply say and return my gaze out the window. The mysterious caller has left me unnerved. I grab at the back of my head and mess my hair up further. My dishevelled appearance will hopefully distract anyone who looks at me from the blood that is rushing to my cheeks and face. "The hell with going out and getting rained on," I confidently announce. The menacing storm that is approaching from the southwest coughs a bout of thunder. Taking up residence in the lounge room seems like the most comfortable right now.

Jayden begins scrolling through the recently added television shows and movies on the media centre laptop that is connected to the television. Mel walks past with a large bag of rubbish from the kitchen which gives him just enough time to select *Game of Thrones*. The score which accompanies the opening credits of the television show begins to play and everyone hums along in time. "Nope. I have already seen this." He taps the back button and returns to the homepage that lists the newest media that has been added to the system. He curiously watches Mel as she walks toward the foyer and laughs. "It looks like you watched a movie called *Eastern Boys*. What the hell is that about?"

Bryce reads the description of the movie courtesy of the synopsis that is being displayed on the television screen. "Jesus Christ. Don't they teach you how to read at your private school?"

The front door slams shut which startles me. "It is actually a really good movie." I chirp. "It is about a gang of migrants from some old Soviet eastern bloc country that fucks over a gay bloke. The dude tried to solicit sex from one of the gang members at the train station." I do a double-take and ponder my recent experiences inside the public toilets and roll my eyes for added effect and dramatically point at the screen. "Look at the Rotten Tomatoes score of eighty-seven. There is no reason to judge it." The faceless men and women behind the Rotten Tomatoes scoring system seem to know everything. I point at the screen again so the uninterested eyes of my friends will hopefully provide some validation with a simple nod or at least will offer some sort of clue that they agree with me.

"I am not judging you mate. It looks interesting enough." Jayden says and then begins to scroll through more movies that are stored on the clustered hard drives. "*Nymphomaniac*, hey? Is that on your top-ten list, Chezdon? I read a review of this movie somewhere. It is supposedly long as hell. Shia LaBeouf fucks some chick in it and you can see his little cock." Jayden coughs and clears his throat.

Bryce begins to laugh hysterically and we wait for his glee to subside before contributes to the conversation. "Where do you come up with this shit? Have you watched it? How would you know that Shia LaBeouf has a small cock unless you took an active interest in it, mate?"

"It is the word on the street." Jayden insists. He crosses his arms and then his legs. "I also read that LaBeouf got raped when he was putting on some sort of art exhibit somewhere. It was during some sort of live show in public. How can that be possible?"

Bryce takes a keen interest in his phone and begins to read something on its screen out loud. "One woman who came with her boyfriend, who was outside the door when this happened, whipped my legs for ten minutes and then stripped my clothing and proceeded to rape me. What the fuck?" Bryce looks mortified as he reads an article presumably about Shia LaBeouf to us verbatim. "People just decided to do whatever they wanted to him. Since he was in an artistic moment, the bloke couldn't say no or even punch someone in the face when they touched him up?"

"Madness." The story puzzles me and I ponder the ridiculousness of the situation in general. The front door slams shut and it startles me again.

Bryce continues to read out loud. "Hashtag I-AM-SORRY involves LaBeouf sitting silently behind a desk in a room in the Los Angeles Cohen gallery with a paper bag bearing the legend 'I am not famous anymore' over his head. For five days, members of the public queued to be able to sit alone with him in a room with a prop of their choice." We all start to laugh in unison. "How many films can he ride a motorbike in and pretend he is cool? This is such a joke. Who would want to waste their time sitting with this bloke?"

Jayden grasps his hands behind his head and looks to be very comfortable with his feet resting on top of the glass table. "I guess that just means that you can stroke his cock and shove a broom handle up his arse. Why wouldn't he rip the bag off and punch the person who raped him?" Jayden offers in a very animated way. "Things like this make me really angry. What a dickhead."

Mel stops next to the television and looks concerned. "Who was raped?" Mel asks us with a sense of concern in her voice having to overhear the tail-end of our conversation.

"Shia" I curtly respond.

"Oh, is she okay?" Mel asks and appears interested.

Bryce makes it known that this person is the bloke from the *Transformers* movie franchise and from what Jayden articulated, the movie, *Nymphomaniac*. I add that he will be just fine and was just part of an art installation that went wrong for too many reasons to list. Mel manages an uncomfortable laugh. "I am going to open a bottle of wine. Does anyone care for a glass?"

"It is only 2:30 PM you know," I interject knowing full well that time doesn't matter when it involves the consumption of alcohol in this household. "I will have a glass, please." I offer Mel a wide smile and show her my teeth. Bryce and Jayden also respond in the affirmative. I did promise alcohol to my friends on the way home and fortunately, Mel is delivering.

"Chezdon, you just reminded me that you need to visit the dentist soon. I will make an appointment for you. Bryce, do you know the house rule?" Mel asks. "There is only one rule."

"The rule is if you start drinking alcohol in this place, we aren't allowed to leave unless it is straight home via Uber," Jayden replies as the rule has been ingrained into his memory. "Safety is Mel's number one priority."

"That sounds like a Qantas safety message," I respond knowing that even Qantas wouldn't let a gaggle of teenagers get into the wine so early in the afternoon despite their desire for increased market share. Perhaps booze will take the edge off. I need to distract myself from thinking about nuisance phone calls and public toilets.

Bryce watches Jayden pulls on a few strands of his exposed underarm hair. "What is your drink of choice you freak? Alcohol from a cardboard box mate?" Jayden quickly crosses his arms over his chest.

Jayden chuckles and swats Bryce's chest. "My drink of choice is your mother's milk. I love sucking it from her hard-hairy nipples." Jayden squeals and laughs before scrolling through the list of movies again. He stops when he sees *Mysterious Skin* and begins to read the synopsis out loud which will prove to Bryce that he knows how to read. "Aliens, Joseph Gordon-Levitt. Let's watch this."

Mel returns holding two wine glasses by their stems. Bryce offers his thoughts on the movie in a monotonal voice. "Not to spoil the movie for you mate, but your idol Joseph Gordon-Levitt gets butt-raped and plays a teenage male whore. It will be a bit like art imitating life for you I suppose mate." Mel sets the two glasses of red wine carefully on the glass table and begins to laugh. I then explode into hysterics as Bryce starts to cackle.

"Whatever." Jayden selects *The Shining* and taps play on the integrated remote. "You remind me of the fucked up little boy in this film Bryce."

Mel returns with a glass of wine and hands it to me. "Thanks, Mel." She places the bottle on top of the newspaper and then retreats to the kitchen. We drink wine and provide running commentary about the movie since we have all seen before. Half an hour later, I empty the last of the bottle into Bryce's glass and I am tasked to retrieve another one. I walk to the wine refrigerator, taking care not to touch any of the bottles that my father has deemed off limits. The understanding is not to drink anything from the Barossa Valley. Those regional varietals are always in short supply here only because so many bottles are consumed by my father and Mel on a regular basis. Instead, I remove a bottle of Marsh Estate, a wine produced in the Hunter Valley, not far from Sydney. The rain begins to pelt against the windows with force. The front door slams again, which startles me. I return to the lounge room holding the neck of the open bottle of wine at the same time my father walks in.

"Hey, Daniel. How were the races?" Jayden immediately stands and shakes my father's hand. "Have you met our esteemed peer

Bryce yet? He is a tad antisocial, I know, and he apologises for not standing up." Daniel insists on being called by his and detests formality in the family home.

"I am just fine, Jayden, thanks. It was a good day at the races. Tom Waterhouse will not be retiring anytime soon." Tom Waterhouse is the CEO of the betting agency that my father places wagers with. "Yes, I know Bryce. How are you doing, mate?" Bryce stands up and shakes my father's hand whilst holding his glass of wine with his left hand. "Hopefully my favourite son is keeping you boys entertained." It was more of a statement and not a question. He is not looking for a detailed answer. Daniel walks to the kitchen and after hearing the clinking of glasses and some chatter in the distance, I am not surprised when he returns holding an empty red wine glass. "I will have some of that Marsh if you would be so kind, mate." He sets the glass on the table near Bryce.

Bryce slowly pours wine into the depths of my father's glass. "This particular varietal has the distinction of being the only wine in the Hunter Valley region that is only irrigated by rain. Therefore, it will taste earthy. Even dirty." Daniel has long insisted that if we are going to drink his wine that we appreciate the story behind what we are gulping from our crystal glasses.

The scene in *The Shining* where the funny looking wife is explaining to the doctor that Jack Nicholson broke their son's arm is playing out on the television. "Look at that doctor, she looks mortified." My father blurts out and pours the wine in his glass down his throat. "It amuses me that the wife can act so blasé about her son being abused. She smokes a pack of cigarettes whilst telling the sordid story and that only takes thirty seconds." He sets his empty glass near Bryce again. "Does Chezdon tell you boys that I physically abuse him?"

"Only emotionally," I say and offer a smile. "I only say you abused me before I started puberty though." We both look at the television and laugh.

Bryce casually refills not only Daniel's wine glass but his own. Jayden grabs the wine bottle from him. "Oi!" Daniel shouts and gets Jayden's attention. "Jayden, you should only refill your glass when it is empty. This is one of the few things that upset me as you do not want to disrespect the wine. It will make for a different tasting experience as the wine opens up in the bottle and you don't want to mix it." Jayden gulps what is left in his glass and then fills it. "Look at this bloody weather. I had to leave the races early as the rain killed the track. The bastards were probably going to cancel the rest of the races anyway."

"Why would they do that?" Jayden asks. He pushes his nose into the depths of the wine glass and snorts.

"Management would be fearful that the horses would get spooked by the thunder and lightning." Daniel drinks from his glass and looks out the window. "Also, there would be public outrage if a horse was struck by lightning."

Mel returns holding an empty glass by its stem and kisses Daniel on his cheek. "Why are you bothering the boys, leave them alone and let them have fun." Mel pours what is left of the bottle in her glass and takes a sip.

"He isn't bothering us, Mel." Jayden clarifies. "In fact, I am keen to hear more about the races and how your business is going." Jayden's parents are getting divorced and his father recently moved out of the family home to Western Australia which is thousands of kilometres away. Since the separation, Jayden has adopted my father as his own and now kisses Daniel's arse whenever he has the opportunity.

Both Daniel and Mel sit down next to Jayden. My father starts a conversation with Jayden about horse racing and the wild world of business. Feeling sombre, I walk to the wine refrigerator and retrieve another bottle, refill my glass and then offer Bryce a top-up. I move the empty bottle that we just finished to the side of the newspaper. "Another dead soldier."

Having sat in an awkward position with Mel and Daniel obstructing my view of the television, I lean to the side and recline back onto Bryce, put my feet up and assume a comfortable position. "Thanks, mate, I knew you would be good for something someday." I raise my glass and acknowledge my newfound human pillow from over my shoulder.

My father recants boring stories about his business which mainly involves difficult conversations with Chinese and Malaysian suppliers. Mel nods her head two hundred times and zones out staring at the television and sips from her glass. Jayden somehow manages to devise a thousand questions to ask and Daniel is happy to keep pouring wine and continues to answer them as fast as Jayden can ask them. It doesn't take long before Daniel is on his feet and removing another bottle of Marsh Estate from the wine refrigerator though.

Time passes and the movie continues to play. Daniel and Jayden continue to talk as I lean against Bryce with a glass of wine in my hand. I have wondered how my father would react if he found out that I am gay. For a moment, I consider interrupting the story he is telling Jayden about corrupt overseas business practices. I can tell him a fact that I doubt that he has considered. The same goes for Jayden. I promised myself some time ago that if Jayden asked me a direct question about my sexuality, I would answer him truthfully. He just never has. Neither has Daniel. Finally, my father excuses himself from question time. Mel follows him from the living room with the only open bottle of wine, which encourages me to follow them to the kitchen to retrieve yet another bottle.

"Hey Chez, I messaged Austin saying that we are chilling out. Can he come around?" Jayden asks as I return with the uncorked wine bottle. Austin is another friend from school and is the type of person that is friends with everybody. Everyone likes the boy and he is very easy to get along with.

With the alcohol now integrating itself with my blood, I decide, what the hell. "Yeah, tell Austin to come over mate." I reach over and pick up my phone from the glass table after setting the bottle of wine down on the newspaper. I skim messages that have arrived over the last few hours and notice that three of them are from Austin. He was quizzing me as to what I am up to. He must have surmised that Jayden would be with me since we always seem to be hanging out nowadays. I exchange a few text messages with Austin and he confirms that he will come around shortly.

Daniel begins to get nervous when I invite too many people over to the apartment. On the day of my birthday last year, four of my mates and I thought it would be a good idea to start drinking my father's wine. Each of us then thought it would be fun to invite four of our mutual friends around to my apartment when my father was out at the horse races. When he returned home there were eighteen boys and two girls having the party of the year in this place. Guests were found having sex in my room. I was aware of what was happening but because I was drunk, I didn't give a fuck. Another boy and girl were caught by my father in his bedroom having sex. I don't know how many times he proclaimed that I disrespected the property after the party finished ahead of schedule and everyone was thrown out. He will go to the grave repeating that he saw some 'slut fuck a boy like Damien Oliver would ride a bloody horse.' Damien Oliver is one of the most prolific Australian horse jockeys and even nearly a year later I am reminded weekly of the specifics of my last birthday party. I continually swear something like that will never happen again when my father sees a mere handful of my friends in the apartment.

I review a series of messages from a phone number that is not saved in my contact list and quickly ascertain that it is James. He has announced that he has finished work and wants to meet for a drink today. I look up and mumble. "Today? Not tomorrow?" Feeling buzzed, I respond and suggest that we meet at the Belgian Beer Cafe, which is next to my apartment building.

"What are you doing arsehole?" Jayden shouts. Bryce is trying to pull on Jayden's exposed armpit hair. "Stop it. Chez, pass me the bottle, please."

I comply and hand Jayden the bottle and he refills his glass. Memories of the snails which are drowned in garlic and butter that is served at the restaurant next door that I told James to meet me at momentarily overwhelms me. "Oh, Jesus," I utter which draws the attention of both Bryce and Jayden and they both offer me a quizzical look. I must be buzzed. What did I suggest? I quickly read my sent messages. "Shit." His last message said that he would be downstairs in twenty minutes. "Shit," I mutter again.

I look up at the television and to discover that Jack Nicholson has frozen to death in the hedge maze. The credits for the movie are now scrolling up the television. "Hey Jayden, did Austin say when he will get here?"

"About twenty minutes." Jayden turns and looks at me. "Why?"

"I need your help. I need to fuck off outside quickly but I need you to distract my father and Mel if they come out here. You know the rules. If they catch me outside of the apartment after getting into the wine, I will be fucked." Not fucked like how Jack Torrance met his demise in the snow at the end of *The Shining*, but it will be a fate worse than death.

Bryce places his phone on the cushion next to him. He looks at Jayden and then they both look at me. "Where do you need to go that is so important, mate?" Bryce smiles and licks the rim of his wine glass suggestively. "I am very keen to know."

I think that I can manage to have a quick pint of orange juice with James whilst I leave my friends in the flat. It is with that silly thought that I come to realise that the red wine has impaired my judgement. My usually good critical thinking and time management skills are now rubbish. If I am away and Jayden starts asking Daniel a further one thousand questions about work and Austin turns up, things will not end well. Bryce doesn't know Austin from a bar of soap either. More bloody drama. I slide towards Bryce, grab the bottle and pour myself another glass of wine, which gives me some time to consider my options. "Never mind, don't worry about it. I was just going to step out and meet James quickly." I hope my simple explanation will satisfy his curiosity as I take a sip.

"Who the hell is James?" Jayden asks. "I have never heard you mention a James. Do we even know a James?" Jayden scratches his head and then his armpit. "Is there even a James at our school?"

"I don't know anyone called James," Bryce injects and stares at Jayden. He then tries to tug one of Jayden's errant armpit hairs again.

I return to the security of my phone and attempt to tap out a message on my phone as Jayden shouts in pain. "Hold on!" I demand and then send another message to James, asking him to meet me here. I glance at my watch and then look at my friends who are both staring at me. Jayden is rubbing his armpit. Whatever happens, at least it will be entertaining. "James is just a bloke that I was talking to at the Emporium earlier," I say as innocently as possible. "I am just trying to expand my social circle.".

After taking a few seconds to process what I said, Jayden speaks. "What school does this kid go to?" An apt question, indeed. Jayden appears intrigued and shoves his nose into his wine glass and snorts. James hasn't even agreed to come to my apartment so I may be creating a drama for no reason at all. "When did you have time to talk to anyone earlier?"

My eyes dart from the left and to the right searching for the right answer. I decide it is not in my interest to spin some lie so I come clean. "James is the bloke that sold me the clothes at Armani Exchange. We just started chatting and he seems pretty cool." I take a sip of wine and set the glass gently down on top of the newspaper.

Jayden looks at Bryce who then looks at his phone and laughs. Like a dog with a bone, Jayden continues to probe. "You couldn't have been out shopping for fifteen minutes and now some retail slut is your new mate?" Jayden eyes have opened wide. "How old is this bloke?" At least by explaining the situation right now, my friends will not be so shocked that they embarrass me and themselves if he does agree to come around.

"Mate, I don't know. I didn't ask him how old he is. He is in his twenties, I guess. Why do you care? I thought it would be fun to have a drink with him." I never thought that the wine would lead me to make such a spontaneous decision. Another message arrives from James. He proclaims that he is keen to come around now and asks for my address. I respond with the relevant details.

I recount my brief interaction with James to my interested friends. I explain that James simply asked me if I wanted to get a drink as some sort of thank you for helping him make his sales target. I finish the story by raising my voice along with my glass as their laughter nearly drowns out my story.

Jayden looks at his vibrating phone. "Austin will be here in one minute." Jayden's lips skew to the right. I know that he is pondering what to say next. He swirls the red wine in his glass and sets his phone on the glass table.

The video intercom on the wall rings obnoxiously, startling me. The video display comes to life. I walk over to it and see Austin's smiling face staring into the camera. I pick up the receiver that is attached to the intercom unit and yell a protracted "Wassup!" I press the button that briefly unlocks the front door of the residential tower, which will allow my friend to access to the building. That single press of a button also permits him to ride the elevator to my home on the 72nd floor. Austin has been to my apartment many times in the past so he doesn't need any further instruction. I walk to the foyer and out of sight of my friends and wait by the front door holding my glass of wine. Bryce and Jayden continue to laugh hysterically in the living room at my expense.

A knock on the door is followed by me quickly opening it which reveals Austin. His dark brown eyes pair well with his ripped blue skinny jeans and white shirt. My attention is then drawn to his silver DC shoes and then his blond wavy hair which looks a bit more wild than usual today. He always dresses very trendily when he isn't forced to wear the school uniform on weekdays. We exchange our usual greeting, "Sup!" I follow him as he walks past me through the foyer and into the apartment which gives me time to check out his arse.

"Hey Austin, do you want some wine, mate?" Jayden offers him an open bottle. Austin looks around awkwardly. It then dawns on me that I should be playing the role of host, and not Jayden.

"Austin, this is Bryce Pistorius. Bryce, this is Austin McGuire." Bryce stands up and shakes Austin's hand. He compliments Austin on his shoes. This breaks the ice and the teenagers begin talking about where to find distinctively colourful clothes in the southern suburbs of Melbourne. Jayden jogs into the kitchen and quickly returns with an empty wine glass, fills it and hands it to Austin. The conversation quickly turns to the much-maligned topic of footy. Austin and Bryce quickly find that they have something in common. They roar in unison when they learn that they both support the Carlton Football Club. Technically, Jayden and I should be mortal enemies with Austin and Bryce since we support the Collingwood Magpies, as there is a robust rivalry between the two teams.

"How did the two of you meet?" I take a sip of wine as the inevitable question is asked by Austin. His dark eyes dart back and forth between Bryce and me. I thought Austin would ask Bryce if he is related to Oskar Pistorius, the Olympian that murdered his wife since Bryce has a South African accent and they share the same surname.

I grab the bottle of wine by its neck. My friends all watch me pour wine into my glass. I open my mouth to answer the question but Jayden raises his hand and interrupts me. "Believe me mate that can wait. You should ask Chez how he met the other bloke that is turning up here." Jayden slowly raises his glass to his lips and drinks wine slowly whilst keeping his blue eyes focused on me.

The video intercom rings again and the monitor comes to life. "Oh fuck. Wait a minute." At first, I believe that I have been saved by the bell, but then realise I am just delaying the inevitable. I walk to the video intercom wondering how this is going to end up. Daniel and Mel are not going to stay hidden forever as they will wonder for whom the bell tolls and what all the commotion in the lounge room is all about. Fuck my life. The messes that I create.

"This is going to be awesome!" Bryce shouts. "There is nothing too sinister about how I met Chezdon mate, we met at an athletic carnival about a year ago. Did I mention you have some pretty cool shoes?" Bryce compliments Austin's silver shoes yet again as I answer the video intercom.

"Are strippers coming or something? I don't understand." Austin asks looking confused. I turn around and look at him after seeing James appear on the screen. He is looking at the small camera mounted on the keypad mounted on the outside wall near the entrance to the building. I pause and wonder if pressing the entry button will potentially be the worst decision that I have ever made or if I am just overthinking things as per usual. What could possibly happen? We are young adults after all. The wine has given me courage.

"Press the button!" Jayden yells. "Press it, press it, press it." Jayden and Bryce begin to chant.

"Who is it, Miranda Kerr?" Austin asks and begins walking towards me. I think of my father betting on races and how once he said that you win some and you lose some but you should never regret the choices that you make in the end. I press the entry button. The video display goes black before Austin can look over my shoulder. "I am so confused."

I turn around and place my hand on Austin's shoulder. He steps back. "It is just a guy I know called James. He wanted to catch up for a drink at some point so I am killing two birds with one stone." I glance over Austin's shoulder and raise my voice. "Besides, why should you blokes care?" I look at Austin. He quickly pours wine down his throat and then licks his lips.

"I don't know anyone called James. Does he go to our school? Catch up for a drink? I didn't realise you were some barfly. What a laugh!" Austin smirks. Jayden realises there is no wine in his glass and reaches for the bottle sitting innocuously on the glass table. Bryce begins scrolling through the available movies stored on the media centre. He selects the movie *Mysterious Skin* which we discussed earlier and presses play. "I am so confused, I don't know anyone called James," Austin repeats out loud. He pushes his blond fringe off his forehead. He indicates to Jayden with hand signals to pass the bottle of wine that he is holding.

"Just drink up mate and go with the flow," Jayden adds. There is a loud knock on the door. I take a deep breath and walk quickly to the foyer. I take another deep breath before opening the door. What have I done?

"Hey." I look at James. Laughter erupts from the lounge room behind me. "Sorry mate, I am sure you were not expecting to come around to my place only to find my obnoxious friends. They are harmless though."

James looks over my shoulder. I turn my head and find Jayden standing behind me and quickly return my attention to James. "Sorry mate, come in, please. It is good to see you again."

"It has been, what? A whole four hours or something like that?" James smiles and walks past me. He looks Jayden up and down. "Is this your brother?"

"No, thank Christ." I laugh uncomfortably. "This is my mate, Jayden McKenzie." I grimace and point at Jayden. He looks like he is going to start laughing hysterically again. "Jayden, this is James, um. I don't know your surname."

James looks at Jayden. "Wow, you look young mate. Sorry. It is good to meet you." James shakes Jayden's hand. I explain that we have been drinking for a few hours and not to take our antics too seriously. James follows me into the lounge room. Jayden stands curiously behind us with his nose stuck in his wine glass. I introduce Bryce and Austin to James. Neither one of them stands up, but simultaneously say "Sup!" and look at each other for a second before taking a drink.

"Okay. I didn't realise that I was going to be hanging out with One Direction today." James says. If he was trying to break the ice, his attempt will have failed miserably. Jayden would take some offence since he considers himself a performance artist and not a manufactured pop star in the making.

Jayden begins to sing a One Direction song. "I still don't know what the hell is going on. Who are you?" Austin demands after pushing his hand on Jayden's mouth. "I am just so confused." Austin finishes the rest of the wine that is in his glass and reaches for the empty bottle. "What do you do James and how did you end up here today?"

Bryce stands up and walks toward the kitchen. "I will get another bottle. Do you want some wine, James?"

"No thanks. I don't like wine. But yeah, I met Chezdon earlier today when he was shopping. We were going to catch up for a drink tomorrow but now I am here. So yeah." James can't stop starting at Austin. "How do you know each other?"

Austin continues to smell the inside of his empty glass and stares out the window. "We go to school together. Well, we don't go to school with this bloke." Austin motions at Bryce as he walks around the corner holding an uncorked bottle of wine. Bryce begins to refill the empty glasses.

"Where do you go? Melbourne?" James asks as he looks out the window at the Melbourne city skyline. "This is a great view."

Jayden holds out the empty glass so Bryce can fill it. "I bet you like the view mate." Jayden winks at Bryce. They both start to chuckle.

I follow Austin's lead and shove my nose inside the glass of wine. The smell of oak transports me back to a more innocent time when I was forced to go on a wine tasting tour with Mel and Daniel in the Yarra Valley, north of Melbourne. Austin stands up and holds out his glass before answering. "Yeah, we go to Melbourne. Great guess." Bryce pours more blood of the gods.

James finally stops starting at Austin long enough to engage in small talk with Bryce. "Where do you go, mate?"

"St Kevin's." Bryce curtly replies and reverts his attention back to the muted movie which is playing.

"Where is that? Can I get a glass of water?" James begins to fidget. I walk around the corner into the kitchen.

"Toorak. It is a damned all-boys school. It is a great place if you like boys." I nearly drop a bottle of water as I close the refrigerator door after hearing Bryce's remark. He obviously noticed James leering at Austin.

"Oh, I see. I have never heard of that University. Is it some trade school?" James says. He catches my eye as I walk into the living room holding a bottle of water in one hand and my glass of wine in the other. I would have thought that Bryce telling him it is an all-boys school would have let the cat out of the bag.

Jayden laughs and sets his glass down hard on the table. "No, you fool, it is a boy's college. He is in year eleven." Bryce begins to laugh hysterically again. His laughter is contagious and Austin joins the frivolity. "At least you picked us right.

Melbourne Grammar is the place to be." Austin gives Jayden a fist bump and they roll their eyes.

I hand James the water bottle just as he incredulously shouts "Grammar? I thought you went to Melbourne University!" This verbal exchange is so ridiculous I can't help but chuckle.

Daniel and Mel walk into the lounge room. My father looks at us one-by-one. "Hey boys, please keep the crowd limited to just you lot. I don't want this to turn into a party."

Mel stands next to James looks at him in the eyes and extends her hand. "Hi. I don't think I know you." I feel like running out of the apartment, going outside and jumping into the river. I drop my head and realise this is not going to end well as I look at my shoes.

"How old are you James if you don't mind me asking?" Jayden queries what I am confident that everyone is curious to learn. I knew one of my friends would ask James this question at some point, but I certainly did not want the topic broached in front of my father.

James drinks most of the water from the bottle before answering. "Twenty-five."

"What the fuck?" My father goes quiet and appears that he is considering his words. Austin returns to sniffing the contents of his wine glass. Bryce finds a sudden interest in the television. Jayden begins to chew on his bottom lip and takes a sudden interest in the painting hanging above him on the wall.

I need to start talking to distract everyone. I need to get control of the conversation before this gets out of hand. "Pretty cool painting isn't it Jayden?" Jayden looks at me and swirls the red wine in his glass. "The artist, Adam Cullen, died not long ago thanks to a long bout with both heroin addiction and alcohol.

He won the Archibald Prize too." I regurgitate as much as I can remember about the painter. Daniel has told countless people about this painting and the tragic life of the artist.

My father refills his wine glass. "You don't find it odd hanging out with a bunch of sixteen-year-olds on a Saturday afternoon, James?" I am so embarrassed. Fuck my life.

"Look, well, umm, you know, I have to go. It was nice meeting everyone but I have to go." James looks like he is going to hyperventilate as he rubs his neck. I follow him as he walks to the front door of the apartment, opens it and leaves. I catch up to him in the hallway as he stands near the elevator door, the riotous laughter is filtered as the front door slams behind me. James rapidly presses the 'down' button at least ten times. He looks like he would rather be held captive by ISIS instead of being here right now. I want to tell him that I can empathise as when I return to the lounge room, I will be facing my own judgement and perhaps even a beheading.

"Message me?" I ask. The bell announces that the elevator has arrived and the doors slide open. James turns and tosses the empty water bottle at me. It bounces off my knee as I attempt to catch it mid-air. He walks into the elevator and disappears behind the closing doors, presumably never to be heard from again.

Innocence Waning

5. **Austin**

I recover the plastic water bottle that was thrown at me and sheepishly return to my apartment, closing the door gently behind me. Lightning strikes nearby and the crackling sound resonates through me. Predictably, a thunderous sound follows rumbling in from the southwest indicating that the squall is nearly upon us. Riotous laughter has evolved into a spirited conversation in the lounge room. I lean against the closed door and take a moment to consider what is in store for me before returning to see my jury and executioners.

Nearly three years ago and almost to the day, I recollect another lazy Saturday afternoon that was filled with angst in this apartment. I had just returned home with my father after a game of football that had been abandoned because of the unpredictable Melbourne weather. Instead of proving my masculinity on the rugby pitch with my peers and running my arse off through the mud chasing an ovoid shaped ball, we instead had an early lunch at McDonald's and drove home. My birth mother did not expect her loving husband and only son to return home so early. That was evident since we found her enjoying a session of intimacy with some other bloke. Shouting and foul language that a thirteen-year-old teenage boy should not have been privy to by three mature adults was the result. I also had the pleasure of watching my mother's breasts bounce up and down as she took refuge from the lounge room since she was getting fucked where Bryce is currently sitting. Her lover scrambled to find his clothes and dress his naked body. Their clothes were strewn over the kitchen floor and the lounge room. I recall the sound of lightning crashing nearby and the resulting sound of thunder reverberating against the glass just as intensely that day as it does now. My mother slammed the door as she left not long after her lover fled after exchanging insults with Daniel. I never spoke with my mother again after that stormy day despite her many attempts at reaching out. Instead of her, I am left with the haunting sounds of the lighting and thunder after locking the front door which snaps me out of my delirium.

I sheepishly return to the lounge room and the gaze of my friends. The adults are nowhere to be found. *Mysterious Skin* is still playing on the television. Ignoring the movie and the chatter, I walk to the kitchen to retrieve another bottle of wine. More alcohol in my bloodstream will calm me down a bit. From the kitchen, as I extract the cork from the wine bottle, I overhear my friends gossiping. Bryce had previously lowered the volume of the television so everyone could share hyperbole and conjecture without raising their voices. I remove a clean large Riedel wine glass from the cabinet and try to read my father's mind. He knows that I invited a twenty-five-year-old man around that nobody except for me knows. He wouldn't be pleased about that. In hindsight, it probably wasn't the best decision that I have ever made and vow to blame my bad decision making on the wine. Being somewhat intoxicated at least will dull any innuendo and concerns about my sanity. My decision making hopefully will be the only thing that is called into question. The cork is finally exhumed from the bottle and the wine is delicately poured into a fresh glass with my trembling hand. It is time to face the music.

Walking back into the lounge room, I give my undivided attention to the movie. The scene ironically involves Joseph Gordon-Levitt acting out his role as an indifferent male prostitute with perfection. I remain on edge with my nose pushed completely into the glass, smelling the wine. I consider asking Bryce to change the movie to something with a lighter storyline since he is holding the integrated remote control but reconsider it since my friends seem to be absorbed by the movie. Even Megan Fox running around like an idiot being chased by Transformers would be better than the rape scene that is taking place on-screen, which acts as the catalyst for

Jayden to speak. "Mate, do you have anything that you want to say?"

Austin is picking at his teeth with his fingernail and Bryce begins to study the ceiling. I wonder if he notices the irregularities in the plastering. Repairs were carried out three years ago after inanimate objects that my mother threw at Daniel damaged it. Whatever wasn't nailed down was thrown on that tempestuous day. I shudder when I recall the vivid memories of violence. I still don't know how my mother managed to throw something and hit the ceiling with it. Given her awful throwing ability, I am astonished that she managed to avoid smashing one of the many panes of glass which not only form our Western wall but facilitates our view out over the Melbourne skyline and beyond.

I offer commentary. "Look, we all do crazy shit when we have been drinking and I haven't done anything that bad. Don't worry about it and just watch the movie." I begin to scrutinise the ceiling myself and can spot the areas that were repaired. After lifting my glass of wine and placing it under my nose, I inhale as hard as I can which yields a cough. The smell of alcohol overpowers my sense of smell and I cough again before emptying the contents of my glass down my dry throat. "What do you want me to say? That I am into guys?" I pause and reach for Jayden's glass of wine which is sitting on the glass table near where I am standing. I pick it up, smell it and then vacate his glass of wine, gulping it all down with the hope that it will soothe my nerves. I can't believe that I am going to say it. All eyes are on me. "Well, I do like guys and if you have a problem with that, you can fucking leave."

Bryce raises his glass. "Hear! hear! It is no big deal Chez, but of course, I already knew. Carry on everyone, nothing to see here."

Austin doesn't look fazed. "I really don't care Chezdon and being that it is time for drunken confessions, I do too. I would rather this trivia not be shared, you know, but now that the cat is out of the bag, I suppose I shouldn't be bothered either. You said it, Bryce. Carry on, there is nothing to see here." He takes a sip of wine and stares out the window.

Jayden starts to laugh nervously and crosses his arms. "Mate, why didn't you tell me?" He cocks his head to the right.

"What difference does it make?" I force a laugh before being distracted by more wine that almost magically appears in my glass thanks to Bryce. Thoughts quickly revert to Jayden and I masturbating next to each other only a few months ago and how much I enjoyed watching him. I briefly close my eyes and briefly shake my head back and forth.

Jayden places his feet on the glass table again. "I don't give a fuck if you are gay. I am just shocked you couldn't be bothered to tell me." He extends his hand toward me and I hand him the wine glass that I previously took. He refills it. "I don't want the glass, I wanted to shake your hand."

I set the glass on the table in front of Jayden. "I promised myself that if you ever asked me if I like guys that I would answer the question. You just never asked. What difference does it make anyway?" I grab Jayden's hand and squeeze it before we fist bump. With confession time over for the time being, I walk to the window and watch the drops of rain hitting the panes of glass. Bolts of lightning strike land in the distance. A crackling boom first causes the windows to vibrate and then my body.

I mumble, "what have I done?" I feel relieved that I confessed my sexuality but I am still concerned that the dynamics will change between my friends and me. What will be said when the news gets out in the wild at school? I pull my phone from my back pocket and immediately see a message that would have arrived during the most stressful conversation of my life. It is James suggesting that we meet tomorrow as originally planned. I scratch my head and quickly respond in the affirmative before returning my phone to my rear pocket.

Jayden looks at Austin and smirks. I nearly forgot that he proclaimed that he is gay. I was so absorbed in my own little world that I ignored the confession of my friend. "Austin, you are too beautiful to like guys. Chicks around the world have already started to cry." Jayden drinks from his glass and puts his feet back on the table.

Austin continues to give the television his undivided attention and chews on his fingernail. He looks perturbed and first crosses his arms and then his legs. "That is supposed to work to my advantage but all of the wrong people seem to take notice of me lately."

I find my confidence and interrupt the conversation. "What are you saying, Austin? That my arse isn't round enough? My jeans are not skinny enough and my fringe is not long enough?" Adding some levity to the conversation will surely lighten the mood.

Jayden snickers. "Honestly Chez, I can imagine you getting it up the arse. Not Austin though. He just looks like he would break in half." Jayden stares at Austin and continues. "So, would you hook up with Chezdon?"

"Well, no. He wouldn't want me anyway, he likes older guys." All the eyes in the room look at me simultaneously. My transgression allowing James to come around and meet me and this rogue gallery of teenagers in my humble abode is the number one news story again. "What was that all about with James anyway mate?" Austin takes a sip of wine and wipes his lips with the back of his hand.

Innocence Waning

"I reckon that I am just horny. He messaged me so I am going to see him tomorrow even after all that shit went down earlier if you can believe it. I blame this awkward situation on this fine wine and finally mustering up the courage to come out. Maybe it is just a curious case of bad timing and a coincidence so many random things are playing out simultaneously. We need more wine I reckon." I smile. "Hell, I need more wine." I look around expecting a waiter to conveniently appear. I resign to the fact that I will need to serve myself but Bryce stands up and staggers to the kitchen. Mel walks into the lounge room which takes me by surprise. I forgot that the adults were still around.

"We are going shopping. Please do not burn this place down whilst we are out boys." Mel looks at me whilst she speaks. They have mastered the art of not being confrontational and avoiding discussing the obvious. This is most likely why my father never realised that my mother was cheating on him until it was far too late. "Don't worry we will get something for dinner." My father shuffles into the lounge room rattling a set of keys and holding his wallet. Mel follows Daniel to the foyer and not long after the front door slams shut. Thunder rumbles in the distance.

Jayden begins to feel around inside the pocket of his bastardised shorts. He pulls out the small plastic bag of white powder that was taken from my father's room earlier and tosses it onto the glass table. "Bryce and my faggy friends, look what we have here!" Jayden announces with glee and rubs his hands together as a mad scientist would.

Austin reaches over and grabs the small plastic bag. He intently looks at it and shakes the contents. "Where the hell did you get this?"

Bryce begins to shake his head and a smile gradually forms on his round face. "This is turning out to be one of the most bizarre but more interesting days I have ever had. You see Austin, young Jayden here stole that baggie from Daniel's room earlier. This is when Chezdon was going through his drawer taking his stash of cash so he can buy a new phone." Bryce chuckles whilst Austin shakes the bag of coke again.

"Mate, I am not trying to be the fun police because I have wanted to try coke, but I don't think Daniel is going to be very happy to find his drugs and cash missing. This will end in tears, mate. Trust me." Austin appears concerned after eulogising his words of wisdom.

Jayden smiles. "You worry too much, pretty boy. I have a cunning plan. Let's do this shit." Jayden looks possessed and is hell-bent on snorting the powder. "Look, I will solve the problem and replace it all. Trust me."

"Have you even ever done coke mate?" Bryce asks quizzically. "There is no need to lie either after Chez and Austin made their admissions earlier, nobody is going to judge you."

"No, I haven't," Jayden admits. "I am excited now though. I really want to do this."

"Well, I haven't either." Bryce then looks curiously at Austin. "Have you matey?"

"Nope, but I am keen. I want to see what it does to me. I just don't want Daniel to go ballistic and kill Chezdon or beat up Mel when he finds his drugs are missing. That is all." Austin looks at me.

"I haven't had the pleasure of ever dabbling with the stuff either. I am not even sure if excitement is the right word." I laugh. "Jayden has an interesting plan. He told us earlier and I think it will work."

Innocence Waning

"That is the spirit. Bryce, another round of wine my good man." Jayden opens the plastic bag and empties some of the powder on the glass table. He proceeds to push it all together into a mound using his ATM card. A picture of Hilary Clinton is on the front of newspaper glaring at us with scornful eyes. Bryce walks around the table and begins to methodically refill glasses with wine. We anxiously crowd around Jayden, knocking into one another. Jayden acts out what we have all seen collectively at least one hundred times in various movies. Praise Hollywood. He begins to separate the mound of cocaine into four smaller ones and then like a magician, uses the plastic bank card to transform each of the mounts into lines that appear equal, approximately five centimetres in length. We watch Jayden act like we know what he is doing and exchange amused and eager looks between one another. Jayden is in his own world. The only commentary is coming from the television. I reach for the remote control whilst Jayden continues to design four equal lines. I change the media content from the movie and instead opt for music to accompany the mood. I queue up the catalogue of Muse. My choice seems to be appreciated by my friends judging by the nodding of their heads collectively in the affirmative.

"Done," Jayden announces. He leans back and licks the edge of his ATM card. His reaction is like a baby who chews on a lemon for the first time. He licks his lips suggestively at Bryce and winks. "Does anyone have any cash?"

"I do." Austin is the first to volunteer a twenty dollar note. He pulls it from his pocket and hands it to Jayden. He rolls the polymer banknote into what could be confused with a bright orange straw. "Thanks, Daniel. Here is to you mate!" Jayden picks up his glass, raises it in my direction as if toasting me is the same as thanking my father directly for supplying the cocaine. The next sound I hear mimics a nasal decongestant being snorted up Jayden's nose. If the pollen count was higher today, this snorting sound would have been anticipated but the sound one makes snorting powder off a glass table up your nostril doesn't sound very nice. Jayden experiences no problems using the orange twenty dollar note as the loading mechanism and inhales a line of white powder in one action. It is a vision that looks ludicrous and one that I will not soon forget. I wonder if the person who has their picture imprinted on the polymer note would disapprove like I know Hillary Clinton would.

Jayden hands the crude straw to Austin. He slams his body into to me indicating that I should move over and I comply. Austin moves into Jayden's former position. "So, what is your cunning plan to deal with replenishing these party favours, Jayden?" He then leans forward. He takes three long deep snorts as I gaze out the window long enough to see a lightning bolt strike land in the distance. Austin snorts every possible speck of powder off the glass table that was originally part of his line. The sound of the thunder consumes me and I sip from my glass of wine.

"It is all very simple, Austin." Jayden smiles. They each sniff and wipe their noses with their fingers in unison. "We simply replace the contents of the little plastic bag with flour or something like that. I then put it back where I found it. Simple. What is Daniel going to do? Write a letter of complaint to the drug dealer?" Bryce laughs uproariously and sets his glass of wine down on the table.

Austin coughs whilst rubbing his nose and manages a hearty chortle. "It all seems so simple but I guess that will work." Austin coughs and then sniffs again and wipes his nose. He looks at the side of his finger and seems satisfied when he finds mucous glistening on it. He was probably expecting blood.

"Give me that note and move over!" I screech. The stress that I have experienced today is beginning to take its toll. I never thought I would be so enthusiastic to do drugs. The boys shuffle to the left and Austin hands me the orange straw. I finish my glass of wine and then lean forward, greedily snorting the line in one fluid motion like I an experienced coke fiend would. "Goddamn, I say! Goddamn!" Why Uma Thurman's character from *Pulp Fiction* suddenly comes to mind makes me laugh out loud. I immediately wipe the bottom of my nose with my finger.

"Are you sure that you have never done this before mate?" Bryce quizzes me with a look of intrigue and licks his lips. "You look like you are in your element. Move over bitches."

"Seriously I haven't. It has just been a tense day shopping, meeting new people and coming out of the closet. You know what I mean? It is enough to make any normal teenager be driven to drugs and alcohol." We laugh and I hand the polymer straw to Bryce. He takes the helm in front of the last line of white powder. The human vacuum turns on briefly and instantly evidence of drugs occupying pride and place on the glass table disappears up Bryce's nose. He picks up the small plastic bag and shakes it. "What are we going to do with the rest of this? Save it for later?" I put a finger over one nostril and snort hard and swallow the snot that ends up in my mouth.

Jayden licks the edge of his ATM card again and takes the orange straw from Bryce. He then unrolls the twenty-dollar note. "First, I thought we would do the rest, but it is better to be safe than sorry, so um, Chezdon get up mate. Follow me."

I stand up and shuffle to the side so Jayden's can pass. He shoves the twenty-dollar note into his pocket as he stands and walks to the kitchen and we follow him. In the excitement, Austin seems to have forgotten that the money belongs to him. "Do you have any flour?" Jayden asks.

"I am not sure." I begin to rummage around in the cabinets looking for the baking powder or anything that looks white and powdery. I finally find a small bag of flour after knocking a bottle of cayenne pepper onto the floor. "Shit." I pass the bag of flour to Jayden who then sources a small spoon from the drawer of utensils. I begin to wipe up the mess that I made. Jayden cuts the bag of flour open and scoops out a small portion of the powder and puts it in the small plastic bag. He seals it before tossing it on the marble kitchen countertop.

"Voila. That should be enough." Jayden decrees. "The problem is officially solved." I pick up the sealed mixed bag of drugs and traverse to my father's room. It would be prudent to return the cash that I took earlier from the drawer too. I don't want him to think that I have been in that drawer for any reason even though he did tell me where I can find a stash of cash earlier.

I return to the lounge room hoping to pour a glass of wine only to find the open bottle along with all the empty bottles missing. My friends have relocated the empties and lined up the bottles on the kitchen counter near where we store the rubbish. Austin is guzzling water from a large glass bottle.

"I need to piss." Austin allows every drop of water from the bottle to drip into his mouth before walking around the corner and out of sight.

"Do you like sucking cock?" Jayden asks whilst he swirls the wine in his glass.

"I wouldn't know." I laugh and wipe my nose with the back of my hand. "Maybe James would have blown us all if the parentals weren't around. He does look like he would be into such a thing."

"I think if you and Austin hooked up it would be hot. I would pay to watch that." Jayden takes a sip of wine and rolls his eyes. "I could make a fortune filming a porn of you two and selling it on the internet."

Innocence Waning

"I heard that arsehole!" Austin walks back into the kitchen and picks up his wine glass.

"Jesus man, is your bladder as small as your dick?" Jayden looks dumbfounded. " You were only gone for a minute."

"It is my mutant ability. Why waste time dragging out the ancient art of urination?" Austin leaves the kitchen. He tries to sing along to the Muse song that is playing; a song that sober people can't even figure out unless they look up the lyrics online. With some additional effort, I focus my eyes on the screen of my phone and read messages that recently arrived. My father wants to know if my friends have any dietary requirements, to which I respond in the negative. James wants to confirm the details of our date tomorrow at the Grace Darling Bar in Collingwood and I respond in the affirmative.

The conversation becomes more raucous. Bryce starts a deep and meaningful conversation about the existence of not only God but man and why the Earth and humankind would be better off if a great plague wiped out ninety percent of the population. Intriguing thoughts coming from a Jew, which Austin is quick to point out. I return to the lounge room feeling hyper and thirsty. Bryce is drinking directly from a bottle of wine and given that I am feeling the effects of the alcohol I assume that Bryce and Jayden are experiencing the same. I try to stay focused. I remember that Austin arrived after the party started so he hasn't drunk the same volume as everyone else. I need to encourage him to consume more to catch up. I return to the kitchen and pull a bottle of San Pellegrino from the refrigerator and polish it off in a series of continuous gulps before walking to the bathroom.

The conversation remains lively and a myriad of topics are debated after I return. Hot topics like the terrorism that recently took place in Sydney, ISIS, the current government and gay marriage are all debated. When the conversation becomes too lively, Bryce successfully guides it to the banal. We resort to gossip and discussing who is hot and who is not, the size of Kim Kardashian's arse and other pop culture trivia. Austin shares his opinion that Kayne West is a fag. Bryce declares that he wants to fuck Nicole Kidman. Jayden emphatically states that he is going to dump his girlfriend. He continues to say she will only let him touch her tits which I find fascinating since Jayden bragged in the past about having sex with her. We collectively stop laughing when the front door slams shut. A flat-bed trolley is pushed past us with boxes of food, beverages, toilet paper and cleaning products delicately balanced on it. The adults must have raided Costco for supplies.

"You boys seem to be having fun." My father looks at me suspiciously. Mel pushes the trolley into the kitchen after my father stops to quiz me.

"Nobody else is coming over, don't worry," I reassure my father. He looks annoyed. It must be because he hasn't had the pleasure of gambling and drinking all day like us. "Jayden is going to break-up with his girlfriend because she has small tits."

Mel scoffs. "Don't be so shallow, Jayden. Since when did you find a girlfriend anyway?"

Everyone besides Jayden chuckles. The adults begin to put groceries away and we retreat to the lounge room. Minutes later, they interrupt our ramblings by walking past us and going out onto the balcony with a massive amount of raw meat. We all follow like ravenous dogs after being asked how we like our respective steaks cooked.

My father turns the knob on the gas bottle, fires up the barbeque and quickly closes the massive stainless-steel lid. "How much have you boys had to drink?"

"Not enough," Bryce claims. "In fact, I wouldn't mind a little more wine." He staggers back inside after saying he likes his meat prepared medium rare.

"It is all good Daniel. I had a late start compared to these blokes." Austin then skips back inside after he says he will have his steak prepared in the same way Bryce requested his.

"Same here." Jayden follows the others inside and like a thirsty animal, stands next to Bryce as he uncorks another bottle.

I am left alone with my father on the balcony feeling drunk. "Who is that James character and how did you meet him?" He opens the lid of the barbeque after looking at the thermostat. Appearing satisfied with the temperature he starts layering uncooked meat on the grill, which immediately begins to sizzle.

"He seemed cool and I just started talking to him when I was shopping earlier," I say innocently. "I also like his earrings. I want earrings like his."

"You should probably get to know someone for more than an hour before inviting them around. Since your friends were here, I am not too bothered just so you know. I just don't want to end up robbed or you be taken advantage of." Two additional steaks are tossed onto the hot grill. These would be for Daniel and Mel as they prefer their steaks cooked rare. I am relieved that nobody asked for their steak to be prepared well-done. If only to save Bryce from embarrassing himself carrying on about the overpopulation of the world and how he is a hypocrite.

"I understand. It will not happen again." I turn around and step inside.

"Do you want my advice?" Daniel asks. I quickly turn around and lick my lips. "Not like I offer it much, but consider it a lesson learned."

"Sure." I fold my arms across my chest and sway from side to side.

"If you are going to keep drinking tonight, drink a pint of water in between each glass of wine. You will not only be the last one standing but you will not feel like hell tomorrow." He begins to flip the steaks one at a time.

I can't feel like death the next day since I am planning on going on a date. My mind wanders as I ponder how my life has evolved over the last day. I have two dates I suddenly remember and smile. "A very good idea my one and only father." I bolt into the living room in time to consult with my friends about the next music that should be played. Bryce selects the debut album by *5 Seconds of Summer* and I do not argue with his choice.

"Hey Chezdon, it is your favourite band!" Bryce yells over the opening riff of the first song on the album. "Which one of them would you fuck if you could make a wish and it would come true right now?" Jayden suddenly takes an interest in our stupid conversation.

I don't know precisely where Mel is, but I choose not to answer the question. I laugh and then fumble around in my back pocket, removing my phone. A new message is waiting to be read and I use that as an excuse to ignore the inappropriate question as it would be hard to nominate just one of the band members that I want to fuck. James has messaged saying that he is looking forward to seeing me tomorrow and really hopes that I don't end up grounded. I smile and stick out my tongue. I assume that he doesn't have to worry about being grounded. At least I hope not.

Innocence Waning

Bryce slaps me on my back which makes me yelp in pain. "You have posters of this band up in your room, mate. Surely it isn't just for their music since you are a fan of Muse." Bryce continues his interrogation. "Just tell us. It is okay, we will not judge you. I don't think." Bryce takes a sip of wine.

"I think I need more wine." I walk into the kitchen. Mel is placing the elements of what seems to be a salad in a large crystal bowl. I hunt around in the wine refrigerator. After finding another bottle of Marsh Estate, I return to the living room without making eye contact with Mel.

"Can you admit it, mate?" Bryce pushes his glass and the corkscrew in my direction. "Confess, goddamnit!" Bryce shoves his wine glass even closer to me as I deftly remove the cork from the bottle. It produces a loud popping sound. I contemplate the message that James sent me and begin to refill the wine glasses.

"I would have the drummer." I finally say in a meek voice not loud enough to carry. If it does, I really doubt Mel will know what we are chatting about. She wouldn't care about the drunken ramblings of teenage boys anyway. Of course, Bryce might be getting too rambunctious and she would eavesdrop just for her own amusement especially if he starts carrying on about genocide again.

"Ashton Irwin?" Austin interjects with a renewed sense of enthusiasm and pushes his glass towards me. "What I would do to him if I had one night. No, wait, just five seconds are all I would need. It would be bliss."

Jayden starts to laugh. "You cum in five seconds? That is no surprise at all, mate." Bryce bursts out laughing which is infectious.

"I knew it. Still, I don't mind their music." Bryce muses whilst I refill his glass. "Just don't tell anyone."

"He looks so perfect standing there in his black skinny jeans and underwear." Austin attempts to sing along but fails miserably. My father walks past us holding the plate of cooked flesh. "And I know now that I'm so down. Sing it!" Austin shouts. "Too bad you don't have a guitar, Jayden. You could play it."

"Children, can we eat at the table now and be somewhat civilised?" My father politely requests. The steaks are plated up and placed on the long black marble dining table that inhabits what could be dead space in the apartment between the kitchen, the living room and the panes of glass.

We converge upon the dining room table, all holding a wine glass. Bryce guzzles the contents of his quickly and sits down. Mel places a large bowl of colourful produce on the table and then returns to the kitchen and begins to retrieve plates and silverware from the cabinet. "Fuck, I am starving." Bryce summarises what I am feeling.

"I didn't really expect for this to turn into the Jimi Hendrix experience tonight boys." My father looks at us and judging by the blank look on our faces realises we have no clue what the hell the Jimi Hendrix experience is. Bryce starts laughing again. "Just try to keep it under control. I don't want to end up getting shit from your parents or have the Department of Children's Services pounding on the front door. I would prefer if everyone stayed here tonight especially if you are going to drink more." Bryce continues to laugh. He picks a cherry tomato from the salad bowl and throws it up in the air, catching it in his mouth.

"It is 5:30 PM, let's get on it. It is getting late!" Jayden shouts after looking at his watch. Mel sets a plate in front of him.

Innocence Waning

"Don't worry Daniel," Jayden places his hand on my father's shoulder. "We are good for the long haul. If my mother asks, my friend Charlie and I drank a box of wine in the Sir Robert Menzies reserve near my house that he stole from his parents. No worries."

"Hey, I know where that is. It is close to where I live." Austin adds. Mel sets a plate in front of him.

"That is reassuring." Daniel removes Jayden's hand from his shoulder. "I would hope that you can keep it under control so you don't have to bore anyone with that alibi." My father reaches for the bottle of wine after Mel sets an empty Riedel glass in front of him.

"You have a friend called Charlie? His parents named him after cocaine. How funny." Bryce snickers and then wipes his nose with a cloth serviette.

I smile and motion for Bryce to settle down. "Just eat your food mate. Relax." I insist.

I stand up and walk to the refrigerator and retrieve a bottle of San Pellegrino sparkling water. I drink the contents of the 750ml bottle in thirty seconds flat. I put the empty bottle down next to the growing graveyard of empty wine and water bottles only to see my father watching me intensely. He offers me an approving nod of his head. "Does anyone want anything whilst I am up?" I am ignored and return to the table and take my seat.

Mel follows me and sits down. "School starts up again on Monday. I am sure everyone is excited." She extracts salad from the glass bowl using large silver tongs.

"That is an understatement." Bryce is the first to respond. " I can hardly wait. Not."

"Hopefully you can say the school holidays have been filled with new experiences." Mel continues to allocate salad to her plate. "After all, life is about doing new things."

Everyone simultaneously stares at Jayden who is playing with the slab of meat on his plate. He looks at me and makes a sound that resembles a pig inhaling its feed. "Nothing too interesting I must admit." I take a sudden interest in cutting a portion of my steak into four strips, taking care to cut the pieces all the same length, mimicking the process that I bore witness to earlier in the day. "Nothing really new or two exciting."

"Austin admitted that he wants to fuck the drummer from *5 Seconds of Summer*." Bryce slurs. "Admit it, Austin."

"Revelations and experiences are different, mate," Jayden says before placing a morsel of steak into his mouth. "I am not very hungry. Is it okay if I save this for later, Mel? Maybe even breakfast?"

Mel being the most accommodating host in all of Melbourne is quickly on her feet. She grabs Jayden's plate and walks to the kitchen and pulls an industrial sized roll of plastic wrap from the cupboard.

Jayden takes a sip of wine. "Chezdon never said which member of *5 Seconds of Summer* he would fuck, I don't think."

My father looks mortified. "This is not an appropriate conversation to have over dinner, Jayden. Just calm down a bit, mate." He looks at Bryce. "You too, mate."

"Whoops. Sorry." Jayden raises the glass of wine to his nose, smells it and closes his eyes. "This smells wonderful."

Innocence Waning

Bryce stops giggling and begins to eat. "This is damned good food. Thanks, Daniel. Thanks, Mel."

"Yeah, I am not too hungry either Mel." After eating four small strips of steak, I admit. "It must have been the big old burrito that I had for lunch." Maybe the coke is affecting my appetite.

"I bet you wish you had a big old burrito for lunch. Sorry, I don't mean to be rude. I apologise." Austin backpedals and shoves a strip of steak into his mouth. "What are we talking about again?"

Jayden stands up and stumbles into the living room. He uses the integrated remote to scroll through the available music on the media centre. "It is time to change this. Sorry, Chezdon." Jayden looks at Austin. "Oh Ashton, Oh Ashton, use my arse as a drum, Ashton Irwin."

"Oh, give it a rest mate." Austin wipes his mouth with a serviette and stands up. "I really appreciate the hospitality, Daniel and Mel. Many thanks." He picks up his dish and silverware, only to be intercepted by Mel who takes everything from him and returns to the kitchen.

~

I slowly open my eyes and listen to Katy Perry singing and put my hand on my thumping chest. My heart is beating so fast heart, it could break free of my torso at any time and splatter against the ceiling. My clammy skin feels like it is on fire. It takes a minute of irregular panting before I manage to focus my eyes and deduce that I am in my bedroom. Music videos are being screened on the television. The public broadcaster screens this form of entertainment every Friday and Saturday night and they continue into the early morning of the following day. I now have the perspective of time. I urgently look for my watch on my bedside table only to find that is still strapped to my wrist. Feeling like I am standing at the gates of hell, and after sleeping on sheets that are soaked with my sweat, I feel like my bladder is going to explode. My elbow bashes into a body next to me. I turn to the right and discover Austin sleeping on my bed only wearing his boxer briefs. His body is being illuminated by the light emanating from the television which makes his skin glow. My eyes move down his glistening body and I inspect his bulge. I don't spend much time staring at it though as vacating my bladder is my number one priority. I roll out of bed and kick Bryce in the side by accident. He is sleeping on a mound of my filthy worn clothes which have been collecting on the floor since the last time the cleaner turned up. Bryce has wine-stained lips which have taken on a morbid hue courtesy of the moonlight shining into the room. He is snoring like a savage animal and somehow managed to wad up my dirty underwear, socks and a few shirts and balled them up into an improvised pillow. There isn't enough time to find the humour in the situation as I stumble over Bryce taking a moment to notice the waning moon hanging over the Melbourne skyline. I stumble over more clothes, books and other rubbish, in a desperate attempt to get to my bathroom. I find solace as my bare feet step on the cold white tiles as I walk into my bathroom and stand next to Jayden who is asleep on the floor naked. There is purple vomit floating the toilet bowl however some of the puke rests not only next to him but on his arm. After exposing my penis to the cool air, the feeling of relief is pure and utter bliss as I vacate my bladder. I take my time shaking the remaining vestiges of urine from my dangling manhood before tucking it behind my briefs again. I pause to look at my best friend sleeping on the floor next to me with his exposed phallus and neatly trimmed pubic hair on display. When the noisome odour from his barf finally overwhelms me, I drop to my knees and lunge toward the large porcelain telephone. The contents of my stomach speak into it loudly; up and out over and over until there is nothing left to purge. Rather than collapse next to Jayden and share the cold floor with him, I stagger to my feet and wash my mouth out with water directly from the tap. After pouring mouthwash into my mouth, I gargle and spit before ripping toilet paper away from the roll. First, I wipe the tears from my face and then blow my nose wondering if any of the cocaine is still in my nostrils somehow.

Abandoning Jayden and his flaccid cock after tossing the toilet paper into the commode, I stumble to the kitchen and retrieve a much-needed cold bottle of sparkling water from the refrigerator. Splintered memories begin to cycle through my aching head as I try to remember everything that happened last night. Memories from the time Austin thanked my parents for his meal are evading me. Twelve empty bottles of wine and numerous empty bottles of water are formed neatly on the counter now reminding me of my excesses. Did we drink a case of wine? Fuck. Barely able to perform simple math, I calculate that my peers and I consumed at least nine of the empty bottles of wine, which would explain why the feeling of death is overwhelming me right now. I find temporary relief when I press the cold glass water bottle against my forehead and then roll it around my neck, letting it rest on my collar briefly before gulping the sparkling water. A sense of absolute bliss overwhelms me after I set the open bottle down gently on the countertop. I step back and lean my haggard body against the refrigerator so I don't collapse.

After wobbling back to my smelly bedroom, I cautiously get back in bed and lay down next to Austin. I gently slide my hand over his shimmering warm chest. Propping myself using my arm, I find the courage to lick his erect nipple. I get lost in the moment and admire his body and listen to his rhythmic heavy breathing. I place my ear on his chest and find the sound of his rapid heartbeat. My finger traces a line on his moist chest from his nipple to his belly button. The back of my hand lightly brushes his skin as it travels further down his navel. I turn my head and focus on his angelic face before my free hand finds his cock which is being concealed behind cotton black boxer briefs. Emboldened, my hand slides down the front of his Bonds underwear first finding pubic hair and then his lazy penis. My hand continues its adventure into the nether region and lightly fondles his ball sack. I start to feel dizzy and my hand quickly retreats from its sordid journey. I quickly stumble back to the toilet with a sense of urgency. My mouth insists on making another urgent call using the large porcelain telephone. What is left in my stomach is liberated which then causes me to violently dry heave multiple times and be left panting like a dog? Feeling absolutely spent, exhausted and dizzy, I fall back only to find comfort when my naked back is pressed against the cold tiles next to Jayden. I am envious that he found such a cold and magical place to rest earlier as the frigid floor quickly cools me down as I drift off to sleep.

Innocence Waning

6. **Relief**

The walk to Port Melbourne along my usual jogging path is warm yet pleasant. I regret not wearing my sunglasses as I sit back, relax and sip the frothed milk and taste the roasted beans from the balcony of the usual café at the end of the tram line. My watch advises me there is just enough time left to get a natural high from caffeine before my morning appointment inside the public toilet with the stranger. In a case of good timing for a change, there are no messages or social media notifications distracting me from what I want.

The intensity of the oppressive sun is burning my neck and exposed shoulders. A few sunbathers on Sandridge Beach stare at my glistening white skin from afar and point at me. I am confident they are laughing at how my untanned shoulders contrast against my tanned arms but I really don't give a fuck. I take some time to feel the sand, look at the bay and admire the architecture of the beachfront property. Even with my dawdling, I have just enough time to get to Westgate Park before my untoward meeting is scheduled to commence.

Normally, the small parking lot is at capacity. There are no cars here today which will mean that there will be few people in the park which will potentially interrupt proceedings. Am I just lucky? Maybe it is a coincidence or something that I should find queer? The sun is shining and the weather is glorious. There are a few black clouds on the horizon floating in from the southwest though that look ominous, which is concerning. It is as quiet as a morgue as I enter the picnic area near the public toilet. I check the time again on my phone only to learn that it is 10:30 AM exactly. My bladder is legitimately full and I have a legitimate reason to visit the shithouse. The cracked screen of my phone lights up and chirps as I had set an alarm to remind me of my date with destiny.

Innocence Waning

I leave the watchful gaze of the bright sun and step through the open door of the public toilet. My eyes thank me for the more subdued light in the small smelly room. The now familiar metal trough remains in stasis waiting to drink my urine. A man slowly turns his head and grins at me as I walk forward the eager trough. I slow my pace and nervously rub the back of my hot damp neck which has been burned by the sun. The stranger continues to smile as I step onto the metal grate at the base of the trough. Despite urgently needing to vacate my bladder, I stare into the eyes of the stranger who is now standing next to me. I am certain that he is the bloke which so boldly gave me the piece of paper yesterday. He nods his head and then stares at my crotch with vacant and dead eyes.

My new acquaintance reverts his gaze from my crotch and looks down at his massive throbbing erect penis proudly. It looks like an inverted exclamation point, something that resembles a punctuation mark used on a menu in a Mexican cantina. Despite my bladder causing me extreme duress, I resist the urge to pull out my cock and piss. I shuffle closer to the stranger; the shifting of my weight causes an odd sounding clunk to resonate from the metal trough. An alarm sounds and water begins to cascade down the back of the trough, effectively washing away the stale urine, spit and anything else that has been deposited in it. The flowing water stirs up a horrible smell and pipes begin to rattle. Not to be thwarted by these distractions, I reach over and grab the shaft of the stranger's throbbing cock. Not having experience with a foreskin, I gently push it down and examine the pink penis head. My small soft hand gently slides down the shaft of the cock until its movement is arrested by big balls and pubic hair. My hand is so small that my index finger and thumb cannot touch whilst gripping the huge schlong which leaves me feeling inadequate as I caress the flesh.

The pipes continue to rattle yielding a horrible clunking noise. My stomach and my left thigh begin to heat up. Is this what it feels like to self-immolate? My insides are beginning to feel as hot as my neck and face. The ambient noise in this dark room begins to become unbearably loud as I continue to stroke the stranger's dick. An excruciating pain in my bladder lurches me from my dream state and back to consciousness.

Like a pig, I return to the real world sprawled out on my bathroom floor rolling in a puddle of urine. I pissed myself during the dream sequence. Jayden kicked me in his rush to put his head in the toilet bowl. He begins to shout into the big porcelain telephone in the same manner that I did earlier. The wretched noise that Jayden is producing drowns out the sounds of snoring and music emanating from my bedroom.

The urine which has saturated my underwear is cooling down, much to the relief of my body but I find it disgusting. Reality begins to take hold as I come out of my stupor. I am further revolted when I find Jayden's vomit on my torso and left leg. The retching sounds continue as Jayden's head is swallowed by the toilet bowl. I extricate myself from ground zero and prop myself up against the glass wall of the shower stall. The thumping pain in my head matches beats in time with my heart. "Fuck me," I whimper. "Fuck." Messaging my head provides no relief. Urine runs down both of my legs as I use every bit of strength that I have left in reserve to stay standing up. Much like legs of red wine would run down the side of a Riedel glass, my body now feels like it will soon fall victim to gravity. The feeling of nausea returns and the room starts to spin again.

Without any concern for modesty or decorum, I pull off my saturated boxer briefs and step away from them. I leave them in a puddle of bodily fluids next to my best friend who continues to retch with his head in the toilet bowl. I try to ignore the dream that continues to play on a loop in my mind and will myself to get into the shower stall with my cock pointing at the ceiling. An ice-cold shower will make me feel better and hopefully cool my burning body down.

Innocence Waning

Freezing water has never felt so good as it splashes off my scorching skin. Out of desperation, I open my mouth and drink from the ejaculating showerhead, propping myself up against the tiled wall in the process hoping that my equilibrium will stabilise. Jayden rolls away from the toilet bowl and collapses against the cabinet under one of the sinks. He stares at me but I don't think in his condition he is watching me.

All my senses are overwhelmed. Before I can reconcile the memories of the previous day, night and now morning, gravity once again grips me and pulls me slowly to the floor. My naked back presses against the wet ceramic tiles until I finally sit on my bare arse. I hold my knees close to my chin as I look up to the shower head. It continues to ejaculate on my face and from the safety of the floor, I close my eyes.

7. **Struggle**

Huffing water up my nose unexpectedly and the taste of gastric acid in my mouth evokes a fit of coughing and wakes me from my siesta. The horrific sounds that Bryce is now making as he pays his respects to the stained porcelain telephone begins to overwhelm me. I have been sleeping in the shower stall with the water spraying down on me for some time, evidenced by the wrinkled skin on my fingers. I wonder how long I have been napping. Without any concern for modesty, I stand up and turn off the flow of water and then exit the shower stall. After emerging from my glass sarcophagus, I retrieve a towel and wrap it around my waist. Bryce remains on his knees retching at a volume that would intimidate even Cerberus as he struggles to return his indulgences into the grateful toilet.

I rub my hair and then my sensitive skin with the red towel and wrap it around my waist again. After pulling my electronic toothbrush from the charger, I apply a dollop of Colgate toothpaste to the brushing head and begin to polish my teeth and then my tongue. The whirring sound of my personal dental hygienist drowns out the moans and spitting noises that Bryce is producing. I kick the soaking bath mat into the corner of the room so I can stand on the cold white tiles. I notice purple puke on the floor near my feet and remember that it came out of Jayden's naked body. I place my hand on my side and recall why my body hurts so much. Propping myself using the sink, I stare into my bloodshot green eyes and take long deep breaths, and try once again to reconcile what is going on in this cesspit. My nasal passage is remarkably clear for a change, which I attribute to the white powder that I inhaled. This is the only positive that I can find as my body pulses with pain. Memories begin to selectively reveal themselves to me and wince as I rub my rib cage. After returning my toothbrush to its lonely docking station is when I notice that Bryce has a black swastika haphazardly drawn on his naked back. I remember thinking it would be funny if Jayden vandalised his skin after he passed out on my bedroom floor. Given how appalling I feel, the humour if there ever was any associated with this prank, is unrealised.

I stagger into my bedroom and let the wet red towel fall off me naturally on the floor. My modesty was abandoned in the filthy bathroom as my feet are massaged by the soft carpet fibres. The sight of Austin sleeping on my bed evokes my memory again. I distinctly recollect how my fingers felt as I ran them over his warm moist skin. How he smelled like lavender and how his nipple tasted like salt before I had to flee to the bathroom. Fond memories cause blood to begin to rush to my penis and my heart begins to race faster. I turn my attention to Jayden who is sleeping on the floor near my feet looking like one of my soiled pairs of boxer briefs. I remind myself to pull underwear on. Sometime after Jayden spewed, he managed to find his skinny shorts and dress. I am left only with the fleeting memory of his naked body as I concentrate so I can step into a clean pair of underwear and not fall. I stumble around to the side of the bed that I sleep on and fall backwards, which wakes Austin up.

"What the hell?" Austin rubs his eyes before he stretches his arms over his head. He takes an interest in what is being broadcast on television. At some point, the channel was changed from the Australian public broadcaster to the mainstream Channel Seven. *Weekend Sunrise* is screening which makes me deduce that it is early Sunday morning. The faux enthusiasm by the hosts of the breakfast show makes me close my eyes. I want to go back to sleep and maybe sleep for a week. Once a commercial begins to air during the break, I open my eyes and watch Austin's stretch his arms over his head again, snapping his knuckles and finally yawning. Bryce continues to cough and heave in the bathroom and flushes the toilet. I focus on Austin's armpit and do not let the background sound effects distract me. I reminisce about touching his pubic hair and then holding his flaccid cock as he slept. It doesn't matter how awful I may feel; the sight of his armpit hair improves my mood and I feel blood returning to my limp dick yet again.

Despite feeling like I am on fire, I take refuge under the damp sheet. Knowing that my dick is stirring forces me to sacrifice the bliss of the cold air blowing in from the vent over my bedroom door. "What a night." My assessment encourages Austin's arms to collapse at his side. "How are you feeling?"

Austin turns his head towards the bathroom where Bryce seems to be frozen praying to the god of porcelain. "Oh mate, certainly not as bad as him." The sounds of coughing, spitting, moaning along with Jayden's snoring makes me reminisce about the last time that I visited Melbourne Zoo.

"Jesus Christ mate. Who needs to go to the zoo when you have these two animals to stare at?" I try to interject some humour which is either not funny or not understood, as Austin turns his head to look at me. Even though my body feels like I have been hit by a car, my penis is painfully erect. Austin smiles and produces a loud growling sound and then giggles.

Austin rolls off my bed and groans as he stands on his feet. He sorts through clothes that have been discarded on the floor, tossing anything that doesn't belong to him in the corner. He finds his blue skinny jeans and extracts his phone from the back pocket. I stare at his hairless white skin and then his brown eyes. He is absorbed into the world within his phone and finally scratches his butt. I am confident that I have ever been this horny before and I desperately need to jerk off. My imagination kicks in and I visualise putting my hard cock inside Austin's bulbous arse. He scratches his bum again. My dick begins to throb under the sheet, gently moving it up and down. I must still be affected the drug as my animalistic lust would mimic something primal that I have never felt before. "I've got to go," Austin announces. "My mother is pissed off." I watch Austin finish dressing and feel a sense of melancholy overwhelm me as he covers himself up with clothes. "Thank Christ that I sent her a message last night otherwise she would have called the cops."

"How is your mother?" I am hoping that small talk about her will calm my penis. "How is Chloe?" Certainly, talking about his obnoxious sister will kill my erection.

"They are fine." Austin slips his feet into the silver DC shoes and swipes the black beanie that is resting on the speaker next to the television. He rolls the woollen hat onto his head, which tames his hair. "I've gotta zip. It was fun. Cya mate."

Quoting the final words of one of the many recently deposed Australian Prime Ministers, Austin leaves my smelly bedroom and closes the door behind him. Some banter is then exchanged between him and Mel in the hallway. I am not surprised to hear her chirpy voice as she is always up early, even on the weekend. Once my erection has subsided, I slither out from under the security of the bedsheet and grab my black skinny jeans off the floor. Searching my pockets for my phone, I growl when I can't find it. I sit back on my bed again and try to get comfortable and distract myself by watching television. Feeling anxious and not being able to relax, I throw the bedsheet off me and begin to hunt for my phone.

I pick up a dirty hoodie that Bryce was previously sleeping on and pull it over my head. After emerging from my reeking bedroom and into the relative order of the apartment, I breathe in the air which smells like lemon. The citrus smell is much preferable to what four boys produced behind my closed bedroom door. A renewed sense of calm overwhelms me as I walk around the unit which is now devoid of any evidence that good times were had last night. Mel has tidied the place up. There are no empty bottles sitting on the counter. Only a note next to my phone which has a shattered screen. "Fuck!" I shout. The note that Mel left me suggests that I drink lots of water and take a vitamin.

I pull two bottles of San Pellegrino from the refrigerator and return to my bedroom. Sounds of animals at the zoo greet me as I prop the door open thinking fresh air can only improve the smell. Bryce continues to hold on to the toilet bowl like a bus driver would grasp a steering wheel and is snoring. Looking around, I scratch run my hand through my hair and then massage the back of my neck. "Jesus, what a fucking mess."

I walk into the bathroom and gently shake Bryce and whisper reassuring words in his ear. I begin to massage his bare shoulders, but he doesn't wake up. I pour cold sparkling water on his head and slap the swastika drawn on his back which jolts him back to the land of the living. Bryce shakes his head back and forth and then slowly gets to his feet and props himself up against the bathroom wall. Looking crazed, he sits on the edge of the toilet and stares at me like a lemur. "Fuck man, I feel like shit!"

"It was a full-on night." I hand Bryce a glass bottle of water. "Here you go. A gift from Mel."

"Thanks, mate." He sets a new world record drinking 750ml of sparkling water and then stands up again. "What the hell happened last night? Where is my shirt?" He pulls his phone from his pocket and then mutters something in Yiddish. "Do you have an iPhone charger?"

"Sorry mate, this is an Android house." My giggling doesn't improve Bryce's mood. "It would seem there are some clothes in the laundry room. Mel left a note saying some clothes were soiled after our boozing last night."

Innocence Waning

"Goddamn, I hope nobody spewed on me as I can remember absolutely fuck all." I follow Bryce from my bathroom, past Jayden who remains sleeping on the floor and into the hallway and run into my father who smiles. He looks amused.

"I hope your hangover is worth it today boys." My father says as soon as he sees us. "If you are going to draw a swastika on someone's back, at least draw it properly. The arms are going the wrong direction."

Bryce doesn't have a clue what Daniel is talking about and darts into the laundry room. He sorts through the laundry that Mel kindly washed and finds his shirt. Free of stains or bodily fluids, Bryce pulls it on. "Please thank Mel for me." He looks at Daniel. "Mate, I really need to borrow a phone. My parents are going to kill me."

The look of fear on Bryce's face subsides after my father hands him his mobile phone after he unlocks it. At some point in the call to his mother, Bryce sighs and smiles. He must have been reminded that he informed his parents that he was staying over. I do remember him making that drunken call last night now. "I will be home soon." He ends the call and hands the phone back to my father. "Thank you, Daniel, for the hospitality."

Bryce shakes hands with my father, offers his thanks again and says all he wants to do is go home to his comfortable bed. I suggest that we can open another bottle of wine and have some eggs. After making my suggestion, he looks like he is about to projectile vomit into the laundry room sink. He quickly regains his composure though and limps down the hallway. The front door slams not long later. It startles me as per usual and puts me into a heightened state of awareness. I glance at my watch.

Briskly walking into my bedroom of discontent I stop to admire the sleeping animal called Jayden on the floor. My room still smells awful. Red wine, sweat, spew, urine, shit and everything else that escaped from our bodies are producing a toxic smell. If I want to get to Westgate Park for the prearranged meeting with the stranger, I must leave this place soon. As I attempt to make myself look presentable, I come to the realisation that my sexuality has been inhibited for sixteen years and has now come to a pinnacle of sorts. I am now facing the impatient stare of the clock on my bedroom wall and have a renewed enthusiasm to get my arse to the nature reserve.

I pause to observe my best friend take a breath, snore, gargle, and gasp as he continues to sleep on my bedroom floor. I step around him and leave not only the smell of my bedroom behind but also the security of my apartment. My journey to Westgate Park is first encumbered by the sun as I leave my apartment tower in Southbank. I can barely muster the energy to walk and decide to catch the tram. Running is just not possible. "Shit!" I shout when I realise that I left my broken phone at home. I walk to the tram stop near the casino and hop on the tram at Clarendon Street illegally since I also left my transport card in my room. I try to relax but cannot seem to get any focus as I wipe the sweat from my brow with the sleeve of my dirty hoodie. The tram makes annoying dinging sounds as it squeals down the tracks towards Beacon Cove and I lose myself in the moment with my eyes closed. What I hopefully find in the public toilet at Westgate Park will be something new and like doing a line of cocaine, I hope it is a memory that lasts for my lifetime. The tram suddenly comes to a screeching halt and my eyes go wide. The conductor announces that we have come to the end of the line at Beacon Cove and that everyone should alight from the tram.

Walking into the sunshine reminds me of not only my dream from earlier but also why I love Melbourne. "Four Seasons in One Day" is not just a song by *Crowded House* but is an anthem that plays on repeat living in this city, since the weather is so unpredictable. The sun begins to burn my neck for real this time. Five minutes later, the sun is covered by clouds and rain begins to fall, cooling my face and neck. Not having any energy to run, I walk past Sandridge Beach. The last stretch of the footpath that I traverse is bordered by dirt, where I am forced to follow the road and the loud pollution-billowing trucks driving to the docks for the last part of my journey.

Having left my common sense behind in my bedroom with Jayden, my transport card and my phone, I anxiously stride down the winding dirt path into Westgate Park. I walk under an ornamental bridge and quickly find my way into a clearing near familiar picnic tables where I finally stop to take a breath. The public toilet is within spitting distance and nearly collide with a police officer once I turn the corner. The Victoria Police are securing the area with yellow tape. I watch a policeman escort a familiar looking bloke from the public toilet with wrists cuffed behind him. He is escorted through the clearing by the constabulary. I follow and watch the cops push the now familiar stranger into the back of what I assume to be an unmarked police car. The blokes who normally languish in their motorcars alone in the small parking lot turnover their ignitions in unison and slowly leave, assuming their company is no longer welcome in the public reserve. Despite the legacy of alcohol and drugs in my system, I quickly come to the realisation that I dodged a bullet. I glance towards the sky to see clouds overhead. After closing my eyes drops of rain begin to splash against my face.

8. Supernormal

Feeling both emotionally and physically exhausted, the walk back to the tram platform at Beacon Cove is equally tedious and tiresome. Without being burdened by technology or money to assist my endeavours to get home, I get lost in my own thoughts. Seeing that the transit police are inspecting the tickets of the wayward passengers boarding the tram reminds me of all the bad decisions that I have made since waking up today. Forgetting to bring my public transport card with me now officially ranks at the top of the list of epic failures for the day so far. If I was on top of my game, I would try to sweet-talk my way past the transit police and on to the tram where I could be ushered back to Southbank in air-conditioned comfort. Normally, I would communicate my tale of woe but appearing dishevelled and wearing a filthy hoodie doesn't help my confidence so I resign to the fact that I will be walking home. My frustration level seems to be linked to the rising ambient temperature and I regret not wearing fewer clothes. I push up on the thick cotton sleeves of my hoodie and begin to tramp up the path that follows the tram tracks. Forty minutes later I am walking amongst the shadows that the high-rise towers provide in Southbank.

Upon returning home, my father confronts me in the foyer before I can close the front door. "Where the hell did you go? You left Jayden here and you just swanned off to hell knows where!" Yet another bad decision that I have made today which can be added to the growing list of failures. My head begins to throb.

"Sorry, I went to check in on Austin as he was sick and having a rest in Federation Square." I lie however my father has a knack for catching me out when I tell a lie. "Also-"

"That is bullshit," my father shouts and interrupts my story. It is rare that he becomes so annoyed with me that he swears. I must be really off my game today and I blame it on the hangover and coming down from the drugs. "I know your damn phone is off. I saw it this morning in the kitchen. How would Austin get in contact with you? Do tell!" Daniel looks pissed off and grinds his teeth. "Don't bullshit me, Chezdon!"

"Sorry, I just feel like shit and needed some air. I couldn't stand the stink in my bedroom." This seems like a plausible excuse as I backtrack from being caught out telling an untruth. "It is disgusting in there and I just couldn't take it any longer."

"I don't know what is wrong with you Chezdon, but sort yourself out. You look awful and please put on some clean clothes. Look after yourself and more importantly look after your mate. Act like an adult for a change." I rub the back of my head as Daniel finishes his lecture. He suddenly grabs a set of keys from the tray on the table across from the front door and leaves. I let the door slam shut and then lock it.

I shuffle to my bedroom and find Jayden laying under the bedsheet on my bed watching television. "Hey. How are you feeling?" I wonder if he will be upset at me for going walkabout like my father is. "It is turning out to be a nice day."

Jayden rubs his temple with his index finger. "Like I have been hit by a cricket ball. At least I didn't end up like Phil Hughes." Jayden cracking a joke at the expense of a cricketer who recently died gives me the perspective that life could be much worse. I ponder what little I know of Phil Hughes who was hit on the head by a cricket ball last year. The sad memory suddenly puts my present circumstances into perspective. My dead phone on my desk catches my eye. My father must have brought it into this hellishly smelling room earlier when he found Jayden, but not his favourite son. I retrieve the phone in one deft swoop and plug a charging cable into it.

"I bet you are happy that you didn't buy a new phone yesterday mate." Jayden's eyes dart from his own phone to the television. I begin to feel deprived of technology and contact with the outside world. "Look at this mate. This photo has the most likes of anything that I have ever posted." Jayden thrusts the screen of his phone in my face. I first make out a white arse. It takes some time for me to realise that the photo is of me mooning the camera. I am looking back over my shoulder and sticking my tongue out." A feeling of dread begins to build in my stomach. I wonder what else happened last night that I do not remember.

"Jesus, you posted a picture of my arse?" I have managed to keep anything besides my exposed face, arms and legs off the Internet until now. All the effort seems to be in vain. "Hopefully that is it." I huff to make it seem like I remember the photo being taken and the circumstances. I grab Jayden's phone out of his hand start swiping at the screen, which shows me all the pictures that were taken last night. Memories quickly return after finding fifty photographs that have been posted on both Instagram and Twitter which memorialised our drunken antics for the world to see. Finding the humour in the silliness which was captured makes me chuckle. The highlights are the photographs of Austin sticking his tongue in my ear, Jayden getting a piggyback ride courtesy of Bryce and of course, my bare white arse mooning the camera. A thirty-second video also makes its world premiere which features me dancing on our black marble dining room table badly. Near the end of the video, I fall off the table and wither on the floor in pain. A resounding thud can be heard and then the obligatory swear words. It was this tomfoolery which sent my precious phone flying into the kitchen and crashing on the cold tiled floor. With the mystery of my broken phone screen solved without the need to involve Columbo, I swipe back to the photo of my arse and notice it has been 'liked' 769 times in less than twelve hours. I toss the Samsung Galaxy S4 which I originally loaned to Jayden a few months ago back onto his chest and sigh.

Jayden scratches his armpit and then pushes his hair off his forehead. "What are you looking for Chez?"

"My bloody phone screen is shattered. I have an old Galaxy S2 in here somewhere." I rummage through junk in the bottom drawer next to my bed. "If you remember I gave you that old Galaxy but you never returned it, so I am forced to use some really old tech now." I continue to move junk from side to side in the drawer. "The camera in this phone is broken as it was damaged in the washing machine."

"The washing machine?" Jayden laughs. "I am surprised it works at all."

"Me too. My father reckons that it is because after it was rescued, it dried out for a week and it wasn't turned on. Believe me mate, I never thought it would work." I close the bottom desk drawer and slide the one above it open, continuing the hunt for my old phone. "I know for a fact that Apple shit would never survive after being drowned."

Jayden laughs again. "Who put it in the washer? Your dodgy cleaner?"

"Actually, I did." I remove an old Mars bar wrapper from the drawer and toss it on the ground.

"Since when do you do your own washing?"

I stand up and face Jayden. "After school, I stopped for a curry at Southgate one day." I know this story is going to lead to me being ridiculed but it will hopefully distract Jayden enough so he doesn't ask me to explain why I left earlier. "The curry didn't agree with me and I couldn't get home fast enough. Let's just say that I couldn't get to the toilet in time. I thought I would clean up after myself by doing my own washing. In my rush to get into the shower, I put my trousers, phone, and my wallet into the washing machine. I simply forgot to take everything out of my pockets. The money and my bank card survived, but nothing else did. Or so I thought." Jayden begins to laugh hysterically. "That is the last time that I did my own wash and I certainly didn't buy a curry from that shitty shop again." I walk to my desk and begin to rummage through the open drawer whilst Jayden continues to laugh. Luckily, I find the Galaxy S2 and thrust it into the waiting charging cable next to my bed. I pull off my smelly and sweaty hoodie and make an audible grunt as I toss it on the floor before collapsing next to Jayden. I begin to pull apart my damaged phone with the intention of liberating the SIM card.

"Jesus mate. You stink!" Jayden lurches to the left. "You smell like old sweaty socks and wine mate."

I fumble with my broken phone and push my nose close to my armpit. I inhale and then look at Jayden. "You have purple stained lips." I do stink.

Jayden begins to lick his lips and then rubs at them violently with his finger before turning his attention to the television. The recent episode of *Game of Thrones* is being replayed. King Tommen Baratheon has just finished having sex with Queen Margaery Tyrell. It is a controversial scene as the actor who plays Tommen is only sixteen in real life. He looks exuberant portraying a typical horny teenager though. "You would so have your way with Tommen," Jayden says with a Cheshire cat-like grin on his face. "Or maybe not, he is only sixteen after all so he is far too young for you mate."

"Fuck you!" I power on the previously retired phone after inserting the SIM card and notice that it now has one percent of battery power in reserve. The 4G signal is located and the Morrison wireless network is discovered. Notifications of all types begin to flood in and the device begins to have a seizure. Missed calls, text messages, e-mails, alerts from Twitter,

Instagram, Facebook, and Snapchat all appear on the display simultaneously. The phone purrs like a cat as the seemingly endless notifications appear and the device continues to vibrate out of control. Feeling overwhelmed, I start to catch up with my digital life. "Thanks, arsehole. I now have these random kids adding me on Instagram. They are also messaging me on Twitter since you posted that photo of my bare arse wanting to see more."

"It is hilarious-" A wry smile envelopes Jayden's face as he pauses and begins to gesticulate. "Really hilarious photo, don't take it so seriously mate. It isn't like I posted a dick-pic. You were in your element and you certainly didn't care at the time so just relax and take a breath."

"It has been retweeted and shared, so I guess that I have to live with it." I exhale a noticeable sigh. The first thought that comes to mind is my father seeing the arse of his only son and namesake on some social media feed. "Whatever! I am over it." I turn my attention to my phone and continue to read and respond to messages. One communication is from James expressing hope that I am feeling 'groovy' and reminds me that we have plans later once he finishes work. I respond saying that I am 'just fine and dandy' and that I will meet him at the bar that he suggested. "So, what is your plan for today?" I ask Jayden after I send the last of the messages that require some attention. I toss the charging phone back onto the bedside table and stare at Jayden who is fondling his right nipple.

"Not much really. Mother is at some party this afternoon. Do you want to get lunch and just chill out? I don't have to be back until around six. I am so not in the mood for school tomorrow."

"Sure. How are you feeling?" I get off my bed and attempt to reconcile my fuzzy mind with my weary body. After the long and tumultuous wander, where the members of the public no doubt confused me with a zombie who managed to sweat out the excesses of the previous evening from every pore in my body, I am feeling fine for the most part. I certainly need a shower before going back out in public.

"Not that bad. I am fucking starving though, so let's get the fuck out of here." Jayden throws the bedsheet to the side, hops up and meets me at my closet. He enthusiastically pulls a white shirt off a hanger and pulls it over his head. "I had a shower after you went walkabout, so get the fuck ready mate."

I take a pair of grey skinny jeans and a black 5 Seconds of Summer concert singlet from my closet and a pair of underwear from an open drawer. I jog into my bathroom and slide the doors closed. Jayden and I have seen each other naked before but I still like to have privacy when I shower. After washing the sweat and filth from my body I blow dry my hair. I apply some product to my blonde fringe and get dressed. Returning to my bedroom, at first, I am affronted by the horrible smell and am reminded just how toxic my room is. Transported back to reality, Jayden exclaims "Fuck off!" as he stands up.

"What?" I look incredulously at Jayden as I begin to collect dirty and soiled clothes from the floor. I toss them all into a mound near my bed so the cleaner will know to attend to them when she next turns up.

"Seriously? Are you going to wear that shirt out in public? "For Christ's sake Chezdon."

"What is wrong with it? Considering what you wear most of the time, this is tame. Don't you like my white shoulders? Every man and his fucking dog have now seen my white arse thanks to you, so I thought I would just help fill in the blanks." Jayden has a contrary opinion because girls will check me out and ignore him as per usual.

Innocence Waning

"Whatever you say, mate. Let's go!" I follow Jayden to the foyer where I find my black Havaianas flip flops placed neatly in the corner and slide them on my feet. I notice that my toenails could use a clipping before taking a set of keys from the silver dish on the table. Food right now trumps any further desire to attend to my personal hygiene.

Our journey to find sustenance takes us across the Southbank pedestrian bridge, through the underground tunnel that passes under Flinders Street Station and out into the chaos of Elizabeth Street in what is considered the centre of the city of Melbourne. A sensory overload of sweaty bodies, familiar fast-food branding, rubbish in the gutter, traffic, and squealing trams are met with indignation as we weave between pedestrians, prams and the local police presence. We debate the merits of each restaurant that we walk past. Huxtaburger is a no-go zone since one of the hamburgers is named after Bill Cosby and Jayden hates the 'rapist' so he refuses to eat there. I veto "Lord of the Fries" only because I think the name is stupid and makes me think of a movie that is on my list that I haven't yet watched. We walk up Flinders Lane and agree to go to Supernormal so that we can eat delicious lobster rolls. I originally discovered this goodness at the now defunct Big Day Out festival a few years back. The lobster rolls were being sold as a takeaway by this restaurant to the concert-goers. They are both amazing and addictive. Last month, I tried to reproduce the published recipe with a very disappointing result; an adventure which proved beyond the shadow of a doubt that my destiny does not involve anything having to do with the culinary arts. Reminiscing about the amazing food and the sweaty shirtless guys from the festival not only makes me forget about what bands were playing that day but also the restaurant that we were fiending for as I walk past it. Jayden must have shouted at me three times before I snapped back to reality and noticed that I wandered past and jog back to him and past the open the door of the restaurant.

We are seated at the long bar on high red stools by a hostess that has a face that looks like a grumpy cat. We promptly get stares from the patrons seated to the left and right of us before being noticed by the wait staff. The looks of consternation on their collective faces as to why teenagers would want to eat at such a venue no doubt mystifies the onlookers where the average age of the customer base is thirty. This trivia provides some amusement as I scoot closer to the bar on the stool with noticeable effort. "Your finest vintage of Diet Coke please my lovely." This is my request when the bar lady asks what I would like to drink. Jayden insists on a full-strength Coca-Cola and requests a double. The older woman seated next to Jayden laughs.

Jayden quietly scrolls though notifications on his phone. I check my own device and read a rather sullen message from Bryce. The content doesn't register in my mind properly after skimming it for the first time since I am not totally with it. I must think about the meaning of the words and after taking a beat, start to laugh hysterically. I muffle the noise I am making with my arm. It isn't long before I can't control myself and my laughter becomes louder as I convert the words using my colourful imagination into pictures. My laughter is contagious. The bar lady begins to giggle whilst she looks at her colleague all the while whispering something to him. It is then when I notice the bloke to the right of me looking at me with an inquisitive gaze. "What the hell? What is so damned funny?" Jayden demands whilst trying to look at the screen of my phone. I put the device into flight mode and place it upside down on the bar, desperately trying to regain my composure. "What the hell?" Jayden asks again.

I stop laughing long enough to take a breath about the same time the 2015 vintage Diet Coke is set in front of me. I gulp it down in record time and swallow the ice cubes, using my free hand to motion for another round. "Were you the one that drew the swastika on Bryce's back?"

"No, that was Austin. Don't you remember those two arguing about all the bullshit going on in the Middle East last night?" Jayden appears intrigued. "Why do you ask?"

"I don't remember much about that conversation but that is not the point. I saw the swastika on his back this morning. My father saw it too and made some comment that it was drawn incorrectly. Anyway, Bryce had to turn up to supervise some youth swim class at his school this morning and he didn't know that was drawn on his back." I pause to watch Jayden both pucker and then tighten his lips and shift them to the right, a result of him being pensive. "He went to the pool with no shirt on, not knowing what was on his back. Both the children and parents saw Austin's artwork and there was outrage, to say the least."

"Oh yeah, I have a mental picture of his back mate. I put that photo on Instagram too. So why should anyone care? Austin was just having a laugh whilst Bryce was passed out."

"He goes to a Jewish school, you idiot." I roll my eyes and grab the empty glass.

"Oh shit!" Jayden reconstructs his pensive look again. "That is bad. That is so wrong." My best mate reflects thoughtfully and then takes a drink of his full-strength Coca-Cola.

"His mother had to turn up and collect him. He got lectured and was nearly thrown out of school. Good thing that Austin drew it the wrong way. I guess it has a different meaning that way so he could blame it on a prank that he knew nothing about. Anyway, he is not very happy and is the shit." I feel bad for Bryce but then find the humour in the situation again. It is just the inconvenient timing of his responsibilities at school on a weekend after a huge night of all things that caused this drama. Jayden swipes at the screen of his phone. He stares at the photo of Bryce that he posted on Instagram and shows it to me. "A masterpiece." Jayden muses. Bryce passed out on the floor of my room with my soiled underwear adorning his head like a crown of thorns with the reverse swastika drawn on his back.

We both begin to laugh in unison. If we were drinking alcohol we would have been cut off and thrown out of the restaurant. Instead, the bar lady turns up and asks us if we want a top-up of soft drinks and then asks us if we are ready to order. Only two words are exclaimed simultaneously. The words "lobster" and "roll" are blurted out and then we confirm that we want two of the amazing offerings each to commence our gourmet lunch experience.

Jayden sits up as straight as he can on the stool and stretches his arms over his head. "What a night mate. That James bloke seems like a sketchy character. Hell, he wouldn't even have a drink with us. You can't trust a bloke that will not take a drink when offered."

I follow Jayden's lead and stretch my arms over my head and try to snap the tension out of my neck by pushing my head to its side. I accidentally knock into the man sitting on the stool next to me with my elbow and quickly put my arms down. The outsider glances at me and turns away. Feeling self-conscious, I put my nose as close to my armpit and inhale. Not detecting an odour, I put it down to teenage enthusiasm distracting him with an elbow to the ribs instead of a stench. "I dunno. There is something about James that intrigues me."

"How could you possibly be intrigued by that idiot?"

"I really can't say. I don't know. It just seemed like a good idea to invite him around and all. It is probably like Austin drawing the reverse swastika on Bryce's back. I think the wine just made us act like fools." I start to question as to why I even bothered to respond to the message James sent me earlier, however, justify it in my mind that I just shouldn't be rude and I would like a beer. A tasty cold beer would probably make me feel better.

"Do you reckon you will bother seeing him again? There are plenty of other guys that aren't so sketchy mate; ones that obviously aren't as-" Jayden pauses, "um... old and experienced." He utters the last word implying a slew of other connotations but remains politically correct as the woman sitting next to him is eavesdropping. I wonder why the members of the public prefer to listen to boring teenage dramas instead of living lives of their own. Another glass of Diet Coke is placed in front of me. I gulp it all down and swallow the ice cubes again, motioning to the bar lady that I am very interested in yet another round.

"I am seeing him later today." I lick the rim of the empty glass. "For what it matters."

"What the fuck are you thinking mate? That bloke is twenty-five years old and is just some silly retail slut. You know he only wants one thing. Is that all you want you whore? To get it up the arse?" I continue to lick the rim of the glass and focus on the back of my throat that is now freezing. The bar lady begins to pour another round in a clean glass from an open can.

"Since it matters to you so much, I haven't ever had it up the arse as you so eloquently put it. Who is to say that that I don't want to give it to him up the arse?" The man sitting next to me shifts his weight and moves his body closer to me so he can hear every word of our conversation. "Jesus Christ, what is it of your business anyway, Jayden?"

"I just don't want you abducted or fucked over mate. That is all. Whatever makes you happy I guess." Jayden understands that he is not going to talk me out of my liaison. His facial expression morphs into one that includes a sullen look and I feel relieved. I don't want to talk about sex with Jayden any longer. Another glass of Diet Coke is placed in front of me and the bar lady winks. I manage a smile and I roll my eyes, which ultimately rest on Jayden.

The lobster rolls are delivered and devoured in between grunts and gasps which translate as how 'damn' good they are. We are so pleased that we order two more of the delightful lobster rolls. Jayden slides off the stool and stands upright. He puts his arms behind his back and tries to crack it. "Goddamn, these rolls are good. I will be right back, I need to hang a leak."

"You are all class." I grab my phone and take it off flight mode, being conscious that the device did not have a full charge when I left home earlier today. Alerts once again flood in, along with a message from Bryce saying he is going to 'kick Austin's faggity arse' and as I am about to respond, I am distracted by the man sitting next to me tapping my bare shoulder with his finger. "Excuse me, are you in that band?"

I finish tapping out a few words of encouragement to Bryce and suggest that Austin meant no harm. Whatever good it will do is unknown but I tap to send it anyway and then look at the stranger on my right. "What band?" My eyes meet those of the curious restaurant patron. He is holding some sort of mixed alcoholic drink in his hand and I am immediately distracted by the ice cubes glistening in the light. He then looks at my shirt and points at the *5 Seconds of Summer* logo. "That band?"

I smile and state matter-of-factly, "believe me mate, I am certainly not Luke Hemmings or Michael Clifford from *5 Seconds of Summer*." I don't know why I start to name the individual band members or why I am speaking so rapidly. I reach for the empty glass of Diet Coke and look at the wall of spirits behind the bar hoping that the gentleman will not ask me any further questions. I have suddenly become the victim of the awkward feeling of being overly self-conscious.

"Well, you look familiar. What university do you boys attend?"

I briefly wonder why the diner wants to continue a conversation with me and ignore the beautiful woman that he is with. I remind myself of one of the lessons learned from yesterday with James. I should not represent myself as being something that I am not. I, therefore, do not lie and simply ignore the question as I don't want to admit that I am really in Year 11. "Why are you so interested mate?" I ask but it sounds rude after coming out of my mouth.

Before I can correct how I phrased it or even apologise, he responds. "Not at all. Sorry to intrude, but we couldn't help but overhear you blokes and I just wanted to say that age is relative. If you like someone, age shouldn't matter." With that fatherly advice, the gentleman turns away and sips his alcoholic beverage from the glass in his hand.

I gently place a hand on his shoulder. "Sorry mate, I didn't mean to sound like a dick. That came out wrong. Sorry." My sincerity should be obvious by the look on my face. The gentle touch of his shoulder causes him to turn and face me once again.

"No worries, it is all good. My name is Shaun by the way." Shaun bends his arm and partially extends it in my direction, eager to shake my hand. I reciprocate and say, "Chezdon. It is good to meet you mate. Again, I apologise."

"That is a unique name. I have only ever heard of one other person named Chezdon in my life." After a dramatic pause which allows Shaun to sip his drink, he continues. "It sounds like you blokes had a big night last night. It was hard not to overhear." He takes another drink and stares at me, obviously waiting for an answer.

I quickly muse about what Jayden and I discussed since sitting down at the bar. There was plenty of amusing banter but also a few offensive themes. I feel my face starting to get hot once again and I am confident that it is turning red. "Oh sorry about that. My mate can get enthusiastic at times. But yeah, it was a big night. I am still feeling the pain."

For a few seconds' memories of the night that has come and gone overwhelm me once again. Before I am consumed by my midnight memories, Shaun introduces me to the woman sitting next to him who was ignored during our brief chat. She says she is his sister and just as I exclaim "g'day!" and shake her hand, Jayden appears in my periphery looking exasperated. I then introduce my friend to Shaun, and his lovely sister, Liz, who takes an interest in the lobster roll being placed in front of him by the now familiar staff. In what would be the most inventive way in recent memory to distract me from speaking with strangers, Jayden pokes me in the side so hard, his finger presses on one of my ribs. He repeats this until I give him my undivided attention and nearly scream in pain. "What goddamnit? What the fuck, mate?"

"You are just always chatting up randoms. It is like cancer." Jayden shoves the tip of the lobster roll into his mouth which is suggestive. Both the imagery and the smell of the buttery roll makes me fondly recall Austin's scent earlier in the day. I start to salivate and unconsciously begin to collect the remaining bits of lobster that have fallen onto my white plate and shove them into my gaping mouth.

"I wasn't chatting anyone up. I just having a conversation with the bloke sitting next to me whilst you were out messaging, pissing and posting status updates. Is that a crime?" I follow Jayden's lead and start to eat the last of my lobster roll. I watch him swallow and lick his lips suggestively once again and wink at me. "So, what do you want to do after this? When are you meeting up with the retail slut?"

"Not until around six." I feel a sense of fatigue setting in as I become more relaxed perched on the stool. After ordering another Diet Coke, which I learn is really Pepsi Max, I float the idea of seeing a movie to bide the time. The discussion turns into a heated argument about what to see. "It is no secret what happens in 'Furious Seven' and I can't be bothered watching Vin Diesel. Besides, I can't stand The Rock. I exclaim after Jayden suggests we view the latest incarnation of the franchise that managed to drag out longer than Paul Walker's life. "Let's watch 'Woman in Gold.'" My enthusiasm for visiting the cinema increases exponentially.

Jayden quickly reads the synopsis of 'Woman in Gold' on his phone whilst chewing on the last of his lobster roll. "Fuck off, why do you always want to watch such serious shit mate? Why can't you just go and watch some light-hearted comedy or a silly movie like the rest of the normal kids in the world like to do?"

I roll my eyes and return to sipping from my glass of Pepsi Max since we are seemingly at an impasse. There is movement by my new friends to the right as they find their feet and begin to gather their belongings. Whilst I am distracted, Jayden startles me by sticking his finger violently into my ribcage again. Shocked, I bark out a sharp high-pitched "Jesus!" and turn my head and sneer at my best mate.

"There is an advance screening of *Unfriended* today at the cinema. How about that?" Jayden was talking about wanting to see this movie earlier in the week. It is a masterpiece about a group of teenagers terrorised by an online stalker that should be dead. The mysterious protagonist makes life difficult for these teenagers whilst sitting they sit in front of their computers. It seems like a very uninteresting and predictably boring story. A tale of cyber-stalking that apparently turns deadly, just like the stigma behind online dating if the hysterical media can be believed. A hand gently touches my bare shoulder which startles me yet again. I nearly hop off the seat but refrain from shouting an explicative or some form of blasphemy. The high dosage of caffeine that I have ingested must be affecting my nervous system. Shaun rests his hand on my shoulder. His skin feels refreshingly cold against mine.

"If you want to see 'Woman in Gold', give me a shout sometime, Chezdon." Shaun removes his hand and uses it to retrieve a business card from his pocket. He places it next to my empty plate. I grab the card assuming Jayden will take it and raise my hand before saying "Cya" as I catch Shaun's gaze and then the eyes of Liz.

I gyrate around to face Jayden who is picking up the individual morsels of crayfish off his plate and shoving them into his mouth using his fingers. "I really have nothing to say." He takes a dramatic pause and finds some words to add. "Let's get the fuck out of here."

After requesting the bill from the friendly bar lady, I drink what is left in my glass of Pepsi Max. I am in no rush to leave and am content just chewing on ice cubes. They are not only cooling down my insides but the base sound of the crunching relaxes me. After a few minutes, the docket arrives on a small plastic tray. I am bemused by the line item that totals $30 for non-alcoholic drinks. Feeling ripped off, I pull some cash carefully from my pocket and toss it onto the tray before we stagger out of the restaurant rubbing our stomachs.

We walk to Federation Square where we purchase Slurpee's from the 7-11. My love affair with ice continues as we quickly traverse the public space looking for familiar faces that would be languishing about on this beautiful warm Melbourne day.

Innocence Waning

After only finding tourists feeding the seagulls and so-called street performers, we walk to Collins Place and purchase movie tickets. I notice a franchise of Guzman Y Gomez and reconcile my finances in my head. Burritos and drinks there would have been much cheaper than the iced glasses of flavourless Diet Pepsi at Supernormal. I get lost in the moment thinking about how ridiculously expensive things are. The seagulls in Federation Square may be loud and obnoxious but the birds are indeed the smart ones as in the end they manage to eat and drink for free.

We wait patiently for the movie to commence in the small air-conditioned cinema. At capacity, the room holds no more than fifty people and I can count on my hand how many people have paid to see this masterpiece. Another $17 can be flushed down the toilet as about fifteen minutes into the flick, I decide that the movie would have made a good candidate to pirate. It is not ground-breaking and is very boring. If I didn't have so much caffeine in me, I would try to go to sleep but unable to, my eyes are left to be tortured. My mind, fortunately, drifts first to exploring Austin's body earlier amongst my damp sheets and how the light that was being emitted from the television made his skin appear effervescent. Ignoring the ridiculous movie, I close my eyes and try to will my penis to settle from its current erect state. My imagination gets the best of me though and I begin to wonder yet again how it would have felt to shove my cock in Austin's arse. How long could I pound him for before I cum? Would it feel better than fucking a peach? I asked myself these questions and cannot even fathom an answer. Given my drug-fucked, drunk and horny state early in the morning, I assume if the feeling of being sick didn't inconveniently overwhelm me at the time, I would have tried to have my wayward way with my attractive friend regardless of what state the other guests in my room were in. I take a deep breath and scratch my eyelids in frustration.

My daydreaming is interrupted by a hand smacking on my chest. I react by screaming since I am so highly strung. Jayden lowers his face into the palms of his hands and begins to giggle. His noise combined with my shrill gasp proves to be a very rude and unwelcome distraction for the other patrons enjoying the cinematic experience. Two girls in unison turn around to shush us. Instead of looking either one of them in the eyes, I look down at my crotch. My erection is situated so awkwardly that it hurts and the cockhead is rubbing against my skinny jeans with impunity. I attempt to shift my weight and adjust it which then turns out to be a futile exercise. Cleverly, I use the fact that Jayden is distracted by laughing uncontrollably into his forearm as an opportunity to shove my hand into my pants and adjust my manhood in the relative privacy of darkness. With an extended deep breath, I find relief and I try to focus on the grown adults acting like teenagers on the big screen. As my physical pain has thankfully passed, I try to make sense of the movie. Why don't these characters just don't turn off their damn computers and unplug their router? You can't be stalked online if you aren't online. Thinking critically about what is playing out on the screen just manages to frustrate me more and it is a state that I remain until the movie mercifully comes to a predictable end.

The credits roll. I yawn and the lights in the theatre are returned to normal. The teenage girls that were seated in front of us stand up and give Jayden a death stare. This just encourages him to slap my shoulder, laugh and carry on one last time as the girls walk away from us down the aisle. "Let's get the hell out of here!" I exclaim after standing up and walking briskly towards the door without waiting for Jayden to acknowledge me.

Matriculating from the cinema and into the plaza, I take my phone out of flight mode and patiently wait for the messages and notifications to appear. One message that takes me by surprise is James announcing that he is leaving work early and that he is keen to meet ahead of schedule. After scrolling through Twitter notifications and reading comments about my white arse being visually appealing and random girls sending their greetings, Jayden catches up with me. "Hey, I better get back to the homestead. Mother thinks I should be home to get ready for school tomorrow. What a laugh. Did you like the movie, mate?"

I continue to read my Twitter feed and don't bother looking at Jayden. "The movie was shit. I get to pick the film next time." I look up and find Jayden's blue doe eyes staring at me and I give him a hug. "Okay, mate. See you tomorrow." I pat him on the back and walk backwards, wave and then jog to the tram stop.

Whilst the tram squeaks and comes to a stop at the platform outside of the cinema, I exchange messages with James. I predict being at the bar in Collingwood, which is where he wants to meet me in fifteen minutes. The iconic method of Melbourne public transport travels the opposite way from where Jayden is travelling and away from the central business district. The tram rattles and hums until I arrive at Smith Street, not far from the nominated bar. Most Melburnians consider this suburb as a haven for hipsters and an enclave of LGBTI-friendly bars and clubs and of course the home of the dreaded Collingwood Magpies footy team. The Grace Darling Hotel is where I am meant to meet James and it is only seconds away by foot once I alight from the tram. I haven't taken the time to overthink this date so when I arrive and find James wearing sunglasses and sitting outside at a table puffing on a cigarette, I can't help but chuckle. Two pints of beer are sitting on coasters in front of him.

"Hey mate. I bet you like Coopers Green. After last night, I would assume you would drink anything and everything though." James smiles, stands up and extends his hand. I shake it and immediately decrease the pressure that I am exerting as it feels like I am squeezing a pancake. I don't want to break him just yet. I pick up the pint glass and take a drink of the tasty beer before sitting down on the wooden bench.

"That is nice. I needed that. Thanks, mate. It is good to see you again. I honestly didn't think that I would ever hear from you again." The next sip of beer that I take is intentionally slow. It gives me time to look at James closely. He is wearing a white collared shirt which is what I assume what he wore to work. The material is thin enough for me to notice that he has tattoos on his chest and piercings in his nipples.

"I have to admit Chezdon, I did have second thoughts about this but I think you are pretty cool and you couldn't really control what happened yesterday." James takes a long drag from his cigarette. He flicks ashes into the tray and then takes a drink from his pint glass.

"Our party yesterday was not exactly planned, but the best ones are not, I guess." I take another drink and structure my thoughts into words. The smell of cigarette smoke begins to irritate my nose. "Apologies for having to deal with my parents. They weren't supposed to be around, but they are pretty cool and harmless for the most part." I glance at the table next to us where four blokes are seated and staring at us. Feelings of self-consciousness begin to overwhelm me again and I begin to question my motives for being here. I distract myself by playing with my hair and looking at the pedestrians that are walking past.

"You are so well spoken for your age. You act like you are in University by the way you carry yourself. It is so cool. You are kinda hot too." James winks at me before taking another drag from the cigarette and drinks the rest of the beer in the pint glass.

"Thanks. I think." My thirst which is directly proportional to my anxiety level encourages me to finish the remaining beer in my glass in record time as I ponder what to say next. Normally I am not at such a loss for words. "I would shout the next round; however, I am afraid dressed like this, the barperson probably will ask me for my I.D., and that would not end well." I quickly shove my hand into my pocket and arch my back.

"Don't worry about it, I will get the round." James takes the last drag of his cigarette which exhausts the tobacco in the cancer stick. Although he blows the smoke away from me as he gets up, a gust of wind blows some of the white haze back on me, along with a few ashes as a consolation prize. "I'll be right back."

I start to tap and swipe on the screen of my phone and appear to look busy. I don't want to make eye contact with the group of blokes at the table next to me even though they are doing their best to get my attention. After responding to a few messages, I send a friendly query to Bryce quizzing him as to the outcome of the battle of Berlin at the Jewish pool earlier and whether he survived the Blitz intact. Searching for a way to waste time, I also message Austin and ask him how he is feeling after our night of debauchery. At least if the conversation dies a slow death or if I start losing interest in James, hopefully, I will be inundated with incoming messages and they will provide me with a legitimate exit strategy. It would sound pathetic to have to blame the fact that I must leave because my parents expect me home at a reasonable hour on a Sunday night.

My drinking partner returns with what I assume to be another pint of Coopers Green. I greedily begin drinking the beer as soon as he hands it to me. Before I know it, I have consumed half a pint long before James has even sat down. Another cigarette is liberated from its box. Whilst watching James light it, I decide that he looks like a caricature of how movies and television shows typically portray a camp homosexual twenty-something. I wonder how the mannerisms on display by James and the associated preconceived stereotype has classified us to the group of very curious blokes at the table next to us. Do they care what our motivation for being at this bar on a sunny Sunday afternoon is? I doubt that I appear that I am even close to being of the legal drinking age of eighteen but I am knocking back the amber ale with a vengeance whilst my admirer plays catch-up. If I was sitting at the other table and looking at us right now, I would find the circumstances not only intriguing but ridiculous and criminal at the same time just judging from our body language. "Let me ask you this." James pauses to inhale smoke, holds it in for what seems like an eternity and then exhales, not taking as much care now to segregate me from the second-hand plume. "Who is fucking who between your mates?"

"What do you mean?" I take an interest in the craftsmanship of my pint glass.

"Who is sleeping with who?" James takes another drag. His blue eyes find mine. "I have an idea of who is fucking who."

I consider his bold question and briefly recall the events from last night. I smile and chuckle. "Jayden has a girlfriend. Bryce is single. I think Austin is single."

"Wait, hold up. Who is who?" James inhales more smoke and quickly spits it out. "Who is the chunkier one of the three amigos?"

The word chunkier makes me think of the character of Fat Bastard from the Austin Powers movies. "You mean Bryce?" I ask. "He plays rugby and is really the only one of us that plays any sport, so I would not call him chunky."

"Yeah, that is his name." James takes another drag and then drinks some ale. "He seems pretty cool. He is cute too."

A feeling of disappointment begins to overcome me. I surmise that James wanted to just meet me as he wanted an introduction to one of my friends. "Do you have a thing for his type? Sorry to tell you though James, he is straight." My self-esteem nosedives in a matter of seconds. I return my attention to rotating my pint of beer on its axis. Instead of looking directly at James, I focus on the edge of the glass that is glistening in the sunlight.

James exhales more smoke before continuing. "Bryce is cute. I just wanted to make sure that you were not with him as I wanted him to be sloppy seconds if things do not work out between us." He takes a drink of beer and stares at me.

Shocked, I look to the right and catch the gaze of all four blokes who continue to gawk at me from the other table. My eyes then find James. He is holding his beer with one hand and a burning cigarette with the other. His eyes jerk up to mine and I am determined to stare him down until he flinches. Fortunately for me, as I am still on a caffeine high, it is only a matter of seconds until I win the staring contest. I smile and retort. "The only other gay boy is Austin."

"He is the one that gave me a hard time that dresses like a slut, right?" James rolls his eyes and places the cigarette between his lips suggestively.

I wait for him to finish molesting the ciggy. He eventually smothers the burning end into the ashtray whilst I finish drinking my beer. "No, the male slut is my best mate, Jayden. I think it would be good if you knew him better before referring to him a slut though." The serious look on my face combined with my icy glare unsettles James a bit. He shifts his weight and quickly glances at the blokes sitting next to us. I patiently wait for him to pull yet another cigarette from the pack and light it. I continue to turn my pint glass on its axis and scrutinise his facial features.

"Sorry, Chezdon." Another cloud of smoke passes near my head. " I meant no offence."

"It is cool. I am just stirring you up. Austin is the blond guy with the obnoxious shoes, Jayden is the male slut with the black skinny shorts and the chunky one is Bryce. They are all good kids." James still appears unsettled as my body language was no doubt indicating that I was either upset or annoyed which would be masquerading the unease of the situation that I have put myself in.

I lean back and begin to pull my right leg up so I can rest it on my left knee. "Sorry mate. No reason to go." James quickly takes a drag from the cigarette and lowers it so it burns under the table.

I flash a wry smile at James. "I am not going anywhere. But I think you are. I am empty after all." He takes another drag from the cigarette before standing up and walking back into the bar.

Finally, I have a chance to be alone with my thoughts and enjoy the ambience whilst James is presumably buying another round of drinks. I begin to wonder what I will be doing ten years from now and consider the chances that I will be sitting at this pub with my same friends or perhaps a new set of acquaintances that I met at University or even from some place of work. Everyone seems to be so familiar chatting about their personal dramas which are not too much different than what I speak about with my friends. It is all just varying degrees of importance, at least on a scale that is affected by perception. I begin to eavesdrop on tales of horrible bosses, relationship breakdowns, cheating boyfriends, parents dying of cancer, financial problems, an HIV diagnosis and an observation that the price of beer is too expensive. Most of the complaints originate from the table of blokes to the right of me. I then don't hear chatter about sport, arts, culture, politics or anything positive; just tales of woe which puts me in an introspective mood as I consider life and my future.

James walks from the bar and back towards our table holding two pints of beer. "Wow, you look serious. Who died?" He must have noticed the look of consternation on my face as he sets the pint glasses down at the same time."

I sigh and scratch the back of my neck. "Nobody. I was just thinking about life and times. Out of curiosity, do you hang out here with groups of mates on occasion or do you just come here for dates?" My throat suddenly feels dry. It needs to be quenched by beer as the words are not coming out considerately, either because I am becoming a bit drunk or just because I am now feeling circumspect.

"I don't have many friends in Melbourne as I just moved here from Perth a few months ago, so I really can't say, sorry." James takes a beat to light another cigarette. "I just like coming here as it is close to where I live, I can smoke outside and drink of course and not worry about much."

"Fair enough." Either we will continue drinking and boring conversation that just summarises high-level facts that you would find on a Facebook profile will bring this to a natural end or I must try again to push things to the next level. "From what you read in the newspaper, you would think that the mining boom in Western Australia would be providing a fair amount of opportunities, not only in retail for the cashed-up housewives, but it would have made Perth more of an exciting city to live in. Is that the case?" My perception of Perth is disjointed and confused and what I know of the city has come from Jayden's mouth.

James stares at me with a blank look on his face. His mouth falls open slightly. He probably thinks that I am just a teenage wanker after that diatribe. "Right, are you sure that you are only sixteen?" He puffs on the cigarette and chases the smoke that he inhaled with beer. His question is overheard by two of the blokes to my right who once again take an interest in me and start whispering to one another. "Perth is a shithole mate. I lived there with my boyfriend for four years. There is nothing to do there besides have sex and get drunk." He sips from the pint of beer and sets the glass down gently. "Before you ask, we broke up just because we grew apart and no longer had any common interests."

I hadn't planned on asking about the breakdown of his relationship or his revelation. James must have noticed an amused look on my face as I wondered what sort of interests he could have possibly in common with the other bloke that he lived with as he just doesn't seem very interesting at all. I muse that they must have shared a common appreciation for tobacco, beer and of course sex as he alluded to. After taking another sip, he asks, "What is so funny?"

"Nothing mate. I was just hoping to get some insight as I am supposed to be going to Perth with my parents in the winter and I was just looking for some inside knowledge." I lie as I want to distract myself from imagining him having sex with somebody else and try to steer the conversation back to something banal.

"Here is the deal." James takes what will be the final drag on his cigarette. This gives him time to collect his thoughts before extinguishing it in the tray. "I don't have any more cash on me, so if you want to know more about Perth you have to come back to my place. I have wine there and I know how much you like your wine. Besides, I need to get these shoes off of me, they are new and giving me blisters. After I go to the toilet, would you be keen?"

Many thoughts rush through my head as I finish drinking what is left in my pint glass. Is he out of money? Does he really have blisters? Does he want to ravage my young body? "Sure, go piss. Then we can fuck off." The blokes at the table next to us start cheering. I overhear one of them shout, "I knew it!" before James stands up and toddles back into the bar.

I check the clock on the display of my phone. As I feared with the natural light fading it is now officially evening and exactly 6:00 PM. I need to be home by 8:00 PM to avoid being given a hard time, punished and most importantly avoid another argument with my father. There is no harm in going to wherever James lives, which I assume is nearby. He previously mentioned that this bar is local to where he lives. James emerges from the doorway of the bar for the last time. "Ready to go?"

"Do you feel like a new man?" I ask trying to act clever. Judging by the look on his face, he didn't understand the underlying humour but I laugh at my own joke.

We stumble at times for a couple hundred metres from the bar into a nearby residential housing block. After exchanging some small talk about the suburb of Collingwood, I admit that I support the Magpies in the footy. I get the impression that James doesn't even know what footy is, let alone what a magpie would be in the wild if one swooped down and pecked him on the head. I begin to question this home visit and wonder if it is a good idea. James then suddenly announces that we have arrived at his humble abode and that we need to climb a flight of stairs to what I find his small studio apartment which he graciously grants me entry into. I look around at the modest furniture and decorations whilst he removes his shoes. Where a refrigerator is meant to be is just a vacant space in the open plan kitchen. "You don't have a refrigerator?" I ask. I continue to inspect the free-flowing mess of organised chaos with varying degrees of purpose resting on the floor. I am startled when James comes from behind me and wraps his arms around my chest. I smell nicotine as he exhales near my ear. He whispers, "I have wanted to do this since the minute I met you." He sticks his tongue in my ear after he chews playfully on my earlobe. He then begins to nibble on the back of my neck, all the while feeling my chest with both of his hands.

Although I was taken aback at first, it only takes a second for me to begin living in the moment. My erection rapidly resurrects itself as James continues to gently kiss, lick and suck on the side my neck. Without warning, he releases his hands from their gentle grip on my chest. His fingers first move to caress the skin exposed by my singlet before he thrusts both of his hands behind my shirt and begins to squeeze my hard nipples. His breathing accelerates as he sticks his tongue far into my ear. I can't help but to giggle and squirm as he increases the pressure on my nipples. The smell of tobacco begins to overpower my sense of smell as his tongue finds its way from my ear to my neck and then to my flushed cheek. As I turn around he removes his hands from inside my shirt and mercifully, he stops squeezing my nipples as our mouths smash together. I haphazardly attempt to insert my tongue into his gaping mouth. Thoughts of licking the floor of the bar that I was just at come to mind as the smell of cigarettes and the taste of cheap beer distracts me as I experience my first kiss with a guy. His arms glide down the sides of my body at the same time until his hands are firmly squeezing both of my arse cheeks. He forcefully draws my torso closer with my arse in his clutches which leaves my hard cock grinding against his. His mouth is ravenous and I accept his tongue which then explores the back of my mouth and then my teeth. His engorged pulsing penis throbs against my own cock through his trousers as he aligns with my body so he can once again grab my arse violently and heave my body into his. He returns to sucking on my neck which I find mind-blowing and get lost in the bliss of this new-found ecstasy that I have never experienced before. The tight grip on my butt is slowly released and his hands make their way gradually up my back. He gently feels my soft warm skin and pulls my shirt up and sucks on my right nipple whilst exploring my moist armpits with his hands.

Tired of going along for the ride, I grab his arse and then muster the courage to feel the outline of his erect cock using my hand whilst he continues to explore my mouth with his tongue. Saliva drips off my chin as James abandons my mouth before crouching down on his knees. He pushes his nose on the noticeable bulge hidden behind my skinny jeans and inhales deeply through his nose. The smell of my crotch would be much more appealing than the tobacco, beer and nicotine I have the pleasure of smelling. My ball sack rests in stasis in a tortured state, imprisoned behind the mere fabric of my jeans and boxer briefs. I want him to pull the zipper down and liberate my dick from its prison. Before I can demand that he do so and suck my eager cock, he looks up at me and simply says, "hot."

I suck in air using my open mouth as James stands up, rubbing my crotch. After kissing me on the lips he says, "I will be right back." He then staggers into the bathroom and closes the door behind him. Confused, I don't know what to say or do next. The feeling then devolves into one of disappointment that our raunchy activities either were put on hiatus or have ended abruptly. When he doesn't return from the bathroom after a few minutes, I can only assume that he is taking a shit. I sit down on a chair after manipulating my hard cock and look around again at the mess that personifies the home life of James.

Another minute or so passes. I consider taking my cock out and having a quick wank and blowing on some old slices of pizza that are still in a delivery box sitting on the coffee table. Finally, I hear the toilet flush and assume that James will be returning soon so I resist the urge to pull my hard dick out of my pants. I watch the door with my undivided attention but it does not open. More time passes and my raging boner becomes exhausted as I continue to wait for James to emerge from behind the closed door. The toilet flushes again and my excitement returns and my cock begins to stir yet again. More time passes and being left to my own devices I stand up and then wander around the small apartment. I find an open bottle of vodka next to the microwave. I take a swig directly from the bottle, only to kill the taste of tobacco and stale beer from my mouth. I nearly gag after swallowing fermented potatoes but it does eradicate the horrible tastes. My eyes go wide when I hear what sounds like a shower being turned on from behind the closed bathroom door. Vexed as to why this sexually charged experience has come to such a dramatic if not abrupt end, I first wonder if I did something wrong. Maybe my pubic region smelled awful after James took a mighty whiff through my dirty skinnies and that is the reason why he had to flee. Confused, but with a heightened sense of courage and curiosity fuelled by my alcohol consumption, I quietly walk to the bathroom door and gently turn the knob. Using my shoulder, I push on the door gently, so I can poke my head in and see what is going on.

Time begins to move in slow motion. Water is flowing from the shower nozzle. James has his naked torso propped up against the wall and is squatting. He is trying to align the lip of a two-litre plastic bottle of Pepsi that has been filled presumably with water with his arsehole. It takes what seems to forever for him to complete the act and for the marriage to be consummated. He squeezes the bottle as hard as he can whilst his penis sways back and forth like a pendulum. The water in the plastic bottle forcefully explodes into his anus. Dumbfounded, I decide to look at his naked body and it is only then I notice how many tattoos he has. James remains squatting with his eyes closed and holds a volume of water inside of him. My pronounced gasp alerts him that he has an audience. With wide eyes, which become a permanent fixture on his face, James looks up. He resembles a kangaroo caught in headlights and shouts, "get the fuck out of here!" I watch water trickle down both of his shaved legs. After the shock and indignation of seeing me watch him carry out this hygienic task passes, the remaining dirty water from his bowels is forced out with a loud fart. He remains squatting in a vulnerable position with a look of dread in his dull blue eyes.

I quickly retreat to the living room, closing the bathroom door behind me. My original feelings of shock and awe evolve into amusement. Having realised that he was cleaning himself out from the inside in preparation for me having sex with him was not only presumptuous but is also humorous. During the last year, I have read many articles about how to prepare my young body for the act of love. I never considered that it would be undertaken in such a sexually charged moment and assumed it would be more planned. He could have cleaned himself out before going to the bar, it wasn't like he was in a rush to meet me.

A feeling of relief overwhelms me. From the moment that James first excused himself and went to his bathroom, I was very close to blowing my load. I was fearful that if he tried to undo my jeans, I would have ejaculated onto his face within seconds after my penis was liberated from its jail. Fortunately, with the benefit of hindsight along with the imagery of him shoving the large plastic bottle of Pepsi up his arse, I feel like I dodged a bullet. Would I have liked to lose my virginity under these circumstances? It is a moment in my life that will be branded into my warped mind until the day I die. These last few minutes include events that I cannot un-see and I decide it would be best to avoid an awkward conversation and just get the fuck out of this shithole. Since the lust of the early evening has come and gone and it will certainly not be replaced with romance let alone sex, I remove my phone from of my back pocket and leave.

The slow-motion bathroom imagery seems like it played out for hours even though it lasted for even a minute. I can only smile and lick my lips as I walk back toward Smith Street and inevitably past the outdoor tables at the bar where I previously enjoyed pints of beer with James. Lost in my own world and overwhelmed with conflicting feelings of amusement and lust, at first when I hear "Oi!" being shouted, I ignore it. After I hear it repeated, I identify the bloke that is shouting at me. He is one of the drinkers that were sitting next to us earlier. Feeling emboldened as knowing the bloke that is shouting 'oi!" is not only the alpha male of the group but also the one that took such an interest in me earlier, I walk over and casually say, "hey, what's up boys?"

The alpha male who looks like he visits the gym daily is the first to respond. "G'day mate. That was quick." He looks me up and down whilst his friends giggle. The wind catches my hair and I press it against my head with both hands.

Confused at the question, I clear my throat. "What was?" I feel like I am playing the role of the dumb blond. I clear my throat again. The vodka has left it feeling peculiar. "What was quick?"

One of the drinkers introduces himself as Damien and extends his hand. I shake it and tell him my name. After the pleasantries are out of the way, he continues. "That bloke that you were with, he is a bit of a tragic fag. Us boys drink here all the time and we always see him sitting outside smoking with some new random guy that he has picked up from god knows where." Damien then points at the guy that was shouting at me just minutes ago and takes a drink before finishes filling me in on his previous observations of James. "Tom here sees him on the gay dating apps all the time. He is always here before taking someone back to what I guess is his place to fuck. Sorry to be so crass, mate." I always wondered if I should download an application like Grindr to find some dates, but have avoided it.

Innocence Waning

I briefly ponder the time that these blokes are wasting gossiping at this bar. I consider sharing my personal business and the many stories that I have actively been a part of over the weekend with these strangers. I am confident that I can amuse these blokes by revealing what transpired only minutes ago. My thoughts once again turn to cricket and the late and great Richie Benaud. I choose to say only what would be both considered positive and necessary at this bizarre moment. Something that would be considered useful but poignant.

"Nothing happened boys." My audience hangs on every word, looking for a tragic story that belongs on a gossip website. "I am not a Pepsi kind of guy, I like Coke." With that enigmatic statement that summarises my weekend, I farewell the nosey revellers with a wave of my hand and then walk towards the Smith Street tram stop with a smile plastered my face.

9. **Nandos**

The pouring rain saturates both me and my stuffed backpack from the top down as the blustery wind plays havoc with the cheap umbrella that feebly protects my body. I briskly walk to St Kilda Road doing my best to take cover wherever possible and avoid the torrential rain whilst remaining vigilant. Hopping over puddles so that I don't end up slipping and falling on my arse, my freshly cleaned and pressed school uniform is left to be abused like a battered piece of fish. Mud and water are splashed onto me as motorcars drive past and turn into a five-star hotel. I am sprayed wantonly as I adeptly slog from the Southbank Promenade which protects me from the weather momentarily by enabling me to take refuge and transit through the Southgate food court and ultimately wander past the infamous fast food Indian takeaway place which caused me so much anguish a few months ago. My exodus is to the nominated place where I was told I could be picked up by Austin's mother since neither Daniel nor Mel were around this morning to act as my personal chauffeur to school. I was prepared to beg for a ride but in the end, a text to Austin sufficed which saved me the indignity of getting a lecture from my father for not being better prepared for events that are beyond my control. The wait for an Uber mimicked that of forty days and nights because of a transport workers union strike today in Melbourne. The selfish taxi union followed suit and they are striking for the day along with the tram drivers which is causing transport chaos. Under my breath, I curse the unions and their industrial action as the wind once again retards my umbrella. I fall into the Plexiglas enclosure of a vacant tram stop and wait, segregated from the driving rain.

A black BMW X5 screeches to a stop in front of me. It isn't too often that you see motorcars being driven on the designated tram tracks in Melbourne but with the public transport not operating today because of industrial action, Austin's mother obviously thought it would be prudent to use the tram lane as her own private expressway to our school. I accidentally smack Austin with my wet backpack as I thrust my body into the back seat of the SUV. After dropping my broken umbrella on the floor and unintentionally pushing my elbow into Austin's ribcage, I notice his mother staring at me through the rear-view mirror. "Hi, Julie."

"Ouch! Mate, how much crap do you have in that?" Austin extends his hand. I shake it at the same time he sticks out his tongue and erratically wobbles his head in silence. I feign a smile despite feeling generally uncomfortable because of my wet shirt sticking to my body. "What did you get up to yesterday?"

"Remember that guy James who stopped by on Saturday?" Austin's eyes open wide and his eyebrows move up and disappear under his blond fringe. "I caught up with him briefly. Oh, Jayden and I went to Supernormal before going to see the movie *Unfriended*."

Not realising that the other two pairs of ears that are travelling in the front seat are hanging on every word that I utter, I am taken aback when Austin's mother interjects. "I love Supernormal. Did you order a lobster roll? They are to die for." I once again see Julie looking at me in the rear-view mirror.

Austin's sister turns around and places her hand on my damp knee. "Oh my god, *Unfriended*. I so want to see that movie. What did you think?"

"The lobster rolls were pretty awesome and the movie was average, to say the least. The movie is worth seeing and it is a bit of a laugh if anything. It was a really short movie so there wasn't much character development, but I reckon you don't go to see a movie like that to analyse it." I do my best to remain politically correct considering I am getting a free ride to school. "Yeah, I did!" I exclaim. "Jayden ate three lobster rolls. They are so good." I shoved three rolls down my mouth too but I don't want to come across as a pig.

"So, when is the wedding?" Is Julie speaking to me? I surmise that I appear stunned and at a loss for words as she stares at me through the rear-view mirror again. I assume she is making some sort of insinuation about Jayden and I being overly close. My silence provokes her to add additional clarity after clearing her throat. "I mean your mother's wedding."

I obviously have missed some gossip over the weekend as I was in a drunken stupor and chasing cock. I know for a fact that Daniel and Mel are not getting married anytime soon, so I am at a loss as to what Julie is talking about. Then it hits me like a ton of bricks. Julie is talking about my birth mother. After my parents separated, she remained active as a Melbourne socialite and persisted in maintaining her relationships with the parents of my friends and acquaintances. Julie would be aware that I do not speak with my mother though. "Not sure." My uncomfortable demeanour is noticed by Austin who cuts in and starts making not only small talk with his mother but then his sister. He provides a timely distraction which allows me to be alone with my thoughts and stare out the window until a sharp left turn is made, which throws me into Austin. The car comes to an abrupt stop outside of school where we are safely dropped off without the fear of being drenched by the falling rain.

"Thanks for the ride, I appreciate it, Julie." I throw the door of the X5 open and slide out, leaving a trail of moisture behind me on the seat as a snail would.

As I wait for Austin to disembark, the front passenger window is lowered. Chloe sticks her head out and looks me up and down like she is inspecting a side of beef. "You have a nice arse." Her comment is met with a blank look of bemusement and I shudder. Austin starts to chuckle and slams the car door closed. "You know, from the Instagram post on Saturday night. I love it!" If the commentary is starting so early from Austin's conservative sister, I will have to mentally prepare myself for what is in store for me behind the school gates. I disregard the surprising yet new-found knowledge that my mother is getting married and resolve to talk about it with my father and Mel later. It is not a big deal. It isn't like I plan on going to her wedding and silently wish her and whatever bloke that is silly enough to marry her good luck and a happy life.

After walking past the iron gates and onto school property, I am approached by friends, acquaintances and many teenagers that I would not know from a bar of soap. I am asked to fill in the blanks about the 'fucking awesome' party that I threw over the weekend. Austin is also asked to give his observations since it is understood that he was in attendance. He was nearly as prolific with the tweets and posting of pictures on Instagram as Jayden so he cannot escape from the interrogations. I am forced to defend why I didn't invite various classmates and make empty promises as I proclaim that I will be throwing another party sooner rather than later. Was my impromptu gathering of four, and briefly five people at one point even a party? I silently wonder however since my peers who must have nothing else incredibly interesting in their own little worlds interpret things differently. Both fact and fiction travel long and far throughout the corridors of Melbourne Grammar School. Photographic evidence uploaded to the various social media platforms are hypothesized and remarked on both online and within the physical realm that is truly outside of my control. Gossip and innuendo fuelled by both Austin and Jayden exaggerating the extent as to how our 'good times' evolved add fuel to the burning fire. Stories spread like wildfire and it doesn't take long before Bryce sends me a message saying tales of our debauchery found their way into the social media feeds of the unwashed masses far beyond my school.

The dark clouds gradually give way to sunshine as I stare out the window. Not feeling enthused to concern myself with the lecture on ancient history, my thoughts wander to my mother. I wonder what type of bloke would be interested in marrying such a bitch; a woman who is so morally bankrupt and ridiculous that her only son cannot even be bothered to speak with her. The question will never be answered as my opinion of her will not change despite the happy announcement that I heard in the day. I silently promise myself yet again to tell my father the gossip that I unexpectedly learned later and be done with it.

Stepping outside of the school grounds coincides with exhaling a deep breath. Feeling revitalised with the sun shining on my face and the tedious day that consisted of one thousand questions about my personal life is now finished for the most part. "Bastards," I mutter under my breath as I recall that the trams are still not running because of the industrial dispute. Just as I begin to cross over St Kilda Road, my phone vibrates in my hand. I message appears from Austin who asks if I want to go to Nandos with him and more importantly that he is offering to buy. Generous offers to buy me Portuguese chicken are made only every other blue moon and I can't help but smile. After responding in the affirmative, I cross St Kilda Road again and wait for Austin on the corner. For five minutes I am left to my own devices checking my usual social media feeds until Austin dashes across the street, avoiding a speeding taxi.

Austin scratches at his earlobe. "Is Jayden coming?" The first words out of his mouth confuse me. Why should it matter?

I smirk. "No, why? Are you hard for Jayden?" Austin and my best friend are merely acquaintances if that and have never gone out of their way to hang out with each other.

"I want to talk to you about something important and I didn't want him listening in. I want your opinion and no I am not fucking hard for him as you put it." Austin leads the way and I follow him down the road in direction of the Nandos that is curiously located in the Alfred Hospital shopping plaza. I always wondered how many people on their deathbed request some take away chicken and extra hot Piri Piri sauce to be brought to them in the in the hospital. "You mentioned earlier that you saw that bloke James yesterday, how did that go?"

Not feeling encumbered by the truth for a change, I detail the events, not leaving any detail out of my story. When we are finally standing in the queue at Nandos and waiting to order, Austin finally expresses what I assume is shock by exclaiming "Oh, God!" multiple times. He hangs on every word and detail until just before the dramatic conclusion. Before I can describe how James cleaned himself out using a two litre Pepsi bottle, Austin is asked to order. Half of a chicken, coleslaw and a 600ml bottle of Coca-Cola. I start to laugh which confuses Austin who raises his eyebrows suggesting that I might be deranged. He doesn't realise what I perceive to be so funny until we sit down and I share the details of the Pepsi bottle experience. Austin immediately begins to laugh and twirls the 600ml bottle of Coke in front of him on the table. "Jesus, mate. I couldn't imagine 600ml of water being squirted up my arse let alone two litres. That is crazy."

I chortle. "I assume that he was going to have multiple goes at cleaning himself out but I didn't stick around to find out." After purposefully grinning I start to drink from my bottle of Diet Coke.

"That is full on." Austin begins to twirl the large wooden cockerel that has the number four imprinted on it. It is meant to provide the server with a clue as to where to deliver the food. "What did he do?"

Austin's brown eyes stare at me intently as I begin to speak again. "He got angry, swore at me and told me to get the fuck out. In hindsight, I believe he just wanted me to stop staring at him in the bathroom, but I just got the hell out of there. Even if I wanted to fuck him, after seeing his performance in the shower, which was better than the *Unfriended* movie, by the way, I was not in the mood. He also smelled like nicotine. It wasn't attractive at so I left as I said and just went home." Austin doesn't blink and seems to be enthralled in my tragic tale.

"Do you think you will see him again?" Austin asks with a curious inflexion to his voice. "Do you want to see him again?"

"No. I will never see him again and have no desire to. He sent me a message earlier just saying 'hey' but I didn't reply and I don't intend to. Fuck him. He should remember that I have school to attend anyway." I smile and Austin laughs. Our respective orders of spicy chicken and coleslaw are delivered to our table. I immediately begin to devour my lunch using a plastic cutlery. "I should probably just message him and say that I am not interested. It would be the right thing to do." I pull the leg off the chicken carcass and start to gnaw on it. "Why do you ask?" I ask in between bites.

Austin finishes the remaining Coke in the plastic bottle and sets it down gently on the table. "About six months ago." Austin pauses and then nervously laughs before looking around the restaurant. "I can't believe I am telling you this. Anyway, I downloaded 'Grindr' and made a profile which said that I am eighteen. I posted a picture of me wearing a beaning so that none of my hair was visible in my profile. I would have been mortified if I was spotted on the street or worse since it is all GPS based." Austin pauses, looks around the restaurant again and lowers his voice. "I started to meet up with random guys that are on that app. I made it clear on my profile that I didn't want sex and just was looking for friends and have some people to talk to if you can believe it. Eventually, I started to meet guys for coffee. The twenty-somethings always wanted to meet around a gym funnily enough. There was never any mention of getting a drink, which is why I find the situation that played out with you and James so interesting. It was just a coffee meet where I was measured up and judged in a matter of seconds. These blokes and there were quite a few of them, always wanted to go back to their place to fuck even though I was crystal clear that I wasn't looking for sex. Most of these guys were pretty tragic like that guy James, so I expanded my scope and started meeting up with the thirty-somethings. Then the forty-somethings which are certainly more interesting and tame. Strangely, a few were married with kids. One wanted to be a guide in my corrupt life, or as he described it. A few offered me cash for sex after I said I just was interested in having a chat and drinking coffee." Stunned, I interrupt Austin. "Speaking of drinks, do you fancy another round?" He nods his head and begins to twirl his empty bottle of Coke on the table once again.

Standing in the queue again gives me time to contemplate everything Austin told me. Even as I tap my debit card on the machine to pay for the bottles of Coke, I am still trying to figure out what motivated Austin to meet up with so many random blokes. It has made me realise that there is so much you don't know what happens in the private lives of your friends. I return to the table and set the bottle of Coke in front of Austin. "Sorry mate, I worked up a thirst listening to that. Don't stop, please continue." I smile which hopefully gives Austin the reassurance I feel he needs right now to continue.

Austin twists the cap off the bottle and drinks half of it down his mouth without taking a breath. My phone vibrates in my lap. Another message appears from James; however, I ignore my phone as Austin begins to speak again. "I just want you to know how much fun that I had on Saturday. I think it was one of the best days of my life."

I chuckle, interrupting Austin. "Wow mate, you need to get out more." I flash him a wide grin so that he knows that I am joking. I sip from my bottle of Coke. It isn't usual that I order a full-strength soda, but I am craving sugar for some reason.

"Not to give you an even bigger head mate, but I think you are a really cool guy." I didn't foresee a compliment. I look around to see if someone is filming me for a reaction and speculate that I am going to end up as the star of some prank YouTube video. Austin pours the rest of the Coke down his throat. "I am pissed off at you though mate."

"What did I do?" My eyes go wide in anticipation of an answer and my heart starts beating quickly as I am at a loss as to how I upset Austin.

"I didn't know that you liked guys until you made your announcement on Saturday. I have always liked you and think you are kind of hot." Austin takes a deep breath and exhales slowly. He stares at the empty bottle of Coke intently and begins to twirl it on its side. "I thought that if I asked you out after we both proclaimed that we are homos that you might not only say yes but also save me from this destructive cycle that I am in of just meeting up with random old gay blokes just to have a chat. I had about a minute to figure this all out before that dickhead James turned up at your apartment, and we know how that turned out." With his assessment over, Austin begins to play with his hair whilst glaring at me with an intense stare. Recollecting the events from Saturday, it is fair to say that James appeared at a very awkward moment in our young lives. Austin surprises me and continues with his diatribe looking flustered which immediately stops my daydream. "All the big talk from Jayden about how you like older guys just made me feel really jealous. It is a feeling that I have never felt before and it is pissing me off. I have been fuming all day since you said this morning that you went out with James last night. I know what these blokes want, so you don't know how refreshing it is to learn that you didn't get fucked, or worse."

"Wow, I don't know what to say." I start picking at the chicken carcass in front of me and finding some more white meat, pull it from a bone with some skin. "I wasn't expecting you to say all of that Austin. I really don't know what to say."

"I think we are both mature enough so whatever happens after we leave here; our friendship will be fine. However just so you know, I have given this plenty of thought. I just want to ask you if you would be interested in going out on a proper date with me, or are you just into older guys? Will a mature sixteen-year-old do it for you?" Austin smiles and folds his hands in front of him as he sets them on the table. Memories of his nearly naked body in my bed return and I feel the blood rushing to my penis. I take a deep breath as I ponder this unexpected situation and Austin's words.

"I have always had a thing for you Austin, I just didn't know that you liked guys. One reason why I am interested in older blokes is simply that they don't go to our school. I don't really want to play in the sandbox with the babies in the corridors of Melbourne Grammar daily." A devastated look appears on Austin's face as he is interpreting my words before I can finish my diatribe. I move my right hand and place it on his knee under the table and start to rub it. "You are right though, we are both mature enough and I would love to go out on a proper date with you." Austin's big brown eyes look to be filled with relief and a smile immediately forms on his face.

Austin's voice crackles and coughs. "Really? Jesus. I am so sweaty right now. I don't know what to say. I will be right back though, I need to go to the toilet." Austin puts his arm under the table and squeezes the top of my hand which is still resting on his knee before he stands up and walks off. I use the next few minutes to put this new phase of my life into perspective which calms my hard dick. I consider the ramifications of dating a guy, let alone one that is a friend that goes to my school. I have feelings of lust for Austin, and going on a date and taking part in what plays out in romantic comedies just don't seem to be something that I want, if I even know what I want at this awkward time of my life. Austin returns and doesn't sit down. "Do you want to get the fuck out of here?"

I wipe my mouth with my serviette, grab my backpack and stand up. "Do you want to go back to my place and watch the latest episode of *Game of Thrones*?'"

"Fuck yeah! Let's go." Austin hits me with his backpack and snickers. "That is for making me think you were going to tell me to fuck off earlier." He smiles.

I remain quiet for several minutes. Without trams and a lack of available cabs to service our needs, we walk back to my apartment in Southbank. After the proclamations and the agreement on our way forward at Nandos, or what I will now refer to as the 'Nandos Accord' for all posterity, how we interact with one another thankfully doesn't change. After snapping out of my initial pensive state, there are no additional awkward silences. We are certainly not lost for words when discussing and at times debating various politics and even banal celebrities. Austin as mature as me and I feel that dating him will work out. I never even considered Austin as boyfriend material until now. We walk down the footpath and I consider how much more stable he seems compared to James and find that amusing because James is nine years older than Austin. As he talks about the government's border protection and asylum seeker policy, I begin to contemplate what Austin was really looking for during his multiple meetings with the older legion of Grindr suitors. Perhaps he just wanted to talk with gay guys about something more than the high price of coffee in Melbourne. He is an attractive guy that is quite popular but perhaps they are not very strong friendships. I begin to consider how superficial his friendship is even with Jayden and recognise a pattern of how he has developed his social circle. I don't think there is much depth to his friendships as I once again begin hanging on every word that he is saying, "-so fuck the government."

I try to change the topic. "So, you never hooked up with any of the Grindr guys then?" I smile. My query seems to take Austin by surprise.

"No mate. Well, I kissed a couple of them and one grabbed my arse. Half of them wanted to fuck me though and they made that clear in the first few minutes after meeting them. The other half just wanted to talk about their boring lives. A few of them bought me dinner, on what I guess would be considered a date. I thought that when they wanted to give me a kiss or squeeze my arse, I should at least allow them that as a thank you." Austin begins to unravel his tie and in the process of putting it in his backpack, hits me with it again. "Whoops."

"So, it begins. I am going to be the abused wife in this relationship if I don't have dinner waiting for you I see. Don't hit me! I will be better, I promise. Just let me squeeze your arse!" I shout and put my hands up in front of my face. Austin laughs and pushes me. I end up on my back sprawled out on top of the wet grass. "Don't hit me again." I shriek. "Please, help!" A woman pushes a baby carriage past us. I throw my arms over my head whilst laying on the grass and plead in the direction of the witness. "Please help, this abusive man is sending me back to the kitchen to slave over a hot greasy pan. Please!"

"Comedy central in real life." Austin offers the comment to the lady as she passes next to him who nods her head in agreement and smile. He then picks up my heavy backpack off the grass. "Come along now. Your hot kitchen awaits you."

I hop up and snatch my backpack from Austin and continue the journey to my apartment via the arts district. Time flies as we chat about nonsense until we arrive at my front door. After opening it, a very appetizing smell envelops me. Mel must be cooking from one of her many celebrity chef cookbooks. We drop our bags in the foyer and walk to the kitchen. "What's cooking Mel?" I start to look through the refrigerator, hoping to find something for us to drink.

"I am trying to follow a lamb recipe from the Heston Blumenthal book. It is taking bloody forever." She is carefully inserting sliced cloves of garlic into the fat of the lamb. I retrieve cans of Cherry Dr Pepper and hand one to Austin before closing the refrigerator door.

"Do you want some help, Mel?" Austin kindly offers and she immediately refuses it. Mel wants to be responsible for creating this gourmet masterpiece and explains that she can execute the prep work without any assistance. Besides, she considers cooking complex meals as a hobby.

I walk to the living room and request the Foxtel cable feed to go live on the integrated remote control. After falling onto the lounge holding my can of soft drink, Austin follows. He collapses close enough to me so that our arms touch. Given the size of the lounge, Mel will probably think this is weird, but I don't move. I begin to scroll through what has been recorded recently and play the latest episode of *Game of Thrones*. I turn up the sound as "A Song of Ice and Fire" begins to play and the cast is introduced on the television screen.

We remain quiet and absorbed in the show, which is the penultimate episode of the season. When Stannis Baratheon decides to burn his daughter alive, Austin becomes enraged. He uses profane words are used and his negative opinion of the fictional character is articulated. "Burn in hell Stannis!"

"Shhhh!" I want to hear the dialogue. Austin's vitriolic reaction to this storyline encourages Mel to come into the room. She would be intrigued by what is causing such an emotional teenage reaction. In another case of bad timing, her curiosity is piqued just as The Red Woman, Melisandre, is starting a fire under feet the feet of a young girl that is tied to a stake. Mel doesn't appear very interested in watching the adolescent immolate unlike her counterpart on the television. The look on her face implies that she is also aware of the inside joke that my father and I have shared for so long about Mel looking like the Red Woman too. She quickly loses interest in what Austin was originally so excited about and returns to the kitchen to attend to the dead lamb.

Austin smacks my shoulder. "She looks pissed."

I blow the sound of "shhh!" again and the final minute of the show is enjoyed in silence. We both shout "Jesus Christ!" in unison as the credits begin to roll. I pull my phone from my pocket and message my father saying that Mel knows about our inside joke and briefly add that I heard gossip that his ex-wife is engaged to be married. As soon as I tap to send, new messages arrive. One from Jayden requesting my status and my location. The other is from James.

"He is persistent." Austin surprises me when he whispers into my ear whilst reading the message over my shoulder. "What a psycho."

"Yeah, I know." I place my phone on my lap and try to compose myself. James is a non-issue for me but he is obviously an annoyance for Austin. I want to address this elephant in the room as I don't want the first hour of our dating to descend into drama. I quickly tap out a message to James thanking him for the pints and the chat and simply say that I don't think things will work out between us. I show the message to Austin who nods his head before I tap send. "Okay, one down. Don't be worried about James, mate. I am finished with him." I then craft a follow-up message to my father saying Austin's mom told me that 'Voldemort' who I refer to as my mother, is seemingly getting married.

"So, you really didn't know that your mother was planning on another round of matrimonial bliss then?" Austin looks at me incredulously. "That is shocking."

I stand up to stretch and notice Austin staring at my exposed navel as my shirt is pulled up momentarily. "It was certainly news to me. You know I don't speak to Voldemort. I wouldn't have a clue what the bitch does and I really don't care."

I shrug my shoulders and walk towards my room with the intention of changing out of my sweat-soaked shirt and school uniform. Austin stands up and follows me. A feeling of anxiety overwhelms me as I briefly stop in the laundry room to retrieve clean clothes. Getting undressed in front of Austin in the recent past seemed natural but now it has other connotations. I pick up a large stack of folded clothes that have been laundered which belong to me and notice there are small items in a blue plastic tray that is positioned on the corner of the shelf. Before the cleaner does our laundry, she always checks the pockets and puts anything that she finds in separate trays that have our names affixed to the sides. Besides a handful of coins, which I ignore, I notice the business card that Shaun passed me at Supernormal before leaving with his sister. I walk past Austin who is waiting patiently for me and into my room, placing my laundered clothes on my properly dressed bed. The smell of vomit, lewdness, and filth has been vanquished by chemicals and the strong arm of our cleaner. Lustful thoughts quickly return as I fondly recall waking up next to Austin the other night. With my back to him, I unbutton my white shirt, pull it off and discard it on the floor. I am startled when I feel his hands lightly touch me on both of my sides and then feel his warm breath on my neck just before he licks it. Heavy breathing through his nose acts as a precursor for him to start passionately kissing my neck. His warm hands begin to explore my naked torso as I gasp as blood begins to rapidly rush to my penis. Austin is shocked as I break his embrace and quickly turn around, only to lock my arms around his body as I pull him tight against me. I don't care that he can feel my erection at first poking him and then grinding against his thigh as I start to explore his mouth with my tongue. Eventually, I move my hands up his outreached arms and grasp the back of his head, violently drawing his face towards mine. I assault his lips with my gaping mouth which ultimately evolves in me trying to consume his salty face.

"Oh my god. Sorry!" Our passionate session is interrupted by the exclamation of a female voice. I return to the real world and rest my chin on Austin's shoulder only to see the Red Woman briefly as she walks away from my open bedroom door.

"Shit!" I take a deep breath and wipe my mouth on Austin's shoulder. "Timing is just fucked today." I continue to hold Austin but pull my face far enough away so our noses are gently touching. "That was nice." I smile and examine his retinas. "I can't wait to do that again when there is more, um, privacy."

"Jesus, I have wanted to do that for ages." Austin lowers his head and gently places it on my shoulder. "Just don't change, Chez."

I am left to consider how a caterpillar will evolve into a butterfly after his ambiguous comment about changing. I reluctantly release Austin from my clutches and turn around once again. With my back-facing Austin and my open bedroom door, I pull off my trousers and quickly hop into a pair of black skinny jeans. After pulling on a clean black shirt, my erection is effectively cloaked. I twirl around and face Austin. "We should probably go talk to Mel."

"Awkward!" Austin gasps and scratches his earlobe. "Maybe I should just go."

"Well, um, just stay here then. I will be back soon." I scratch my head as I walk from my room and toward the kitchen where I hear a hand blender at work. Upon rounding the corner and getting Mel's attention, she immediately turns off the appliance and begins to speak in a hushed voice.

"Chez, first off, I am a big girl and I don't need you to chase me down to explain yourself. I know what I saw." I open my mouth to interrupt her but she anticipates it. "No, wait please, let me finish. I don't need consoling or talked to about what I just saw, but I hope someday that you trust me enough just to talk to me. I am trying hard to be your friend and I want to help you out when I can. It is called transparency. The more that I know, the easier it is to make your life more comfortable."

I stare at the white tiled kitchen floor and rub my chin. "Sorry."

"There is nothing for you to be sorry about Chez. Just try to trust me and talk to me from time to time. I have some experience with situations that involve the heart you know. Not as many years as that woman on *Game of Thrones*, but I am sure that you know what I mean."

"Oh, sorry about that too." I can't help but smile as I continue to count kitchen tiles.

"Again, there is nothing for you to be sorry about." Mel reaches for a glass of red wine and takes an extended taste of it before continuing. "I know that you and your father have your little inside jokes. I am happy that you do. I would be concerned if you did not. Don't worry about that." Mel takes another sip of wine. "How long have you and Austin been together?"

"About one hour." I can feel my face turning red and my heart begins to race. "We decided to get together today." I look up at Mel who is holding the glass of wine under her nose and I cough.

"What are you doing talking to me then? Go be with him and spend time with him. Can I give you some unsolicited advice?" Mel drinks the last of the wine in the glass and sets it down on the counter.

Feeling overwhelmed by how cool and calm Mel is being, a smile returns to my face. "Sure."

"We all have five senses. Some say there is a sixth called Umami but that isn't the point. Every time you see Austin use your senses and discover something new that you like about him and tell him. Once you stop bothering to do that, reconsider what you want. You have a very strong personality Chezdon and I see how easy it is for you to suck people into your world. I want you to be doing it for the right reasons with Austin." Mel begins to pour wine into the glass and suddenly gives me a directive. "Now go, and talk to me later if you want." She smiles. "Austin is more than welcome to stay for dinner too."

I walk back to my room and hear the hand blender roar back to life in the distance. As I pull on my shirt, I curse the damp fabric that is bunching up in my armpit. My worry about being caught in a passionate moment with my friend is now a thing of the past. Austin is noticeably surprised to see me return so quickly and stands up. "Is Mel fucked off? Should I go?"

"No, it is all good." I shuffle toward Austin. He gasps when I push him onto my bed and then climb on top of him. I lean down and kiss him lightly on the mouth and then notice he is wearing some type of fragrance. "I really like the smell of whatever you are wearing. What perfume is it?"

Austin leans his head back into my pillow and chuckles. "It is cologne you fool, and it is called Tom Ford Black. It isn't perfume." He grabs me by my waist and pulls me back. He kisses me on my lips. "You are a funny bastard."

I push my nose into Austin's neck and silently confirm my feelings for his cologne. "I really like how you smell." My green eyes stare into Austin's big brown irises and I momentarily resist the urge to chew on his nose. My tongue rudely pushes past his teeth and I use it to explore his warm mouth. Resting my forearms on his chest, I fumble with the buttons on his white shirt as I struggle to maintain balance whilst I savagely make out with my new lover. I somehow manage to get four buttons undone and get my hands inside of his shirt in one fluid motion. Perched on top of his legs, which gives me the ability to undo the rest of the shirt buttons, I greedily lean down and start sucking on his exposed left nipple and then move to the right one. Playful squeaks rapidly evolve into loud grunts, and I must put my hand over Austin's mouth as I realise that once again I have left my bedroom door open. I muster the courage to gently lick his chest, starting in the area between his nipples and then gradually move toward his belly button. With my new offensive tact, his grunts quickly turn into squeaks once again as I lick and suck on his slightly hairy navel above the black band of his underwear. I provide Austin with one last opportunity to put a stop to my indecent advance by retreating from him to close my bedroom door. My erection is being constrained, if not strangled conveniently on the right side by my skinny jeans and my shirt is covering the bulge. Austin is not as lucky as he is obviously hard as the loose cotton trousers that he wore to school today aren't doing him any favours.

The obnoxious ringing of the video intercom in the foyer coincides with me shutting my bedroom door. The sound of the buzzer not only startles me but is extremely irritating and interrupts my lustful advance at least for a moment. I climb first on my bed and then Austin. As I lean in and kiss him my wayward plan to get into his pants is thwarted by Mel shouting. "Chezdon, it is for you!" I close my eyes and take a deep breath.

"Really?" I mutter to Austin and look towards the ceiling. "Fuck. I will be right back." Austin rolls his eyes and reaches for the remote control which is resting on my bedside table. He powers on the television as I walk from my room and towards where the video intercom is mounted on the wall.

I pass Mel who offers a wink. "Good luck." When I see it is James who is displayed on the video intercom, all I can do is huff and manhandle my throbbing bulge. He appears to be impatiently waiting for what I assume to be an exchange of words as he is tapping his fingers on the wall of the building. I dodged a bullet earlier when I was caught making out with Austin thinking that would lead to an awkward conversation with Mel, however, I know this chat is certainly going to be uncomfortable with James.

I pause after lifting the receiver and ponder what James is trying to prove turning up unannounced. Finally, I manage a simple "G'day, mate" which startles James from what I notice. "What are you doing here?" It seems like an obvious question.

"Hi. Ummm." After his salutation, there are many seconds of excruciating silence. "Can I talk to you?" James looks uncomfortable speaking to the keypad and the camera mounted on the wall. He knows that I can see him but he can't see me.

My penis begins to soften against the pressure of the denim. "You could have just rung me on my mobile mate. What's up?" I am grateful it is no longer my cock.

James begins tapping on the wall again. "Can I come up and talk?" He stares intently at the camera lens.

Although I might have thought it was a good idea on Saturday whilst under the influence of wine to allow James up, my sober and pragmatic self now knows it would be a terrible idea being unaware of his agenda. After informing him via text message that I wasn't interested earlier, I would have assumed that he would not solicit further contact. Austin emerges from my bedroom dressed to face the public and is approaching me. He would be curious to see who not only broke our sexual tension but also who rudely just stopped around to see me. I know I would be. "How about if I come down and see you. I will be there in a few minutes." I slam the receiver back on its cradle and look at Austin. "You know it is going to get stranger. Do you want to come down with me and see what he fucking wants?"

"Didn't he get the message or something? What a psycho." Austin looks both perturbed and pissed off. "Sure, let's do this." Austin quickly turns around and walks back to my bedroom and I follow. We find our shoes and pull them on.

Austin picks up the cricket bat that is resting upright against the wall in the corner of my room near my bed. "Hey, that is pretty cool. My father got it for me and is signed by Michael Clarke." He is my favourite cricketer and the captain of the Australian national team.

"Let's see if James knows who Michael Clarke is." Austin rests the bat on his shoulder and walks from my bedroom and I follow him to the front door, where I grab a set of keys and we leave the apartment.

"What are you going to do? Beat up the bloke up with the bat?" The wry grin on my face makes light of the situation and noticeably calms Austin down. "Mate, he isn't here to kill me. I am sure he just wants to tell me off. Besides, I have you with me which he will not expect, so all will be good." I smile at Austin at the same time a dinging sound announces that the elevator has arrived. "We can walk out of the car park exit also and then meet him at the front of the building so he will not see us both coming."

Austin uses the cricket bat to prop himself up. "Great idea. Let's surprise the cunt."

"I never thought of you as being so hardcore, Austin." I brush an errant blond hair from Austin's shoulder with my hand.

"I just don't want such a nice day ruined by that arsehole. That is all." Austin adjusts his messy hair in the mirror whilst we descend to one of the lower levels of the building. His tough talking is a stark contrast to the vain teenager that I am now watching primp his hair. If you are going to maim someone with a cricket bat, I suppose you should look good for the camera that will take your photo at the police station. Austin doesn't notice me begin to chuckle.

We exit on the level of the car park that I have access to and walk down the various access ramps, exiting the building past a security guard. We walk around the building on the footpath and I am the first to see James leaning against a tree smoking a cigarette. "Hey, what's up?" I hope that my friendly interrogatory provides enough of a distraction for James not to care that Austin is standing behind me brandishing a cricket bat.

James takes a drag of his cigarette and then flicks it into the gutter. Littering is a pet peeve of mine and it really annoys me when I see people dropping rubbish in my neighbourhood. "Did you bring the twink to bash me or something?"

I turn around to see Austin standing not far behind me with the bat resting on his shoulder. "Oh him? No, mate. We are just off to hit some cricket balls." With conviction, I lie. James tilts his head to the left.

"Yeah right. Dressed like that. Sure." James removes a soft pack of cigarettes from his pocket. After a dramatic pause, he removes a cancer stick, lights it and takes what seems forever for him to inhale the smoke.

Not feeling comfortable during the long silence, I try to move the proceedings along. "What did you want to talk about?"

James exhales a plume of smoke in my direction. "I just came by to collect the money that you owe me." He finally educates us as to what was so important that he needed to see me in person, which leaves me confused.

I scratch the back of my head. "Since when do I owe you money?"

James flicks the end of the cigarette and an ash falls on the footpath. "You owe me thirty dollars."

"What the hell for?" My frustration would be obvious. I turn around and make a confused face for Austin. He shrugs his shoulders and rolls his eyes.

When James starts to speak again, I quickly turn to face him. "That is how much the beer cost that I bought for you yesterday. I want my fucking money back."

"Are you serious? You make a personal visit to shake me down for thirty dollars? If I had fucked you would you still want this cash?" I am mortified and can't believe this is what he came over for to discuss in person. "Can you message me your banking details and I will make a transfer. That isn't a problem."

"Yeah, I am serious, and I want the money now." James takes another drag from the cigarette." You are such a cocktease and an arrogant dick. A fuck from you would be worth about five dollars, don't give yourself so much credit." I can't help but smile as this conversation is so absurd.

Austin stands next to me and our shoulders briefly touch. He begins to tap the cricket bat on the concrete floor. "Whoa! Let's dial this back. There is no reason to be rude. Hold this." I grab the cricket bat and he rummages through his pocket. "I have never heard of anything so ridiculous." In between scraps of paper, a to-do list and the remains of a roll of Mentos, Austin retrieves some Australian currency and begins tossing it on the ground. First, a blue note, then three pink notes and then completes the transaction by tossing five gold coins on the ground, which scatter in all directions when they strike the concrete. One curiously rolls into the gutter and rests next to the burned-out cigarette butt that James earlier flicked away. "Anything else arsehole?" Austin grasps the cricket bat and rests it on his shoulder.

"You are such a cunt. You are a cunt too Chezdon." James takes yet another drag of his cigarette and then flicks it at me unexpectedly. The filter end of the ciggy hits my arm and falls to the ground. James bends down and begins to retrieve the plastic banknotes and coins. "You are so stupid, Chezdon. You have no idea what you are missing out on."

I grin. "What is that? Fucking around with a loser?" Speaking the truth comes easily as James waddles like a duck picking up coins. He looks up at me. "You are right though. If it wasn't for you James, I wouldn't have realised what I am missing out on." I look at Austin and put my hand on his shoulder.

James stands up holding his bounty. "Yeah, what is that?"

I turn and kiss Austin on his cheek.

"Fuck!" Noticeably enraged, James takes four steps toward us as Austin grasps the cricket bat and demonstrates that he is not afraid to swing it. James then retreats and shouts "fuck!" at the top of his lungs. In what plays out next happens in slow motion as he once again advances at us with a look of fury on his face. James must have assumed that Austin would not have the fortitude to swing the bat as it crashes into our attackers' arm. The volume of the thud and the resulting shout of "fuck!" is identical to his previous outburst. The resulting scream is riddled with equal amounts of pain and frustration. James falls to the concrete and ends up in the gutter with the butt of his cigarette. The coins and banknotes that he was previously clutching follow him and once again scatter.

"If I see you again, I will be swinging this at your head." Austin points the bat in the direction of James as he slowly stands up, holding his left arm. "Now fuck off!" Austin steps backwards and eventually turns around and I follow him. When he gets to the corner he stops and gyrates in place to face James again, who is once again collecting money from the gutter. " James!" Austin shouts. James looks up. "There is a 7-11 over there." Austin points with the cricket bat. "They have a sale going on two-litre bottles of Pepsi. Use some of those coins."

James lowers his head and looks not only physically but emotionally spent. Austin wraps his arm around me and I stumble as he pulls me to his side. He rests the bat on his shoulder again and escorts me around the corner.

Innocence Waning

10. **Mel**

We turn the corner and the sound of a jackhammer coincidentally ends leaving behind a battered bloke to collect his newfound riches from the damp gutter. The clamour originating from the construction site on the other side of the road mercifully ends. I surmise that the clock just passed 5:00 PM if the workers are downing their tools and finishing for the day. The trams and taxis must now be running as per the published timeline as the industrial action would have ended. Projecting my contempt for James to my disdain of the transport union, I try to think of something positive. I feel a sense of gratitude that the construction union bothered to work today considering the poor weather that Melbourne offered up earlier. The building site will be ready that much earlier and the daily racket which I loathe will finally come to an end that much sooner.

Mimicking the new state of the building works, Austin has remained quiet since abandoning his thirty dollars and the altercation where he dispatched his foe with necessary roughness. Traversing past my residential tower, I strategically remain one step behind Austin and follow him down the dusty street. The temperature has noticeably dropped since we first confronted James. The dark clouds returned overhead since we played our innings of cricket only minutes ago. A drop of rain first hits my face and then another one splatters on my lower arm, which was only recently struck by a burning cigarette.

"Can you please hold this?" Austin hands me the cricket bat. I feel relieved that he has started to speak again. I was beginning to think that he was in shock and was just going to wander around the neighbourhood like a zombie with no destination in mind.

Austin removes the black beanie which he borrowed the morning after our party the other night from his right pocket. Thanks to the stupor that I was in yesterday, I completely forgot that Austin took this beanie with him when he left. I wanted to wear it when walking to school and was upset when I couldn't find it. I feel a sense of joy knowing that it has been found and that Austin indeed has it. I watch him pull the black piece of fabric over his head and like he has the benefit of looking in a mirror whilst he is walking, easily pulls his wavy blond fringe out and moves it so it rests over his left eye. "Let's get a coffee. I need one after that nightmare."

"Sure." I follow Austin and his wide eyes after he issues his proclamation. I cross the street and enter a café that strangely I have never been to before, despite it being in the shadow of my residential tower. I wish Austin said he wanted alcohol as I am agitated after our run-in with James. Coffee is certainly not going to calm me down right now.

We are advised that the café is closing for the day however the server happily sells us two coffees in takeaway cups He asserts that we are welcome to stay inside and relax if we can excuse the noise the staff are making cleaning the place up. I thank our host and let him know that we will take him up on his kind invitation as Austin taps his debit card against the terminal and pays for our hot caffeinated drinks. I once again follow Austin to a table in the corner which is away from the staff and rest the cricket bat against the cold stone wall before taking a seat at the table.

I carefully remove the plastic lid from the hot cardboard cup as I need the coffee to cool down substantially before drinking it. Austin takes a sip of his hot beverage after adding some sugar without flinching. "I have never been in a fight before." He looks to the right and begins to inspect the stone wall. Tears begin to well up in his eyes. I really hope he doesn't start to cry.

I am relieved that we did not get maimed by James and attempt to lighten the mood. "Thank you for doing what you did. James deserved to get his arse kicked if only because he tossed that cigarette in the street." The recent events seem to be taking more of a toll on Austin then any physical injury that James had to endure. For once in my life, I am at a loss for words as I search for something insightful to say. "We must have set a world record and remained relatively drama-free for a whole hour in our new relationship if you don't count Mel catching us making out of course." Austin slowly moves his gaze from the stone wall and back to me. A wry grin forms on his face however that lasts for but a second before he looks down at his lap wipes at his eyes and snorts back mucous. I stand up and start to walk around the table thinking that giving him a bit of reassurance by putting my hand on his back would be the best thing to do.

"No, sit down. No public displays of affection please." Austin wipes his eyes and sniffs again. "I will be fine. Are there any other fucked up guys that are going to pop up in your life anytime soon? I can't deal with this sort of shit again. All of this stress is going to make me have a breakout."

I did notice Austin with a few new pimples today however they do not distract from his general good looks. Briefly, I muse just how many products he has at home that is devoted just to his skin and acne management as it is evident that he takes it very seriously. I return to my chair and sit down behind my steaming cardboard cup again. "I am so sorry. I promise nobody else is going to pop up and cause any drama. I owe you thirty dollars now though." I smile and rub my arm.

Austin wipes at his eyes with the back of his hand again. He pulls off the black beanie and rubs his eyes with it and takes a few deep breaths. I appreciate that the situation that we both just experienced with James was intense, but I do not understand why Austin is becoming so emotional. I remember him being just fine when I put my hand on his knee under the table at Nandos, so I repeat that covert action and fortunately do not receive any form of protest whilst Austin composes himself. "Earlier you said that you have felt something for me for a while. I really hope that you aren't just playing fucking mind games with me, Chez. I sure as hell know you are good at doing that." I silently forgive his snipe as he starts to sip from his cup of coffee.

I swirl the contents of my cup like it is red wine in a glass and take a sip. The coffee has cooled down substantially so I continue to gulp it down and recall the apt advice that Mel offered me earlier. Using my hand, I apply additional pressure to Austin's knee, which causes him to raise his big brown eyes and stare at me again. Realising that I need to take control of this awkward situation, I begin to speak. "I like seeing you with my beanie on your head. Your face looks really cute when your hair pokes out from it." Austin smiles and a feeling of relief overcomes me. I continue to gaze into his eyes. "I know all of this drama with James and what just played out is my fault. I get it, but if I look at the positive side, the dickhead just was the catalyst that brought us closer together."

Austin sniffs once again. "I can't remember the last time that I became so emotional. I really hate being like this. You probably think that I am just some silly fag or just some sook." He looks down at his coffee before taking a deep breath and continuing. "Last year in May, I was at home with my mother and sister one night." He takes another deep breath. I start to scratch his knee which gives him some encouragement to continue. "To make a long story short, there was a knock at the door and the next thing I remember was my mother screaming. Three men had forced their way into our house. One was holding an axe, one had a machete and the other bastard had a shotgun. They were shouting at us to open the safe and they were waving their weapons around. Of course, I was scared shitless but I was also confused as I didn't know that we had a safe. That sense of confusion was then magnified by my mother who claimed ignorance to the masked men." Austin wipes at his eyes again with the beanie. "That was the understanding at least until one of the blokes chased down Chloe and grabbed her and forced her to the floor. He put the machete against her throat."

I give him time to compose himself again by filling the void of silence with my outrage. "Jesus Christ! What did they do to your sister? This is shocking." I grasp my cup of coffee with both hands patiently waiting for Austin to continue and after some time passes, set it down and then start to scratch his knee again under the table.

He turns his head and stares at the stone wall. "The cunt that grabbed her started to grope her and tear her clothes off. Fortunately, that persuaded my mother to open her fucking mouth. She admitted that we have a safe and that she would open it. After that, at least in my mind, things are a bit hazy but I know that I started mouthing off and abusing the animals, telling them to leave Chloe alone and shit like that. One of the men shoved me and I fell backwards into the corner of an iron and glass table, which cut the fuck out of my back. I ended up on my arse screaming in pain and bleeding all over the place whilst the arsehole stood over me pressing the barrel of the shotgun into my head. I thought it was game over for me." Austin wipes his eyes with the beanie again and takes two long deep breaths. I am not only captivated but genuinely shocked and continue to scratch his knee. I pick up my cup of coffee and attempt another sip and then find there is nothing left to drink. I can not to move or even breathe as I wait for Austin to speak whilst I remain a prisoner of time and sit on the edge of my chair.

"Obviously, we all survived the ordeal. They got into the safe, took a bunch of shit and then left."

"Fuck." I am at a loss for words for the second time today. "I guess that is what the scar on your back is from. I was going to ask you after seeing it yesterday morning but you left so quickly that I didn't really have the chance." From memory, the scar isn't really that bad and given it is located between his shoulder blade and spine, I imagine it would have been more painful if anything. Knowing how vain Austin is, he is probably more outraged that the scar has marked his body instead of the fact that it represents a horrible moment in his young life.

"You noticed it? I guess you were paying attention to me then."

Austin turns to head to look at me and I smile. "I wasn't just paying attention, I was checking you out mate." Austin grins. After that tale of woe, I am glad that his mood has improved a bit. "I am so sorry that you and your family had to go through that."

"I am self-conscious about that scar and I was actually afraid that you did notice it and you were going to ask me about it. That is why I fucked off so quickly. I don't like being quizzed for obvious reasons as it brings back some bad memories. Even the ridiculous lie that I tell people about how I got it manages to upset me." I continue to scratch Austin's knee, not really knowing what to say next. "This is why I not only took the cricket bat with me when we went to talk with James but why I was so hell-bent on not being a victim again when he came at us. I wasn't going to let that arsehole do me in, let alone assault you. I was not about to let another violent situation spiral out of control when I had the ability to do something about it. He is lucky I didn't smash his skull in."

It is like I placed the last piece of a puzzle and I see the whole picture for the first time. "I totally understand Austin. I am so sorry that I put you in that situation. Did the coppers ever catch the arseholes?"

"They did actually. My uncle was behind it all and when my father drinks heavily he carries on about it. The arseholes are all in jail though, that is what is important. I guess this is why those fucking animals didn't rape and kill us all I assume, they were just hell-bent on getting into the safe and leave. It was on the news too. They just left our family's name out of it since the sordid story involved victimised teenagers. I really hate that word now - victim." The café staff start cleaning the table next to us, which distracts Austin.

"What was in the safe? Michael Jackson's glove? It is like a scene from *Pulp Fiction*." I lean in close to Austin and start scratching at his knee energetically. "Come on. Let's get the fuck out of here." I stand up and stretch. My back pops multiple times whilst I look around the small café. Austin gets close enough to me so that I can smell his cologne and gently pats my arse signifying that I should start walking. I grab the bat and continue to process all the shocking revelations as we walk back to my apartment in silence. We avoid being knocked down by a yellow taxi which rushes past us as we illegally cross the small street not paying attention to the traffic. The bright lights of the foyer of my residential tower beckon me after I tap the fob on the security panel and the front doors slide open. This is the same panel that has the one-eyed camera that spied on James earlier. My thoughts drift again as we get in the elevator. Will James will ever feature in my life again?

"You are unusually quiet. It is a nice change." Austin grins whilst staring at the LED screen that displays not only the short-term weather forecast in Melbourne but reports the breaking news along with the floor number that we are currently travelling past.

"I was just thinking what a cool guy you are and that you smell so damn good. You certainly didn't deserve to go through that hell. Nobody deserves to be terrorised." The elevator stops and the door opens at the same time my verbal diarrhoea concludes. Austin follows me out into the corridor before the elevator door closes. He rushes to catch me as I use the key that has been rubbing against my leg for the last hour to open the apartment door.

The strong smells of thyme and garlic first greet us and then I hear the twittering sounds of familiar voices. I leave the cricket bat in the foyer leaning against the wall as I recognise one of the voices being that of my father. We walk into the living room and I see Daniel sitting contently on the L-shaped lounge next to Mel. A bottle of wine open and they are gossiping about one of Mel's friends who is having an affair.

"Hey, boys! How was school today?" My father gets up to shake Austin's hand. Perhaps it was the emotionally-charged afternoon or because I am feeling a sense of mortality, I give my father a hug after he offers Austin his hearty salutations. My father is rigid and noticeably shocked but after a second, embraces me. "What happened? What do I need to know?"

"Nothing," I say. My father would be suspicious as I never show any affection towards him. "I just appreciate you. It is just good to be alive." I release Daniel and feeling emboldened for a Monday, promptly retrieve two wine glasses from the kitchen and upon returning to the lounge room, hand one to Austin.

"It is Monday, Chezdon." Daniel still looks surprised that I gave him a hug. "For Christ's sake."

"Don't worry, dad. It is only a glass of wine." I clutch the bottle of Baileys Shiraz by its neck and pour Austin a glass. I then greedily fill my vessel nearly to the brim. "May I be so bold as to make a toast?"

My father and Austin are both at a loss for words as Mel stands up. "Yes, please Chezdon, please do. Just not to Ned Kelly."

The wine is from Glenrowan in upper Victoria, which is where infamous Australian bushranger is from.

"What I learned today is that you can be snuffed out at any moment. Anyone can be knocked down by a car or tram. When you are taking your last breath, you will regret that you didn't tell the people that you love what they mean to you from time to time. Dad, Mel, I love you both and I just want to say thanks for always being there for me and just being amazing."

My father's eyes open wide which is a rare occurrence. He gazes at Austin as his eyebrows shift up his head suspiciously. "Austin, has he been drinking today? What the hell has happened?"

I deny Austin the opportunity to respond with anything witty and instead cast my eyes on his round face and raise my glass in his direction. "Austin, to you mate. Thanks for making me look at life differently." I reach out and first tap my glass against Austin's, then clink Mel's and finally follow-on and chink my father's glass twice by accident. After smelling the wine quickly, I take a drink of Ned Kelly's blood. As I lick my lips, I set the glass of wine on the table and shuffle past Daniel and embrace Mel. "Sorry for being such a dickhead, I do love you."

Nobody knows what to say after my toast and unexpected proclamations. Everyone gives their attention to the muted Sky News broadcast on the television. I pick up my wine glass and after taking another sip, walk to the kitchen. Far away from the confused faces that I left behind, I take a quiet moment to gather my thoughts and close my eyes.

I overhear my father ask Austin whether I nearly got hit by a tram or if something more sinister happened in my life today. As not to make Austin feel uncomfortable and feel obligated to answer Daniel, I return to the living room nearly as quickly as I left with a newfound feeling of enthusiasm. "Father, it is all good. Life is good. Don't worry." I take a sip of the wine and my eyes once again find Austin's. "Do you want to stay for dinner? Mel said you are more than welcome. Something smells delicious and I know that you don't want to bugger off. Just say yes."

"Whatever you are making smells great, Mel. I will phone my mother just to make sure that I can. She might have something planned for me." I literally cross my fingers using my free hand. I quietly hope that Julie doesn't make Austin go home as I really want to spend some quality time with him on the first official day that we proclaimed to be dating. I want our teenage union to be defined by positive and happy experiences and not mired in drama and forged in despair. My lustful feelings for Austin have gone through a metamorphosis in the last few hours and they have evolved into something which I can't really comprehend. I just want to be around Austin. It is as simple as that.

"Come along now you damned fool, our phones are in my room." Not wanting to look back and catch the incredulous stare of my father, I walk around the corner and towards my bedroom. Austin follows behind me. I allow him to walk past me in the hallway before he crosses into my bedroom. I follow him, this time remembering to close the door behind me, having learned my lesson from earlier in the day. Austin sets his glass of wine cautiously on my desk, taking care not to place it on any pieces of paper or books before picking up his phone. After swiping in all directions quickly, he places a call. Feeling emboldened, I take a few steps toward Austin and place my wine glass next to his. My ear is close enough to his handset to hear the ubiquitous ringing sound emanating from his phone.

I startle Austin by wiping my moist lips on his white shirt. "What the absolute fuck?" Austin is shocked and then embarrassed when he realises that his mother heard at least the last word of his profane question.

"Excuse me?" Julie asks her son in a harsh yet inquisitive voice. I can help but laugh.

"Sorry about that mum. Can I stay at Chezdon's tonight for dinner or am I required for something at home?" Austin looks irritated as he asks his mother's permission. His sour look is exasperated further after I wipe my lips on his white shirt again, which leaves another noticeable wine stain on the fabric. I start to unbutton his shirt and can hear his mother droning on although I can't decipher what she is saying with her posh Australian accent. One sentence quickly blends into two, then four and then eight. Austin waits for her to take a breath before he can get a word in and takes a step back to thwart me from unbuttoning his stained shirt. He learns that any effort to keep me away from him will be futile whilst trying to communicate with his mother. "Well, can you pick me up later then?" Julie begins to ramble once again. I take the opportunity to pull Austin's shirt up releasing it from the constraint of his trousers and the pressure of his belt. He sits on my bed and lets me have my way. "No, they have already had some wine, so that isn't a good idea. I will just get a train or something. I don't have any money on me though." More noise spews over the phone as I try to pull Austin's shirt off him. He fumbles his phone onto his lap and misses a few sentences of his mother's diatribe. He deftly pushes the phone back against his ear and starts to bark into it. "He hasn't said anything, I don't know." Obviously frustrated, Austin continues to respond to a barrage of questions which gives me the chance to first sit next to his naked torso and then slither behind him. I examine the tragic scar on his back that he is so self-conscious about. I am no medical expert but when he was originally wounded, it does look like the laceration have bled a fair amount and that it would have hurt like hell. The assault took place a year ago, yet the prominent pink scar still contrasts starkly with his white skin. Soon I will show him a scar of my own which I keep secret and tell him the story behind it. It is only fair.

I begin to run my finger over the scar tissue. Austin's body twitches but it doesn't distract him enough to stop responding to his mother's interrogation. "Okay, don't worry about it. I will find out. I will message you if I leave, or if I am going to stay here. Bye!" With that exclamation, Austin ends the call, tosses his phone on my bed and wraps his arms around me. "Having a good look?"

"Yeah. I just want to know everything about you. I don't care about some scar. You are just so hot." After my frank admission, I know that my face has gone red and my fragmented statements must have sounded very juvenile.

"Just don't tell Jayden what I told you about what happened to my family. That isn't his business."

"I wouldn't know what you are talking about." I roll my eyes indicating that the information will never leave my mouth. "What is this you said to Julie about staying over?" I smile.

"My mother at first had words to say about both Mel and Daniel drinking on Monday. She had to admit that she had gotten stuck in the wine herself as she was making some pasta sauce, so she can't drive and pick me up later. My father is out drinking with his colleagues and she doesn't want me dealing with the train station late at night, let alone walking to the tram stop in the rain. She said just to stay over if I can since everyone is apparently getting drunk on a Monday night." Austin scoffs, stands up and reaches for his glass of wine. He takes a drink and then turns to look down at me. I look straight ahead and stare at his crotch. "This has been a very bizarre day and I will assure you. I never thought in my wildest dreams all of this would happen or did I expect it all to play out the way it has only to watch you sit there and leer at my crotch. I want something more from your Chezdon."

I look up at Austin. "What is your mother's problem with the train at night?" I give him a cheeky grin, ignoring his proclamation.

"I reckon that you are like the sun burning bright and you are nearly red-hot right now. It is just that your rays of light are not just blinding me, you are burning up with sexual energy. I am afraid that if I give in to you on the same day that we get into a relationship of sorts that you will quickly burn out and scorch me at the same time if that makes sense. Hell, I could quickly burn up in your wake and be left devastated. I certainly never expected to be standing here before you in your room with my shirt off right now when I woke up this morning, let alone beating up the guy that I thought that you were fucking. This isn't normal. Nobody can exist living on a high of hormones for hours, if not days, which is what I have been doing."

I slowly stand up and place my warm hands on his cold chest and slowing move them up his body until they are resting in his armpits. Perspiration as the result of his stress and excitement begins to be absorbed by my skin. I shuffle closer so that my lips are close to his. "We should find you a clean shirt and wash the one you wore today. You are a size twenty-eight, right?"

Despite being deep in Austin's personal space, he doesn't move and whispers. "Twenty-eight, twenty-nine. It depends. Why?"

"You can borrow a pair of my trousers for tomorrow. I can clean everything else. There is no reason to stress out, I will not pressure you into doing anything that you don't want to do. I never will." I kiss Austin on the cheek and then push my nose into his neck and smell his cologne again. I close my eyes and lose my balance briefly which makes us falls back against the wall. He opens his mouth to accept my tongue which goes exploring like Captain Cook once again inside its dark wet recesses. My hands grasp his thighs and then grasp his buttocks. Using all my strength, I pull Austin towards me. I pull him back toward my bed, however, lose my balance once again and we collapse on top of my bed.

"What were you saying about finding me a shirt?" Feeling like I am running on an empty tank of fuel, I relent and let Austin break my embrace. He rolls off my bed and walks to my open closet and searches for something that he likes. Much like Jayden has grown accustomed to doing without even asking, after a few seconds, Austin locates a slim fitting red cotton shirt and pulls it over his head. Red is the colour of power and he is exerting it over me right now which is driving me mad. I intently watch him as he walks to the bathroom. He plays with his hair which gives me a chance to admire him with the bright light shining overhead. His dirty blond hair, red shirt, and white skin match perfectly. I am so turned on that the blood begins to rush to my penis again.

Austin finishes preening his hair by applying styling putty and secures it with hairspray. He innocently rubs one of his blemishes before returning to my bedroom, not realising that I was watching everything that he was doing. I reach for my glass of wine and depress a button on the remote to scroll through available channels on the television. I continue to hold the now empty glass instead of what I really want to embrace for the time being. Austin sits at my desk and starts to browse the papers that I have scattered haphazardly over it. When he finds nothing interesting to read is when he discovers his voice. "Shouldn't we actually do some study?"

School completely slipped my mind with the angst, drama, sex, alcohol, and violence on offer which proves that life is certainly more interesting compared to what you find on television.

Since today is the first day of the new term, I am relieved that not much happened at school and thankfully not many schoolwork was assigned. Fortunately, I have nothing that is due tomorrow. "Is there anything that you need to hand in tomorrow?"

"No, but I should probably do some reading. When is dinner? I am so hungry."

"Good question." I scratch the top my head. My ravenous hunger is the result of the fleeting taste of Piri Piri sauce in my mouth that is left over from my late lunch at Nandos. Despite having enjoyed Coca-Cola, coffee, red wine and Austin's saliva over the last few hours, nothing has managed to eradicate the taste from my tongue. "Let's go and find out."

Austin follows me as I make the now familiar journey from my bedroom to the kitchen. Daniel is sitting at the marble dining room table reading something on his Samsung tablet. I smile as I recall dancing on this table the other night and falling off it and then turn my attention towards Mel who appears to be reducing some sort of sauce. She pours a small amount of wine from the open bottle onto an aluminium tray that contains the lamb droppings and then fills her wine glass with what remains in the bottle. "Something smells great." A large leg of lamb is resting on a wooden cutting board.

I am about to ask Mel how much longer it is before we can devour her creation but then hold my tongue. Austin and I instead intently watch Mel prepare a gravy. I assume that we are only minutes away from our fine dining experience. I have watched her cook multiple times and have asked her enough questions to feel confident that the epicurean side of me knows the answer but I still manage a single query for validation. "What were you using the pressure cooker for Mel?"

Mel turns around and sips from her glass of wine. "I had to make a lamb stock. It is a bit of a pain in the arse really, but it is rich and smells nice. It is the base for this gravy."

The pleasant conversation is interrupted by the video intercom obnoxiously ringing again, which startles me as usual. My heart begins to race as I wonder if James has returned for another innings of cricket. Before I can announce that I will attend to our visitor, Daniel is walking toward the irritating colour monitor. I wish there was some easy way to disable the intercom and consider how long I would be disciplined for if I rip the goddamned device off the wall. I follow my father, who is still holding his glass of wine as he approaches the insolent device.

"Jesus Christ, the police are here!" My father exclaims and then turns around. A stern look quickly takes form on his face and he naturally assumes that I have done something criminal judging from the poisonous stare that he offers me. The obnoxious sound of the intercom repeats as a drop of sweat rolls down my back. Daniel pours what is left in his Riedel glass down his throat before picking up the receiver.

"Good evening constables, how can I help you?" The shitty technology doesn't broadcast the sound at a volume so you can snoop on a conversation if you happen to be close to the receiver, unlike Austin's phone.

"Yes, he is my son. Is he being charged with something?" My heart skips a beat as I silently stare at my father. "That is fine, he is here. You are welcome to come up and have a chat. I am sure that he can assist you with your enquiries." After offering my services, Daniel presses a button which grants the constables entry to our floor of the building before returning the receiver to the cradle on the wall. Austin and Mel meander into the living room at the same time Daniel turns around and points his finger at me. "I don't know what has happened but you two bastards have two minutes to educate us." He glances at his watch before grimacing at Austin. Daniel offers his synopsis. "There has been no complaint against Chezdon, but they want him to assist with their enquiries. Apparently, Chezdon's boyfriend beat up someone on the street outside this building with a cricket bat."

Mel sets her glass of wine on the table softly. "Austin, we don't have much time. Is this true?"

Austin looks dazed. "He attacked us." Mel nods her head as Austin begins to blurt out words. "He was going to bash us."

"What do you mean? Give me the high-level facts." Mel touches Austin on his arm with two fingers. "It will be fine. I won't let anything happen to you. We only have about a minute until they are here." Daniel is staring at his watch and tapping his foot.

Austin suddenly speaks hurriedly. "Do you remember that bloke called James that turned up here on Saturday? Well, he bought Chezdon some beers yesterday so he came around earlier today asking Chez for thirty dollars as payment. He was a dickhead to even ask but we met up with him earlier to give him the money. We called each other some bad names. He was a bit offended so he attacked us." Austin lowers his head and he stares at the floor. "I warned him to stay away because I had the cricket bat. In the end, I hit him with it."

There is a loud knocking on the front door. Daniel waves his right hand in a circular motion. He has gesticulated in this manner when I have droned on endlessly in the past and is bored. "Okay, fair enough. Were there any other witnesses? How long were you on the street with James?" Mel folds her arms and tilts her head to the right and appears to be deep in thought.

Austin responds quickly which would surely please my father. "Five minutes, I reckon. James smoked a few cigarettes whilst we were talking, so maybe a few minutes longer." Austin shifts his weight from one foot to the other repeatedly. He might have to pee. I fondly recall our joking on Saturday that he has a small bladder. The loud rapping on the front door returns and I secretly hope that this chat with the cops will be quick as I am fearful that Austin will piss his pants. "I don't think there were any witnesses."

Mel walks past us and into the foyer. She opens the door and greets the two police officers. After exchanging pleasantries, she invites them inside, extending her arm and motioning in the only direction that they can move. A constable points at the cricket bat that is propped up near the front door as Mel ushers the officers into our reception area. "Constables, before we begin, let me introduce myself. My name is Melissa Peterson and I am a criminal barrister. This fine gentleman to my left in the periphery is Daniel Morrison, the father and legal guardian to Chezdon Morrison, who is the minor child that you wish to make queries of today. I believe we can assist you with your questions and you are more than welcome to make them here, in our home, if you can afford everyone the respect that they deserve. Chezdon, will you please sit here with me?" Mel extends her arm and points at the red two-seated sofa near us. I stand next to Mel and when I begin to sit down, she does the same and we rest on arses on the red leather that is rarely used. I have never seen her in action professionally; the law is more of a hobby for her as she would rather spend her days following recipes in the Heston Blumenthal cookbook instead of dealing with the law. I feel at ease with her sitting next to me during this unforeseen meeting.

I stand up and extend my hand to the constables. I shake the hand of the female constable and smile, and then enthusiastically shake the hand of the male officer, who appears to be her supervisor and grips my hand so hard I wince. "Hi, I am Chezdon." After introducing myself, I sit down next to Mel once again. "How can I assist?" I glance at Austin and first notice his wide eyes. He is playing with his hair, which he seems to do when he is nervous I have noticed today. Daniel stares at his watch. I know he was looking forward to eating lamb and of course consuming a few bottles of red wine with the fragrant meal.

With the thought of dinner now on my mind, the smell of thyme that is emanating makes my stomach grumble. The male constable speaks with a bored country drawl. "Chezdon mate, we have received a complaint from a James Bateman that your boyfriend assaulted him outside of this building with a cricket bat. Are you able to identify this person? We would like to interview him. Can you please tell us what happened?" This is the second time that the coppers have referred to Austin as my boyfriend. I still haven't gotten used to even having a boyfriend or even if I should be referring to Austin as one. This ambiguity is causing me more stress than being questions by the local constabulary.

I take a deep breath which produces a sigh as I exhale and glance at my father. I can only imagine what he is thinking about now that it has been inferred that I have a boyfriend. Mel places her hand on my knee and begins to speak as I open my mouth. "Constables, can we please save each other some precious time and cut to the chase? As a family, we would like to eat our dinner soon and I am confident that you have more important things to deal with today." Mel appears uninterested as she crosses her legs. She has been away from her glass of wine for a few minutes now and I am confident that she is missing it.

The female constable obviously doesn't like Mel trying to control this interview. "Mrs Peterson, we take violence very seriously as I am sure that you aware. We will conduct our inquiry now and take what we need or we will invite you to come down and speak with us at the station." She then gazes at me with her small notebook and pen ready. "Chezdon, please continue. Can you please identify the person that allegedly assaulted Mr Bateman?"

I am relieved that the copper first identified our supposed victim as James as I never asked him his surname. I don't know how I would have reacted if I learned his last name was Pepsi or some variant of a soft drink. "It certainly was not an assault and the person that you want to question is standing right there." I point at Austin.

Mel stands up. "Constables, unless you are going to charge Chezdon with an offence, that is all he will be saying. I will be representing Austin in the same way I did with Chezdon though." Mel squints at Austin and motions to him. She places her hand on Austin's shoulder. "We can easily finish this now if you trust me, and just tell the constables exactly what you told us earlier. They will ask if you want to be questioned with your mother and father present. That is up to you." The female copper appears irritated. She opens her mouth to interrupt before Austin and I voluntarily swap places.

"It will be fine." I squeeze Austin's shoulder after he sits down.

"Your name is Austin? What is your surname?" The female constable is again ready with her pen.

"McGuire."

"Mr McGuire, are you comfortable speaking with us now with Mrs Peterson supervising and advising? We can drive you to your home and question you with your legal guardians present if you wish. Whilst you consider this, can you please provide us with your home address."

Austin looks at Daniel, who has taken an interest in the view of the Melbourne skyline before returning his attention to Mel. "Just tell them what you told us earlier, I promise you this will end quickly." She repeats her original advice with a calm yet soothing voice.

My alleged boyfriend looks at the female constable. "I am happy to continue here. How can I be of help?" After providing his home address as being in the affluent suburb of Toorak, the officers look at one another. By the snide looks on their faces, I am sure they are both wondering if Austin is the son of Eddie McGuire, the president of the Collingwood Football Club and the former CEO of Channel Nine Australia. I struggle to contain my laughter knowing that he is not a member of that celebrated family.

The male constable who no longer appears bored opens his notebook and clicks the button on the tip of a pen. "There has been an allegation that you assaulted Mr Bateman. Can you please tell us about this?"

Austin looks at Mel who smiles and nods. He recounts the specifics of how our interaction today with James took place on the street below. Austin becomes animated and starts to gesticulate, which is humorous to watch as a spectator. He quickly becomes morose and appears to be experiencing regret as he admits that he smacked James with the cricket bat. "If James was so badly hurt and felt so threatened, why would he hang around to pick up numerous banknotes and coins off the street?" It is an interesting question he posed and leaves everyone in the room staring at Mel.

Mel clears her throat. "Constables, as we all know, one is permitted to defend oneself to a reasonable degree. Having not witnessed the act myself, it would be imprudent of me to comment upon whether what Austin did amounts to being reasonable. However, I will simply highlight that under the

Child Protection Act of 1966, it is an offence for an adult to assault a child, even in a rage. We do have lawful chastisement; of course, however, Mr Bateman is not the parent or legal guardian of Austin McGuire." Mel speaks like she is reading from a textbook. Both Austin and I look at each other and then at Daniel who is pursuing his lips. I wonder if my father thinking about lawful chastisement and how he can legally kick my arse later. "I would suggest constables that you ask Mr Bateman as to whether he wants to pursue an erroneous allegation against Mr McGuire. If he does, we will then be asking the court for an assault against minor charge to be levied against him."

The male constable has been writing continuously. Sometime after Mel stops speaking and finishes writing notes, he clears his throat and looks at Mel. "Mrs Petersen, you are not in front of the judge, so if you would please calm down and keep the theatrics to a minimum we would appreciate it." The copper then looks at Austin. "I have two questions Austin if you don't mind. How long were both you and Chezdon outside speaking with Mr Bateman before you allegedly hit him with the cricket bat? Were there any other witnesses?"

Without looking at Mel, Austin immediately responds. "James smoked two cigarettes whilst we were chatting with him. He tossed one of the ciggies into the gutter. He smoked another one after that and flicked it at Chezdon." Austin pauses to consider the facts before continuing. "Chezdon later said James deserved to be hit with the bat simply because he littered after we walked off. James picked up one of the coins in the gutter which was next to one of his cigarette butts." Austin takes a breath and looks up at the ceiling and then back to the male constable who continues to write in his little notebook. "I don't know about any witnesses, but there is a construction site across the street and the workers were knocking off for the day. I reckon we were talking with James for around five minutes before the alleged incident took place." Everyone keeps using the word alleged. It is now officially the word of the day.

Mel once again places her hand gently on Austin's shoulder. "Constables, it is obvious that Mr Bateman never felt threatened by these two boys and continued a conversation with them whilst smoking multiple cigarettes. Although it can't be proven as only three people know for a fact what dialogue was exchanged and although I would imagine it to be colourful in nature, it doesn't give the explicit right to Mr Bateman to attack these boys out of rage."

The male constable holds up his hand to interrupt Mel. "I have heard enough. We will have a conversation with Mr Bateman and explain to him that everyone should just avoid one another in the future. I am sure that he will not want to pursue this after we explain to him what you kindly articulated to us about the assault against minor charge. I am confident that he will see reason. Thank you, Austin. Can you join us downstairs to identify the cigarette butt in the gutter if you wouldn't mind?"

"Austin, I will go downstairs with you. It looks like this has been finalised. Constables, thank you for your time and your kind attention. I am grateful that we could settle this ridiculous matter. It looks like my lamb will not go cold after all. Before we go, can I offer you anything to drink?" I really doubt that Mel inferring that she wants to open a bottle of wine and share sordid stories involving stupid criminals with the coppers.

"Thanks, Ms Petersen, but we are fine. Shall we?" The male constable begins to walk toward the front door. The female constable initially follows him but stops to look at the painting of 'Growler' hanging on the wall. When he notices her distracted the cop offers her some insight. "That painting was featured in the winning apartment on *The Block* which is why it looks familiar. It is signed though so I doubt it is the same one."

190

I can't but offer some additional information to our local constabulary about the troubled and now deceased artist. "Yes, it is a piece by Adam Cullen who led a very tragic life and is an Archibald Prize-winning painter. He died not long ago from living an unhealthy lifestyle. A bit like I foresee James ending up if he doesn't make some better life choices. You may want to tell that to him also constables." Everyone is now staring at me. I look at my father and then at the female constable and shrug my shoulders. "What? It is just my opinion of course. Oh, and Austin isn't related to Eddie McGuire." Mel smiles and then laughs.

The male copper smiles and opens our front door. "Don't worry about that Chezdon. I will be having a strong word or two with Mr Bateman. Have a nice night. Your dinner smells wonderful by the way." He then glances at his colleague. "Let's go." He looks at Mel. "If you can join us outside on the street with Austin, I promise that you will be back and enjoying your dinner in a few minutes." The male constable holds the door open for his colleague who wanders slowly into the corridor. Mel follows and then Austin who pauses at the door and offers me a smirk. He sticks his tongue out and rolls it into a taco and crosses his eyes. He is the last to leave the apartment, playing with his blond fringe as he lets the door close gently behind him. I am left alone with my father who has had plenty of time to consider the notion of legal chastisement. I take another deep breath before walking into the living room.

Daniel is holding his Samsung tablet in one hand and a glass of wine in the other. I have no idea what he is thinking, but I feel it is in my interest to coax his thoughts out of him so there is not another awkward display when Mel and Austin return. "Well, that was interesting. Mel certainly knows her shit." It takes him a while to find my statement more interesting than whatever he is reading.

"She does know her shit and that is why I love her. That could have ended badly Chezdon, I hope that you know that."

I take an interest in the carpet under the glass table and start to count the different colours of fibres whilst acknowledging my father by nodding. "Yeah, I know."

Thirsty from the courtroom scene that played out in our reception area, my father pours the contents of his glass of wine down his throat seamlessly. I am still on edge about the boyfriend comment that was made twice by the constable. I hope that my father was distracted by the ridiculous situation and the drama that unfolded and forgets how Austin was classified by James. I scowl when I recall telling James that my parents aren't aware of my sexual orientation and how I asked him to keep it secret before he turned up here on Saturday. I quickly get lost in my own thoughts thinking about how James tried to stir up shit and out me. Lost in my own world, I didn't notice that Daniel had gotten up, refilled his wine glass and then returned to sit next to me until I feel a thud, which interrupts my contemplative state.

My father takes a sip of wine. "Chezdon, please just remember that you are a teenager and a clever one at that. Don't try to grow up before you have to." Daniel gulps another few mouthfuls of wine before setting the glass gently on the table. "The only things that I want from you is for you to lead your life as a good person and for you to enjoy every day. You don't have to worry about me judging you for decisions that you make in your personal life. I wouldn't care if all the sudden you declared you hate cricket, the government, joined a religious cult, went vegan and decided that you wanted a sex change. I would still love you and not judge you. Nothing would change. I just hope that you communicate with me so I can give you the best advice and give you the best mentoring that I possibly can. Mel is here for you too. Hell, the same applies to your friends if they ever need anyone to talk to. Just know that you can talk to us about anything. I don't ask for much from you besides this."

I am overwhelmed by my father's diatribe and his attitude. He has never uttered anything so heartfelt and I never imagined that he would be so accommodating to my life choices. "Thanks." I don't know what else to say as he picks up his wine glass and I return to counting the various colours that make up the rug under the table. The front door closes and I hear Mel and Austin chatting as they walk through the foyer. My mouth is dry and my breathing is much faster than normal.

Mel walks into the living room with Austin following behind her. She immediately locates her glass of wine but starts speaking before she takes a drink. "That is sorted thank Christ. The coppers took the cigarette butts into evidence. They only asked Austin for his mobile phone number in case there are follow-up questions." Mel looks at Austin and puts her arm around him. "You did really good mate, and it will all be fine. Thank you for trusting me." Mel finally consumes wine and after the rim of the glass parts company from her lips, she smiles. Wine to her is like a blood to a vampire. "Just call me if you get into a tricky situation like that again. Promise me?" She pulls a business card from her pocket and hands it to Austin.

Austin nods. "Thank you so much, Mel, I really appreciate what you did. That was just amazing."

"No worries. I will send your parents a bill. It is seven hundred dollars per hour, but I will give you the friends and family discount." Mel pats Austin on the back and walks toward the kitchen. "Just kidding." She announces out of sight before returning with a bottle of wine, which she deftly opens thanks to the ingenious screw-cap. Mel fills Daniel's empty glass and then hers. "We can finally eat. After that, I am bloody hungry."

I stand up and wrap my arm around Austin and glance at my father. Daniel retrieves his glass of wine and stares out the window. "Austin, don't be pissed off at me. I am really appreciative of what you did earlier as who knows what that lunatic would have done to us." My father turns around and sips from the wine glass. "Dad, just so you know, Austin is my boyfriend. We have been together now for four hours plus or minus, and I really hope that when I wake up tomorrow, he will still consider me his boyfriend after all of this bullshit." I smile and feel genuinely happy as I know don't expect my father to go berserk after our chat earlier.

Daniel looks at Austin. "I always knew you had great taste Chezdon. Now can we please eat?" He pours all the wine that is in his glass down his mouth as he walks over and stands in front of us. Daniel extends his hand and Austin grasps it. "Welcome to the family, mate." My father walks toward the kitchen and Mel follows him.

Austin looks at me in disbelief. "I hope you are worth it." He takes a deep breath.

"I know I am."

Innocence Waning

11. Kafka

The marble dining room table is being used for feasting instead of being danced upon for a change. The medium-rare lamb is as succulent as Austin's lips and almost as tasty when paired with the local red wine. Fine dining at the Morrison household usually involves robust discussion about politics which ultimately devolves into calling various leaders, both domestically and internationally, obscene names which always is amusing. Tonight, around the table, the chatter plays out as per the nightly script. In between the words Austin chooses to compliment Mel on the meal and repeatedly nodding his head, we collectively attempt to solve the nuanced problems of the world with a knife and fork in each hand. Austin noticeably is restraining himself in fear that if he dares to contradict Daniel or Mel's right-wing conservative beliefs that he will be admonished, or worse, I feel. Mel aptly slices meat from the leg of the lamb that we have named Dolly in between gulps of wine from the large crystal glass. Dolly was sacrificed to fulfil our dietary requirements and when matched with the hearty rich dark gravy, it tastes wonderful. After finishing two large glasses of Bailey's Shiraz, I notice the ghost of the Australian bushranger, Ned Kelly, now dancing on the table as our discussion of political politics becomes more enthusiastic.

Austin dramatically raises his hand which immediately silent my father. "Daniel, my mother wants to know if you are going to Kelly's wedding." Austin knows that I do not speak with my mother, and at first, I find it appalling that he would ask Daniel a question that could potentially cause outrage. My shock quickly morphs into curiosity as I tap my glass of wine against my nose and wait for an answer. I wonder if Austin has been affected by the spirit of Ned Kelly. His ghost stops dancing on the table long enough to take an interest in the question also.

The room goes silent for a noticeable period and I chew on a morsel of lamb for much longer than I need to. Daniel gulps wine from his glass and abruptly places it on the table. "Austin, please don't take this the wrong way as I am happy to discuss anything and everything with you, and I sincerely hope that you will forgive me for saying this, but you need to tell your mother that she needs to stop stirring shit up. Her life seems to be a daily audition for *The Real Housewives of Melbourne* who just feeds off conflict and drama. Honestly Austin, I don't know how your father puts up with her." Daniel takes a drink and I hope with it, his honest assessment of Julie McGuire has finished. Mel continues to eat her twice baked potatoes with lamb reduction and judging from the look on her face, appears to be amused. "What I find fascinating about your mother is that she could have called me, sent me a text, e-mail or all the above which I know she can do, and frequently does by the way, as she is always sending spam and trying to guilt people into donating for whatever cause she is championing. Instead, she uses you as her pawn to try to stir some shit up here. Julie knows goddamned well that I am not going to Kelly's wedding. Hell, I only found out about it today when Chezdon sent me a message about it. Do you think either one of us is counting the goddamned days down with giddy anticipation?" My father is obviously agitated and takes another gulp of wine. I feel like I need to interject or else his soliloquy will continue all night.

Interrupting my father is always a risk and seeing how much Mel is entertained by his diatribe, that and how mortified Austin looks, calls me to arms. "Austin, that sums it up really. Voldemort is not loved too much around this place, so I guess you can tell Julie the answer is no." I reach to grab the wine bottle and extend my arm as far as I can to refill my father's glass and strategically attempt to distract him. "So, dad, are you going to China anytime soon?" I hope by mentioning Asia, he will become distracted and begin to provide expert commentary as to what he really thinks of his subordinates there.

Daniel takes another drink. I close my eyes as I wait for him to start to speak again waiting for him to utter the first word to see if my subterfuge was successful or not. "Kelly and your mother should both keep auditioning for *The Real Housewives of Melbourne* as they will have something to do with their lives instead of trying to fuck around with me." My father was friends with Austin's dad until a few years ago. Obviously, my mother and Julie McGuire have stayed in touch and remain close, probably just to irritate my father if you subscribe to his opinion on our family dynamics. The adults were best mates of sorts when my parents were married even before I was friends with Austin. Thankfully our friendship developed independently of our respective parents' squabbling and having a falling out.

"My mother is a drama queen, I know." Austin looks frustrated. He will not let this topic go and I know he is quite aware that if he continues, he is going to get another unsolicited assessment of Julie McGuire. "Sorry, but my mother told me that I need to tell you something as this information should come from someone that you actually like, and not via e-mail or anything like that." I assume that my father likes Austin after his positive reaction to my earlier revelation that he is my nearly one-day-old boyfriend.

My father appears intrigued and picks up the wine glass and begins to swirl its contents around. This is a habit that I have also recently acquired, which leads me to believe that I would look rather sinister doing it. Daniel looks quite menacing as his mouth appears distorted as I stare at it through the crystal. "Okay, I will bite. What important information do I need to know?" Daniel takes another drink. His curiosity got the best of him, much like the fabled cat.

Austin delicately places his fork on the plate and then wipes his lips with the black cloth serviette that was previously resting on his lap. "Your ex-wife has M-S." Austin is interrupted with his mouth still agape. He has more to say.

"What the!" Mel exclaims. Mel rarely says anything about my mother as it just leads to unnecessary tension. Since she handled my parents' divorce proceedings she feels she should not get involved in any discussion involving Kelly. "Whether it is true or not, oh Jesus. Christ." Mel appears lost for words and as a Barrister, I am surprised. I pause to take note of this moment so that I can give her a hard time later. I will remind her that she was so shocked that she could not speak but then the horrible news registers in my mind belatedly. Voldemort is going to die. After scratching my eyebrow a few times, I consider what to say next as I am now also speechless.

Austin picks up his fork again and is about to poke a morsel of lamb before he decides it is time to finish the message from Julie. "My mother says that she is getting married. It is all rush-rush because the doctors expect her to be in a wheelchair full-time shortly. Kelly doesn't want to be pushed down the aisle. That is all I know, so don't shoot the messenger."

My father looks exasperated and continues to inhale the air from the depths of his large empty wine glass. "Sorry Austin, I hope I didn't come across like a dickhead. My anger and frustration with those women have nothing to do with you, and it doesn't do much good for me to talk rubbish about your mother, so I apologise. Please tell Julie that you passed on the message and that we are giving it the attention that it deserves."

Feeling confused, I want more information. "Isn't M-S what Michael J. Fox has?" I consider his character in *The Good Wife* which I watch with Mel every week religiously.

"No Chez, Fox has Parkinson's. M-S is short for Multiple Sclerosis and it is a disease of the nervous system. It really doesn't end well so I wish her luck." Mel utters and starts to swirl the wine in her glass as vigorously as when I last masturbated. My thirst for red wine intensifies and I pour another glass. Without thinking, I raise it in the direction of the ghost of Ned Kelly who takes notice and beings to dance on the table near Daniel.

"Wow, that it is a bit tragic." I mimic my father and inhale the air from the wine glass and think about getting Austin off. The tragic news about my mother strangely doesn't bother me and in fact, it is distracting me from enjoying the amazing meal.

"What do they have you reading this term? Have you been told yet?" Daniel puts an end to the topic of mortality and fortunately, does not provide any parting comments about either of the maternal figures in our young lives.

Austin and I are in the same English Literature class and he appears relieved that the topic has changed. I let him answer whilst I first look at the deep hues of the wine that is left in my glass and then enjoy a taste. "The first tale is called *The Metamorphosis* by a bloke called Kafka."

Immediately, begins to start laughing hysterically. At first, I surmise that he going to fall off his chair and more alarmingly spill his wine on the floor as he buckles over not bothering to try to control himself. When the amusement passes, which takes a few minutes and gives me the opportunity to enjoy a few mouthfuls of the twice cooked potatoes and pungent yet aromatic gravy, I pause to stare out the window at the Melbourne skyline and wonder what it would feel like putting my penis inside Austin's arsehole. My wild imagination rapidly gets me hard and I hope that the spirited conversation which will commence soon will distract the table long enough, so I can adjust my painful erection which is pushed awkwardly behind the black denim.

"The irony is really amusing me Austin. I pay good after-tax dollars for Chezdon to go to a private school. Jesus Christ!" My father raises his voice and holds the empty glass of wine to his side. "What a load of shit and I can't believe that school is making you read that garbage. I can sum up that assignment quickly boys, so make some mental notes and you will be guaranteed a high distinction for anything you write about bloody Kafka. The main character in that novella is really a caricature of your father, Austin. *The Metamorphosis* is about a depressed salesman who undergoes what some people think is a horrifying yet surreal transformation." I don't think anyone notices me rolling my eyes as my father steps back on his soapbox which gives me the opportunity to force my hand into my jeans under the table and adjust my cock without anyone noticing.

Since Daniel associated the main character of this novella with Austin's father, I am looking forward to reading the story now as it seemed very boring judging from the synopsis on the back cover of the book. My father fills his empty glass with wine before educating us further. "Kafka is from Prague, which I had the displeasure of visiting not long ago after I had to go to Budapest to get the dodgy Hungarian office in line. Prague is not only gloomy but claustrophobic. However, the Czechs celebrate Kafka like he is a national hero that repelled the invading German armies, when all he was, is a social outcast that spent his days brunching, much like what your father does these days Austin."

Half-way through Daniel's damning assessment of Kafka and after having a go at Austin's father, Mel sets her glass of wine down, covers her mouth and begins to chuckle. She continues long past my father finishes his rant about Kevin McGuire, what is being taught at Melbourne Grammar and poor old Kafka who I assume is dead and buried. My father takes another drink of wine and snickers. "The Czechs even built a museum to honour old Kafka. What is in it that would be interesting? Who would know though as I would think it would be as boring as the man himself. What I found fascinating though is outside of the museum is a piece of art by another Czech bloke that features two men urinating into a pond in the shape of the Czech Republic. If you send a text message to a number that is advertised near the installation, the statues will move their bronze cocks and spell out the number with their urine. That sums up the Czech Republic." I feel the need to relieve my bladder after the sublime description of a country that I doubt I will ever visit.

Mel continues to cackle. Even I find the humour in this nonsense. "Austin, welcome to the Morrison family." I reach for my wine glass and then make a standing offer. "Join us for dinner whenever you want, it is never dull." Daniel finally resumes eating his meal. "You mentioned earlier that you should do some reading tonight. Are you going to get stuck in the Kafka now? I know I am intrigued by this assignment." I now want to read about this tragic yet depressed salesman and see what sort of transformation he undergoes and further understand the graphic description associated with Kevin McGuire.

"No, I don't think I have much desire to read tonight. You are a funny guy Daniel. You should open for Josh Thomas at the Melbourne Comedy Festival." Austin decides he wants more wine and picks up the bottle not knowing it is empty. Mel is quick to stand up and source a new vintage from the wine refrigerator whilst continuing to giggle. I am vexed as to whether Austin is being serious. I assume that the descriptions of Austin's parents are accurate considering he knows them both well. A depressed salesman and a mother that is suited to star on a local reality television program. Austin glances at me curiously, no doubt wishing that he could read my mind. "What a great meal and it was certainly a lively conversation. This sort of thing never happens in my house. To be honest, we hardly ever sit down and eat together as a family, so I really appreciate this."

Mel twists the screwcap off a new bottle of Baileys Shiraz and fluidly begins to refill Austin's glass and then hers. She still has a smile on her face. "There is never a dull moment around here, believe me." She raises her glass. "A toast. To Austin. Thanks for giving me the opportunity to give some shit to the cops. That woman copper was such a bitch. She wouldn't even look at me when we were outside. Don't worry Austin, we will not be telling your parents about what happened earlier. Not like we speak with them anyway." Wine glasses kiss; multiple chinking sounds resonate throughout the room.

"Really? I would never have thought." Austin takes a sip of wine and rolls his eyes

Obviously amused, my father begins to chortle. Not at the same volume that he achieved when he first heard about Kafka being taught to our impressionable minds courtesy of his after-tax income though. He harshly wipes at his mouth with his serviette and then slaps Austin on his back with enthusiasm. "You are a good kid Austin. I am glad you can manage to put up with my only son. You are certainly quality compared to those parents of yours." I believe the wine is starting to affect my father and he is no longer measuring the full impact of the words he spews. The look on his face immediately changes and it appears he immediately realised that he may have crossed the invisible line. "Do me a favour. Take that cricket bat you beat up that bloke with home with you as a souvenir of this momentous day. Not only can it be a symbol of lessons learned all around, but it can also serve as an icon symbolising a positive and happy way forward with Chezdon. Every time you see it, know that you have a family in Southbank that you can always depend on. Is that okay with you Chez? I will get you another bat signed by Michael Clarke. Hell, I will get you one signed by the whole goddamned team."

"Yeah, that is cool. Will you take it Austin?" Even though I am buzzed, I know what my father is doing. Earlier Austin commented that I can play mind games with people but my father is the master manipulator. By sending the bat home with Austin, he is effectively sending a message to his parents saying that he has essentially won and will always be one-up on them. At least, that is what I assume.

"Yeah sure. I don't even like cricket, but I am sure it will be valuable some day since Michael Clarke signed it." Austin smiles.

"Spoken like a true capitalist. Kafka will be turning in his grave." Daniel pats Austin on the shoulder and then wipes his mouth for the last time with the black serviette before standing up. "That was amazing Mel, thank you." He walks over and grasps Mel's shoulders. He leans down and kisses her gently on the cheek. I know this is all a show for Austin as the adults never engage in any sort of display of affection in front of me. He will certainly report all of this newly discovered intelligence to his mother when she asks him one thousand questions.

"That was so good Mel. Thank you!" I follow my father's example, wipe my mouth briskly with the serviette before abandoning it. I then walk around to the other side of the table and kiss Mel on her right cheek. Mel will not mind being used as a pawn to advance our happy family narrative and ham it up a bit, which I know will please my father. I excuse myself to go to the restroom, leaving Austin and Mel alone at the table so they can talk about what I assume will be James and everything else that I no longer want to think about. The full stomach of food and wine has given me courage and I am not too concerned what is said about me any longer after having earlier confessed to my father that I am gay. Nothing else that is said now can even come close to the magnitude of that revelation.

Innocence Waning

After I finish urinating, I am conscious to wipe my arse. I rub the Nivea sports deodorant chemical around the holiest of holes and roll some of the chemicals under my ball sack, as I want to feel clean, fresh and confident, knowing there is a high probability I will be spending the night in the same bed as Austin. With all the walking around today, I decide to change my underwear. The cotton has absorbed a fair amount of sweat and should I get into a vulnerable position later, I don't want any horrible odour of my private areas to deter Austin should he be motivated to get on with sexy times. I consider taking a few minutes to masturbate but instead reserve my hot load as I am hopeful that I can deposit it somewhere inside Austin later.

After getting dressed, I abandon my shoes and then notice my phone resting on the bed comfortably. I have been separated from it for what seems to be an eternity. With one of the most dramatic days of my life nearly over, I casually grab the device, quietly wondering what has been happening outside of Southbank. Ten missed calls and forty new messages greet me after waking up the display. The vast majority of the text messages are from Jayden who is concerned that I have been kidnapped. There are a few missed calls from the dreaded private number and my frustration level increases immediately as I remember that someone keeps ringing and hanging up on me. I immediately tap out a message to Jayden and tell him to calm down and then write that I left my phone in my room whilst I was dealing with some family stuff, which is true. I explain in a few words that Voldemort announced that she is getting married and it caused a stir in the happy Morrison household. A follow-up message explains that my father has been on his soapbox and telling us the way things should be in the world. My best mate will certainly understand the comments regarding my father since he is my one friend that goads him on and has heard his spiel many times. Jayden also things that Daniel is hilarious. I toss my phone back on the bed next to Austin's. Thoughts of what I want to do to Austin immediately flood my imagination and I lose track of time staring at my bedsheets, only to have my lurid thoughts interrupted by Austin as he walks into my messy bedroom. I lift my head and smile. "Hey, hottie." I don't know why I chose that term of endearment, but it appears to please him as he smiles.

Austin puts his hands on my thighs and softly kisses my cheek. After withdrawing his hands, he walks towards my bathroom and slides the mirrored doors closed. "What a day!" I hear him shout. The toilet flushes not long later and the two mirrored doors open once again. Before leaving, he spots the small bottle of Nivea deodorant that I recently applied to my groin area near the sink. He grabs it, removes the cap off and then pulls up the left side of the shirt that he earlier borrowed and rolls the chemical on his armpit. He then repeats the process on the other side of his body.

"What are you doing mate? Are you going to hang out here, go home or what?" I sit on the bed and then quickly realise that action may be too suggestive. I quickly stand up and then sit on the chair at my desk. I cross my legs and attempt to look relaxed and uninterested.

"I will just stay here if that is okay. Mel said she will make up the spare room." In my mind, I curse the bitch for thwarting my evil and lustful plans. I will have a hard word with her, and I predict that she is expecting it, which will entertain her to no end. Everyone is playing a game and I hope to win Austin as the prize.

"That is cool." I casually say and then focus my attention on my laptop. I feign some interest in the Windows login screen, but I never type my password. "We can watch a movie in here if you want. You can sleep in here also, that would be cool. Like you did on Saturday. It was nice waking up next to you. Nothing has to happen."

Innocence Waning

Austin walks over to the bed and lays down on it. He reaches out to grab his phone, makes some swiping gestures on its display and then looks at it intently for a few seconds, which encourages me to turn my attention back to my laptop. I log in and appear disinterested and scroll through countless unwanted e-mail. I spend a few minutes deleting spam messages whilst Austin re-connects to the world digitally. Eventually, I hear an ominous sigh and a light thud. I turn around and notice that Austin has tossed his phone onto the bed. It is out of reach and he is laying down with his hands interlocked behind his head. He appears relaxed for the first time all day. "I just messaged my mother and said I am staying here tonight."

My heart begins to beat faster, and I can hear the dull thudding sound as it beats inside my chest. I press both the windows icon and the 'L' key simultaneously which locks my laptop and after closing the bedroom door, I join Austin on my bed. I reach for the remote control and power on the Samsung television and we both get an idea of what is playing by looking at the Smart Hub summary screen. "Do you want to watch a movie? Looks like it is just rubbish on free-to-air."

"Sure."

I press the 'source' button which allows me to wirelessly connect to the media centre in the living room which gives me access to the collection of movies, recorded television and music. I deftly place the remote control on Austin's chest. "Happy one day anniversary. Your choice."

Austin presses the down arrow and scrolls through the 'Movies' folder. Whilst he considers various titles to play, I decide it is time to reveal something about myself. "Not to bring up a bad memory, but I am happy that you shared the tale of the home invasion with me earlier. Thanks for trusting me."

"No worries." Austin continues to scroll through the list of cinematic masterpieces saved for all posterity. "What do you want to watch?"

Not caring about watching a movie, I ignore the innocent question. "I also have a scar that has a story, and I pretty sure that you haven't seen it." This piques Austin's interest. He stops pressing the 'down arrow' button and turns his head to look at me. "Really, where is it?"

"Well, first the story." Austin appears interested and I attempt to find my words which is proving difficult because of the wine. As my mouth is dry, I roll off my bed and walk to the bathroom. I quickly swallow water from the sink tap before returning to take my previous position next to Austin before commencing with story time. "Do you remember last year at school when Jayden and I were mucking around; when I picked him up and injured my back and missed a week of school?"

Austin looks confused again, no doubt trying to associate my back being pulled out with the concept of a scar. "The story I spun last year was a lie. Nothing happened to my back. Originally, I thought there was something wrong with it, but it was something more fucked up. My ball rotated in its sack and twisted up after that physical exertion. As it didn't untwist fast enough, I ended up in the emergency room the following night and the doctors at the Alfred Hospital removed my left nut as it had died. It was strangled to death if you can believe it. I was out of school for the next week as I couldn't walk and needed time to recover. Nobody obviously knows this trivia as it is embarrassing. I was in so much pain and doped up on codeine that I wasn't even in the mood for Nandos."

"Jesus man. Why didn't you go to the hospital after it happened?" Austin appears shocked and is hanging on every word I have to say. "Fuck me."

"It had happened before, but after I took some painkillers in the past, it always sorted itself out naturally after a few hours of pain. I just thought this was normal, but the next day when I couldn't walk, and after a fair number of painkillers were not working, I told rang Mel and she took me to the hospital. They told me if I waited much longer I would have ended up with blood poisoning and probably died. That was scary."

"Are you fertile? I mean, would you be able to knock up a chick?" Austin is really interested in the specifics. "Fuck, that is awful."

"Of course, I still have one working nut. I just seem to make less of a mess. My father thought that my voice would change after the surgery. I think he was surprised when it didn't." Austin laughs. I feel like I am manipulating Austin in a way, and decide to see how far I can go with it. "Want to see the scar?"

"Um... sure." Austin's go wide, and his eyebrows disappear behind his fringe again. I first unbutton my black skinny jeans and proceed to unzip them. I carefully pull the denim off me, being careful not to pull off my clean boxer briefs off in the process. Once the jeans are clear from my feet they are discarded on the floor. Looking truly captivated, Austin props himself up and rests on his elbow facing me.

"I just figured I would tell you this now as if we ever have an intimate moment-" I pause. "I hope when we do, and you notice that I am missing a nut, or that I have a scar on the sack, I don't want the intimacy delayed for question and answers."

"Fair enough." Austin is certainly interested in my own tale of woe. "Jesus."

I consider just pulling my blue Bonds underwear down exposing my junk and closing my eyes, so Austin can have a look at the whole box and dice. I think back to the painful recovery period after the emergency surgery and the pain that I experienced walking, which quashes any hope for my cock to suddenly become engorged and really embarrass myself during this vulnerable time. Instead, I roll onto my side and face Austin and rest my head on a pillow. I strategically grab the cotton fabric of my underwear that is between my legs and pull it out and then to the right, liberating my slightly hairy testicle. Austin moves his head very close to the prize and touches the fine scar tissue with a single finger. "Jesus, that must have hurt." Feeling self-conscious now that I have shared my embarrassing loss with Austin, I banish the sheath of my manhood back into exile back behind the safety of the blue cotton briefs.

"It was a bitch. The first day after the surgery was horrible. My father literally had to drag me to the toilet when I needed to use it. He also had to put my arse in the bathtub, so I could clean myself. Strangely, I didn't feel self-conscious at all after that as I guess the pain and immobility were far more important to me, unlike now." I roll back onto my back and interlock my hands behind my head. "After that near-death experience, I thought that you have to live every day without having any regrets." I roll back to the right and grab Austin and try to sit on top of him, but he pushes me away. I make another attempt to break his defences by first kissing his ear and then biting his earlobe before I try to force my tongue into his mouth. He thwarts my efforts again and pushes me away, this time force.

"Can't we just chill out? You can hold me or my hand if you want, but I am not in the mood for anything else. It would be nice to be with you and not have you just try to molest me every third minute. It has been a long and ridiculous day and I am tired. I told you before I am not going to have sex with you on our first date if you can even consider today a date. God, we only got together this afternoon and look at everything that has happened. You must be drunk if you think you are going to fuck me right now." Austin starts to pull back the sheets and slides his body under them still clothed. He makes a fair point and I really don't think that if I was questioned by the police for an assault that I would be up for sex. I follow Austin's lead and get under the sheets and then slither next to him slowly. I push my arm under his pillow and put my other arm on his chest. After a few seconds and he doesn't push me away, I slide my hand in between his shirt and navel and then try to pull his shirt off him.

"Jesus Christ, can you please calm down and just lay next to me." Austin pulls his shirt down, covering his exposed naval. "Fuck."

"What is the big deal? I thought you just slept in your underwear. At least you did the other night."

"Just stop Chezdon. I promise I will not ask you for much, but just this one time, do this for me. Just relax and chill out." His eyes go wide again so I oblige and reason with myself that patience is indeed a virtue. I will get what I want in time and relish in the buzz that I am experiencing from the wine. I sit up and pull my shirt off. I toss it on the floor next to my discarded skinny jeans. Ignoring Austin who is staring at me intently, I find my phone and then sit back and start to read messages. First, I ignore the ones sent by Jayden and intently focus my eyes to read the words that Bryce sent. After a few minutes of reviewing messages, all similar in length of text that Kafka has written, I chuckle. Austin jerks his head and stares at me. "What?"

"Do you remember Bryce telling us about his father shaking his mother and her getting pissed off and going to their holiday home?" I shouldn't be laughing. This is tragic. Tragically funny though.

"No, I don't."

"Oh yeah, you weren't with us at the time. He told us about this over lunch on Saturday. Well, his father likes to hold his mother when they sleep and she has a habit of farting on him and waking him up. He got pissed off the other night and shook her after it happened, so she got pissed off, packed a bag and went to their house in Sorrento. Anyway, it seems she came back earlier and now wants a divorce. Bryce is devastated." Judging by the frown on Austin's face, he doesn't seem amused.

"That is sad and really sucks, and you laughed? You are a monster without a heart." I didn't think Austin would react in such a way so I must backpedal.

"I only laughed because I thought of the original story and how he told it. I think it is cool that a married couple sleeps like that. I really hope that years from now, I am holding you all night. I don't care if you fart on me and wake me up. It does suck that she is leaving though. I feel bad for Bryce." I smile and raise my eyebrows, but that doesn't placate Austin.

"Violence against women isn't a laughing matter." I need to put an end to this conversation as soon as this isn't very positive pillow talk.

"I totally agree. Absolutely. One hundred per cent. Violence against boys isn't a laughing matter either, and I would never do that to you." Hopefully, that statement mollifies Austin however he still appears agitated.

"Great conversation to have in bed, Chez, only hours ago, I beat up some bloke. Open mouth. Insert foot. Anything else you want to say?" Now is the time to say nothing. I know Richie Benaud would say the bare minimum.

"Sorry." I revert my attention back to my phone and send Bryce a message expressing my manufactured outrage. I then ask if he wants to catch up on Saturday for lunch, which is turning into a weekly engagement. Austin finds the remote control and resumes the task of scrolling through movies available on the media centre. I respond to Jayden's messages and detail some of the highlights of the day. Instead of providing a one-line update about the relationship status between Austin and me, I instead activate the camera, extend my arm and take a photo of us next to each other in bed. Austin is holding the remote and I am in a state of undress under the duvet. I send the photo to Jayden knowing his reaction will be as timeless as the wind.

"What are you doing?" Austin stops scrolling through the selection of movies and attempts to grab my phone from my hand.

"Just messaging Jayden, I sent him a photo of us. Look." I tap the photo that is part of our messaging dialogue. Austin looks intently at the display.

"Well, I guess people were going to find out about us eventually. So much for keeping my sexuality under wraps." Austin seems defeated and looks exhausted.

Seconds after sending the message, my phone begins to vibrate as I grasp it in my hand. "It is Jayden. He rarely rings."

"Of course, it is. I really don't think he is ringing to ask you if you read any of the Kafka tonight." Austin must be settling down and feeling more comfortable as his sardonic wit is on display again. "Just answer it or he will hassle us all night."

"Hola, amigo." This is the first time that I have ever answered the phone using a Spanish greeting. Jayden immediately begins speaking and doesn't stop talking for at least a minute.

Periodically he uses blasphemy strategically. He expresses his shocked indignation as reading into the meaning of getting a photo of Austin and me in bed on a Monday night like some old 'married couple' begins to ask questions that I am not given an opportunity to answer. Commentary ensues and after he repeats the word 'shocking' ten times, I decide that it would be funny to respond with, "can you repeat that? You broke up for most of that."

Austin begins to giggle as he is aware that I heard every word that Jayden spewed. He was shouting so loudly over the phone that not only his neighbours but his father who lives 3,000 kilometres away would have heard him. Jayden proceeds to use more colourful language, repeating most of what he originally uttered verbatim and just before he runs out of breath he ends his commentary. "I was only joking the other day when I said that the two of you would be hot if you hooked up. How did this happen? I am so confused. I just saw you last night and now you in bed with Austin? What happened to James?"

Finally, being afforded the opportunity to say something, I articulate to the highlights of my date with James, the subsequent rendezvous at his dirty flat, Austin's confessional at Nandos, James making his unplanned visit to shake me down for thirty dollars and how Austin eventually knocked him down with the cricket bat. I finish the comprehensive update by explaining how the courtroom drama that played out in my apartment with the police and Mel. "Did I catch you up mate? Now you see why I have been a bit distracted and not paying attention to my phone since leaving school today. Oh yeah, my mother is getting married and has M-S also."

"Jesus Christ mate. So much drama, this is so fucked up that it all must be true. You should write it all down and sell it as a book. You would make a fortune." I ponder that statement for a few seconds as I do believe it would make for a good story but my writing skills are not my strongest asset. "I have heard enough. I think I am going to go steal one a Valium from my mother, so I can chill out after hearing all of this shit."

"You do that mate. We got stuck into the wine with the parentals earlier, so maybe you should too. Oh, Bryce's mother is asking for a divorce. I forgot to mention that to you."

"Jesus. It is all happening. Well, I am going to go now and read some more of this Kafka bullshit. What a loser." Suppressing my laugh is futile and I erupt into hysterics. Tears quickly form in my eyes as I attempt to convey some of the random facts in between breaths that my father muttered about Frank Kafka. Austin begins to laugh. "I think you need my mother's Valium mate, I don't know what you find so fucking funny."

My laughter subsides to the point that I can speak coherently. "When you rang, Austin said you certainly weren't calling to talk about bloody Kafka. He was fucking wrong."

"Go do whatever you are going to do with Austin. Go see if your father has a drawer of Valium's and have one, you need a few, mate. Talk to you tomorrow at lunch. Later." Jayden doesn't give me the chance to fare him well before ending the call.

"Are we going to watch a movie, or are you going to gossip all night?" Austin has stopped pushing the down button on the remote and appears to be ready to play one of the *Harry Potter* movies. The face of Voldemort flashes before me and I momentarily feel a sense of sadness knowing that my mother is going to exit this life in pain. Within minutes of the movie starting, both the stressors of the day and the wine overwhelms me and I fall into a deep sleep.

12. Cinema

The annoying sound that I previously nominated as my morning alarm on my phone recalls me to the land of the living, begrudgingly. Austin is using my shoulder as a pillow. I really did spend the night with him and it wasn't just a dream. The memories from the last few days' rushes back into my head and I am happy that it wasn't just some ridiculous dream sequence. I attempt to locate my phone which is causing the untimely racket and curse myself for forgetting to connect the device to the charger before I passed out last night. After finding the source of the ridiculously noisy alarm under my pillow causes Austin to stir. I fumble with the phone to mute the alarm from blaring and Austin lifts his head off me, leaving behind a clear pool of saliva on my chest. He rolls onto his back and wipes at his mouth with the back of his hand. "Good morning Chezdon."

Judging from the amount of drool that he left on my warm shoulder, I assume that he must have enjoyed a deep sleep. "Good morning. It is nice to see you smiling first thing." I feign a smile and try to ignore the pounding taking place in my head. A wonderful throbbing headache and a painful shoulder as the result of it being used as a pillow to start what will be a long day. I roll out of bed and toddle to the bathroom. After locating a box of painkillers in the cabinet and popping out two pills, I wash them down by sucking greedily on the sink tap. My wine-stained lips are then scrubbed vigorously with a towel which is then used to wipe slobber that is dripping down my chest before returning to bed. The alarm wakes me up daily at 6:45 AM which leaves plenty of time to get ready for school and have a coffee. Today I just want to hide under the sheets and from the world with Austin. With my head back on the pillow, I check the display of my phone. A message appears from my father which he sent two hours ago saying that he will take us to school and to be ready to go at 7:45 AM. How my father wakes up so early in the morning after staying up so late at night drinking wine is a mystery. I was hoping that both my father and Mel left long before my alarm went off, so I could have tried to coerce Austin into ditching school. Now that I have returned to my comfortable bed and his smiling face, I am not going to want to go anywhere anytime soon.

"Had a bit too much wine, did you?" Austin is tapping a message in which he announces to his mother that everything is indeed fine, and he is being taken to school by Daniel. She would have no clue that her son spent the night in the same bed with his newfound love and I am confident that she has no idea that he is gay. I would love to be a fly on the wall when that conversation inevitably takes place.

I yawn and scratch the side of my head. "I probably did enjoy my fair share of wine. But what a day yesterday was. Jesus." I look around for the remote control but can't locate it. Instead, I press the "up" button on the other small white control that issues a command for the electric blinds to raise in my room. "It looks like it is going to be a beautiful day." It will be great if my headache subsides before I get to school so I can appreciate the lovely conditions on offer outside just a little bit more.

"You have an interesting routine in the morning, I like watching you, Chez." Austin has been keenly observing me since he woke. I was hoping that he was just satisfying his morning horniness and feasting his eyes on the object of his desire as I shuffled around only wearing boxer briefs. When I woke up I felt his stiff morning wood poking my leg which is why I assume he was quick to roll off me once he got his bearings.

"I am certainly more interesting compared to the morning news, so feel free to watch me any morning you bloody voyeur." I grab a pillow and hit Austin in the face with it. I save him the embarrassment of having to admit that he has an erection, which he obviously doesn't want to show me sadly, and proclaim that I will have a quick shower and practice my morning hygiene ritual giving him time to wake up and thus, calm his cock down.

Usually, I stand in the shower stall for at least fifteen minutes, robbing the whales that breed off the south coast of Australia the water that they need to survive, of course after it is delivered to me via the desalinization plant. Not knowing how long it will take Austin to get ready, I constrain my morning routine to mere minutes and spend most of the time drinking the water that is ejaculating on my face from the shower nozzle. I feel claustrophobic behind the closed sliding mirrored doors after I leave the shower stall, dry off and then use the hair drier to eradicate the remaining moisture first from the hair on my head and then my armpit, and finally squat down and blow dry my arsehole. I imagine that someday someone will watch this routine and die of laughter. My morning ritual as Austin likes to call it works though. After Nivea is applied to my dry underarms, I once again dab a small amount under my lopsided ball sack and push the applicator ball lightly into my arsehole which leaves some chemical behind on the holiest of holes. I apply some cortisone cream to my face to keep my eczema under control and then rub moisturizer to my face, wiping any excess cream on my shoulders before quickly rubbing a sticky product around my hair. I emerge from the unhygienic bathroom with my towel wrapped around my waist to find Austin watching the weekday version of the *Sunrise* morning show. The hosts are interviewing a previous winner of *X-Factor*. "There are clean towels under the sink, and I will find you some clean clothes that you can wear." Austin enthusiastically rolls off the bed, still wearing the standard-issue trousers from yesterday that is part of our boring school uniform. "I will leave everything that you will need on the bed. Just throw your dirty clothes in the sink in the laundry room and someone will sort them out. I will meet you in the kitchen. I need coffee." I feel like I should go out of the way, so Austin has some privacy. I don't want to endure an awkward conversation where he asks for it. As I couldn't even get his shirt off last night, I presume he doesn't want me checking him out or judging his own morning routine.

"Yes sir, thank you my Führer." He stops walking to the bathroom long enough to kiss me on the lips. I immediately smell both lamb and red wine emanating from his mouth, which makes me both hungry and thirsty. After he disappears behind the sliding mirrored doors of the bathroom, I get dressed and then find a spare pair of trousers and a white shirt for Austin whilst contemplating the kiss. Fortunately, we have similar builds and are of similar height, so he will not look awkward wearing my altered trousers. I leave the clothes, along with some black socks and a clean pair of black Bonds underwear on my bed next to the pillow that he also salivated on. I know how much he likes the colour black, but I leave the drawer of socks and underwear open. He can choose something himself if he decides he wants an alternative, but I reckon he will like my suggestions. The shower turns on again after the toilet is flushed. For a moment, I consider throwing the sliding bathroom doors open and checking him out but being a realist know that will not end well. It is more important to feed my body with some coffee and perhaps even take another painkiller instead of perving on Austin.

En route to the kitchen, I stop in the laundry room to retrieve the coins from the plastic tray so that I have money for the vending machine at school. After dropping my wadded wet towel into the sink, I pour the contents of the blue plastic tray, which includes scraps of folded paper that I wrote notes on and Shaun's business card into my backpack that Mel considerately left next to my favourite black school shoes. I hear my father shouting at someone on the phone in the study and then find Mel in the living room reading the newspaper holding a cup of coffee. "Good morning. The coffee is fresh as of five minutes ago," Mel doesn't look up from the broadsheet. She knows what I am on the hunt for, as I usually crave coffee the morning after indulging in the wine bottle the night before with dinner.

"Good morning." I walk to the kitchen and locate a ceramic cup and fill it to the brim. Whilst waiting for it to cool down, I raid the refrigerator and find can of Cherry Dr Pepper and drink every drop of it before grabbing a banana from the green glass bowl on the countertop and begin to peel it. Mel walks into the kitchen with her empty red cup and sets it close to me on the counter.

"How are you feeling today?" Mel begins to pour black coffee into the cup.

"Like hell. I woke up thinking I dreamt about all the drama that took place yesterday. I was shocked when I saw Austin next to me. All of that really happened. Full on." Mel chuckles before sipping the steaming coffee from the cup.

"I see Austin didn't sleep in the spare bedroom." Mel begins to peel a banana. I then recall her clever game last night of suggesting that Austin can sleep in the guest bedroom and enjoy some privacy. My face quickly turns red from embarrassment as I know what she is thinking. "It isn't my business Chezdon, just be safe."

I insert the banana as far as it will go into my mouth and then slowly pull it out. I suggestively lick my lips and end the salacious routine with a chuckle and a wink. "Don't worry, nothing happened, he wouldn't even take off his shirt."

"I don't need to know the intimate details. Just be safe when you have sex and for God's sake, don't film any acts or take any photos of your bits." Somehow Mel manages to drink the whole cup of steaming coffee after eating the banana. The woman is a coffee and red wine consumption machine.

"Yeah, I know. I love it when you remind me though. Can you draw up a consent form, so I can have it signed like the bloke did in *Fifty Shades of Grey*? I can carry one around in my back pocket with a pen, so I am ready to go when sexy times are on offer." I sip coffee from my mug.

Mel bursts out laughing. "You are a little shit. You are funny though. This is very unlike you first thing in the morning. You must be happy."

"Happiness is subjective. I don't know what I am right now. Life just seems to be going so fast, I don't know what to think." I take another sip. "Will I get the friends and family discount if I get you to draw up that sexual consent form?" I smile.

"No mate. You will be paying the seven hundred dollars per hour. I will bill you for the time it takes me to consider the law also, so save up your gold coins." Mel pours refreshes the cup of coffee as my father enters the kitchen dressed in a suit and tie.

"Are you ready to go?" My father barks. "Get your arse moving."

"Good morning to you." My headache feels as if it is starting to wane as quickly as my innocence. "Do you have fifty dollars on you that I can have?" My father retrieves a mug from the cabinet and fills it with coffee.

"What do you need it for?" Daniel drinks the steaming beverage as quickly as Mel does. Why his tongue doesn't object to being scorched is indeed a mystery. I am beginning to surmise that both Mel and Daniel are wine and coffee robots and high levels of stimulants and depressants do not phase them.

"I owe Austin thirty dollars after the cricket bat debacle yesterday and I owe Jayden a lunch." I run my hand through my sticky hair and then adjust the fringe in the mirror that acts as the splashback over the gas stove in the kitchen.

"So, you aren't going to buy your boyfriend lunch?" I shudder when my father says the word 'boyfriend' as I still haven't grown accustomed to our new union, let alone my father being so comfortable with saying the word. "Speaking of your boyfriend, where is Austin?" I noticeably cringe and scratch my neck.

"He is getting ready, he knows that we need to leave soon. What is the rush anyway?" I take another sip of coffee and look intently at my father who then glances at his watch.

"Time is money, we have places to be." If my father has meetings to conduct or has scheduled calls to shout at people, I can understand his urgency. I am about to volunteer to go check on Austin, but he walks into the kitchen on cue. "Good morning Austin, do you want some coffee?"

"You say 'good morning' to him but not to me. I see how it works around here." I drink the last of the coffee and ponder a way to stir up my father. With a clearer head and feeling much more relaxed with the headache subsiding, I feel like giving him some shit.

"Austin looks ready to go and is smiling, which makes it a good morning. I don't know what he did to you last night Chezdon behind closed doors but keep up the good work."

Innocence Waning

Mel beats me in expressing a shocked gasping sound by a microsecond. "Daniel! Jesus Christ. That isn't your business, stop stirring people up."

I am surprised when Austin opens his mouth, not giving me time to retort. "Yeah Daniel, you are starting to sound like my mother." He must be in a great mood as he got my father back with a very apt comment. Both Mel and I laugh and make bellowing noises validating Austin's successful verbal jab."

"Well done mate. I knew I liked you." Daniel smiles and drinks the last of the coffee in his mug. "Let's go. Chez, where is your tie? Where is your goddamned jacket?"

I grab a bottle of water from the refrigerator and toss it at Austin and then take another one for my personal use. "My tie is in my bag and my jacket is resting on the chair."

My father opens his wallet and hands Austin thirty dollars. "Here is the money that my favourite son owes you." He then turns towards me and hands me forty dollars. "Take your boyfriends out to Nandos or whatever it is you eat these days."

The irony of my father mentioning Nandos is not lost on either Austin or I and we both smile. "Thanks, Daniel. I need to correct you though. Please re-phrase your statement to say 'take your boyfriend and Jayden out to Nandos' as having one love interest is complicated enough. If I dated Jayden I would be forced to get into his mother's supply of Valium." I fold the cash and push it into my pocket.

"Bloody crazy women. Can we go now please?" Daniel begins to shake the keys in his hand.

Bags, jackets, additional sets of keys and even the cricket bat are collected by various members of my now extended family as we leave the apartment. We travel down together via the lift and into the parking structure without saying a word and get into the black Porsche Cayenne. After we drive from the secure building, I feel vexed and ask my father a question. "Dad, is Mel going with you to your meetings today?"

"No, we are going to get breakfast. The place where we had our first date nearly was nearly burned down by an arsonist last night. I thought we would go there this morning and relive some of the good old days. Fortunately, the prick was crash-tackled before he could light a match after pouring petrol on the wall of the place." We drive down one of the designated lanes for cars once we turn onto St Kilda Road, unlike Julie McGuire who raced down the deserted tram tracks yesterday morning at this time in the torrential rain.

"Jesus, that is awful. Where did you have your first date, Daniel?" Austin appears interested and I suspect is looking for an idea as to where we can go on our first official planned date, which is something that we need to discuss.

"The Vineyard in St Kilda. Have you ever heard of it?" Daniel mutes the Triple-M morning drive broadcast which is playing on the radio. Coincidentally, Eddie McGuire hosts this program.

"No, I haven't. But isn't it really just a wine bar?" Austin inquires. The place is called 'The Vineyard' after all so one would assume that wine would be flogged to anyone with a thirst.

"They serve breakfast, lunch, and dinner there, but yes, it is a wine bar of sorts."

"So, you are going to the wine bar at 7:45 AM on a Tuesday morning? Isn't it a bit early for you both to be getting stuck into the piss?" This makes Mel laugh and it appears that my father is embarrassed as it takes him a couple of seconds to consider his response.

"I might have a beer with my eggs. It is never too early for a beer." My father looks at Mel. "You agree with me, don't you?" Mel doesn't say a word.

I feel like getting revenge on my father for what he said in the kitchen earlier. Austin made a successful jab so now it is my turn. "Austin, will you go out on a date with me? It will be our first official date too."

Austin smiles. "I thought you would never ask."

"We can ditch school and go over to The Vineyard. It seems like it would be a perfect first date venue." The look on Daniel's face changes slightly. I believe he was expecting a serious proposition and the comment doesn't seem to phase him. "Just kidding, maybe tonight you want to go see the movie *Woman in Gold* over on Collins Street."

Austin contemplates my question and chews on the inside of his mouth. "I wish I could but I should go home after school. I don't want to fall behind after doing full all last night. I need to start reading the bloody Kafka."

"Denied!" My father shouts and fortunately does not provide any further insight into Kafka or compare anyone to Austin's father.

"Well then, let's plan something at lunch when we are away from these meddling adults." Austin nods his head in agreement all the while keeping his eyes glued to his phone and the social media feeds. The remainder of the short trip is commentated by Eddie McGuire who is unmuted. There is plenty of chatter about the sport on the radio before an old song by Pearl Jam is played. By the time Eddie Vedder is finished singing about Jeremy speaking in class, we come to a stop outside of school. We quickly get out with our bags and Austin takes the cricket bat with him. "Thanks, Father!" I shout. "Have a good day. See you later Mel."

"Thanks again for the hospitality. Cya." Austin closes the car door. My father in one last act of defiance blows the car horn for five seconds which causes both our peers and strangers alike to stare at the Black Cayenne and then us, wondering what the hell is happening. My parental unit then drives off and I wonder if my father will really have an alcoholic beverage with his breakfast at the wine bar. It wouldn't surprise me.

I stand on the side of the road outside of school sharing an awkward moment with Austin as we don't know how to part ways. Hugging him would not be appreciated and I wonder if he would hit me with the cricket bat if I put on a public display of affection for all and sundry to see. I simply pat him on the shoulder. "See you in Lit, hot boy. I am looking forward to lunch with you later. By the way, you look really nice today."

"Thanks. You do too. Don't take this the wrong way, but your bed is comfortable. I had such a great sleep with the air conditioning on. It was the best sleep of my life until I woke up and had to look at you." My mouth drops open. "Just kidding! Cya Chez." Austin pats me on the shoulder and walks past me. He is on fire this morning and is doing a good job winding everyone up. After adjusting my backpack, I walk quickly to get to my usual seat in Chemistry class.

Each minute seems to draw out like hours. Notes are dutifully taken, and I participate in discussions like usual. I drift off when the lecturer drones on about coefficients and inverse cosine in a subsequent class and begin to ponder the decisions that I have made over the last few days. I certainly didn't want to have an ongoing relationship with James and I was just looking for a good time when I thought he was a sane individual. Now I am in the early stages of hopefully being in a sexual relationship with a friend. I wonder when I will have sex or some sort of fun with a guy. Distracting myself from lurid thoughts, I think back to the last time I went for a run. My body and mind would benefit from some exercise so after the final bell, I consider going home to change and then going for a run to Westgate Park. Certainly, there will be someone there that will be happy to get me off but then I remember the look on the face of the bloke that was getting escorted away from the public toilet by the Police. If I learned anything from the drama that unfolded yesterday is that I need to stay safe and not get into a position that requires Mel to be speaking to the cops about something disgraceful that I have done. As I continue to scribble notes in a daze, my mechanical pencil runs out of lead. I begin to rummage through the pockets of my backpack looking for more lead. Instead, I find a pen resting against Shaun's business card that I tossed into my bag earlier along with the cache of gold dollar coins. I slyly remove my phone from my bag and look at the Palace Cinemas website at an uncomfortable angle as I am forced to conceal my technology under my desk. I check the session times for when *Woman in Gold* is screening and discover that there is only one session later today and one tomorrow before its run comes to an end. I sigh loud enough for the nerd with greasy curly hair that sits in front of me to turn around and 'shhhh!' me as he is captivated by the exciting discussion about math.

Whilst walking to Lit class, my stomach rumbles. Nandos chicken comes to mind since my father was kind enough to plant the seed earlier. I need to first endure a lecture about how wonderful Franz Kafka is from the teacher and see both Jayden and Austin before we are released for lunch. Austin is already seated in class when I arrive and only seconds later Jayden appears. "Chezdon Morrison! The man!" Jayden's familiar booming voice startles me. He approaches me and gives me a hug. "You bloody dirty dog!"

"What are you on about freak? Before you talk shit, do you want to go to the cinema later? There is something that I want to see." Austin is staring at us from afar.

"Let me guess, you want to see some dramatic foreign shit with subtitles. Haven't you experienced enough drama lately?" Jayden puts his hand on my back and shoves me to the back of the class. He obviously wants to talk before class starts. "I can't today mate. I must force myself to read this Kafka shit, but I also have an appointment with the doctor about my allergies. I am going to start getting shots to hopefully manage the reactions. Joy hey?"

Well, that sucks balls. Do you want to get Nandos for lunch? My shout." Jayden has been spending most the time that we have been conversing staring at Austin, who is returning the favour.

"You would know all about sucking balls now. But yeah mate, I am keen." Jayden continues to stare at Austin. "Is your boyfriend going to be joining us?"

Normally I wouldn't look around when someone uses the word 'boyfriend' but I do this time to see if anyone is paying attention to us or bothering to eavesdrop on our banal conversation. "Yeah, he is."

"Figures. I hope that I can schedule some much-needed Chez-time later in the week then. I miss hanging out with you." Jayden confesses in a whiny voice.

"You saw me most of yesterday arsehole, what are you on about?" I watch our teacher shuffling papers at the front of the class. Everyone scrambles for their assigned seat. "Meet outside of class after all of this Kafka shit is over with."

Jayden laughs. "What do you have against Kafka?"

Innocence Waning

"Don't worry about it. Talk later." With those words, we part company and go to our respective desks. Like the math lecturer, the teacher drones on endlessly and provides a different perspective on Franz Kafka than my father did. This class would be much more interesting if my father taught it and then instead of taking notes, I start writing down ideas involving my forthcoming date with Austin. I spend most of the class ignoring what is being said about *The Metamorphosis* and brainstorm on a piece of scrap paper. Fortunately, I was not called on to provide an opinion or add any sort of insight to the discussion. When the bell rings and we are dismissed, I feel like I have devised an awesome itinerary and I can't wait to share it with Austin. I am confident that he will be impressed.

I wait for Austin to approach me as he leaves via the back of the room. We exit into the hallway together and are immediately approached by Jayden. "Hello, my fag friends. Some interesting stuff in class don't you reckon? What do you think of Kafka, Chez?"

"Please don't get him started mate. You should ask his father what he thinks if you want a good laugh." Austin waves the red flag in front of the bull.

"What is up with that? The two of you are playing happy households now. I left Chezdon on Sunday night and he was busy chasing that bloke James' arse around the city and one day later the two of you have moved in together. I am just gobsmacked!" Jayden continues as we walk from the school grounds and towards Nandos. "Does Daniel know one of you is fucking the other? Why the hell are you carrying that cricket bat?" Jayden looks at Austin who seems to be finished asking questions for now at least.

Jayden's crassness is hilarious, and I can't help but giggle. "Yeah dad knows what is going on behind closed doors, he is fine with that."

"Some things are just not your business Jayden." Austin looks flustered.

"Hey mate, can you give me a minute or so that I can speak with Austin about something?" I do want to ask Austin out on our first date without Jayden providing analysis or his opinion.

"Secret men's business, so soon. It should be expected as you are an old married couple after a day. Thanks for the photo by the way. I jerked off to it." Jayden continues to walk after we stop. "I will meet you on the corner."

I adjust my backpack so the straps rest on both of my shoulders. "Hi." I smile at Austin.

"Hi." Austin smiles back.

"Um, I was wondering if you would like to join me on an official date on Friday. We can do a few rounds of bowling, then get sushi at Nobu and finally see a play at the Melbourne Theatre Company." The expression on Austin's face doesn't change as I ask my first boyfriend out on our first official date. "Or we can do what you want to do. It is up to you." I shrug my shoulders and then look down the road at Jayden who is pointing at his watch.

"Can't, I am busy. Sorry." Austin succinctly says without any emotion.

"Well, maybe you want to go out on Saturday then. If you are keen, we can meet up with Bryce for lunch and then make a day of it." It is hard to negotiate when I am not getting any sort of feedback to work with.

230

"Can't, I am busy. Sorry." Austin repeats and curiously the look on his face doesn't change. I wonder if he is pissed off at me and think back and wonder if I offended him in some way.

"How about the 13th of October, which is six months away. Can you fit me into your busy schedule then?" I feel like acting like a smart arse will break this impasse one way or another.

"Can't, I am busy. Sorry." Austin repeats yet again but then explodes into laughter. "You should have seen the look on your face Chez. Hilarious!" Austin continues to laugh. "Sounds perfect. Friday, it is then." He puts his arm around me and we start to walk toward Jayden, Austin guides me along the footpath as I recover from the body blows of repeated rejection.

"Arsehole! You are on fire today." Once again, I am sucked into Austin's trap. "Don't read much into this, but if you want to bring your stuff on Friday, you can spend the night again. Being that you liked my bed so much. The theatre is only a five-minute walk from my apartment." I am not sure Austin appreciates how much thought I put into this. I hope he doesn't just think I am trying to get his pants off in bed once again, but with all the venues associated with the date that I have planned to be only minutes away from where I live, a strategy was considered when I made this plan.

As we approach Jayden, Austin simply says, "sounds great mate" and then taps Jayden on the arse with his cricket bat. "Let's go, I am hungry."

Lunch is a hurried affair where we all consume extra hot peri peri chicken, coleslaw and wash it all down with Coke. We recount Austin's dealings with the police, James and the Pepsi bottle and educating Jayden on Kafka, thanks to the trivia that was shared with us by Daniel last night. I really hope that Jayden uses some of the trivia and disrupts the Lit class tomorrow. We walk quickly back to school which gives me little time to talk about my mother and how I feel bad knowing how she will end up. Before we all go our separate ways, both Jayden and Austin encourage me to reach out to Voldemort. They feel that I will regret it in later life if I don't. I seriously consider their words as I walk to the library to have a productive study period alone with my thoughts.

I spend some time reading the math study guide but feeling unmotivated, instead doodle pictures of the various characters from South Park. Suddenly experiencing a light bulb moment after staring at my rendition of Eric Cartman, I know what I need to do. I pull my phone out of my backpack and tap out an e-mail to my mother suggesting it is the time that we meet up and have a chat. Voldemort has sent me numerous e-mails over the years, but I have never responded. If the M-S hasn't put her in a wheelchair yet, the shock of getting an e-mail from me just might. After pressing 'send' and feeling empowered, I locate Shaun's business card and send him a message. He previously commented he would happily see *Woman in Gold* with me when we were chatting at Supernormal the other day. After I press 'send' I wonder if he will bother responding. His business card says he is a psychiatrist, and I selfishly think it would be nice to have someone to talk about all this personal drama with. Even though I think that I am navigating the ups and downs of my adolescent life quite well now, I reckon we all need someone to talk to that can provide an unbiased assessment of things. Not long after sending the message, Shaun responds in the affirmative and suggests attending the screening of the movie tomorrow night.

I respond that I will make time and that the last showing for the film is at the Palace Cinema on Collins Street at 6:30 PM. His office is also on Collins Street, so it will be convenient for him. He quickly replies by saying that works for him and suggests meeting at the bar at the Pei Modern Restaurant, which is next to the cinema at 6:00 PM for a quick drink. I roll my eyes when presented with yet another situation that involves meeting an older guy at a bar. Thinking rationally, meeting a few minutes before a movie starts, doesn't mean that I must try to evade the question of my age with either Shaun or the barman, and decide to just order a Coke when the time comes.

After the tedious study period ends, whilst walking to my next class I ring Nobu Restaurant at the Crown Casino and make a booking for two on Friday at 6:00 PM at the sushi bar. A feeling of satisfaction overwhelms me as I walk into the last classroom on the schedule for the day knowing that I am trying to reconcile with my mother. Having also unburdened myself of my secret involving my sexuality, I surmise that this is how it feels to truly act like an adult.

13. **Metamorphosis**

The remainder of the school day passes like the blink of an eye. My mood improves exponentially as the dusty feeling of my wine hangover subsides not long after I have started to digest the half of a chicken and coleslaw that I indulged on during my lunch break. After the final bell of the day sounds, I stop and have a pleasant conversation with friends that I hadn't enjoyed words with for weeks. Besides talking about sport and gesticulating wildly whilst doing so, I casually comment that I am going to plan yet another get-together sometime soon which will rival the party that I spontaneously threw last Saturday which has been discussed in the school halls and across the digital divide of social media. My occasional mates languish on the footpath outside the iron school gates, waiting to be collected. They express their fervour with fist-bumps and give me brisk hugs before I turn my back to school and begin the short amble to the tram platform on St Kilda Road.

The pleasant weather has allowed the gardeners to complete their daily duties today as the grass that borders the footpath has been cut. The spoils of their human labour are strewn all over the place like debris in an Iraqi battlefield though. The repulsive smell of the pungent freshly-cut grass would certainly cause Jayden unease; he would hold his nose and then flee across the road to get as far away from the odour of rotting grass as quickly as humanly possible. I seriously doubt he languished on the side of the road waiting for his ride suffering in silence, which is the reason why I am now walking the footpath alone. After boarding the air-conditioned hulking carriage which slowly glides toward the centre of Melbourne, a sense of discontent overtakes me, and I feel pissed off that Jayden wouldn't accompany me to the cinema. It works out for the best though as I am determined to go home and complete all my required reading. I will finalise my required studies and complete the associated assignments that have been thrust upon me and not just fuck around. I am going out tomorrow evening with Shaun to see the movie anyway, so I shouldn't be so pissed off, but I am.

The walk home is uneventful. I spend my idle time responding to messages and catching up on my social media feeds. Doing my best to finalise all the outstanding digital conversations en route to Southbank, or at least get to the point that my presence will not be missed is my priority. I author the last message to Austin saying that I miss his smell and articulate that I really enjoyed the brief time that I spent with him earlier. I visualise Austin smiling as I tap to send the message. Quickly, I delete the last few words and alter it; revising it to say that I am looking forward to taking him out on Friday. Abandoning my digital life, I attach my phone to the charging cable and toss it on my unmade bed. The serenity around me produces a yawn as I stop and stare at the Melbourne skyline from the window. I leave my bedroom door open for a change, knowing that I will not be disturbed. Enjoying the whole of our home by myself for a change affords me the luxury for the first time in over a week to casually strip off my school uniform and be naked. My clothes are haphazardly tossed on top of the growing mound of worn apparel near my bed. Not satisfied with the look of the mass of garments on the floor, I gather them up and take them to the laundry room and place the mound next to the sink. I organise the pile of filthy apparel that needs the attention of our part-time cleaner after noticing Austin's attire was deposited in the sink as per my request earlier. I find his white boxer briefs after some searching; they were rolled into a wad and hidden inside his grubby trousers along with his dirty socks and the shirt that he abandoned this morning. Smiling, I take a very keen interest in his Bonds underwear. I hold them at eye-level only to discover they are riddled with yellow stains. The once fresh cum from presumably this morning has dried and the cotton fabric has stuck together. I am disappointed that he would not watch him pleasure himself after I woke up looking for some action but then I recall an excruciating headache that I was enduring and assume that it would have distracted me sufficiently from his equally throbbing cock. Assuming again that everything is going to work out for the best and if I am patient, my brain knows that if I am going to have a sexual relationship with Austin. It will happen naturally and I know that I shouldn't rush him or even myself for that matter. After quickly smelling the front of his underwear and not noticing a scent, I wad it up and push the underwear inside of the leg of the trousers that he left behind. When the cleaner sorts the dry cleaning from the laundry, I wonder if she will be shocked. She has seen my soiled jocks numerous times before, so I doubt there will be many surprises but you never know. I always use my underwear to clean up the mess up after jerking off which leads me to believe that our cleaner is used to gifts like this.

I stride to the kitchen wearing my birthday suit to retrieve a bottle of sparkling water. The cold bubbly liquid revitalises my innards and after stopping to quietly look at the Melbourne skyline outside again for some time and giving my arse a good scratching, I return to my room and close my bedroom door. It is finally time to study. I read and write diligently for hours unencumbered by technology, teenage angst or the various characters that manage to occupy the virtual centre stage in my young life. When I finish reading the last published line of *The Metamorphosis* I spontaneously laugh out loud. I grasp what my father was referring to when making the comparison between the main character in the novella who is called Gregor, the travelling salesman who morphs into an insect for no apparent reason. When Gregor changes, his family feels a sense of relief. The father figure in the novella fires the cleaning lady, which I secretly wish my father would do to our domestic help since she seems so lazy. The final scene of the story demonstrates how the character Greta has managed to grow up to be a fine-looking babe, which makes her parents go about the task of finding her a husband. Greta could be compared to Austin as he would look like a well-figured lady if I dressed him up like a girl, just with better hair I muse. My mind wanders again and I think of how I want to ravage Austin and explore his various orifices, but quickly banish my lurid thoughts by returning to the kitchen to retrieve another bottle of sparkling water. Sipping from the bottle whilst looking at the Melbourne skyline yet again makes me feel claustrophobic in the apartment. I feel restless and deduce if I want to go for a run, I have an hour until the sun sets completely. I decide to get some exercise, so I can really work up an appetite and consider what Kafka wrote about in a much simpler time in far greater detail. After jogging to my bedroom room and dressing in clean shorts and one of my *5 Seconds of Summer* concert shirts, I slip on a pair of running shoes. Quickly transformed into a fitness fanatic, I jog out of the apartment after throwing the front door open, grabbing my keys in the process.

After fleeing from the boredom of the foyer of the building and thus the monotony of study, my run commences at the same place where James was struck by Austin with the cricket bat. The memory evokes a chuckle as I first replay the action in my head on repeat. Being unburdened by my phone and music with only the noises of the city to accompany me on my journey, my imagination reverts to Kafka and Gregor the insect. How its family came to terms with the ridiculous bug and its transformation has some correlation to my recent revelations about my sexuality. Thoughts then evolve to my other classes and ridiculous comments that were uttered by the lecturers today and how they apply a left-wing slant on every topic at my school. Whilst lost in my thoughts and being relatively amused, I run to Port Melbourne via the pedestrian footpath with relative ease. I wave at the café owner who recognises me whilst he stands on the outdoor platform of his Beacon Cove café puffing on a cigarette. I am positive that he is judging me, the Southbank teenage caffeine addict sprinting past him before I predictably turn sharply right and run towards Westgate Park. I am surprised that I have so much energy since I have consumed minimal carbohydrates today. My fuel sources are now solely dependent on adrenaline and the thoughts that my wildly active mind is not only devising but are processing in overdrive. At the perimeter of the nature reserve, I convert my fast run into a slow gait just so that I can spy on the bears that are hibernating inside their motorcars in the parking lot. I then take some time to watch the men wandering around aimlessly and pretending to look around innocently at the flora and fauna. Being far enough away not be noticed, I justify to myself that even if the Police were in the area on the prowl for lurid acts again and suddenly drag a pair of gentlemen from the protection of the trees and bush kicking and screaming, I legitimately look like I have been exercising since my hair, face and shirt are all saturated with sweat. The look of a shocked and mostly innocent teenage boy could be feigned very easily. Whether my motivation to come to this place was just to reminisce about what I could have had enjoyed the other day, which would have been an act of instantaneous gratification, or if it was to prove to myself that I am indeed patient is now an enigma. Noticing the position of the setting sun in the sky, I quietly predict that I have about twenty minutes until the sun fully sets. Having roughly six kilometres to run before I am home seems simple enough. Aspiring to beat the sun disappearing over the horizon, I will myself to abandon the observations of the human zoo and begin my run home. Retreating from the boundary of the nature reserve, I jog and then increase my pace to a run and follow the route that I originally took from Southbank like I have done now many times over the last week. I always knew that I was a creature of habit.

At the far end of Sandridge Beach, I observe a dispersed group of men who have stripped completely naked and are just hanging out on or around their towels or just wandering around aimlessly. Unlike the public toilets, this beach doesn't seem to be a place that you would hook up because of the lack of saltbush in the area and I think that maybe they just congregate there to look at one another slyly. They watch me running past and I wave in the general direction and one of them waves back. His penis sways in the same manner as his arm and it doesn't seem like any of these presumably gay blokes care that motorists, workers at the nearby Webb Dock, or even impressionable teenagers who are running past can see what they have on offer. Like the nude men, I feel a sense of freedom now that my sexuality is no longer captive like a penis in a Speedo. I continue running past the blokes who stand in the shallow water like fish, their oiled bodies perched in the same place so the setting sun shines its weak light on them as they look out over the bay with their hands clasped behind their backs.

My run takes me past barbeques and picnic rings on the foreshore that have always been abandoned when I have travelled past in recent days. I spot a few Muslim families congregated around food where meats are smoking, where the by-product of the hookah fills my lungs and I cough as I watch it be passed around so various burly men in board shorts can have a relaxed tote. The charcoaled meat smells delicious and my stomach begins to grumble as the muscled arms pass the hookah and the women in their headscarves and long robes pour drinks.

As I approach Beacon Cove once again, I wonder if the groups of the gay men and Muslims know whether they are each occupying their respective sections of the beach. It would be difficult not to notice the Muslims as they are rarely seen in Port Melbourne, and the smell of the hookah would give them away. Whether the Muslims realise there are a group of nude gays not far from them without a care in the world intrigues me. Without a god bearing witness, these two groups manage to carry on with their lives and enjoy themselves without any worry of prejudice. A sense of satisfaction overcomes me as I ponder the problems in the world and continue to run up the pedestrian footpath toward Melbourne and intentionally increase my rate of speed knowing that the sun is now waning on the horizon. I finally emerge near Crown Casino in Southbank, puffed and saturated in sweat and act as a wet piece of eye candy for the bored office workers of both sexes that have recently been liberated from their places of employ. I join these office workers along with the tourists and teenagers in walking down the promenade and eventually enter my residential tower at precisely the same time that day officially turns into night.

The silence in the apartment is once again welcomed as I strip off my wet clothes, including my saturated underwear and toss everything into the sink in the laundry room after abandoning my shoes on the floor. Without hesitating, I walk towards my bathroom and feel a sense of calm for a change as the soft beige carpet fibres brush against my sensitive ticklish feet in transit. I stand on the cold white tiles in the shower stall where cool water inevitably washes the sweat from my weeping body. After a quick shower and drying off, I experience a sense of contentment for the first time in ages as I walk around my room naked with my hands clasped behind my back, mimicking the men standing on Sandridge Beach, looking out into the distance towards Sandridge Beach.

Feeling isolated from the world for a change, I want to consult the local news on my laptop. After logging into Windows, my Google Inbox appears. I delete a few spam messages before spotting an e-mail from Lord Voldemort, my illustrious mother. It is a short e-mail where she expresses both her delight and elation that I contacted her and articulates a 'great desire' to meet up with me soon to chat. She suggests Thursday evening if I can manage to travel to her house if it is not too inconvenient, considering my studies and other important commitments of course. Being sensitive to the fact that she probably isn't in the best condition and silently wondering if she is even mobile, I quickly revert conforming that I look forward to visiting her home and ask her to send me the address along with the time that I should be expected. That was simple enough. I open a new tab in the Google Chrome browser and start to type the hyperlink for the amateur porn site that I like to look at daily, but the combination of fatigue, hunger, and pain in my lower legs catches up with me. This discomfort forces me to placate my overwhelming desire for food before I subject my cock to the rigours of my hand.

Knowing that I do not have to walk the runway in a fashion show tonight, I pull on a pair of pink shorts and a black singlet before literally jumping back on to my bed and grabbing my phone in one synchronised action. Having missed numerous calls and text messages from Mel concerns me as I first notice them on the phone display, and immediately ring her back. She probably wants me to pre-heat the oven or something equally important and I patiently listen to the ringing tone and pick at my teeth.

As soon as she answers, I quickly blurt out words. "Sorry I was studying and then running-"

She cuts me off mid-sentence. "It is okay. First, I don't want you to stress, because everything is okay."

"What do you mean? What happened?" My heart starts to race at the same rate as it was earlier when I was running.

"Your father and I were in an accident earlier. We were in the back of an Uber and it got hit by another car. We are banged up, but we will be just fine." Mel speaks with a monotone voice and I immediately wonder why my father hasn't rung me or sent a message. "Don't worry Chez."

"Where are you? I will come right now! How is Dad?" I really don't know what to ask as a million thoughts are racing through my head.

"We are at the Alfred Hospital. I won't lie to you Chez. He has a few injuries as he wasn't wearing his seatbelt. He was on the side of the car that got hit. He isn't in critical condition, so don't worry about him. He will be fine, but he will be in the hospital overnight as he has a few broken ribs and some internal bleeding." Mel continues speaking in a robotic monotonal voice. "He is asleep now, so I am going to stay here until he wakes up and then I will come home for the night. There isn't much point in you coming down here and sitting around at the hospital. It is best if you study and stay at home if you can manage it."

"Fair enough. Are you okay Mel?" It seems as if she rehearsed her speech regarding my father. In answering my question, I wonder if she will react with a bit more emotion.

"I am banged up, but I will be fine. I might walk up the street and have a glass of wine to take the edge off though." Mel laughs which makes me giggle. I know what bar she is referring to as the licensee remains on high alert for the Melbourne Grammar schoolboys walking in and will eject anyone that doesn't possess a state identification or passport to prove that they are of legal drinking age, unlike the vast majority of premises where I get away with boozing underage at least. "Did you have a good day? Have you had dinner?"

Even during the darkest of hours, Mel worries about me and remains upbeat. "My day sounds like it has been much better than yours so don't fuss about me. I haven't had dinner yet but I will grab a dodgy curry from Southgate or something. I will be fine." I grind my teeth together and tears start to well up in my eyes. I wipe the wetness away with my free hand. "Ring me if anything changes please, and maybe I will see you later tonight."

"Otherwise first thing tomorrow morning. Love you, Chez." She ends the call before I can tell her that I love her too. She probably wasn't expecting it and is noticeably distracted however knowing that she will be enjoying some wine does put a smile on my face. My mind drifts back to lunch and whether any of the ambulances that drove past us and up the ramp to the Alfred Emergency Room accommodated my father as a guest. Both my frustration and anger levels rise when I consider that I was eating coleslaw and gossiping whilst Daniel was most likely being hauled into the hospital in the same complex that I was so innocently enjoying my lunch at.

Without bothering to read the missed messages or reviewing what other information I missed during my epic afternoon of study and exercising, I ring Jayden. I assume that he will be shocked to see my name appear on his phone since I rarely ring anyone unless it is important. "Hey mate. What are you doing?"

"Just finished reading bloody Kafka. It was so bullshit. What are you doing?" Jayden is chewing on something, which makes my stomach rumble again and then tears form in my eyes and quickly run down my cheeks as I sob.

I sniff. "Fuck man, I really just need someone to talk to. There is just so much happening now and with my father being in the hospital, I am just feeling numb." I snort back mucous and then wipe my eyes with my arm. "Just so much shit has happened so quickly, I am just not coping." It is hard for me to admit this as I am the one that people look to as being in control all the time. I internalise so many emotions though, that at times I do break down and when I do, they get out of hand. "I just don't know what to do."

Jayden continues to chew on something. "What do you mean your father is in the hospital, is he okay?"

"Supposedly he is. I just spoke with Mel, but they were in a car accident." I move the phone as far away from my face before sniffing again and then return it to my ear after wiping my eyes with the back of my arm again. "He is going to be okay but I guess he is all fucked up."

"I will come around to yours now. Is Austin there?" Jayden asks awkwardly.

"No, why would he be?" I know what Jayden is trying to insinuate, but I blow it off. "I haven't seen him since lunch. Why?" I can't help but sniff again.

"Oh okay. Give me thirty minutes' mate. I will come around. See you soon." Jayden ends the call and I take a long deep breath. I shouldn't be feeling so emotional since everything is technically under control, but all the little things spinning in their places like tops are poised to fall awkwardly.

I roll off my bed and stumble to the laundry room again. I search the pockets of the trousers that I wore today looking for money. Not finding any polymer notes, I sigh when I recall spending all of it buying lunch. Why does everything have to be so goddamned expensive in Melbourne? I find a one-dollar coin and a twenty-cent piece in Austin's trouser pocket. I consider going to the local market to buy a tin of cat food to eat as that is all I can seemingly afford. From memory, there isn't much in the refrigerator. Fresh food is purchased by Mel daily is then consumed leaving the refrigerator bare, but I am sure that I can find a can of soup or something equally boring if I search hard enough. I have a light bulb moment and remember that there is money in my father's drawer. I subsequently wander into his room and look through his nightstand and find the wad of fifty dollar notes that I previously returned on Saturday. Spotting the corner of the plastic bag that contains a mixture of cocaine and flour protruding from under some papers, with a couple of watches discarded on top of the heap acting as paperweights, I remove two fifty-dollar notes and remove the now familiar small plastic bag. I am positive that my father will not care that I have borrowed some money especially considering the circumstances. The hybrid blow will stimulate me and perhaps reverse my morose feelings that have amassed in the last few minutes as I walk to the kitchen with my score.

Sifting through the refrigerator yields nothing appetizing or even appealing to eat. Bottles of water, beer, cider and jars of pre-made sauces occupy the shelves and compartments. I remove a bottle of apple cider and pop the top and it and drink it in thirty seconds flat. Feeling partially refreshed, I repeat the process with a second bottle. My body thanks me for providing it with hydration after the long agonising run. I open the wine refrigerator and remove a bottle of 2007 Rusden 'Black Guts' Shiraz, which was produced in the Barossa Valley and then hunt for a corkscrew. Like the cash from the drawer, my father will not miss a bottle of this wine. There are many cases of it in the storage cage in the basement. The corkscrew grants me access to the magenta-coloured treasure which technically I am not allowed to drink. Wine from the Barossa Valley is off-limits to my young supple lips and I knowingly violate the standing house rule. I fill a wine glass and then take refuge on a bar stool in the kitchen. After a few slurps, I retire to the living room with the glass and play the latest album by *The xx*. I become lost in my dark incongruous thoughts whilst staring out the window listening to the moody music and sipping wine. Fatigue begins to overwhelm me, and I decide to snort some of the leftover drugs from the plastic bag before Jayden turns up. Like an expert illicit drug user now, I replay the sniffing exercise after depositing a mound of the stimulant on the glass table and then manually craft it into two distinct lines with a business card. The obnoxious sound of the video intercom explodes much like my nose wants to with a sneeze after I hurriedly inhale the two lines of white powder that I fashioned. Assuming half of the stash is now flour, I double my previous intake which encourages me to squeeze my nose closed with my fingers and will myself not to sneeze after the drug ends up somewhere within my nasal cavity. The intercom bell buzzes again. I want to rip it off the wall to silence the horrible noise that it makes for all posterity. I find Jayden's smiling face on the video display and press the appropriate buttons granting him access to my floor without uttering anything. The remains of the white powdery substance rest on the table. I disguise it with the newspaper and make sure the small plastic bag is hidden under the broadsheet that Mel was reading earlier this morning. Feeling delighted that I have concealed my excesses, I open the front door at the same time the familiar 'ding' announces that the elevator has arrived and the lift doors open. My neighbours' exit into the corridor, followed by Jayden. I raise my glass in the direction of my middle-aged high-rise neighbours who I only ever see travelling between floors and they nod their heads before disappearing into their apartment. Jayden quickly walks past me and drops his backpack in the foyer before I let the door slam behind him.

"Getting into it so soon? Can I have a glass?" Jayden walks towards the living room and I follow. "So, what the fuck is going on mate? You look like shit."

My hair must look wild and my pink shorts and black singlet don't exactly match. I haven't attended to my general appearance since getting out of the shower. "Sorry to offend, but I went for a run earlier. What did you tell your mother?"

"If you can believe it, I told her the truth. I told her that Daniel and Mel were in a car accident and that I am going to hang out with you. She wanted you to come around to ours but I told her that you will not want to leave your air-conditioned castle in the sky, which is probably true." I follow Jayden into the kitchen and watch him retrieve a wine glass from the overhead cabinet. "Wow, shit from the Barossa Valley tonight, Jesus. You must be feeling like hell. When you talk to your parents next tell them my mother sends them love, hey?"

Innocence Waning

After Jayden pours a glass of wine, we tap our respective glasses together in unison. "That I will do." After taking a drink and sniffing at the product in the glass, I continue. "I e-mailed Voldemort earlier and she responded. I am going to go see her on Thursday." Knowing this is an additional stressor that is now weighing on my mind, I drink the rest of the wine in my glass and then quickly fill it again. Jayden is studying the label of one of the empty bottles of cider that I previously abandoned on the counter.

"That is great news mate. I think if you see Voldemort it will be good for you. I guess you aren't going to do any study tonight then?" Jayden drinks the last drops of cider that were left in a bottle which I assumed that I previously vacated. "Cheers!"

"Funny you say that. When I got home, I did about three hours of study. I read the Kafka shit and then went for a run. When I got back, I felt relaxed and in control of my life and then all of this shit happens." I look at my hair in the mirrored splashback and then feel embarrassed as it looks ridiculous. Jayden will not care though and I have nothing to prove by not being suitably dressed and properly preened around him. "I am waiting for James to unexpectedly turn up for round two of batting practice or some shit like that just to complete this shit of a day." I look at Jayden and chuckle.

"Should I even mention Kafka?" Jayden smiles knowing that he will get a reaction. "What did you think of that shit?"

"Fuck Kafka! I have done enough study for the day and I have every intention of going to school tomorrow just to tell everyone what I think of that ridiculous man and the insect. I will stop around at the Alfred and see my old man at lunch if he is still there. It didn't sound like he is getting out of the hospital anytime soon though so maybe you want to come with?" I pick up my wine glass and the bottle and walk into the living room. I let gravity take hold of me and fall on the lounge, resting my feet on the newspaper that is concealing what is left of the stash of cocaine. I am not sure of how Jayden will react if he sees the white powder, especially since it has only been a few days since we indulged upon the graces of the original score. "I can't believe that bloke turns into a filthy insect. I wonder if that is what Daniel meant about Austin's father."

"Wait, what?" Jayden turns from the window and gives me his undivided attention. "What do you mean?"

"Last night Daniel told Austin that the salesman character in *The Metamorphosis* reminds him of Austin's father. There were some interesting themes in that story. For old Gregor, the filthy insect to meet his demise after being a horrific figure in the lives of that family is rather comical really. I know that my father hates Kevin McGuire with a passion, but when I read the story, it was like various characters in the silly book all came to life. Austin could easily be the Greta chick." I turn up the volume of the music and then carefully place both of my feet on the floor, making sure that I do not move the newspaper.

"Speaking of a bitch." Jayden laughs and puts his feet on the glass table. "Are you actually taking this so-called relationship with Austin seriously or are you just playing with his little insect-like mind? I was watching him stare at you today with his protective big brown bug eyes. He looked like a kangaroo caught in headlights." I notice Jayden is not drinking much wine, but I reach over and grab the bottle so that I can top up his glass like a good host and more importantly pour myself another round.

I take a moment to look out the window and then close my eyes and listen closely to the lyrics of the song that is playing whilst I think about the question regarding Austin. "Fuck my nipples are as hard as a rock and they hurt. Sorry mate." The look on the face of Jayden quickly turns from that of a relaxed amused teenager to one of pure shock and horror as I pull off my black singlet and toss it onto the living room floor. I briefly look down at my nipples and touch each of them with the side of my wine glass and wince. I don't understand why they are so sensitive. "I admit, my new relationship with Austin took me by surprise, especially after I woke up today and realised everything that happened yesterday was not just some silly teenage dream."

"Did you fuck him? Sorry to ask but you were looking really tired this morning mate. Hell, you still do!" Jayden continues to probe me for information after taking a sip of the fine wine. "I just figured that you had a long night of pounding his arse. I can't imagine him putting his dick into you, and I am not even really sure if I want to know the answer tell you the truth." Jayden takes another sip of wine and sets the glass on the table carefully. "Can I change the music? This stuff is making me want to cut myself." Jayden reaches for the remote control before I have a chance to answer.

I swirl the contents inside my glass and inspect the marks that my lips have left on the rim before carefully setting it down on the newspaper. "Go for it mate. Find something more upbeat and I will get us some cheese. I think we have some left." I walk into the kitchen and begin to rifle through the refrigerator desperately hunting for some sharp smelling cheddar knowing that will complement the earthy taste of the red wine. Finding a block of cheese next to the duck eggs, I remove it and find a knife. I use it to slice the hard cheese on a cutting board and then go on the hunt for some crackers, which we seemingly have an endless supply of. The music being played changes in the distance and I pause for a few seconds until I recognise that it is *The Smiths Greatest Hits*. I organise the crackers and slices of cheese into asymmetric lines on a plate, attempting to appear somewhat civilised like a gracious host. Returning to the living room, I see Jayden lounging back comfortably and reading the newspaper, taking an unexpected interest in an article about union corruption. He doesn't look up at me as I place the plate of cheese and crackers on top of the newspaper that is covering the errant powder and the small plastic bag, which was left exposed when Jayden took an interest in reading the news. I take a deep breath and then let gravity take control of my body yet again.

"So, did you fuck him? You never answered." Jayden loses interest in the article or at least feels it is not as interesting as my sex life. "Spending the night with the boy on the same day that you get together hey. You move fast, Chezdon. I am proud of you." Jayden returns his wide blue eyes to the newspaper.

"Believe it or not, we didn't have any sexytimes last night. I actually fell asleep after he put on one of the damned *Harry Potter* movies." I carefully reach for my glass of wine and grab a morsel of cheese, which I consider the start of my long overdue dinner. "It wasn't like I didn't try, but I found his cum stained underwear this morning. I guess he got off whilst I showered." I chuckle and swallow the piece of cheese and drink wine.

"Too much information mate, but it is still good to know. I know it has been a hard day for you, between Voldemort, that car accident and even Austin's shit. I can understand why you probably want a few drinks to take the edge off, but you should probably give the drugs a miss mate." Jayden places the newspaper on the table next to the plate of cheese carefully. "Just take it easy. I don't want to have to visit both you and your old man in the hospital tomorrow."

I lower my head and cover my eyes with my hand as the tears begin to well up again and I manage a single sniff. After a few deep breaths, I regain my composure and take a big whiff of the wine from the glass. "Sorry mate. I was just feeling emotional earlier and you know that doesn't happen often. Not only a minute ago, but after I heard the news about Daniel. I am really overwhelmed which is hard to admit. I was thinking that a little of the blow would just bring me back up." I vanquish the wine left in my glass and reach for another cracker and a piece of cheese. Jayden is staring at me which makes me feel uncomfortable which encourages me to keep talking. "Austin described me as a sun burning red hot with sexual energy and he doesn't want to have sex until we have at least had one date and that isn't happening until Friday." I eat the cracker and slice of cheese and wash it down with some more wine.

"What happened yesterday wasn't a date?" Jayden then grabs a piece of cheese, sits back and crosses his legs, inspecting me. "You are red hot every day of the week mate. I mean from a temperature aspect. It is like you are never cold."

My mind continues to race as I take another sip of wine and reach for another morsel of cheese. "Yesterday was more of a confessional over chicken at the Nandos, then of course cricket batting practice on the street followed by the courtroom of Judge Judy up here later with the coppers." The sharp taste of the cheese cleanses my palate and I reach for another slice. "Honestly, I am just so horny! Look at my nipples, why else would they be so sensitive that they hurt?" Jayden rolls his eyes and then rubs his arm. I can hear his fingernails scratching the epidermis. Another sip of wine is followed by another piece of cheese and the flavours oddly placate me. "When I was on my run earlier, I thought of going into the public toilet with the hope that someone would suck me off if you can believe it." I return the glass of wine to my lips and sip it very slowly so I can observe Jayden's reaction.

"Goddamn mate that is funny. Since we are telling bizarre stories, not long ago I was having a shit in the toilet at the cinema. Some bloke in the stall next to me was having a wank as I saw the shadow on the floor going crazy. I decided to get off too as it was so exciting. Just as I was about to blow, the shadow play next to me stopped, but I carried on, so I stood up and blew all over the door of the shitter. When I sat down on the toilet again, I looked up only to find the bloke next door watching me over the wall of the cubicle. I didn't mind giving a show, but that doesn't mean that I was running back to the same cinema the next day, literally, to do it all over again." Jayden decides to finally put another mouthful of wine in him after conveying his exciting yet sordid story. "You aren't the only one that is horny mate." Morrissey continues to sing a tale of woe through the speakers.

I move the plate of cheese, exposing what is left of the cocaine and the small plastic bag. Leaning forward to pick up the business card that I previously used to organise my lines with, I begin to slowly drag the powder back into an organised mound. "I need to get this back in the bag and add some more flour." I giggle, whilst I rake the white powder into a centralised location. "Now that is a story mate. Jesus Christ!"

Jayden moves quickly and sits next to me whilst carefully holding his wine glass by its stem. He smells like lavender. "Let me help you with that." He takes the business card from my hand after tearing the article on union corruption from the newspaper.

"Hell, I thought you were going to indulge." I flash Jayden a cheeky smile and then lean back as he carefully brushes the stimulant and flour blend onto the torn piece of newspaper. He then slowly transfers it all into the small plastic bag. "You are missing out mate, we can have a party tonight." I smile at Jayden again and place my hand on his knee. "Have some wine." With my hand lingering on Jayden's knee I reach for the bottle of wine and top up my glass and then his. "Fuck! I am so bloody hot!"

"Chezdon, you aren't a bad looking boy, I will admit." Jayden stands up and walks into the kitchen and I follow him. He opens the overhead cabinet door near the refrigerator where the flour is kept and repeats the process that we undertook last Saturday and replenishes Daniel's drug supply. "Or are you talking about your body temperature? You are an arrogant fucker." I watch him spoon a small amount of flour into the plastic bag and then seal it. He tosses it in my direction. "You look like Alex Rider when you don't have a kilogram of product in your hair."

I quickly push the small bag of drugs into my pocket whilst walking to the climate control panel on the wall. I press the down arrow, commanding the air conditioning to cool the apartment further. "No, dickhead, I just feel like I am burning up. I know that I am fucking attractive though. Who the hell is Alex Rider?" As I laugh uncontrollably, Jayden follows me into the living room again. "What class is he in?"

"He is some blond teenage James Bond." Jayden mysteriously proclaims. "Just a character in some movie that I saw on television the other day."

Feeling intrigued, I look for my phone and then realise that I left it in my bedroom. I walk as fast as I can to retrieve it. With the fully charged Samsung technology resting safely in my sweaty hand, I read an update from Mell which says that my father is doing well and that she will be coming home soon. More importantly, I am advised that I should not stress and to continue to study and not worry. A further message from Austin expresses his confidence that I am getting a fair amount of study completed since I have gone quiet from the digital world. He articulates his desire for me to 'be happy' and from his observations, it seems that I am much happier when he is around which in turn makes him happy. After scrolling through messages from others that I randomly communicate in my daily life, my heart immediately begins to beat faster when I see a message is from Shaun. He declares that there is an additional screening for *Woman in Gold* tomorrow night at

9:15 PM and he is hoping that we can see that session just in case he must be at work longer than planned. I forgot about this engagement and feeling a heightened sense of awareness, I return quickly to the living room to find Jayden watching television and chewing on his fingernail. "Score! It is time to party arsehole!" I exclaim and then plot the quickest route to my wine glass and pick it up. "Tonight is going to be an amazing night. Should I just order pizza?" I start to construct the sentences in my head, so I can tell Jayden about my plans with Shaun before he interrupts.

"Any news about Daniel?" Jayden looks concerned as he watches me hold my phone. "Pizza sounds good if you are going to order some."

"Oh yeah, he is doing fine it seems. Mel will be back in a few hours." I spit out the words and then take a much-needed drink. "My old man is as tough as nails. Don't worry about him." I swipe repeated looking for the Domino's Pizza application on my phone.

"Mate, right now I am worried about you. You are all over the place." Jayden continues to watch me intently which makes me feel self-conscious and distracts me from ordering pizza. I spend a few seconds looking at the carpet as I devise a witty yet apt response so hopefully, he stops this line of questioning. "Just take it easy."

Jayden's request motivates me to take a deep breath and reboot my internal operating system. I ignore both my intense hunger and endless thirst and opt to delay taking a much-needed drink. I simply place the glass on the table and sit next to my best friend. "You lied to me," I say with the most serious face that I can muster.

"When? What do you mean?" Jayden quickly forms an incredulous expression with his mouth and decides that wine will quench both his thirst and mirth after my question. "What are you talking about, mate?"

"You told me the other week that you fucked Daria. You told us when you decided to get into the coke the other night." I pause and give Jayden a cheeky look again and squint my eyes, so he can briefly consider his relationship with his girlfriend. "You then said that you never had sex. So, what is it?" After Jayden's comments about taking it easy, I intentionally bring the glass of wine to my nose, take a prolonged sniff of it and then return the glass to the exact spot on the table that I previously found it. Jayden is watching me like a vulture would roadkill so this token act I suspect will placate him. Given that I haven't heard any commentary or associated drama regarding Jayden's girlfriend in a few days, it makes sense to query him, if only to distract me from the melodrama that is playing out in my life. I reach for a piece of cheese and place it carefully on my tongue, closing my mouth in noticeable stages.

Curiously I watch Jayden grab his glass and quickly drink the wine contained in the beautiful vessel. Looking nervous, he urgently reaches for the wine bottle and pours it. "Who cares. I didn't fuck her. I just didn't want you blokes judging me." He intentionally takes a dramatic pause and looks me up and down. "I am really surprised that Austin didn't put out especially if you just lounged around in your pink shorts and just played with your nipples in front of him."

Feeling like I am on fire with my heart thudding at one thousand beats per minute, my minimal dress and slutty appearance have become a distant memory. I intentionally touch one of my nipples and wince again before swallowing the small slice of cheese in my mouth and take a gulp of wine. "You know mate, Austin may be like one of the hottest guys in Melbourne, hell, maybe Australia, but you are the one that is fuckable." During my confessional, I set the glass of wine down delicately. I lean toward Jayden and try to make my lips connect with his but he uses his arms to push me away.

"Chezdon, stop! Mate, stop! I mean it!" Jayden simultaneously shouts at me and attempts to push me again as I try to advance on him with the hopes that I can break his defences. I can't manage to get my mouth to his despite launching a German-style blitzkrieg in the end. "Goddamnit stop, Chezdon! Just get away from me!" His western front fends off my attack and I retreat into the grasp of my lounge and wallow in the disappointment of my defeat. I turn to my old friend, the glass of wine which always accepts the offer of my soft lips without any fuss. "Mate, I really think that you need to calm down and think about taking a break from the bloody wine and drugs. Obviously, you are fucked up right now. Just calm down."

I laugh and hold the glass so it is gently touching my chin. "I am not fucked up. Far from it, mate. Tell me that you haven't thought just once about having sex with me." My body freezes in place as my eyes lock onto Jayden's face as he takes a sudden interest in the television screen. "I mean we have jerked each other off before, what is the harm in doing something else? Hell, you have tried to kiss me in the past."

Jayden quickly drinks what is left in his glass and then reaches for the bottle. Seeing that it is empty and not saying a word, he walks to the kitchen, far away from my intense inquisitive stare. In his absence, memories return and flood my consciousness. I remember watching a particularly hot video online of an abnormally hung bloke putting his dick up the arse of some woman who shouted that she 'wants cock' causes my own dick to stir within my pink shorts as I replay the video in my head. Then remembering seeing Jayden's bulge and how it felt when I first caressed it when he was happy for me to liberate his penis, so I could jerk him off earlier in the year, quickly gives me a raging boner. Not long ago he had no qualms with me unbuttoning his skinny jeans and then stroking his throbbing dick, which quickly shot a hot load of cum. He then returned the favour. Jayden shuffles to the living room as I hear the metal cap being screwed off a wine bottle. As Jayden fills my empty glass, I grab a pillow and put it on my lap so my excited state is not revealed. "So Chezdon, what would you want to do?"

I thought that he would just ignore my proposition. He appears lost in thought as he returns to watching the talking heads on the television and sipping wine. Not knowing what to say, I shrug my shoulders. "What would you want to do Jayden?" I then find some interest in the muted political commentary on the television with Morrissey continuing to wallow in misery over the speakers. I find the modest amount of the wine that Jayden poured to be refreshing as I wait patiently for my best friend to respond. I find it difficult to keep my eyes in focus and hope that my elevated heart rate metabolises the alcohol in my body faster and take a deep breath.

"You make me laugh mate. As if! I need to piss." Jayden walks from the living room and towards the guest bathroom. I push the red pillow resting on my lap hard into my crotch, willing it now by force to succumb to my will. I try to focus on the imagery from Syria that is being broadcast on Sky News instead of the talking heads, which oddly calms my penis quickly. After additional deep breaths and spending time trying to focus my eyes yet again, I realise that I should at least put Austin's dirty clothes, including his cum stained briefs into the washing machine just in case he comes over before Friday. I follow Jayden's path and stumble towards the laundry room.

Walking past the guest bathroom, I faintly hear a muffled gasp, but with *The Smiths* still playing through the speakers not far away, I stop and pause next to the closed door. I attempt to ascertain what is happening and more importantly verify that Jayden is masturbating. I briefly hear yet another stifled gasp followed by a deep breath which confirms my suspicion and blood quickly rushes to my cock. I place my ear at the door and listen to Jayden pleasuring himself. He must assume with the music playing that even if I walked past the guest bathroom that I would not hear him jerking off. The drugs and wine give me courage as my heart beats so strongly that I at first, I believe it will burst from my chest at any second.

Knowing that there is no lock on the guest bathroom door, I throw it open to see Jayden's bare white arse facing me as he quickly ceases masturbating. "What the fuck? Get out of here!" He squats and tries to pull up his skinny jeans without exposing his manhood to me as he shouts out his demand again and more expletives. "Get the fuck out of here. Leave me the fuck alone cunt!"

I take two quick steps towards Jayden and place my hands on his exposed cold thighs as he once again demands that I leave him alone and repeats the same boring expletives and demands that I leave. He starts to masturbate slowly as my hands move from his thighs. I squeeze each of his exposed arse cheeks with some force. Jayden begins to vigorously flog his penis as he substitutes his demands for me to leave with loud moans. Following my instincts, I fall to my knees and spread his butt cheeks apart so that I can inspect his pink hairy arsehole for the first time. Strangely, I have wanted to look closely at one for some time and then wonder how easy it would be for me to insert my dry cock into it. Either because Jayden feels self-conscious with me inspecting his holiest of holes or because he is confident that I will accept what he offers, he shuffles in place and turns around to face me. I pull his skinny jeans and underwear down, bonding his ankles. His hard cock ends up resting a mere centimetre from my face. I place my hand on his wrist and gently guide both it and his hand from his schlong so I can look at his dick. I casually smell and then lick his ball sack. My hand then guides his five inches of uncut flesh into my mouth and Jayden lets out another prolonged moan and taking the cue, I squeeze his balls as I greedily accept his manhood into my mouth repeatedly. I use both of my hands to squeeze his arse cheeks as I pull his body as close as he can possibly get to my face. Jayden screams as he grabs the back of my head and pulls my blond hair out of my scalp. My best friend forces my face against his crotch as his haemorrhaging dick blasts cum down my throat. Fortunately, the drugs have opened my sinuses; my body remains oxygenated as Jayden fills both my throat and mouth with his seed. I gulp it down as fast as I humanly can and nearly choke which causes my hands to squeeze his arse cheeks with as much power as I can muster. As I continue to swallow and gently suckle on his hard cock as an afterthought, my index finger finds his arsehole and I attempt to push it inside of him. Jayden makes a weird squealing noise and then quickly pulls my head off his dick. A drop of his cum falls onto my knee as I look up at him and see his blue eyes curiously watching me. "I like how it tastes." I smile.

I watch cum begin to ooze and immediately place my lips on the tip of his pink cockhead and lick it for insurance against any further assault on me or the floor. He squeals again and jumps in shock. "Chez, no, it is too sensitive." Jayden squats down to pull up his underwear, however, I grab his face and try to kiss him again. "No! not with cum on your lips." Jayden laughs and I quickly not only understand but also appreciate his apprehension. I watch him first pull up his blue boxer briefs and then his skinny jeans up far enough to cover his penis, but not his dark brown pubic hair.

I stand up and our eyes quickly meet. "I guess we both finally got our wish, we got off in the men's toilet." I chuckle as if needing to have small talk will both diffuse the awkward situation but also give me some sort of guidance as to what to do next.

Jayden brushes my bare chest with his left hand and uses his right hand to feel the bulge concealed by my pink shorts. I eagerly watch his hand move down my moist chest and then force its way behind the elastic waistband of both my shorts and underwear and grab onto my hard cock. "Let's go into your bedroom." He then abandons my dick and quickly walks past me with his skinny jeans still unbuttoned.

The taste of cum evolves into a metallic flavour across my palate. I decide to detour to the living room and quickly eat two slices of cheese. I wash it down with the rest of my wine before collecting our wine glasses and the bottle and then traverse into my room, slamming the door closed behind me.

Jayden is casually sitting on the edge of my bed and appears bored. "If you use some mouthwash, you can kiss me if you still want to." Without making eye contact, he smiles and starts to inspect the carpet again. Taking the hint, I walk into my bathroom and find the bottle of purple Listerine and gargle with it. Its harsh flavour is usually bearable however when mixed with the aftertaste of cheddar cheese, red wine and cum makes me gag. I expel the mouthwash into the toilet and keep everything else in me down and quickly return to Jayden without taking the time to flush.

Standing in front of Jayden as he first inspects the noticeable bulge in my pink shorts only centimetres from his face gives me the courage once again after his invitation to lean down and press my lips against his. After a millisecond, he opens his mouth wide enough to allow my tongue access and I begin to explore the inside of his mouth. I simultaneously use my body weight to push him down on my bed and use my hand to feel his thigh as I grind my moist body against his. Although our tongues dance for a matter of minutes as my cock pushes up against his which has returned to life, at first it seems like minutes and then hours of bliss. After pulling off his shirt, my hands once again expose his hard dick to the conditioned air whilst I continue to pass my tongue over every millimetre of his mouth, tongue, cheeks and teeth. I go back down for seconds and begin to lick and suck on his rock-hard penis again and he squeals so I assume that I am doing something right. When he tries to remove my head from his male organ a mere minute later, I know he is going to orgasm yet again. I do not allow him and instead, permit a few drops of cum to drizzle into my mouth. His utterances of blasphemy amuse me, and he must use considerable force to push my head off his cock as he orgasms for the second time. I collapse on the bed next to him and gaze into his blue eyes. "Fuck man! That was hot."

Jayden turns his stare to the ceiling and takes a deep breath. He sits up and feels my bulge again before quickly pulling up on both my pink shorts and briefs and exposes my cock. I feel the air blowing from the vent above on my penis and then the deoxygenated air that he blows from his mouth onto the tip of my circumcised manhood. I can't help but watch with great anticipation as he examines my dickhead before I express my gratitude with a loud moan when he envelopes my shaft with his hot and humid mouth. His head begins to rise and fall on my cock like a well-oiled machine. He grabs my single testicle hard and I squirm. It doesn't take long until I release a sharp gasp and when my breathing becomes laboured, I shoot semen into Jayden's mouth. He quickly spits my life force back up onto my chest and then falls back and licks my thigh. Appearing like he is sampling a new exotic cuisine from the Heston Blumenthal cookbook, he continues to watch my pulsating penis spit out the rest the sperm I have on reserve along with the associated by-product whilst licking his lips. "That didn't taste anything like I thought it would." Jayden looks up at me and then thrusts his body to the rear of the bed and takes a position on his back next to me.

"You never tasted yours?" I slur incredulously. "Yours tastes like a salty mango yoghurt."

Jayden chuckles and begins to inspect the ceiling once again as we both allow our penises to air dry courtesy of the cold recycled air that is blowing on us from the vent above. "No actually. Yours tasted like a salty well-done steak. It must be from all of the shit that you eat and drink." When there is silence, I gently grab my cock, which is still curiously erect and I take a deep breath. "Sorry, that probably wasn't the nicest thing to say after doing that."

I start to inspect the same plain area of the white ceiling that Jayden is staring at. "So, does this mean that you are going to tell me that you do in fact like guys or are we just experimenting?" I sit up and pull my underwear and shorts over my erect penis. I grab my glass of wine and fill it up before taking a few sips whilst Jayden considers his answer. I keep my back facing him, hoping he will not feel like I am putting him on the spot so that he may feel comfortable enough to share his wants and desires. I close my eyes and feel a bit dizzy and take deep breaths until Jayden begins to speak.

"You are just so hard to say no to Chez. I really don't think about guys. Like I don't notice them or go out of my way to check out Brad Pitt or anything, but I do think about you and having sex with you if that makes sense. Maybe I am just obsessed, you know I can get that way sometimes. Can I have my glass?"

I proceed to fold my hands in front of my face and chew on my thumbnail, squinting hard to control my world from spinning out of control. After another deep breath, I reach over and grab Jayden's glass and with some alacrity, turn around and hand it to him. His penis is still exposed and his belly button is not only filled with cum but there is a small amount smeared just under it. "I would so be with you over Austin." Jayden props himself up on my bed so he can hold the wine glass. "We don't have to be boyfriends as such or have that title, but we can enjoy the benefits." I appeal not only to my own desires but I try to read his mind.

Innocence Waning

Jayden tilts his head back far enough, so he can drink what is left in his wine glass without propping himself up. I reach over and grasp his flaccid penis and pull down the foreskin. I inspect his pink cockhead whilst he ponders the moment. My heart continues to race and I decide to placate my dry mouth with some more wine. The alcohol quickly vanquishes the taste of Jayden from my mouth and then the remains of the mouthwash which was lingering like a bad smell. The room starts to spin and I quickly get up and walk with grave intent to the bathroom. Wine, cheese and cum are spewed into the toilet as I make my last emergency call for the night into the porcelain telephone. After I heave again and have a few seconds to contemplate my position in life, I manage to slide one of the mirrored doors closed so that Jayden doesn't have to watch me beg for forgiveness or mercy at the altar. After additional heaving and sacrifices are made to the god that we swore to whilst engaging upon oral sex to, I feel controlled enough to reach over and close the other sliding door, finally giving me the illusion of privacy.

Slowly, I use the toilet bowl as a crutch and after rising to my feet and flush the evidence of my excesses for the day. I feel a sense of ecstasy as I splash cold water on my face repeatedly before greedily filling my tainted mouth with water direct from the tap. After spitting it in the sink and repeating the process a sense of calm overwhelms me. I wipe my eyes with a scrap of toilet paper and blow my nose in my drunken and drug-fucked state. I assume some of the cocaine has been expelled with my mucous and my anxiety curiously rises. Reasoning with myself that there should be enough of the original white power to give myself a much-needed kick so that my party can continue, I empty the contents of the small plastic bag on my bathroom counter and quickly snort it without any sort of plan. Knowing that the mixture is predominantly flour, I know I must uptake it all up my nose to get any sort of effect, which I quickly and methodically execute. After licking what is left of my father's stash from the countertop like a dog with a dry tongue, I find my black towel hanging next to me and wipe the white residue that has dispersed over the outside of my nose, face, lips and that which has affixed itself to my damp chest. After a swig of mouthwash and spitting it back into the toilet, I slide the bathroom doors open only to see Jayden asleep with his soft cock still exposed to the cold air blowing on him from above, pointing towards his belly button. Taking one last drink of wine for the night reminds me that it doesn't mix well with the mouthwash and once again I fight the desire to gag and spew. I forcibly shake Jayden, waking him up and encourage him to shimmy further up to the top of the bed. He obliges and rests his head on the pillow that Austin used just last night and as quickly as he woke up, returns to the land of Nod. I pull his jeans and underwear off and toss them on the floor and literally climb over his naked body, so I can rest my head on my own familiar pillow. Before passing out the body next to me rolls over to embrace me and I fall asleep smelling cherry blossoms.

Innocence Waning

14. **Out**

My eyes open wide and I am confronted by an eerie white haze. I try at first to comprehend the unnatural sound of banging in the distance and then attempt the complex task of trying to understand the muffled shouting of what I finally deduce as being a female voice. I close my eyes and will my dry tongue to lick my equally dehydrated lips and focus on the annoying thumping sound that drums in unison with that of the one inside of my head. Combined with an awkward heaviness within my chest, my recollections take me back to a time where I am floating in a heated pool at my former school in Sydney which leaves me confused. The pounding sound continues and when I first comprehend that my name is being shouted, I begin to scratch at the crust that has formed in corners of my eyes. My green windows to the world are finally able to focus on first the ceiling and then the television. As per usual in the morning, *Sunrise* is screening, and the chirpy disposition of the presenters manages to irritate me within a matter of seconds once I realise where I am. The door to my bedroom is then thrust open after the rhythmic banging and associated shouting ceases.

"Oh Jesus! Chezdon! Jesus!" Mel leaves my room as quickly as she entered it and slams the door behind her. "Get ready for school, we are leaving in thirty minutes!" It then takes several seconds which seem like minutes before I realise that Mel's shock would be attributed to Jayden's naked body lying face down next to me with his arm draped over my chest. The fact that I was also discovered nude with my morning erection prominently on display would have been equally unnerving for Mel and I finally comprehend my surrounds which supersedes how fatigued my mind and body currently feels.

After a few deep breaths, I feel as if I am once again living in the moment and jerk to the right so that I can shake Jayden vigorously until he stirs. "Good morning." Examining Jayden's bloodshot blue eyes makes me wonder if I look as bad as he does.

Jayden rolls over and doesn't feign any sense of shyness even with his erection on display. "Christ, I feel like shit." He places his forearm over his eyes. "Fuck, I don't want to go to school. Do you have anything that I can wear? Do you have any painkillers? I need some water." My best friend begins to moan.

The pounding on the door returns. "Chezdon, get up! Hurry up, I need to speak with you." Mel sounds aggravated as she again raps on my chamber door. "Get your arse moving!"

"I am! Stop hitting the door!" I shout at Mel as loud as I can muster. She would be able to detect my anguished torment and then I clear my throat. "I am getting ready!" I look over at my bedside table and find my phone, and it is out of power as usual. I plug it into the charger and quietly chastise myself under my breath for not ensuring that the silly device was powered the night before. If the alarm had woken us up I wouldn't have endured the embarrassing alternative. "Come on mate, we have thirty minutes to get our arses ready." I shake Jayden again however he doesn't shift the arm that is covering his eyes. As he is not bothering to acknowledge me, I take a moment to look at his hard cock which is convulsing; dancing in place like a nerd would in the corner of a room at a school function.

"No, fuck that!" Jayden rolls over onto his stomach again. "I am not going anywhere. You got me fucked up."

Feeling emboldened, I sit up and caress his cold bare white arse. Jayden doesn't move or say anything. "Come on mate, have a shower. Mel will kill us both if we claim we are too ill to go to school. She will also come back in here soon if she doesn't hear us moving about." I continue to stroke his buttocks like one would knead bread and then shift my weight so I am resting on Jayden's back. This frees my hands so they can spread his butt cheeks open in the same fashion that I did last night when everything started going out of control in the bathroom. He doesn't protest and remains silent whilst I inspect his pink hairy arsehole like it is a fig in the supermarket. I lean in close and inhale the smell of his arse crack and at first, I am confused that it smells more like my sweaty underwear after I have gone for a run instead of anything more nefarious. Fighting back the urge to try to fuck him with my erection that will not subside, I instead slap his bare arse as hard as I can which immediately leaves a red mark, and me with a sore hand.

"Fuck! That hurt you bastard!" Jayden jerks up and turns on his side so his back is facing me. I take the opportunity to slap his arse again as hard as I possibly can. "Fuck! I am getting up. Jesus. I feel like shit! Where are your painkillers?" Jayden slithers off the bed and gets to his feet. I watch him rub his red arse before stumbling into the bathroom and sliding the mirrored doors closed. "Find me some clothes, you bitch!"

The shower turns on. There is some further commotion in my bathroom as Jayden inventories the cabinet shelves no doubt looking for pills that he hopes will eliminate the pain caused by our excesses from last night. I take some interest in my phone once again and tap the encryption code so that it boots up and then toss it onto the table nonchalantly. Memories of the previous night overwhelm my thumping head; thoughts which mimic chickens returning home to roost. The chaotic recollections in my clouded mind encourage me to roll out of bed and then sort through my closet to find some clothes for Jayden to wear. I retrieve some boxer briefs not only for him but also ones for me to temporarily use to conceal my erection.

Innocence Waning

My mobile phone startles me as it begins to vibrate incessantly, alerting me to messages that I have little interest in reading. Finding clean components of the school uniform in my closet, I opt to wear shorts, so Jayden can wear the last clean pair of trousers that I have and then throw the clothes haphazardly on my sweat-stained bed. "Hurry up you fool!" I shout with little emotion to reinforce the perceived urgency and I hope that Mel is within earshot, so it at least appears that I have some motivation to move this circus along.

The water stops flowing from the shower stall and I use that as a cue to lay on my bed and to check my phone. I immediately send a text to Austin communicating my hope that he is having a good morning and to let him know that I look forward to seeing him at school shortly. Fortunately, I only missed a few messages from my new boyfriend and I am confident after reflecting on the chaos that I have created that my lack of participation in social media during the previous evening just demonstrates that I was being studious. I do know that I need to craft a story to tell him so most of the truth is anchored with fact.

Jayden finally slides the door open to the bathroom and I intentionally do not let my eyes drift towards him as he walks toward me. Being aware that my dick has calmed down, I shift off the bed leaving my phone on the charger as I walk past him and into the bathroom, not permitting myself to look at Jayden for fear that it may excite me again. "Did you find the painkillers mate?" I turn to close the sliding mirror doors just in time to witness Jayden drop his towel onto the floor next to my bed. I see the outline of a red handprint on his white arse waving me a fond farewell as I quickly slide the mirrored doors closed.

"Yeah, I did. All good!" Jayden shouts.

I take what would turn out to be a ten-second shower and spend the equal amount of time drying myself. I rush through my usual routine and prepare myself for the day ahead in a frenzy. In a matter of minutes, I am rushing back to my bedroom and getting dressed whilst Jayden nonchalantly does up his tie. I am dressed and throwing the door open to my bedroom before Jayden can say anything however in his debilitated state, I am not surprised that he doesn't provide a running commentary or attempt to make a few jokes.

Spotting Mel in the kitchen with a coffee in one hand and reviewing the 'Letters to the Editor' in the newspaper doesn't surprise me since it is a daily occurrence. "Hey." I shuffle past Mel and open the cabinet door and grab a red mug. "How is Daniel doing?"

Mel turns the page of the newspaper as I pour black coffee into the ceramic cup. "I never thought you would ask. I got home last night and went to your bedroom door, but I thought it would be best not to disturb you since I overheard carnal sounds coming from your room." I decide not to turn around and instead take time to sip the hot coffee, knowing that this is going to be an embarrassing conversation. "Chezdon." I hear the page of the newspaper turn again and then Mel sips her coffee before taking a deep breath. "I don't care if you have sex. You aren't a stupid teenager, but just do us the courtesy of keeping the zoo soundtrack to a minimum so I especially don't have to hear whatever deed you are up to. I know you thought you had the place to yourself, but just think about it." I continue to stand in place looking at the coffee in the mug, waiting for what some viewing a sitcom would consider the punchline. "Jayden, Austin, James. Do yourself a favour and pick one of the above. Your life will be much easier. Speaking of Jayden, let's go."

I quickly gulp what is left in my mug and place it in the sink. "Jayden!" I shout with authority and then jog to my room to retrieve my phone. Jayden is laying on my bed, dressed and seemingly ready to go. "Hurry up, we have to go."

Jayden sits up. "Is she pissed? Where is my bag?"

"By the front door from what I remember. She is fine, don't worry." Jayden then saunters out of the bedroom with no urgency and most likely no energy whilst I collect my books, papers and laptop and speedily force everything into my backpack. Mel starts to shout my name yet again and I run towards the front door which is open. I slam it closed and lock it with the key that I grab off the table as I make my quick exit whilst Mel scowls as me.

We get into the Cayenne and are quickly driven outside of the residential tower and on to the road. Without traffic, we will get to school on time but I keep my opinion about the clock and my thoughts on the matter to myself. "So how is Dad?" Mel looks at me whilst I stare at the red traffic light.

"Oh, I never told you, sorry. I was obviously distracted earlier. He is fine, he will be out of the hospital later today. You should go see him at lunch unless of course the two of you-" Mel pauses and considers her words carefully. "Have big plans to start happy hour early today. What the hell, Chezdon? What has gotten into you lately?" The traffic signal turns green and Mel presses the accelerator down until her foot touches the floor. The car jerks forward and Jayden moans in the backseat.

I turn around and stare at Jayden who is holding the side of his head as he looks out the window, no doubt feeling motion sickness with his hangover. "Stress, Mel." Mel looks at me as she turns onto St Kilda Road. "It just seemed like something to do you know, enjoy some wine last night to take the edge off."

Mel laughs out loud and scowls at me again which makes me feel so uncomfortable that I shift my body weight in my seat. "You need to get your shit under control Chezdon or else you will end up with a drinking problem. Remember in life, you need to do everything in moderation. Don't make me have to have this conversation with you again." Fortunately, the traffic lights all stay the colour green so Mel must focus on the road, other vehicles and pedestrians instead of giving me yet another dirty look. "So, are you two together now? I can't keep track." Jayden moans again.

"The complicated life of a teenager." I simply say to Mel, not knowing how to answer the question. Instead of responding, she chews on the inside of her cheek and focuses on driving us to school, weaving in and out of traffic before turning onto the usual slip road before stopping the car near the school gates. We quickly fare Mel well and converge on the footpath. Jayden appears pale as a ghost and unwell.

"Hold this." Jayden hands me his bag and places his hands on his hips. He slowly walks down the footpath. It is obvious he is taking deep breaths as the erratic ride in the car mixed with his hangover has made him queasy. Another group of boys walk past him and notice that he is not feeling well and most likely in an act of revenge for all the pranks and stirring that Jayden has been responsible for over the years, decide to give Jayden a hard time. The larger boy in the group grabs Jayden from behind and gives him in a bear-hug, effectively picking him up off the ground in the process. "Goddamnit, put me down!" Jayden shouts but the other boy just begins to shake him like he is a rag doll. "I am going to be sick!"

With the threat of spew being an unwelcome addition to the situation, Jayden is quickly dropped onto his feet and the group of boys walk past me smiling and laughing. I walk over to Jayden as he resumes his deep breathing exercise. "Are you going to be okay mate?" I place a hand on his shoulder and suddenly he jerks his body around and walks away from me.

Once on the school grounds, we go different ways and walk to our respective classes. After suffering through boring lectures and quizzes most of the morning, I arrange to meet Austin before English Literature starts at one of the vending machines. I try in vain to insert a five dollar note into the currency slot however the machine rejects it. I stop uttering blasphemy under my breath and exchange mutterings to an enthusiastic question as Austin stands next to me. "Hey there. How are you?"

Austin smiles. Part of his blonde fringe drops down over his right eye and he hurriedly moves it aside. "Great!" Austin proclaims and removes a five dollar note from his pocket and inserts it into the vending machine. "What do you want? My shout."

I want to curse the contraption for not wanting my bank note however my thirst for something carbonated and sugary is overpowering me. "Just a Coke. Thanks, mate." With the credit available in the machine, Austin purchases two cans of Coke. He hands the first one that is ejected to me, which I quickly take and put on the back of my neck. "Feeling hot, are you?"

"Just a long night." Mental images of first dabbling with the white powder again and then fooling around with Jayden begin to bastardise my chain of thought. "Oh, sorry I didn't mention it earlier, but Daniel and Mel were in a car accident yesterday. That is why I went dark last night." It is the truth and I realise that it obviously does not add to the benefit of either of our young lives if I admit to the tomfoolery that happened with Jayden either now standing in front of the vending machine or ever for what it matters.

Austin's eyebrows rise and his blonde fringe drops down over his right eye again almost on cue. "Oh Jesus, are they okay?" He opens the can of soft drink and consumes it in what appears to be one gulp.

I put the can of Coke on my forehead. "Daniel is still in hospital but he will be okay. He is getting out later apparently. Do you want to go see him with me at lunch?"

"Yeah sure. That is really shit. But yeah. We should probably go to class now though." I open the can of Coke and start sipping on it before jogging to catch up to Austin. "Does this mean that you haven't read the Kafka stuff?" Austin looks at me in fear knowing full well that I might explode with unsavoury words about the celebrated author.

"I sure did. I finished reading that shit at about the same time I heard about the accident. I was a good little boy yesterday." Searching for affirmation for doing my studies promptly should put any wayward thoughts from Austin to rest, but to cover myself and tie up loose ends, I volunteer additional information. "Jayden ended up coming over and we got into the wine until Mel got home and we talked about life and times. I was feeling a heightened sense of mortality last night."

Austin tosses his empty can into the rubbish bin outside of our classroom before he enters and I emulate his action after finishing the rest of my drink. "Fair enough. Sorry to hear about that shit. Just know things will only get better." Austin looks at me and smiles before walking to his seat and past Jayden who is slouched at his desk looking exhausted. I walk over to him and crouch down.

"Hey mate, you don't look well. Do you need another painkiller or something?" Providing your peers with any sort of drugs is frowned on by the school for obvious reasons but now, the rule just seems to be ridiculous as do most of the rules that are subjectively applied to the student body.

"I reckon if I had the powdered painkiller that you took before you started in on the drinking last night, I would be feeling fine, but no, I will just suffer in silence." Our teacher enters the room and quickly places his possessions on the desk at the front of the classroom which is a signal for all of us to take our seats. "Thanks though." I quickly shuffle to my small desk and shove my bag under it. I let out a sigh which is loud enough for the two boys that sit in front of me to hear which causes them to turn around and stare at me, both with confused looks on their faces.

Perhaps it was because I just ingested sugar, but I suddenly feel revitalised. In what seems to take a matter of seconds, my hangover appears to have passed and the cobwebs in my head are dusted away. I first match the stare with the boy with the short curly brown hair that has braces and then finds interest in the red-haired boy that resembles the Ron Weasley character in the *Harry Potter* film that Austin was watching the other night. "Be yourself," I say to the red-haired boy. "Everyone else is already taken." There is some snickering from my fellow classmates around me. Strangely Austin is the one that finds my comment to be the most amusing.

"Let's come to order shall we class?" Our teacher breaks up the laughing and regrettably commences the proceedings for the day. "Mister Morrison, it pleases me that you are quoting Oscar Wilde. I look forward to hearing you quote Franz Kafka in a few minutes since you are obviously eager to participate today." Austin continues to chuckle, and I put my hand over my mouth to keep from uttering any further sounds.

"Mister McGuire, if you would be so kind as to control yourself." Our teacher glares sternly at Austin who barely manages to contain his amusement. I take an interest in staring at the desk before the lecturer opens his mouth once again and begins speaking in a monotonal voice. "Firstly, I have an announcement. I wish to inform you that signs are being erected on the bathroom walls as I speak. These signs kindly request that if you wish to use the school bathrooms, the Facilities team requests that should you want to urinate, that you should no longer stand up to do it, but you should sit down to do your business."

There are some gasps followed by laughter from my peers before the monotonal voice continues. "That is the thing with blokes," he tells the class with an element of seriousness in his voice. "The Facilities team has to tidy up after you. You can't just expect someone to clean up your mess and just assume that if you spray all over the bathroom that someone else will deal with it later." I am not sure if this is a new rule or simply a request but it is the stupidest thing that I have heard since the woman who was arrested after playing a version of 'Naked Twister' with her daughter and her friends.

The red-haired boy that looks like Ron Weasley offers his opinion. "Well, at night it is easier to sit and do it because it is easier than aiming in the dark, so I don't see what the problem is to do it at school this way if it makes everyone's jobs just a bit easier." My blood pressure begins to rise as I interpret this deliberate arse-kissing and become angry that our lives are beginning to be managed in such a way by the nanny state.

The monotonal voice of our teacher commences again as I continue to stare at my desk and chew on my thumbnail. "In Germany, there are signs in the toilets that ask men not to stand. There is a term for this also in German, it is *sitzplinker* and it is translated as 'man who pees sitting down' and with that said, yes, let us move on from Germany and to the Czech Republic and discuss Kafka." He starts flipping through pages of a book.

My heart begins to race faster, and I feel an overwhelming desire to add my input to this ridiculous request and lame conversation. After first clearing my throat, which acts as a dog whistle and entices the red-haired boy to turn around in anticipation that there will be fireworks on offer, I let it rip. "This is ridiculous, Sir!" The lecturer looks up with a concerned expression on his face. "Who came up with this ridiculous new rule that was presented as a suggestion, which is just another example of how this school is turning into a nanny state where political correctness has gone mad?" Various members of the class start chucking whilst Ron Weasley stares at me with his mouth agape. "Who asked for you to tell us this nonsense and more importantly why are signs being created and put up asking us to sit down to urinate of all things? This just seems ridiculous. How hard is it to piss in a bowl anyway?"

The monotonal voice of the lecturer begrudgingly starts up again. "Chezdon, this communication came from the headmaster's office. Can we move on to Kafka now if you are done?"

First, I bite my lip, but my anger can only be suppressed for a matter of seconds. "So, the headmaster, who is a female wants to emasculate us males only because she is obviously envious because she can't urinate standing up. She wants to bring us down to her level."

Our teacher appears noticeably uncomfortable. He first tries to silence the class as everyone either starts talking or laughing before he is able to respond. "Chezdon, there is a hint of misogyny in what you just said. Would you like to correct yourself or can we please just move on from this?"

Jayden who is normally as quiet as a mouse in class and only offers an answer to a question when asked directly interjects after cackling loudly. "A hint of misogyny! Really, Sir? Chezdon doesn't like women at all. Just ask Austin." Most of the boys in the class start shouting and make sound effects and for the first time, I feel betrayed that someone would share my private business and it cuts me to the bone. Jayden's comment required no interpretation and knowing that I was just outed for being gay I feel like I not only have to brush it off but go on the offence as our teacher attempts to regain control by motioning for everyone to be quiet repeatedly.

I tap my fingers on the desk whilst my peers leer at me, willing me to at least respond as to being kicked out of the closet. For once, this class filled with non-fiction drama instead of the boring words of Kafka's fiction and after assembling my thoughts, I begin to speak a few decibels louder than usual. "Being an atheist, I always found it relaxing in a way when I had to endure religious studies at this school however now I am grateful." I am not sure if the gasps of various boys indicated that they thought I was going to utter unforgivable blasphemous words however since the school likes to ply us with religion, it is time to use it to my advantage. "Sir, the King James Bible has multiple references to man pissing against the wall as it was just last week we were asked to read '1 Kings:16' which went on about the house of Baasha and how he left not one that pisseth against a wall." Knowing that I am pushing the boundaries of the numerous rules that are already imposed upon us and not wanting to get into a religious debate, I change tactic and stare at Jayden. "That is where this country is going. First, we have the boys in this school pissing whilst sitting down, followed by the pastors and then maybe even the Prime Minister. So much for the leaders of the future who don't stand up and piss against the wall like a man! This is what is wrong with Australia, and when I go to Germany someday, you should know I am going to stand up to piss wherever I decide to go." Some of the boys in the class begin to clap. "Now I will excuse myself as I suspect that I am going to be kicked out right about now."

Innocence Waning

Our teacher looking defeated puts his glasses on and whispers. "Goodbye Mister Morrison." I pick up my bag and walk towards the door.

"Wait!" Austin shouts. Before opening the door, I turn around. Heads are moving back and forth throughout the classroom waiting for something else interesting to play out. "If you translate the word *sitzplinker* in German it actually means 'wimp' so I will stand with Chezdon." Austin stands up and picks up his bag. Other boys in the class follow his lead as I twist the knob on the classroom door. My icy stare then turns to Jayden who remains in his seat as most of the class follows me out into the hallway in an awkward demonstration of support where the word 'wimp' reverberates against the walls over and over. The rogue's gallery of protesting youth scatters shouting their new anti-establishment war cry, knowing that our early lunch break should effectively begin as soon as possible as it is inevitable that we will either be punished or expelled from school later today.

15. Daniel

As I undo my tie and quickly walk out through the open gate and off the school grounds, I hear footfalls and the shuffling of shoes behind me and then the familiar voice of Austin. "Chez, wait up." He places his hand on my shoulder as I continue to traverse along the footpath, having no plan as to where to go or what to do. Before responding I notice the presumably innocent children playing in the park across the road and their respective bored parents sitting on a bench before locking my gaze upon Austin and smiling. "Wouldn't it be nice to be like those kids again?" I point in the direction of the children frolicking on the grass who are trying to hit each other with sticks. "We will probably end up punished or worse." I deliberately move my head from side to side trying to remove the tension from my neck as I swipe the sweat that that was beginning to form on my forehead.

Austin retrieves a small tree branch off the ground and gently scratches my arm with it. "You are precocious Chezdon. We are still just kids. We can still play in the park and not take anything too seriously if that is what we want to do. I am obviously not in the same rush to grow up as you are." Austin tosses the branch over his shoulder and onto the street. A Mercedes passes us a second later. The driver raises his middle finger and beeps the horn, most likely thinking Austin intentionally chucked the branch at his fine motorcar.

I pull my backpack off and awkwardly shove my tie into the top pocket. After returning the heaving bag to my right shoulder, I casually unfasten the top three buttons of my white shirt. The few minutes that I have had to reflect since bolting out of class has caused me to feel a certain amount of mirth. It is very rare that I allow such nonsense that is said in class to bother me however it is the pious look that was on Jayden's smug face that set me off. It irritates me far more than any words that he uttered in class, or those that were written in the gospel, that there is an edict stating how boys should piss. The school has numerous other silly rules that I have never bothered to comment on at least out loud in front of the authority figures. It bothers me that I couldn't keep control in class. My provocative opinions amuse me though, along with some others when I feel like I want to entertain myself and my peers, but they do tend to get me in trouble. I know my big mouth is also my tragic flaw and I wonder how long it will be until I face my reckoning. My phone begins to vibrate in the back pocket of my shorts. I ignore the annoying device and choose to quarantine it and simply wipe the sweat beads off my forehead again using the back of my hand. I roll my eyes at Austin and revert to watching where I am going so I don't trip on the uneven pavement. "That is thought-provoking mate. I never thought of you as being such a deep cunt." Nervously, I grab the back of my head and mess my hair up further.

Austin laughs and after a few seconds, looks up into the leafy trees that cover not only the footpath but the street. "I doubt they will expel you. You just expressed an opinion and essentially walked out of class. I will be in the shit though when I get home if Mister Mackey reports it. The only damning thing you said was that misogynist comment about the headmistress." Austin remains sanguine in what waits for us back at Melbourne Grammar. There is no continuing commentary from him about being castigated by parents and the school for that matter. His calm demeanour quickly settles me down. "Do you want to go to Nandos?"

I look at Austin and then start to giggle. "Mmmkay Austin. Please just sit your arse down on the toilet to piss and be happy about it. You are an evil man for spraying urine on the floor!" I put on a voice resembling Mister Mackey, the dishevelled elementary school guidance counsellor from the cartoon *South Park*. Most students in our English Literature don't bother to refer to him by his proper name. It is just 'Sir' or when we are outside of the class, 'Mister Mackey.'

My pace slows as my circumspection quickly evolves into sheer and utter amusement. I hold my stomach and start laughing so uncontrollably that tears start to well up in my eyes which then finally stream down my face. I attempt to commentate the events that transpired in the last ten minutes, and as I do, I interject every third word with more laughter, until I get to the point that I must drop my bag on the ground in the desperate hope of controlling myself. Austin begins to laugh and attempts to mimic the silly statements that our teacher had to say, starting every statement with 'Mmmkay' like the fictional cartoon character would do as monotonal as humanly possible. "Oh god, I can't take much more, please stop!" Austin starts to laugh as he continues to imitate Mr Mackey again. We halt on the footpath to carry on like fools, it gives a group of the boys who left English Literature after us a chance to catch up to us.

Malcolm, the brown-haired alpha male of the group whom we both know only as an acquaintance, is the first to shout. "Chezdon! That was so awesome mate!" He puts his hand up and I do the same. Our hands smack together and then we fist-bump. He speaks to me like we have been best mates since birth. "That was just amazing mate. You summed up exactly what we were thinking." Malcolm's three friends nod their heads and both Austin and I start smacking their hands which of course are followed by the requisite fist-bumps. "You totally owned Mackey, it was priceless!" The group starts laughing after Austin simply says 'Mmmkay' and then smiles. "What is this shit that Jayden was saying about the two of you though? Was he saying you are gay for each other?"

Austin's face immediately turns a shade of crimson and immediately drops his head. I knew what Jayden had to say in class effectively outed us, but with the hilarity of the moment, I didn't think I would be questioned about it on the street so soon. With nothing to lose, I gaze directly into Malcolm's blue eyes and then quickly glance at the other boys who seem eager for my response. "Yeah, so what. Do you have a problem with that?" Austin looks up at Malcolm and then at me.

Malcolm appears stunned and his eyes convulse toward his friends who then quickly start looking back and forth at one another. The awkward dialogue that has quickly evolved from back-slapping hilarity and fist-bumping action to time-stopping seriousness. "No mate. We just never would have guessed. What the two of you do behind closed doors isn't my business, it is all good." The other three boys nod their heads in unison and repeat in their own words how it is all good and that there are no worries. "What the fuck is Jayden's problem then? You could get him on a bullying charge you know. What he said is just not cool. Isn't he a door knocker?"

I laugh and after rolling my eyes, I wipe more beads of sweat that have accumulated on my forehead with the back of my hand. "You know what, I really don't care what Jayden said. I know far cleverer people than him who have tried to insult me, bully me and call me names throughout my life. Why should I care? It happens to all of us and if that cunt can manage to offend me by saying what he did, I should just cut myself and end it all right here and now."

Austin looks at Malcolm and makes one sound. "Mmmkay." Everyone laughs. "Jayden thrives on schadenfreude because he is just a dickhead."

Malcolm slaps Austin on the shoulder with enthusiasm. "You are a cool bloke Austin." He extends his hand so he can fist-bump us once again. The process is then repeated by his gang of three. "What the hell does that word you just said mean though? You are the walking word of the day mate."

Austin moves his fringe and then scratches the back of his head. "Wow, I wasn't expecting that. Jayden is a fuckwit though, that much is true. He just gets pleasure from others misfortune. That is what that word means." My look of confusion subsides as I add a new word to my vocabulary.

"Malcolm, what is a door knocker?" I ask innocently. I know what he is inferring but I want him to put it in his own words.

Malcolm smiles and stretches his arms over his head. It is obvious looking at him that carbohydrates are not part of his diet and that he visits the gym with some regularity. "You know, a Jehovah's witness. The bastards that come and knock on your door on Saturday morning to talk to you about religion and what-not. Don't they knock on your door?"

I pick up my backpack and slide it over my shoulders anticipating this conversation will end soon. "I live in an apartment tower so they wouldn't be able to get in to knock on my door. But anyway, Jayden is agnostic and lazy so I really doubt he would wander around and do such a thing." I knew there were groups of people that would door knock and preach the word of some God, but I have never seen it happen in person.

Not being content with being silent any longer, Charlie, who previously only contributed only heavy breathing to the conversation and who appears to be losing the war against acne, finally speaks. "Better to be door knocked by some bible bashers instead of goddamned ISIS. I wouldn't want those pricks turning up at my house." Charlie looks relieved that ISIS has never paid a visit to him in whatever suburban area that he lives in.

"You really think ISIS would knock on your door mate?" Malcolm asks with a thoughtful look on his face. The banal conversation causes me to clear my throat and adjust my backpack. "Those arseholes would knock down your door and lop off your ugly head."

I raise my voice with the hope of shutting down the conversation. "Boys, we need to go. We need to be heading to visit my father in the hospital so can I just wish you well now?" The look of agitation on my face causes Austin to look out and watch the children play in the park again however he understands my play on words and chuckles.

The hand smacking and fist-bumping commence to end the final act and I feel self-conscious when Malcolm gives me a hug. He would have felt that my shirt has become saturated with sweat before his followers start to walk away. "What is wrong with your old man? Can I get your number?" Malcolm looks at Austin before continuing. "By the way, if you boys need anything let me know." He hands me his unlocked phone and I retrieve my phone from my back pocket, unlock it, and hand it to Malcolm.

I pinch my lips together and shrug my shoulders as I watch Austin pick up his bag. What could Malcolm possibly be offering? Does he want to beat up Jayden? Perhaps sell us drugs? I am confident that he thinks I am more innocent than I truly am after making such an offer. "He was in a car accident yesterday. He will be fine though. He is just bored if anything sitting around in the bloody hospital." Sometimes the truth is stranger than fiction and as we exchange phones once again before walking away from our new friends waving. I wonder if life will get any stranger before the sun sets.

The irony of my father being in the hospital and me using the term 'he will kill me' when I make a reference to walking out of class makes Austin laugh. I remind him that he, along with others followed me like mice after the Pied Piper and that we need to accept our fate when we return to school. Unfazed, he expresses interest yet again in joining me on my short walk to the hospital. Austin suggests that we purchase many coffees and take Daniel a few cups after I say that we will not have time to go to eat at Nandos and visit the hospital if we plan to return back to school and face our reckoning on time. I should inform Daniel about my shenanigans earlier and as I ponder exactly what to say, a sense of dread quickly envelops me. He will remind me that he pays a substantial amount of money for me to attend this illustrious private institution. I really hope that after the ceremonial offer of roasted beans, the wild and injured beast will be appeased.

I inspect Austin like he is a tomato at the farmers market. We casually walk into the McDonalds and order a cardboard tray full of flat white coffees from the McCafe kiosk. Whilst waiting for the barista to do her duty, I take some time to check the messages that have been delivered to my phone whilst admiring Austin's frame out of the corner of my eye. One message is from Shaun who provides a gentle reminder that we have a movie night planned for this evening which causes my face to turn red. I am embarrassed because I forgot about our arrangement. "Hey Austin, what are your plans later?" I pose my question loud enough for all the patrons that are ordering junk food to hear. Most of the customers in the queue promptly turn around to stare at me. They collectively then glare at Austin who is graciously collecting the tray of coffees from the enthusiastic server behind the counter.

Austin appears embarrassed. It was an innocent question after all. "Let's go!" Austin quickly walks toward the automatic sliding door and I follow him, bemused as we flee into the mild yet crisp Melbourne air with the sun shining on us from above. "Why do you have to be so loud?"

I jog so I can catch up with him with my backpack awkwardly swaying from side to side like a pendulum. "Sorry, I didn't mean it like that. Here, let me take those." I grab the cardboard tray of coffee cups from Austin's cold hands. "Thanks for that, my father will be kicking me out and welcoming you to the family home soon enough if you keep this up." A wide grin forms on my face as Austin takes a moment to wipe the sweat off his forehead with his arm. He then moves his hand to the back of his neck and rubs it vigorously.

Austin appears circumspect and his eyes widen as we continue to traverse along the footpath. The entrance to the hospital is roughly as far as you can throw a cat. "Tonight, I am going to tell my parents not to expect any grandchildren from me and that I like guys. That I like you. I am sure that will go down well." He averts his gaze to the pavement as we walk towards the entrance of the Alfred Hospital. "Keep your phone on and make sure it isn't on silent. I will be ringing you later as I am confident that all hell will break loose." Austin looks at me and places his hand on my shoulder before we walk into the air-conditioned hospital.

"Wow." I wasn't expecting this proclamation from Austin and different scenarios start playing through my mind as to what his parents will say when he makes the confession that he likes cock. His mother will be devastated since she wants him to produce a grandchild and carry on the family name. His father will most likely only be annoyed because his romantic interest is the demon spawn of Daniel Morrison. "Yeah, well. I can go with you if you want. Whatever you need, I am there for you." I remove Austin's hand from my shoulder and then hold it gently before abruptly stopping. "Just promise me that if you don't think you will get a positive outcome after you start talking to your parents that you pull out before it is too late. There is no point in making your life difficult"

Austin stops in time with me. "What do you mean before it is too late?"

"You have to live with them Austin so if you think that the discussion is going to turn out to be shitty and your life will end up being hell and awkward, don't tell them anything especially that your crush is me. It isn't worth it. Just keep fitting in until you can move out. Your sexuality is part of your identity but in this case, the power of your parents will trump it, and you have to admit, your parents are not going to take this confession well."

"What do I have to lose? I can always come and live with you especially since I look at you as more than my crush these days." Austin states matter-of-factly and looks deadly serious before starting to laugh and winking at me. "I will be fine."

I become in my thoughts and play out various scenarios involving Austin in my mind. Returning my gaze to my phone, I discover a message from Mel which provides some much-needed insight as to how to locate my father at the hospital. "I hope so. Maybe because Daniel and Mel were so accommodating and understanding when I made the big announcement that I am a fag, I naturally assume that it should be easy for everyone else, but I still do expect all hell to break loose." Austin begins to gnaw on his fingernail as I continue to read the message from Mel. "We need to go to the west wing on level three." I wrap my hand around Austin's wrist and pull his hand along with the fingernail he is chewing on out of his mouth and use his digit to press the button to call the elevator. "Don't stress, everything will be just fine."

A few minutes later we find ourselves at an information kiosk on level three of the hospital. An attractive nurse that has cat-like features with brown hair pulled back into a ponytail consults her computer and points us in the direction of another kiosk further down the bowels of the wing. As she speaks, she stares at my exposed hairless chest as I forgot that I undid a few too many of the buttons on my shirt because I was so hot earlier. I smile and thank her for her help and we quickly toddle off. A few seconds later Austin quickly wraps his arm around me and laughs. "She was totally checking you out."

"Well, I am one hot piece of chicken." I nudge Austin hard enough and his body knocks into the wall. I begin to strut like a rooster. "Don't shove me, I will spill the coffee!" I casually point out as Austin looks set to ram me into the wall of the corridor.

"Bastard. You win this battle, but I will win the war." Austin takes one of the cups of coffee from the tray and begins to drink it as we arrive at the next kiosk. I announce to the day nurse that I am looking for the bruised and battered Daniel Morrison and we are directed further down the hall to his allocated room.

My father smiles as soon as we enter the shoebox. "Coffee! Give me!" He demands. His face is bruised, swollen and he has a cut over his left eye which has sutures holding it closed. A bandage is taped to his neck but there is no blood on it thankfully. I pass him the tray of three coffees. "You read my mind, many thanks, boys." He proceeds to drink one of the cups as quickly as Mel would in the morning and then retrieves the second one from the tray and calmly sips from it. "I am happy that you came around Chez, I am so bored. You too Austin, it is good to see you mate." My father extends his hand toward Austin and he shakes it.

"It looks like Mel gave you a good beating Daniel. I always knew that I shouldn't piss her off. What did you do?" I smile and my father chuckles. He drinks more of the McDonalds coffee. "Didn't Mel bring you a charger? Is your phone out of power? Is that why you have been so quiet?"

"So many questions." He polishes off the second cup of coffee in three rapid gulps. "Is that cup for me too?" Austin looks at me. My body is so hot. I determined my discomfort can be blamed on Daniel's cocaine that I snorted last night and think the last thing I need is for my heart to beat faster.

"It is all for you. Go for it. What the hell happened?" Daniel begins gulping from the third cup. Austin sits down and crosses his legs at his ankles. The Channel Seven newsreader is giving the midday report on the television, which is on mute. Barack Obama is talking about something on the television which is why I assume my father has it set to silent.

Daniel sips from the third cup of coffee. "Brilliant." He lets out a long sigh. "If you remember, Mel and I were off to The Vineyard restaurant in St Kilda after we dropped the two of you off at school. A long breakfast turned into lunch. Some wine was enjoyed so we left the car in the parking structure in St Kilda and just called for Uber. I had a meeting to go to in Prahran and Mel was seeing a client in the city. The only story I must tell really, which isn't very exciting, is that another vehicle hit the Uber and because I wasn't wearing a seatbelt, or so because they tell me, I ended the ride prematurely all fucked up and have had the pleasure of the fine accommodation, food and service here. My phone broke in the collision, and besides for the obvious inconvenience of enjoying a very quiet time in the hospital, I am motivated to get a new Samsung Galaxy S6 Edge anyway. Mel brought me her old iPhone but that ran out of power quickly and nobody has a charger for that Apple crap, so I have pretty much just sat here watching television and have had a quiet holiday. Life is good." My father begins to cackle loudly which makes both Austin and I laugh. "Hey Chezdon, can you do me a favour?"

"Sure, what do you need?" I look at Daniel and wonder what sort of complex request I will be asked to sort out.

"Can you find me a can of Coke? I really need some sugar." He finishes the last of the coffee and places the empty cup next to the two other empties. Even hearing the innocent version of Coke makes my arsehole tighten and I feel a bead of sweat silently travel down the centre of my clammy back.

Austin stands up. "I will get you a few cans, Daniel. Not a problem."

"Thanks, Austin, but I am hoping that my favourite son can get me a can or three. I would like to talk to you about something." Austin's eyebrows disappear behind his blond fringe and I am left vexed.

"Yeah, no worries, I will be back soon." I casually stroll out of the private hospital room leaving both my father and Austin to speak in riddles, having no idea what is so secret that I cannot enjoy the conversation. I return to the kiosk and locate the cat-woman who was checking me out earlier. I query where I can purchase soft drinks. She enthusiastically gives me directions to the canteen as one option and suggests the infamous Nandos outside of the building as another outlet for sugar. She also takes the time to educate me that Nandos is her 'favourite' restaurant in the area and that she will go downstairs with me if I can wait fifteen minutes until she goes on break. I feel like telling her that the blond haired boy that I left behind with my father and I were at the aforementioned Nandos merely two days ago and how we decided to start a gay relationship, but the wild idea fizzles out and with a smile, I let her know that she is very kind to make such a suggestion but I must be on my way. Waiting for the elevator once again gives me a chance to respond to messages that deserve attention. My eyes once again skim the message from Shaun earlier and I respond to him saying that I am looking forward to seeing the movie and that I will meet him at the restaurant as planned. Before the elevator delivers me to the ground level, Shaun responds to my message, confirming that he is looking forward to it and that he will be at the bar as planned. It doesn't take long to find a vending machine after following the signs to the canteen and fortunately it is retrofitted with a debit card reader. I purchase four bottles of Coke for the exorbitant cost of sixteen dollars, before retracing my steps to the third level of the hospital, past the gawking cat-lady and return to my father's room.

Both Daniel and Austin simultaneously look up at me as I walk in and my father stops talking. "Did I interrupt something?" I pass two bottles of Coke to my father and hand one to Austin. I sit on the empty chair in the corner and open the last bottle of Coke. After quickly drinking the contents of the bottle in silence, I ask, "so, what did I miss?"

Austin glances at my father and is the first to speak. "It is nothing really Chez. We were talking about the home invasion that I told you about the other day. He wasn't sure if you knew about it."

"I was starting to explain a situation to Austin." Daniel pauses to open a bottle of Coke and then takes a sip. "You turned up just in time Chez." My father takes a deep breath and then takes another drink before what I know is going to be a long spiel. "This whole debacle with the accident has given me time to reflect and consider life and how to better live it. Firstly, after thinking a bit about your mother, umm, I mean Voldemort, and how she turned out, I think it is time to pop the big question to Mel." Before my father can say "What do you think?" I make a loud gasp since I was not expecting this question. I look from my father to Austin and he is smiling, but he doesn't say anything.

"It is about goddamned time!" I shout and extend my arm and shake my father's hand. "That is so awesome, when you are out of here, we should throw a big party, assuming, of course, she still wants you and she will actually accept." I laugh which makes my father giggle.

Daniel drinks from his bottle of Coke. "I was really hoping that you had that sort of reaction Chez."

Austin shakes my father's hand. "This is great news, Daniel. Good luck!" Austin smiles.

"Okay then, that isn't it." My father looks around the room and up at the ceiling before twisting the cap off another bottle of Coke and continuing. "The so-called experts at this hospital say that I need to take it easy as my blood pressure is high. Also, don't get alarmed about this, but they also found some skin cancer which I am going to get sorted out. That is why I have this." Daniel taps the bandage affixed to his neck with his index finger.

Austin immediately appears concerned. "What, you have a melanoma? My father had a scare not long ago however it didn't turn out to be cancerous."

When Austin's father is mentioned, Daniel can't help but roll his eyes. "The quacks here seem to think that I will be fine, but yes, it is a melanoma. To sum it up, the five-year survival rate for a melanoma that is 1mm or less is just about 100%. The five-year survival rate for a melanoma that is thicker than 4mm is 55%. The one they found is 3mm, so I am sure that I will be just fine. This is what I get for never wearing sunscreen in the country that produces the most reports of skin cancer in the world. Lesson learned boys!"

"Jesus Christ, I don't know what to say." I simply stand in the same spot in silence and turn my attention to the muted sports report playing out on the television.

"Don't worry Chez, I will be fine. The quacks caught it early and combined with other life choices that I will be making to get my blood pressure down, you will be seeing me for a long time." Daniel appears confident however I start to consider that it isn't a one hundred percent likelihood that he will survive, and tears start to roll down my cheeks. Austin notices that I am becoming overly emotional and hugs me. "Come on boys, get a room!" My father shouts. "I will be fine, don't worry."

I take a deep breath and gently push Austin away. "Yeah, no worries. I wasn't expecting that announcement either. It is a shame it wasn't as thrilling as the first one you made. You need to better your game, Daniel." I quickly wipe my right eye with the back of my hand and take another deep breath. I reach for the bottle of Coke that my father is holding, which he quickly relinquishes and finish the contents of the plastic bottle quickly. "Is there any more news?" I smile and glare at Daniel.

"Actually, there is. That is why I wanted to speak with Austin privately." I notice Austin staring at me. His brown eyes are wider than normal. I feel another bead of sweat roll down the centre of my back. My stomach tenses up somehow predicting that this news is not going to be any better than the last. "With my blood pressure elevated, the quack is saying that I need to lose some weight and relax. I have decided to consult the Board and hire someone to replace me at work. I will keep my seat on the Board, but I will no longer have any operational responsibility. I can then lead a life of leisure playing golf. Why is this a big deal? In the spirit of transparency boys, as you know, Austin's father and I started this business some time ago and he has been really pissed off at me since he sold his shares to me and he feels taken advantage of. Austin, you live in one of the wealthiest suburbs in Melbourne and you would agree that you have a good lifestyle, right?"

Austin nods his head. "Yes, of course, I do."

Daniel continues. "Your father likes to demonise me for everything and anything and just feels like he was wronged somehow. He is so delusional that he thinks that I am responsible for the home invasion that you sadly experienced. In the past, he has said some very horrible and outrageous things about me in public, accusing me of all things of being behind the home invasion. Mel sued him for slander, however, we ultimately settled with an agreement that he would just simply shut the fuck up. I didn't want any money from him, I just wanted him to be quiet and stop saying things that were not true."

Austin begins to scratch his head and then begins to ruffle the hair on the back of his head. He is processing all this information and appears nervous. "So why would my father care if you quit your job?"

"That is the thing. I will get a substantial payout and he will quickly know since the company is public, it will be reported to the Australian Stock Exchange. There will be an announcement that one of the principals is moving on and everyone will know exactly how much money I am receiving to retire. I just wanted to let you know in case your father starts running his big fucking mouth again. I really don't care what he says, as it is all such bullshit, but since I consider you part of our family now, I wanted to be honest with you." Daniel averts his attention to a movie that has started to play silently on Channel Seven overhead.

"Obviously, the home invasion isn't the highlight of my life, and I am happy you said what you did. My father has had some colourful things to say about you Daniel, but none of it bothered me. Business is business. He always said it was your plan to get rid of him and then IPO the company. I won't humiliate myself by even asking you if you had anything to do with the home invasion. I can't even comprehend why you would be motivated to do something like that anyway. It is so criminal and shocking, it offends me just to think about it." Austin looks at me and pushes his fringe off his face. "I guess what I am saying is if my father has anything outrageous to say in the future, it won't bother me." To be a fly on the wall when Austin informs his parents that he is dating me will be even more incendiary now.

I clear my throat and try to think of something clever to say. "From the sound of it, your workplace is a bit like our school.

Just loaded with people who gossip. On that note, since it is confession time, I have something to add." I feel another bead of sweat drip down my back. "Dad, just remain calm when I tell you this. I reckon when you eventually listen to your voicemail that you will have received one from school saying in a roundabout way that I disrupted class and walked out." I avert my eyes toward the floor and start counting the white tiles.

"I was wondering why both of you were here so early. Did you leave early also Austin? What happened?" I look up only to see a thoughtful look on my Daniel's face. The rest and relaxation in the hospital bed have done him some good and I feel an immediate sense of relief because I expected him to go berserk. "Austin can tell me what happened as I am sure it will be more entertaining than if my son tells the story from his biased perspective."

Austin immediately reanimates himself. He must have been thinking about the home invasion. "Sure, Daniel. There is a new policy at school that was announced in English Literature class. The school is saying that if we need to use the restroom we should sit down on the toilet to piss. The cleaners have been complaining about what they have to mop up."

Daniel laughs uncontrollably. "Are you serious? Or are you just taking the piss metaphorically?" He then looks at me.

"I am deadly serious. We were informed that signs were being put up in the toilets instructing us to sit down when we piss in the bathroom." I smile.

Austin scoffs and then continues. "Chezdon took offence with the request and made his opinion known to our teacher and the class. He said that they talk about pissing against the wall in the bible and he certainly will stand up and piss wherever he wants. He made some comment that could be interpreted as being misogynist though since he said that the headmistress can't stand up to piss that she just wants us boys to be at her level when we do the deed. He walked out of class after that and half the guys in the class followed shouting and carrying on."

Immediately my father starts laughing at a volume that I have never heard him reach. The booming sounds emanating from his mouth seems to last for a minute before he can compose himself to speak coherently. "That is so fucked up, it has to be true. I think I am more shocked that Chezdon referred to the bible. I am confident that will not go down well but fuck them. That goddamned school. If they ring me I will remind them of my last donation on top of the fees that I pay, and clean bathrooms should be the least of their worries. This is supposedly one of the best private schools in the Southern Hemisphere. Where do they get the nerve?"

As Daniel rants, I can understand why the doctors instructed him to calm down as his face has turned red and it looks like smoke is going to start coming out of his ears. "Take it easy." I simply say. "Just letting you know as I am sure that I will be disciplined."

"If they try, we will fight that. Don't worry about it Chez, it will be okay. Thanks for letting me know." His red face begins to transform back to normal as he continues to chuckle. Austin who appears circumspect sits on the arm of the chair and crosses his legs, no doubt reminiscing about the sinister events that played out inside his home.

"You mentioned Voldemort earlier Daniel. I e-mailed her and arranged to meet up with her tomorrow night. I thought it would be the right thing to do considering what she is going through." Laughter immediately ceases, and Daniel's mouth drops open. "It is true. I am going to meet her at her house and have a chat."

"Jesus Christ." Daniel is lost for words. "Well, wish her well for me." His relatively positive reaction and kind words take me by surprise.

Austin stands up. "We should get going if we are going to get back to school on time."

"Go!" My father insists with a raised voice. "If the school gives you a hard time, don't say anything. Follow their instructions and we will deal with it tomorrow. I will be home tonight and will talk to Mel about it after I propose marriage." My father grins.

"That sounds so romantic." Austin rolls his eyes and inspects the display on his phone. We all laugh in unison. "Daniel, will you propose after the first or second bottle of wine? Will you tell Mel about what is happening at school before or after sex?"

Daniel once again starts bellowing like a madman as I shake his hand. "See you later mate. Be good." I pick up my bag and we begin to walk towards the door.

"Bye Austin you are a good laugh mate. Love you Chezdon. Be well."

I simply say "I love you too" as I look over my shoulder and then at Austin. As we stumble into the hallway, I brush up against him as he finishes tapping out a message on his phone. I wonder if Austin had any inkling that I wasn't just making what would seem to be a cursory response to my father that I said thousands of times previously as we leave.

Innocence Waning

16. **Struggle**

The walk back to the open wrought iron pedestrian gates bordering Melbourne Grammar is painful as the new shoes that Mel bought for me. They rub incessantly against both of my heels. I have to stop once under the school crest and motto which is translated from Latin into "Pray and Work" to remove my shoes and apply band-aids that I strategically carry in my backpack for emergencies. I pray to the flying spaghetti monster in the sky that the bandages serve a purpose and blood stops blowing on to my socks. Austin and I pass the time reminiscing about everything that transpired at the hospital earlier and of course the random references to Mister Mackey and the silly new rule that us boys need to follow. My stomach noticeably growls like a lion as our peers walk past us eating takeaway from the local McDonalds and Subway franchises. I consider bribing one of my hungry classmates for a mere chicken nugget or even a fry but instead just endure the grumbling sounds. My body is demanding nourishment and something besides Coca-Cola. The smell of fresh bread wafting from the Subway footlongs and the grease of the Quarter Pounders are certainly alluring. I nearly throw in the towel and ditch the rest of the day at school only for some much-needed sustenance elsewhere.

"It's hump day." Austin begins to preen himself using the limited reflection available to him via the glass on his phone. "I am really looking forward to Friday night." I then remember that Friday is our much anticipated first date night and I quietly congratulate myself for sorting out the particulars of what I hope will be a fun and romantic evening.

"Me too." I smile as I pull a sock over my bandaged heel. "What the hell is hump day? I don't think there is time for me to hump you mate unless you want to head to mine and blow this place off." I wink at Austin. "I was hoping you would ask. You look nice today by the way. I like it when your fringe goes to the right instead of the left."

Austin laughs and sets his bag down on the footpath. He begins to straighten his tie and tuck in his white shirt. I am glad that he cares so much about his appearance since I really like looking at him. I almost feel guilty that I appear to be a dishevelled mess who to a random on the street looks to have been sweating like a rapist. Jesus Christ didn't care what he looked like when he was crucified so my appearance as I enter the school grounds is the least of my worries. Anticipating a form of punishment after I finally pull on my socks and return my shoes to my feet after picking up my bag doesn't trouble me in the slightest. "Hump Day is the middle of the day on Wednesday, meaning it is all downhill with respect to the rest of the week. I can't believe you haven't heard that saying before. My father says it all of the time."

"I guess that is true. You are thinking about our five-day school week so I guess even if you consider there are seven days in the week, what you say is certainly true. Happy hump day!" I raise my arms above my head and begin clapping in time like I am at a concert. "I like my definition better though. Can I at least squeeze your arse once for luck?" I wink again at Austin as he picks up his bag feeling satisfied with his appearance and follows me.

"Nope. Later maybe. Certainly, not here." Austin declares matter-of-factly. "Do you think when you get home that Daniel will be betrothed to Mel?"

"Jesus, Austin. You are on fire with the vocabulary today. However, why not say it in German? You sound cute when you are uttering the guttural syllables of that language." It is well known that I am ranked the highest in our class and I wonder sometimes why Austin is not. I rationalise it that I am much more book smart and uptake information easier, a bit like a sponge. Austin can apply what he learns easier and files it all away for future reference. "Yeah, I think they will be engaged when I get home. I am glad that there is some happy news after what just seems to be a sea of shit washing ashore today."

"They are a good couple. I really hope that we can have as much fun and communicate as well as they seem to in the days, weeks, months and hopefully years ahead." Austin catches my gaze for a few seconds and smiles before looking at his watch. "I should go. I will ring you later after I stir some shit up at home." I am reminded that he is going to 'come out' later to his parents which escaped my mind.

"Take care of yourself Austin." I give him a very discrete wave not knowing what to do as he turns and walks off. My stomach rumbles again which I consider a foreboding omen as to what I fear Austin will experience when he has the big talk with his parents later today. Not only about his sexuality but my young self.

I glance at my watch whilst taking a deep breath. I start to walk towards my Economics class. After a prolonged sigh, I come across a few of the boys that were in my English Literature class earlier and as I approach they start to whistle and then one of them shouts. "I will stand and piss where I want!" After a few attempts at chanting in unison, the four boys are then in-sync and repeat the eight-word proclamation as I walk past them as we fist-bump and smack our hands together before I casually walk into Economics class, smiling.

The rest of the day behind the iron gate plods along. Except for the students taking notice of me in between the next class who slap my back and high five me, my stress level decreases as no member of the administration or respective school staff requests my audience. Seemingly, Mister Mackey hasn't made a big deal about my disruption earlier or the mass exodus of students from his class. I begin to surmise that Mister Mackey is a reasonable person and suspect that he doesn't agree with the totalitarian view that boys should be forced to sit and urinate as per an edict from his comrades in the administrative office. Maybe he isn't the deadbeat instructor that I thought he was.

The day of learning ends thankfully without any additional fanfare. Whilst leaving the school grounds at the wrought iron gate I spot Malcolm gesticulating wildly and his droogs chatting amongst themselves. They start laughing when they see me and enthusiastically wave me over. "Hey lads. What's shaking?" I drop my bag on the ground and begin to scratch at the infected pimple that has sprouted on my shoulder under my shirt.

"Hey mate." Malcolm starts the fist-pumping routine with me, and I complete the action with his gang of three. "Did you get into the shits?" Charlie looks preoccupied and is looking down the street, most likely he is waiting for someone to pick him up. I notice the acne on his face and quickly decide that I would rather have one pimple on my shoulder despite the annoying pain.

"No mate. I didn't hear shit from anyone in administration today. Let's hope it stays that way, hey? I told my old man what happened though and he said he would fight the school if they try to punish me because it is so bullshit." Malcolm chuckles and starts sorting through his backpack. "He was mortified at that new shitty rule."

Charlie bends down and scratches his knee and then his hairy shin. I notice some scabs on his limb, most likely suffered from playing a sport. His tibia looks like it has been dented, which makes his shin appear strange and almost cartoon-like. "Hey, I told these blokes earlier, but one of those new signs in the toilet block has already been vandalised." He stands up, rolls his eyes and smiles. "I wouldn't know who did it though, so don't ask."

Malcolm hits Charlie on his shoulder. "It is obvious who did it, dickhead. Not like it matters. Hey, there is Austin." Malcolm extends his arm over my head and waves at Austin as I turn around and make an inviting motion towards him with my arm, effectively waving him over to our sewing circle.

"Hey, what's happening?" Austin nonchalantly says as he arrives at my side. "Someone has already written graffiti on the new stupid sign in the bathroom that I just used." Everyone besides Austin looks at Charlie and begins to laugh. Malcolm slaps his shoulder and finds Austin's observation especially amusing.

"What a laugh. I love it!" Malcolm states with glee. "Hey, there is that dickhead Jayden." Austin and I both turn around and look back through the iron school gates and see Jayden stumbling out onto the footpath with his backpack as fully laden as it possibly can get. "Hey, dickhead!" Malcolm shouts at Jayden. Austin and I both look at each other incredulously. "Hey, dickhead!" Malcolm shouts louder and drops his bag and starts to run towards Jayden. Charlie follows him after dropping his bag on the ground.

Jayden didn't have a chance to get away even if he tried with the tonnage in his backpack and simply raises his hands above his head. Malcolm wraps his arm around Jayden's neck and forcefully escorts him back to our social circle and for Jayden to keep up, he must drag his backpack on the ground. When Charlie catches up to both Jayden and Malcolm, he forcibly takes Jayden's backpack off him and then walks back toward us with purpose. "What the fuck!" Jayden shouts and then once again repeats himself as loud as he can for good measure. Other students in the area take keen interest and begin to watch the commotion knowing that something interesting is about to happen.

By the time, Malcolm has escorted Jayden back to our area, he has relented, no doubt realising that Malcolm and Charlie would drag him over to us by choice and not by chance if he resisted. "Do you have anything to say to Chezdon, arsehole? You need to apologise for being a dickhead." Malcolm takes the black tattered backpack from Charlie and rests it on his shoulder. The weight of the bag doesn't appear to phase Malcolm at all.

"What the fuck you arsehole! What do I need to apologise for? I didn't do shit to you." Jayden appears both flustered and agitated and doesn't seem apprehensive at all in stepping into Malcolm's personal space. He then turns around and shoves me hard before turning back to Malcolm. "Are you Chezdon's bitch now?" Before Malcolm can respond, Jayden turns around and shoves Austin. "You are all a bunch of cocksuckers!" Jayden exclaims with a new sense of venom in his voice and tries to yank his backpack away from Malcolm.

The shouting and swearing attract the attention of other students in the area and they begin to rush over, forming a circle around us. I notice a few taking their phones out and pointing them in our general direction as I get my bearings after being shoved. Austin and I quickly look at one another and I can tell that Austin is concerned. Most likely not for Jayden, but I know he does not want to have an unplanned chat with the administrators. The look on my face also indicates that I am fearful this situation is going to get out of control quickly and Austin picks up on it. "Who gives a shit about him Malcolm?" I look at Jayden with a disapproving stare before continuing. "Sometimes mates can quickly turn into arseholes, so who can be bothered with this one." I steadfastly proclaim, mustering as much confidence as I can with the hope of diffusing the situation. I seemingly dodged a bullet from the administration of the school once today and the last thing I want to be accused of is inciting a riot outside. My response is in turn measured, especially for the cameras which I know are now recording us. A beautiful black Audi R8 pulls up near the group of teenagers that continue to assemble on the street and honks its horn. The son of the parent who is trying to record us simply waves at his mother, obviously more interested in filming our escapades instead of leaving the drama behind.

Jayden quickly turns and shoves me again. As I stumble backwards, I drop my phone so I do not crush it as I tumble over and end up on my back resting on the concrete footpath. Once I have regained my sense of place, I hop up and rush back towards Jayden and shove him as hard as I can into Charlie who nonchalantly shoulder charges Jayden. Charlie treats him as an opposition rugby fullback and Jayden collapses on the concrete sidewalk like a bag of potatoes would if thrown from a truck.

"You pussy! Fuck you mate!" Jayden exclaims whilst laying on the footpath. Malcolm drops Jayden's bag on his stomach causing Jayden to howl in pain after getting the wind knocked out of him. Once he is composed and gets his second wind, a barrage of curses and blasphemy spews from Jayden's mouth, where everyone that he looks at, including the curiously interested spectators with their phones recording every word that Jayden now shouts, is abused for one reason or another. Finally, after he takes a deep breath and stands up slowly, he picks up his backpack and for the benefit of the smartphones and the audience he looks at Austin. "If you want to play happy families with Chezdon, go right ahead faggot! I hope you don't mind that he is a big fucking slut who sucked me off and swallowed my cum last night. Good luck to you. Fucking pussy!" Jayden spits on the ground and with hate in his eyes stares at me as he walks past me, knocking my shoulder hard enough to make me wince. After a second of relief thinking that the drama has concluded, Jayden quickly gyrates his body around and with a murderous impulse and a deranged look on his face places his hands around my throat. The moment in time then resembles a photograph as I remain fixated on Jayden's soft lips and with memories of the previous night rushing back to my head however they are quickly replaced. Knowing that he is apoplectic with rage, I thrust my forehead forward as hard as I can and it meets at first the bridge of my friend's nose and then his head. Screaming, chanting and swearing comes from all directions as my world begins to spin.

I briefly rest my hands on my knees to get my bearings and then pick up my phone. Voices have merged to form white noise. A hand rests on my back gently which as if magic transports me from my delirium and back to reality. I rise up to see Malcolm as rigid as a statue, much like you would find in a photograph that a tourist would have taken at the nearby war memorial. My eyes finally find Austin and I realise that he is the one that is trying to comfort me as I finally stand erect and wipe what I first believe to be sweat off my face and out of my eyes, but when I see the back of my hand, I realise that the crimson red colour substance all over it is in fact blood. All of the outrage and shrieks are on offer because blood was in fact shed. Charlie hands Austin a dirty towel that he pulls from his backpack. Austin at first applies pressure to my forehead before taking Christopher's bottle of water from him. I now can comprehend English vocabulary and the first words that make sense to me are spoken by Malcolm. "It isn't his blood, he is okay I think."

Austin shakes me and I am roused back to life as he continues to wipe my face with the wet towel. The shrill shrieking sounds are muted by the shouting of the onlookers and the cheering of the mob as I watch Jayden stumble away and up the street, pushing past students and onlookers. Someone shouts that Jayden's nose is broken as the smartphones follow him as he slowly staggers up the street swearing at anyone that comes close to him.

A few of the theatre boys that I recognise from the senior campus at first try to restrain Jayden to help him, but after being verbally abused, Malcolm interjects. "Let him go. He isn't worth it." He raises his voice and some smartphones move from Jayden to Malcolm and then back to me. "We are being recorded, it isn't worth it. He isn't worth it. Who cares about the dickhead?" Malcolm retreats into our sewing circle. Various members of the enthused and interested viewing public signal that the spectacle is over and put away their smartphones. There are noticeable groans filled with disappointment as Jayden walks away holding his face with his hand. The driver of the Audi blasts the car horn again and a boy slowly wanders away from us and is driven quickly away. He looks disappointed that he must leave the bloodlust behind.

"Wow, it is all happening today." Austin attempts to lighten the mood. "I didn't expect that to happen. Moaning Myrtle is buggering off at least though. At least he will not be dripping blood all over the bathroom floor at school as I am sure that would mean a new rule." I smile at the reference to Moaning Myrtle, the ghost that haunts the various bathrooms at the Hogwarts School in the Harry Potter saga. Austin continues to wipe my face and refreshes the blood-stained towel with more of the natural spring water from the bottle. My earlier thoughts and convictions that my life has only been complicated needlessly by the splendours of lust and love merge with the miseries of jealousy, hate and self-loathing. I thought that they would weave into a happy sunlit meadow of beauty and butterflies comes to bear and it is only that I know that I have been deluding myself. "Chez, if you have a spare shirt in your bag, you should change."

"If we were in the United States that dickhead would probably come back with a gun and shoot us all." Charlie reflects and scratches the shoulder that he used previously to knock Jayden down with. "God save America." We all chuckle uncomfortably as I start rummaging through my backpack before retrieving a wadded up dirty polo shirt that I wore a few weeks ago, that was stuffed into the bottom of my bag.

"Maybe when ISIS comes knocking at your door mate, you can point them in the direction of dickhead Jayden." Malcolm slaps Charlie on his back. Their laugh is infectious, which causes the other two boys, Christopher and Wyatt to also snicker. I unbutton my shirt and pull it off and am at first taken back by the amount of blood on it. I am lucky that it wasn't my essential life force that was shed.

Austin watches me pull on the filthy polo shirt as random boys whistle at me from afar. He then looks thoughtfully at Malcolm. "Can I ask you a question, Malcolm?" Austin adjusts his backpack. Malcolm opens his eyes wide which encourages Austin to continue. "You seem to care more about Jayden acting like a dickhead compared to Chez or I. What has he done to piss you off so much mate?" This is a valid question and it should provide insight as to why Malcolm and his friends all the sudden have taken such a quick likening to us over the last hour.

"Fair enough." Malcolm picks up his bag and looks at Austin before staring at me before he answers in a solemn tone. "My sister is, well um, she was a lesbian. She was bullied and she killed herself. This is how I ended up here. My parents thought a private school in the city would be more suitable after she took her life than out in the country. When Jayden outed the two of you, he made an enemy for life here mate. I don't put up with this bullying shit." The surprised look on the faces of Malcolm's three friends gives a clear indication that they did not know this piece of trivia. Charlie looks sad. Christopher starts to chew on the inside of his lip and Wyatt pats Malcolm on the back gently. "It just pisses me off and I wanted to kick his arse, but as you said, Chez, he isn't worth it. Besides you did enough damage, hey?" Malcolm takes a deep breath before continuing. "It doesn't look like you are even bothered about what he had to say in class earlier or even just now. Why is that?" All eyes then find their way to me as I try to smooth out the wrinkles on my filthy shirt.

Austin then looks at me with a curious expression. His right eyebrow once again disappears behind his fringe. "They are just words really mate. We keep talking and laughing about ISIS lobbing off heads, and I should be worried or upset about petty things Jayden says to me? My father told me that he has skin cancer today and tomorrow I am seeing my bitch of a mother for the first time in three years. Believe me, mate, there is nothing that Jayden can say that would annoy me as there are more important and sinister things in life. Honestly, it is just a waste of time and that is my struggle." My mouth feels dry and my frustration level rises knowing that we are standing around on the footpath telling tales of woe instead of having fun and developing positive relationships amongst one another. "It is just frustrating, that is all." I take the water bottle from Austin and drink what is left in it.

"It doesn't sound like *Mein Kampf* mate," Austin interjects smiling. "You see that bloke Hitler had a struggle and wrote about his from his cell, I don't think yours compares."

"What is up with you and the German references today mate?" I grin and put my arm around Austin and shake him. For once he doesn't act embarrassed or feign from a public display of affection. "You do make me laugh though." I rub my forehead and wonder how long the act of head-butting will leave my forehead aching. My stomach growls again, reminding me that it should be listened to in the future as it sounded the alarm earlier that danger and drama were brewing.

Austin laughs which makes the rest of our group either smile or chuckle. The remaining onlookers wander off after associating Jayden with various words that you would not call your parents. "Okay lads, see you blokes later and thanks for the entertainment. I was looking forward to watching the UFC this weekend, but now I have no interest. I have to go." Austin notices me staring at him and after breaking away from my embrace, he winks at me before turning around and walking towards the train station. He removes his phone from his back pocket and starts to fiddle with it as he walks away.

"I should get going also, boys." I look around and find my bag and hoist it on to my back. "Thanks for helping out with Jayden. I doubt he will have much to say after that display." I am at a loss for words and this proclamation seems to make sense. "Malcolm, sorry to hear about your sister. That really sucks mate."

"We should party soon, Chez. We heard you throw a good one." Christopher finally says as he stretches his arms behind his back. I am shocked to hear his voice as I thought he was mute. "See you tomorrow, mate."

"Indeed. It would be fun. Soon, I promise mate." I start the fist-pumping routine with Christopher and follow it on with Wyatt. When I get back to Malcolm he decides to give me a hug instead. Whilst being embraced, I slap Malcolm's back hard a few times. "Thanks, mate. You are a good bloke." Malcolm releases me and smiles.

"Anytime Chez. Later bro." Malcolm walks away and is followed by his rugby triumvirate. They retreated towards the train station, following the path that both Jayden and Austin previously took. I pause for a few seconds and squat down to check one of my heels. I collect my thoughts and rub my forehead before pulling off a shoe and peeling down a sock where I find a small dot of blood peeking through a worn band-aid. I return my footwear to where it belongs and walk the opposite direction towards my familiar tram stop knowing that I no longer have a best friend of a few minutes ago. I wipe my eye again knowing it is watering only because Jayden's blood irritated it and I feel hollow as the tram grinds to a stop next to me on the platform.

Innocence Waning

17. **Kinsey**

I deftly insert my key into the lock on the door of my apartment and pause before turning the shard of metal. I drop to my knees and open my backpack and upon finding my bloodied shirt, I decide it is prudent to get rid of it. I quickly walk to the rubbish chute at the opposite end of the corridor and toss it into the dark chasm. No amount of detergent or chemicals I surmise will return the white cotton fabric to its virginal state. Keeping it is a souvenir would be disturbing to anyone that comes across it, including me in the future. I massage my forehead, hoping that the pain will magically disappear as I rub it with my hot hand. I return to the door and deftly twist the key in the lock until I hear the ominous click. I am granted access to my dwelling and then shortly afterwards my bedroom, where I immediately strip off my filthy polo shirt and toss it on the floor.

I consider just collapsing on my unmade bed but decide it would be better to take a shower. I need to cleanse my body of the filth and the remnants of the human secretions left on it which includes Jayden's blood which has dried in between my fingers. I methodically kick my shoes, belt and all of my soiled clothes into the corner of my bathroom and onto the place where Jayden peacefully slept some nights ago. Fond memories of briefly watching my friend snore on the cold white tiles naked next to the toilet quickly take over and encourages the throbbing pain at the front of my skull to intensify. I rifle through my cabinet and find one lonely generic painkiller remaining in its package and quickly toss it down my throat and encourage its quick travel into my body by sucking the water directly from the tap of the faucet. I spot the empty small plastic bag that once had the white powder in it on the countertop next to the sink. I wish that I could go back in time so that some of the illicit drugs were left in the bag for me to inhale right now.

I lose track of time showering and after what turns out to be over an hour of being left alone with my thoughts and the droning hum of the warm water splattering off my body, I emerge from the shower stall first noticing my back in the reflection of the mirror. It has turned red as the result of the water pummelling my delicate skin for a prolonged period. Feeling invigorated, I dry off and return to my unmade bed and crawl under the covers holding my phone and once settled, check to see what is going on in my social circle and beyond.

I count the seconds quietly in my head before I am not only overwhelmed but mortified by a collection of thirty-second videos making their rounds through cyberspace. They depict Jayden from various angles getting head-butted by me. Other video clips depict the aftermath of our skirmish and the heated exchange that led up to blood being shed. Rather than add to the commentary or its associated manufactured outrage, I instead call Bryce who chooses not to answer his phone. Not wanting to participate in the juvenile exchanges online, I give a cursory scan of my unread text messages and finally decide to confirm with Shaun that I am indeed going to go out tonight and that I will meet with him at the bar as originally planned. Despite feeling emotionally drained and physically exhausted I think it would be good for my mental health to extricate myself from my bad teenage dream that I am living. I can't just hibernate within the confines of my soft bed sheets all evening. The adults I quietly decide should be able to frolic at home and have what I hope to be a romantic and happy night once my father returns from the hospital without being exposed to my teenage drama and follies. I close my eyes and hope that my father is still is keen to pop the big question to Mel. With something positive potentially happening today, a smile slowly forms on my face as I will myself to raise my aching head off my pillow and throw the sheets back with some enthusiasm.

My thoughts transport me to an alternate reality. I first dress and then primp and preen myself whilst replaying the vivid memory of my earlier confrontation with Jayden over and over in my mind. I consider different scenarios and what the outcomes would have been if I had made different choices in the heat of the moment. I intentionally find one of the amateur videos that was distributed by the boy that was collected in the Audi R8. It is by far the most professional of the collection being shared on Twitter. I download it and play it on a continuous loop as I first dry and then proceed to style my hair. I watch the video at least ten times before I am satisfied with how far my hair is standing on end, making sure the sides are not puffy and my mane is pushed stylistically-forward. I then work on the shaggy mass of hair at the back of my throbbing head which feels knotted before I dust it with hairspray. Having completed the tedious grooming process, I decided that I can go out into the cold and cruel world confidentially looking older than I really am after abandoning my signature fringe. Shaun believes I am currently in University from memory and I want to keep up this persona and look older. Feeling circumspect, I sigh when I come to the realisation that I could not have reacted any differently after being assaulted by Jayden if I didn't want to possibly end up toes-up at the morgue. I recall the deranged look in his eyes with a sense of horror as he placed his hands on my throat. My level of outrage intensifies as I continue to play the video of him attacking me and watch him put his hands around my delicate neck. The demonic look that forms on his face scares me. His eyes are bulging and I feel the strange sensation of a shiver moving down my spine as I close the video and then all the programs on the phone so that I can conserve battery power.

Picking up my set of keys in the tray by the front door before opening it, encourages me to stop and send a text message to Mel saying that I have gone out and that I will be back around curfew, which is at 10:30 PM on a weeknight. I catch my own eyes staring back at me in the mirror after I look up from my phone and then inspect my forehead. It hurts so much and I am surprised but thankful that there is no mark on it. I then recall the videos showing blood splattering in all directions and what appeared to resemble a pint of the red stuff on my white shirt that I threw away earlier. I am in awe that I escaped unscathed, but as I stare back at my own reflection which doesn't flinch, I watch my face turn a lighter shade of blood-red as my anger rises. My level of disdain for Jayden increases as I think about him trying to choke the life out of me earlier and being unconcerned not only for my own well-being but the fact there were multiple witnesses watching. If I hadn't head-butted him and probably broken his nose, I take some seconds to wonder if he would have choked me until I passed out. Would the gawking crowd watching the nonsense have ever intervened? Everyone just watched the violence playing out from behind a smartphone which is just sad. I assume Austin or Malcolm at a minimum would have somehow pulled Jayden off me though. At least I hope they would have. I stare back into my own green eyes and consider who can really be called a friend after what happened today. If Jayden can act like a deranged arsehole, anyone can devolve into one I suppose. It is then I remember that I do not have any cash in my pocket so I quickly jog to Daniel's room and liberate his drawer of a further $200, which I am sure he will not notice is missing after the experience that he has endured. With cash in hand, I leave the apartment and lock the door behind me, waving at myself in the mirror.

I walk through Southbank Promenade at a casual pace before crossing over the dirty Yarra River. I meander through Federation Square slowly, only so I do not sweat. The only pair of black skinny jeans that were clean that I pulled on earlier are skinnier than the others in my collection and instead of taking a jacket with me, I decided to wear a red and black flannel shirt knowing the temperature is going to drop later in the evening. I did not want to be encumbered by a jacket since I tend to lose them. As I admire the people silly enough to row up the

Yarra River and under the St Kilda Road Bridge, I roll up my sleeves as despite the reasonably cool temperature I feel like my body temperature is rising from stress. I briefly stop in Federation Square to respond to multiple text messages about the unfortunate incident earlier. The task feels more like a necessary chore, but I persevere and send concise yet flippant messages saying that I have gotten on with life and that people need to live in the moment and not dwell in the past. As I have thirty minutes of time to kill before I am supposed to meet Shaun, I call Bryce again.

My friend answers his phone on the third ring. He expresses some surprise that I called since nobody rings one another to chat these days with all of the social media platforms readily available. I tell him about the events of the day, culminating with Jayden going postal and Bryce admits that he has seen the violent videos circulating on Twitter. I laugh after telling him that I am not shocked since our pathetic lives are played out online more and more and the world is left to simply judge and admonish on a whim. We agree to meet for what is turning out to be a standing lunch engagement on Saturday at the Emporium for tacos once again and then we bid each other a warm farewell. After Bryce reassures me that I made the best of a very bad situation and then reassured me once again that I am not a horrible person, I feel a bit better. I decide to stop at the familiar 7-11 franchise and purchase a frozen Coke in Jayden's honour. There are no hard feelings at least from my perspective. I can only hope that after Jayden calms down that he will have a different outlook however when he looks in the mirror at his nose and face, I am sure that will not be the case.

Slurping on my frozen Coke cools me down as I continue my casual walk towards Pei Modern restaurant. The memory of watching the film 'Unfriended' last Sunday at the cinema next to the restaurant I am traversing to brings an unexpected smile to my face. It was just before seeing that so-called scary movie with Jayden that I met Shaun and then the memories of the past week begin to overwhelm me once again. I take another long slurp of the crushed ice and the pain that quickly develops in the back of my head matches what I am experiencing at the front of my head. It is so bad I must stop and massage it and kneel down until the untimely brain freeze passes. Having a desire to eradicate the pain instead of compounding my ongoing misery, I toss the frozen Coke into the first rubbish bin that I find and conclude my slow walk at the doors of Pei Modern near the valet parking area at the Sofitel hotel. I take a moment to admire the Audi R8 that is parked at the valet desk. It is in fact not the same vehicle that I watched usher away my classmate earlier in the day as the interior is a different colour. I pause long enough to catch my reflection in the passenger's side window and upon seeing it, take the opportunity to mess with my hair, at least until the owner of the vehicle deactivates the car alarm, which startles me. I quickly put my hand on my heart at first thinking that I did something to set it off but then I see the owner laughing as he opens the driver's side door. I mutter "bastard" under my breath and smile. "Beautiful car." Still, with my hand on my heart, I say sincerely.

"I know." The professional-looking gentleman sits behind the wheel of the Audi, closes the door and turns it over. I walk toward the entrance to the restaurant and he drives away.

After a few deep breaths, I walk into Pei Modern. I have been in this restaurant before with both my father and Mel ironically before seeing a movie next door, so I know where the bar area is and walk towards it like I am a regular. "Can I help you?" A female voice asks as I make my way to the casual seated area.

I turn around quickly and inspect the middle-aged woman with blond hair. I vaguely remember her from the last time I dined here and I am confident that she is the service manager. "I am just meeting a mate here, I might wait over there for him." I point at one of the empty tables in the bar area. She walks past me and indicates that I should follow her and after welcoming me she hands me a small bar menu along with a long drinks list as I take my seat. She proceeds to fill a glass with water.

"In front of you have a bar menu with a list of specials that we have today and of course the drinks list. Are you dining with us tonight?" I take a second to start counting her white teeth as she smiles before wondering if Shaun made a reservation in the restaurant tonight. I once again roll my virtual dice and take my chances. "Yes, we are, there should be a reservation under Shaun." I grind my teeth and compress my lips together with some force as she walks away. I hope that the accommodating and happy woman doesn't return and quiz me as to what Shaun's surname is as I have forgotten it. I have him listed on my phone as 'Shaun' and his business card is in my backpack at home. I quickly drink the tap water from the small glass as I watch the toothy woman return and quietly hope that I have not made a complete arse out of myself.

"Yes, we have your booking Shaun. Can I get you something to drink? She smiles and flashes her glimmering white teeth at me once again. The dentist I use is across the street in one of the commercial towers and I wonder if she is his patient.

"No, I am Chezdon. Not Shaun. But thanks." I give her a wide smile which puts my teenage white teeth on display for her to admire. "I will have a gin and tonic to start if that is okay?"

I give her the opportunity to refuse me service or at least ask for identification which would prove that I am at least the legal drinking age of eighteen, but the staff at decent restaurants in Australia rarely ever bother to ask. "What gin would you like?" She bends down and opens the menu and points to the many different makers of gin that the bar currently stocks. Her eyes leave mine for a mere second as she flips the page and points to the list of grains flavoured with juniper berries before gazing into my eyes once again.

Innocence Waning

My eyes do not leave hers and confidentially I respond. "Do you have Melbourne Gin Company? It is hard to find these days."

"Why yes. That is a great choice Chezdon." I am taken aback that she remembered my name, however, knowing she has probably never heard such a name before, I am sure that she considers it unique. "What garnish would you like if any?"

"Can you do rosemary and orange if possible?" I smile and show my teeth once again.

"Sure, that is no problem. I will be back shortly." The happy woman picks up the two menus and walks away quickly. I am ecstatic that I have perfected the ancient art of ordering alcoholic beverages. A smile returns to my face knowing that once again I was not asked for identification and begin to twirl the empty glass for mere seconds before the smiling lady returns with a carafe of water and quickly fills the glass to its brim.

"Do you have any San Pellegrino?" I casually ask. I always prefer to drink sparkling water instead of the Melbourne tap unless it is out of desperation.

"Of course, would you like a large bottle?" She retorts showing her teeth and smiling wide.

"But of course," I pull the phone out from between my legs as the smiling lady walks away. A message that arrived five minutes ago from Shaun says that he will be at the restaurant in five minutes and like clockwork, I look up after locking my phone and see Shaun waking through the door. The smiling lady points him in my direction and I stand up and shake his hand after he gets close enough to me. "G'day, mate. How are you doing?"

"Hi, Chez. What a day." Shaun pulls his chair back and begins to sit down and I follow his lead. "People are just crazy. I think I need a drink." Given he consults with crazy people for a living, the reference, in turn, causes me to chuckle. I didn't notice his very square jaw when I first met him. His facial features are unique however his hairstyle can be found on most of the professionals that I saw walking around the city earlier.

The smiling woman quickly returns with a crystal glass filled with gin, tonic and ice. She sets it in front of me just as Shaun finishes his sentence. "I agree." We both look up at the service manager and Shaun expresses interest in getting a glass of whatever I am having. She nods her head and walks back to the bar. I pick up my alcoholic beverage and take a drink. I immediately notice the taste of juniper berries move across my palate. My head throbs and without thinking I rest the chilled glass against it before taking another drink. "Sorry, but I have a massive headache." I look at Shaun and he appears older than what I remember. Dressed in a dark suit gives him more of a conservative appearance which tacks on additional years to his face which I previously estimated as to being mid-thirties when we first met at Supernormal last Sunday.

Shaun bends down and picks up his brown leather bag and rests it on his lap before he starts to rummage through it. Only seconds later he pulls out a small cardboard box. "Are you allergic to codeine?" He pulls a tray of pills out of the box and casually looks at me.

"No, I am not allergic to anything that I know of." I take another sip of my drink. I continue to look at his square jaw as I chew on a cube of ice.

He flexes his arms and proceeds to push a pill through its foil barrier and onto the table and then repeats the process with a second pill. "Here are some Panadine Forte. There is a small amount of codeine in these painkillers, so I am positive that they will sort out your headache." I suspect that the throbbing pain in my head will be a thing of the past shortly as I pop the pills into my mouth and quickly wash them down my throat with my ice-cold alcoholic beverage.

"Thanks. I appreciate that mate. How are you? How is your sister? I would say a long time and no see, but it has been only a few days." The small talk seems appropriate and cute and I replicate what I have seen my father do with his mates. As I am addressing someone potentially as old as my father, I need to turn up the maturity level of not only how I present myself but also the sophistication of the conversation.

Shaun briefly chortles and then crosses his legs under the table after rotating to the side so he can look at me from an angle. "She is great. She told me after we met you that if she wasn't getting married in a week that she would happily give have a go with you as in her words and thinks that you are cute." The smiling woman returns with a glass of gin, tonic and ice and places it in front of Shaun. Our silence encourages her to walk off before he continues speaking. "She reckons that you would be taken though." He picks up his glass and sips his drink after eating the flesh of the orange and discards its rind on the table. "How old are you Chez if you don't mind me asking? We were debating it for hours over a bottle of wine after we last saw you."

Knowing that it would be awkward to speak the truth and not wanting to find out how Shaun would react, I simply lie. "Eighteen if you can believe it." At least the smiling server will not think about ringing the police if she overhears this false confession. "How old are you? You don't look a day over thirty-five mate." I smile and twirl the contents of my small glass.

"Forty-three and after today, I am sure feeling it." My heart starts beating quickly after Shaun's admission. "Excuse me, I am just going to use the toilet." The chair that Shaun is sitting on screeches on the concrete floor as it slides backwards. He takes another drink before setting the glass down and walking off. An awkward feeling overwhelms me as I imagine him vacating his bladder and shaking drops of urine off his dong all the time wondering why this older bloke wants to hang out with a self-professed teenager tonight. A teenager who is lying about being an older teenager no less, who is lucky to pull off looking like he can legally drink alcohol in Australia. Being somewhat mindful that this movie-night is going to end abruptly when Shaun returns, I feel compelled to reach under the table and grab his brown leather bag off of the floor. I begin to rifle through it with the hope of finding a few more painkillers. After unzipping the bag and rummaging between the yellow legal pads of paper, a laptop and a wad of paperwork for what seems to take an eternity, I find a small cardboard box. At first, I believe it will contain the Panadine Forte painkillers that I was offered earlier but it turns out to be a box of Oxycodone. I know this is a painkiller as my father was using it when he had some really bad back pain after a particularly gruelling session of golf a year ago. I open the box and take a sheet of eight pills out of it quickly. I close the box once again and return it to the bottom of the soft leather bag, before placing it on the floor under the table. Desperate to eradicate the pain lingering inside my forehead as quickly as possible, I pop two of the round white pills into my mouth and chase them with what is left in my thick crystal glass. I suck on an ice cube as I catch the eye of the smiling woman and raise two fingers. I shove the remaining pills into my pocket before chewing on the ice. A 'V' for a victory that in-service circles can only be interpreted as another round of two drinks and I am anxious for a refill before the conversation starts up again. Only seconds then pass before I see Shaun making his return journey from the restroom paying attention to his smartphone as he navigates the maze of tables and chairs around me. I continue to chew on the ice which makes a loud crunching sound and swallow the shards as he sits down and drags the chair back towards the table.

We chat about local and then international politics before discussing current affairs. Naturally, the depressing events in the world encourage me to change the topic from terrorism to the ever-changing Melbourne weather and then finally to movies that are currently screening in cinemas. We then agree that we should migrate to the dining room and enjoy some food if we are going to make the last scheduled screening of *Woman in Gold* after we polish off another round of drinks. Watching the movie which has been on my mind for ages is then discussed at Shaun's gentle reminder after getting lost in conversation. We both agree that food is very much needed as Shaun comments that he has heard my stomach growl multiple times during the happy hour. The idea of seeing the film only to escape from reality now seems like a holiday as I feel the pain in the front of my head beginning to subside.

The lady with big white teeth returns and escorts us to our table in the dining room. She pushes the chair into the back of my legs as I sit down and she rushes around the table to repeat the process. Serviettes are then placed in our respective laps and formal menus are placed in front of us. After quickly reviewing the extensive wine list, Shaun asks me if I trust him with selecting a wine and declares that since I am a seemingly poor university student that he will happily pay for the wine and food. After briefly considering the kind offer, I nod my head and tell him that I will follow his lead. I review the dinner menu and say that I am very interested to try the 'native bird dressed with white soy and hibiscus' to which he orders the dish for two when the smiling woman returns along with a bottle of 2010 La Clarte de Haut-Bron Pessac-Leognan from Bordeaux for us to drink. "You don't have a problem with that do you, Chez?" Shaun looks at me curiously like he is evaluating me whilst he sucks the remainder of the gin and tonic from the glass that was graciously placed in front of him by the attentive woman with the big white teeth.

I quickly drink the remaining drops from my glass, accidentally accepting an ice cube into my mouth during the process and then suck on it before spitting it back out into the glass. "Not at all." I take my time to consider the wine and my surrounds as I pull the flesh of the orange from the rind that accompanied the repeat drink order before haphazardly tossing the rind of the fruit back into the glass. "A white Bordeaux. Are you a fan or are you just choosing it just for the hell of it? You don't find much of it going around in restaurants these days." Words that my father has slurred at times at other restaurants occupy my head and fortunately, I only release some of the positive aspects of the varietal in question as not to potentially offend my benefactor. My father would laugh at the notion of drinking a glass of white wine from Bordeaux, and the mere thought makes me chuckle.

"Wow, you know your wines, Chez. I am impressed."

The last three words raise my ire as I didn't realise that I needed to impress Shaun, so I attempt to go on the front foot. "Wine is my life. I haven't ever found a white wine from Bordeaux that is any good, so I am keeping my mind open and I look forward to it." On cue, the lady with the sparkling teeth once arrives at our table and presents the wine. Shaun nods his head indicating that he is satisfied which gives her the green light to begin the process of extracting the cork from the bottle. She then begins to regurgitate a wealth of information about the wine and the specific region of France that the grapes were cultivated as she struggles to remove the cork. Two other servers then appear like clockwork and place plates lovingly in front of us in unison with the celebrated native bird which we ordered which I notice is laying at rest in a compromised position with soy sauce and edible flowers covering its perceived private parts. Shaun sniffs the wine after it is poured into his glass. "Yum. That smells wonderful. We will have that." He then places his glass on the table and the service manager proceeds to partially fill our glasses. Shaun then picks up his glass and raises it in my direction. "To good times."

"To good times," I repeat and tap his glass gently. I slowly bring the glass back to my nose and begin to inhale the vapours that are rising from the fermented grapes. Amazingly, the alcohol content doesn't make me cough and I immediately decide that it is, in fact, a good vintage. I feel embarrassed that I was so hard on this style of wine and greedily drink it, first catching Shaun's eyes staring at me before tilting my head back and ingesting the contents of the glass in one fluid motion. I set the glass down and the lady with the wide smile notices and quickly walks over and begins to refill the glass. "So what is your story? Are you married? Do you have any kids my age?" I smile, which makes Shaun laugh before he takes a drink of the wine and sets the glass softly on the table.

"No, I am not married but I have a lady that I have been dating for many years now. We live together. The only way I can keep one is if I don't apply all of Kinsey's theories into my day-to-day sexual lifecycle." Shaun smells the contents of his glass and then sips from it. "Wow, this is an amazing wine. What do you think?" I briefly think about the movie *Kinsey* that I saw a few years ago, that chronicled the life of the famous sexologist. I smirk when I recall that Liam Neeson played the role of Alfred Kinsey in the movie. I reach for my glass again and wonder what the meaning behind what Shaun just said is as I have no idea what he meant.

My mouth had gone dry sometime in the last few minutes. I drink wine from the glass once again in another fluid movement before setting the glass down gently at the edge of the table which indirectly signals the lady with the wide smile to return and refill it. "It has a very surprising taste. I wasn't expecting this." I scratch my leg and then my stomach before reaching for the glass of wine again and take another sip. "It is really good. Thank you for suggesting it." I eat a piece of the native bird that has been placed in front of me whilst Shaun explains the lack of mental health that his patients' exhibit. Seemingly all of them inevitably end up in the local asylum that is paid for by the generosity of the taxpayer. I then consider Jayden and what played out earlier as I continue to scratch my leg. Jayden needs to see a professional like Shaun for treatment but I avoid sharing any personal experiences or provide any hypothetical situations for his analysis despite a few scenarios running amuck in my head.

Conversation evolves seamlessly from Shaun's boring work to what I am currently studying at university which is easily subverted using motherhood statements involving my old friend Frank Kafka, Post-Keynesian economic theory which was covered after my return to school after lunch today and an off the wall statement about calculus which didn't even make sense to me. Looking at my watch briefly, I excitedly blurt out that *Woman in Gold* is scheduled to start in a mere fifteen minutes. I repeat the timing of the movie, knowing that our plans will distract Shaun from my so-called life at Melbourne University. He raises his glass towards me and I emulate his action and then tap my glass against his. "Why bother? Can't we just chat and enjoy each other's company? This is the most fun that I have had in months."

I bring the glass of wine to my mouth and take a prolonged sip. "You need to get out more mate. Your lady doesn't have you chained to the bed at home I hope. Or maybe she does?" I smile and give him a wink, which makes Shaun chortle again which draws the attention of the couple sitting at the table next to us.

We tap our glasses once again. "You are right Chez, I do need to get out more. Believe me when I say she doesn't have me chained to the bed. I haven't had sex in over a year." Shaun drinks the last of the wine in his glass and then attempts to pour more from the bottle and looks disappointed when he discovers it is empty. "It looks like we need another one." I am left stunned as I hold my glass wondering what it would be like to be with someone for a year and not have any intimate relations.

The smiling woman quickly returns. She presents both the bar menu and the wine list to Shaun. He quickly flips through the alcoholic offerings and then closes the binder. "Trust me, Chez, you will love this." He looks at the service manager. "2006 Rusden 'Black Guts' please."

I look at my lap and scratch my dick. The sudden desire to rub my various itchy body parts is starting to become annoying. I chuckle before looking up at Shaun after he hands the wine list back to the attentive woman. "No worries with that choice mate, I drink that shit all of the time." Feeling my body temperature gradually rising, I know that I need to contain my enthusiasm and not resort to swearing and gesticulating like a madman.

Shaun's mouth drops open briefly before quickly closing it. He then quickly regains his composure. "Have you been to the winery?"

"Yeah, it is a great winery. Whenever I am in the Barossa Valley I go there and see Christian." Christian is the winemaker and the winery is about an hour and a half north of Adelaide in South Australia. I only know this as I have been an unwilling participant in the rented car with Daniel and Mel multiple times as they criss-cross the various wine regions with me in tow whenever they can. Fond memories returns and I recall laughing at both Daniel and Mel because they became so drunk that Jayden had to drive the rented car back to Adelaide with the adults in the back sleep after indulging all day at the various wineries. Jayden only had his 'Learners' license so it was fortunate that the cops didn't pull us over. They would not have been very impressed with the sleeping adults in the back seats as the kids up front bellowing out their rendition of the classic Nirvana album *Nevermind* at full volume with the car windows rolled down. The memory makes me smile.

"What are you thinking about?" Shaun leans his body in closer towards me over the table and holds his glass only centimetres away from his sparkling moist lips. I cease reminiscing about happy times with Jayden and I drink the contents of my glass. "I was just remembering my last visit to the Rusden vineyard." I pause and rotate the wine glass on the table in its place which catches the eye of the lady with the big smile. "I was there with my best mate but we recently had a falling out, so I was thinking about the good old days."

"I see." Shaun sniffs his glass in a way that reminds of how Mel smells the wine. "What happened to you and your mate if you don't mind me asking?"

He notices me roll my eyes and once again brings his glass close to his nose and waits for me to respond. "Before I get into that, you will need to excuse me. I have the smallest bladder in Melbourne. I will be right back." With a certain amount of deftness, I pull my phone out from under my arse and slip it into my back pocket before excusing myself from the table.

I quickly vacate my bladder and then pause to look at myself in the mirror and wonder why I am here. Besides the good food, wine and conversation, a sense of unease begin to overwhelm me as I mess up the back of my hair further. My shirt is starting to absorb the excess perspiration that is bubbling out of my armpits. After taking a few deep breaths and focusing on my green eyes that are staring back at me, I retrieve my phone to review the incoming text messages that I have been ignoring whilst sitting at the table. My phone had vibrated against my perineum and arsehole on multiple occasions as I was chatting and drinking. I was previously partially sitting on the device so I know there is some information to read which will distract me from the awkward situation evolving in the dining room. My father informs me via text that he and Mel are going to stay at the Grand Hyatt hotel this evening as he is now betrothed to the woman in red. I smile widely despite knowing that the Hyatt is only a few hundred metres from where I am at now. I doubt that I will run into them and quickly imagine my father and future stepmother doing everything besides admiring the view out the window and enjoying room service on this much-anticipated evening. Austin is the author of the next text message explaining that he successfully broke out of the closet and liberated the skeleton at the same time. His father is stunned and his mother is not speaking with him and instead went and hid in her room and is having a hushed conversation with her circle of friends on the phone. This information makes me pause and really appreciate both my father and Mel for being so positive and so supportive when I announced both my sexuality and that Austin and I were interested in one another. The next text message from Austin enrages me as his bitch of a mother called him some homophobic names and made some awful remarks about me. Austin concludes that his mother is coming 'to terms' with her only male child's sexuality and hopes that we can meet an hour before school tomorrow to hang out. My lips purse and I dig around the recesses of my mouth with my tongue before responding to Austin. I tell him that I am proud of him and express my regret that he must go through such an uncomfortable situation without me and I convey my hope that his parents will come around quickly. I then try to reassure him that things will return to normal sooner rather than later. Finally, I state that I will be at the 'Market Café' an hour before school starts tomorrow for breakfast and to try to meet me there if possible. Before sliding my phone back in my pocket and returning to the table not only do I set an early alarm so I, in fact, wake up early but I also send one last text to Austin saying that I miss him and that I can't wait to see him tomorrow. Although I am annoyed by the information that Austin shared, it does not supersede the happy news that my father announced in the end. I roll the sleeves of my flannel shirt higher up my arms before stumbling back to the dining room.

My fatigued eyes meet Shaun's bright brown eyes as I quickly sit down and scoot my chair in closer to the table. Awkwardly, I pull the phone out of my back pocket and return it to the warm nurturing embrace between my legs. "There is some happy news to report. My father just announced that he is getting married, so the day has not just been drama and unplanned chaos." I lift my glass of wine and sip from it.

Shaun quickly reaches for his glass whilst I scratch my leg again. "That deserves a toast. I do like hearing happy news since most my day is spent listening to tales of woe. So well done and congratulations. To the future and his happiness." He reaches across the table holding his glass by its stem and I do the same. I notice Shaun staring at me again like he is expecting me to speak. "Cheers!"

The glasses chink and I gulp a mouthful of wine. "With that in mind, I will not bore you as to why I fought with my mate. It was really stupid stuff and as you inferred, there is no point dwelling on tales of woe." I take another sip of the wine and eat the last of the native bird that is on my plate before continuing. "I do have a question for you if you don't mind giving some free therapy to a poor student."

Shaun's eyes open wider and he rests his head on his hand and places his elbow on the table. "Go for it, I am intrigued." The lady with the big smile returns to remove our plates and leaves menus in their place whilst I wonder how to phrase my question. I look at the ceiling for a few seconds and notice a crack in the plaster, which I follow to one of the light fixtures. I find interest in this defect in the building as I start talking whilst looking at the ceiling, instead of looking directly at Shaun. "Why are some people aroused by distasteful things? When I say distasteful, I mean things that the majority of society would consider shocking. Like kiddie porn for example." My eyes move from the ceiling and back to the menu before finding Shaun's gaze on me once again. He rubs his big nose.

"You aren't interested in kiddie porn are you Chez?" Shaun's eyebrows quickly scramble up to his forehead and he scratches his chin before picking up the menu and giving it a cursory glance. I am not sure if he is uncomfortable in general about this topic or finds it wholly interesting. I am sure he has heard other unsavoury things in the privacy of his office, but I feel like I need to immediately answer his question and clarify what I mean.

"No way!" I exclaim before continuing. "That is just an example of something unsavoury, but that is more criminal if anything. Another example is that some people find it arousing to get off in public places. Why is that?" I move closer to the topic that I am interested in and quickly realise that I am not going to outsmart Shaun, so I just blurt out my question. "Let's cut to the chase, recently I have been aroused by imaging getting off with a guy in a public restroom. Just a random hook-up if you know what I mean. I never acted on this, but I came close a few times. What makes me attracted to distasteful situations like this?" I set down the menu and reach for the glass of wine and drink what is left in the glass. This attracts the woman with the big smile and she quickly pours the familiar dark purple Rusden Black Guts direct from the bottle. I reach for the glass of water and take a drink of the essence of life whilst Shaun ponders what I said all the time staring at me which makes me feel uncomfortable.

"Are the two of you ready to order a main dish?" The chirpy service manager inquires whilst I once again examine the crack in the white ceiling.

Shaun orders the duck breast with fermented blueberries and to make things easy, I request the same dish when queried. My stomach has evolved from the rumbling associated with hunger pains to a periodic sharp pain, which is discouraging me from wanting to eat. When the service manager departs after professing that we have made an excellent choice, Shaun picks up right where the conversation previously left off. "How long is a piece of string, Chez?" He chortles again which once again attracts the attention of the couple that is sitting to my right who would have noticed that my eyes have gone wide.

Confused, I look towards the woman with the big smile who is pouring wine at the table next to us. "There isn't an answer to that question." I then watch Shaun take the stem of his wine glass in his hand. "Well, um, there is an infinite number of answers to that question actually."

"That is right. I could answer your question but it would require a far deeper conversation and the explanation and interpretation of Alfred Kinsey's theories. So, you get aroused in the public toilets then? That is interesting. This is the conversation that I like to have along with a good meal. It certainly beats the boring Australian political landscape and the shit Melbourne weather." Shaun drinks the remaining wine in his glass as I feel a brief pain subside in my stomach, which I take as a sign that I shouldn't eat anymore. The lady with the big smile sees Shaun with an empty glass out of the corner of her eye and quickly floats over to not only refill it but asks us if we would like another bottle of sparkling water which I enthusiastically answer in the affirmative. Another member of the staff joins his colleague at our table and quickly sets plates of duck and blueberries in front of us.

Innocence Waning

I scratch my leg again and then quickly withdraw my hand from under the table and put it in front of my mouth to cover a yawn which is desperately trying to escape. When I can speak, I am happy to explain myself with some renewed energy. "I don't think I am so much aroused, but more intrigued. I guess we are all interested in the things that we have never experienced before, whether they are perceived as being politically correct or even unsavoury by popular opinion." I feel another sharp pain come and go within the dark confines of my stomach.

Shaun notices my discomfort before picking up his glass of water and sipping it. "Are you okay?"

"Yeah, I am fine. Just a stomach pain, but it passed." I focus my attention on the glass of water and decide not to drink any more wine after losing my train of thought. I quickly drink all the water in the glass and just as quickly, it is refilled by another smiling and enthusiastic member of the service staff.

As Shaun begins to talk about Alfred Kinsey and the reports on sex that he wrote after World War Two, my thoughts drift and I find it hard to concentrate on what he is saying even though the content is nothing more complex than anything Mr Mackey had to say about Frank Kafka. Shaun's face morphs into that of a fly, which continues to speak whilst taking breaks to sip at the glass of wine whilst I find comfort holding my glass of water and intently listening, but not really understanding. When Shaun inserts the last morsel of the duck breast into his mouth, he stops talking long enough to allow me to politely excuse myself and I stagger back to the bathroom with my phone in my hand and lock myself in the toilet stall. Sitting on the rim of the toilet and taking long deep breaths gives me a brief window of clarity which makes me realise that I am not so much drunk, but that the alcohol that I previously enjoyed is having some sort of convoluted chemical reaction with the Oxycodone that I not only stole from Shaun's bag but greedily took. Feeling lightheaded, at first

I try to unlock my phone using my fingerprint but fail. After multiple failed tries my phone locks for a predetermined amount of time for security reasons. Annoyed and agitated, I start to watch the countdown timer on the screen. Purging everything that I recently put in my body after gently placing my phone on the concrete floor of the bathroom seems like a good idea. It takes a matter of seconds before my dry heaving evolves into a chunky purple explosion that finds its way into the toilet. With tears falling from my eyes and the return of the brief sharp pain in my stomach, I quietly expel the remaining food and beverage in my gut, using every amount of control not to get any of the mess on me. Briefly thinking about how cold my own bathroom floor was after donating the excesses of one of my previous nights at the altar of the porcelain god, I consider getting into the foetal position and going to sleep but being aware of my less than private and sanitary surroundings, I manage to get to my feet after flushing the toilet. After leaving the cubicle with my phone, I return to the familiar mirror and stare into my bloodshot green eyes and take more deep breaths after cleaning out my dirty mouth with the water available from the tap. I quickly blow my nose and wipe the tears from my face before quickly taking notice of my appearance once again in the mirror.

I casually return to the table again and find myself sitting in my chair and scooting it in like I am on auto-pilot. I make a conscious effort not to let Shaun immediately see my bloodshot eyes by examining the uneaten duck on the large white plate in front of me. "Sorry Shaun, I just don't feel very well." I push the chair back once again and with a feeling of self-preservation utter "I just have to go. Sorry." I pause before standing up and once again notice Shaun staring at me as I dig all of the cash out of my pocket and toss it on the table before walking towards the entrance of the restaurant.

Shaun stands up and quickly finds the lady with the toothy smile and they begin their transaction which I assume involves settling the bill. I watch Shaun pull a wallet out of his jacket pocket before I cross the threshold and into the much-needed crisp and cold evening air. The Sofitel hotel valet quickly walks over to me. "Can you get me a cab mate?" I am surprised that I can speak as thoughts only involve sleep and I feel lucid as I stand in the same position and sway left to right and back to left as the hotel valet blows his whistle. I once again try to unlock my phone but can't and it presents me with a countdown timer. It banishes me from using my technology once again. Two hands place themselves on my shoulders from behind just as I believe the swaying will overcome me and knock me over. "I will get you home." A familiar voice that I recognise as Shaun's whispers into my ear. "You will be okay." The yellow cab pulls up in front of us after circling the roundabout in front of the hotel. Shaun opens the back door and I fall in. Feeling numb, I do manage to slur one command before falling asleep. "Eureka Tower in Southbank please."

Returning to consciousness, I first feel a cold hand on the back of my neck and realise there are voices speaking. I am still in the back seat of a taxi and quickly open the door and stumble out of the bright yellow car clutching my phone in my right hand. Some other words are shared between a familiar voice and a man with an Indian accent as I hear a car door slam as I prop myself against the side of a tree. The yellow vehicle then speeds off and Shaun stands next to me and extends his arm, which gives me the courage to extricate myself from my chains binding me to the tree, only to be lead away from the street. I look up and find black sky instead of high rise towers. Shaun is opening a miniature wrought iron gate. The gate is too small to be the one that controls the borders at my school and far too small to be of any use to thwart thieves in the middle of the night, which adds to my overall state of confusion. "Here let me help you." I follow Shaun's lead as I slide my phone into the back pocket of my skinny jeans and focus on climbing two steps towards the red front door of a terrace house which confuses me further as he opens it with little effort. Every action seems to be complex at the moment as I feel the sharp pain return and then subside in my stomach.

Shaun leads me to the residence and that is when I first realise that I am not at my home in Southbank. I am perplexed as to why I did not see high rise towers only a minute or so ago. Each step feels like it takes a kilometre to travel as I am led down a hallway where I hear my own footsteps fall onto the hard wooden floor briefly before I am guided into a small room. I immediately spot a bed that I happily fall back on to. "So itchy. So tired." I mutter. I close my eyes.

A scratching sensation on my bare chest stirs me as I open my eyes and watch Shaun's fingernails move all over my soft exposed skin as he has unbuttoned my flannel shirt. "Does that feel good?" He starts to use his other free hand and moves it gently across my stomach and then over my crotch.

Taking two long deep breaths gives me the ability to focus my eyes and although what he is doing does feel good, I take my hand and try to push him away. He easily grasps my arm and then moves my hand so it touches his crotch after he adjusts himself. He is straddling me on his knees on top of the soft bed. After my hand drops to my side, he unbuckles his belt as I take long and deep breaths and decide what to do next. My thoughts escape me again and I draw a blank. I watch him unzip his grey trousers and unfasten the top button which holds the fabric together only to expose at first plaid and dull coloured boxers. After pulling them down far enough, pubic hair and then a penis that is rapidly growing is on display for me to see. My shock and the general state of malaise causes my heart to beat faster as I watch the engorged penis continue to grow wider, become longer and evolve so that it is pointing towards the unremarkable white ceiling. I look for the crack in the ceiling but cannot find it this time. The man with a face that has features like a fly takes my right arm by the wrist again. "Hold that." My small hand at first gently grips an erect penis and I become fascinated by it as I realise that the tip of my thumb and index finger cannot touch each another as I attempt to grasp the throbbing thing fully. "I thought you would like that." Not understanding what there is to like or why the fly is whispering, or what I should like about the big penis, my hand slides off it and returns back to my side on my command. I stare at the mole on the base of one of the robust and hairy testicles in front of me and for what seems like days think about how nice it would be to have my second testicle back again. I liked having a complete set and curse the doctor who removed mine during my stay at the hospital some time ago. The fly begins to fiddle with my skinny jeans and momentarily after the zipper is pulled down, I feel a rush of cold air against my thigh and then my flaccid cock as the denim fabric is forcibly pulled down along with my boxer briefs exposing my private area for the fly to inspect and fondle. I imagine myself taking the form of the native bird that I ate earlier at the restaurant after I shifted the flowers off its privates for me to eat. It only seems fair that the fly eats me and my privates now after moving the scratchy and constraining fabric away. I take another deep breath and close my eyes knowing that when I wake up this unsavoury dream will have ended.

An intense smell of sweaty socks and fruit jolts me awake as a small glass bottle is shoved into one of my nostrils. I experience a quick rush of blood to my head as I tightly grasp onto the fabric that I am lying face down on and wince. A white-hot pain then sears my arsehole as my eyes first try to focus on something besides the covering on the bed. I make a futile attempt to roll off of my stomach and that is when I once again feel the white-hot pain erupt in the bowels of my lower body and then the burning and stretching of my arsehole again. I let out of scream of sheer and utter pain which results in panic and then I violently kick my legs up repeatedly striking something as I tighten my anus with all my strength and expel the foreign invader from the inside of my body. The horrible pain subsides quickly and the dead weight rolls off my body. I hear some swear words being shouted before the sound of footsteps fade in the distance. A door then slams shut. I push myself up and roll away only to find that when I expelled the invader from my arse that some shit followed blowing a loud and long fart. This resulted in the horrible smell of the crap that I left on the ugly quilt, which recalls me to the land of the living. Resting on my side I again try to get my bearings and slither as far away from the poop that I left on the quilt. I pull on a bedsheet that was previously concealed and use it to wipe in and around my sore arse. It takes a few attempts to clean myself up with the white sheet and that is when I notice that I am also wiping blood from my butthole. I reach for some tissues from the box next to a lamp near me and wad them up and shove them between my arse cheeks. I pull up my skinny jeans and after falling into the bedside table, I knock over a lamp which breaks when it hits the floor. The horrible smell of shit in the confined musty bedroom begins to make me feel nauseated as I stare at the shattered pieces of the glass lamp on the floor. I wantonly stumble for the door and throw it open before retracing my steps back outside and into the crisp and cold air. I hold on to the small closed iron gate and in a moment of clarity know that it isn't the gate that leads out of the school grounds, but away from something more sinister. I figure out how to open it all the while thinking about the symbol on the gate at school. A fleur-de-lys. It symbolises purity and I assume that is why the symbol is not affixed on this gate as there is nothing pure within the confines of the house that I just left. I focus on my breathing and then wander the uneven footpath that runs along the street. I pick a direction at random and then follow it. I walk for a few minutes before remembering that my phone is in my back pocket and after retrieving it, I miraculously unlock it by swiping my fingerprint. I provide my sore body with a moment of relief as I rest my tired frame against a tree. Continuing to breathe in deeply and expelling the tainted breath from my abused body into the night sky takes on a noticeable rhythm as the pain thumping inside of me mimics my fast pulse. I button my shirt up after wondering why I completely unbuttoned it given it is so cold tonight. The pain inside me keeps the sensation of spinning at bay as I navigate to the Uber application on my phone and request a car. My location on the map educates me that I am a few streets away from Jayden's house, so after the Uber application notifies me that a car will collect me in two minutes, I call Jayden to tell him that the fly raped me, but he doesn't answer the phone. I count the seconds as both the pain in my abdomen and the smell of sweaty socks distracts me from not only sleep but from the confusing situation that I find myself in on the side of the road.

~

The final part of Innocence Waning, will be released on 15 November 2019 in paperback (ISBN 978-1-9999612-4-4) and eBook (9878-1-9999612-5-1)

~

Innocence Waning
Chezdon Mitchell
Part II

Made in the USA
Coppell, TX
21 November 2019